A NEW GOD

A NEW GOD

THE BETAVERSE • BOOK 2

MENILIK HENRY DYER

Podium

Rose, you're not a single character. You're a piece of every character.

Cover design by Alexandre Rito

ISBN: 978-1-0394-4285-6

Published in 2024 by Podium Publishing
www.podiumaudio.com

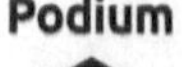

A NEW GOD

CHAPTER 1

PETER

FREEDOM

Peter straightened his back. He'd always been a tall man, but the subtle feeling he got from standing above the guard for the final time somehow made all those centuries behind bars a little more bearable. He smiled as he stood in front of the gate, waiting to be released. He pulled his cufflinks out from his suit arm and suddenly felt more at home. His navy suit better matched his dark features than the orange overalls did.

The guard slid a document toward Peter's lawyer, who picked it up. The lawyer was a skinny man. Or at least he looked like a skinny man in a suit that was designed to make him look a bit bigger. After a few moments of reading, the lawyer passed the document to Peter. "It's your release documents. Sign them and you're free."

Peter did as he was instructed and was handed a clear bag. "What is this?" he asked.

The guard looked up at him, confused. "It's the stuff you had on you when you came in."

"It can't be." He said examining the contents of the bag. Inside he could see a Submariner watch that looked a lot like the one he had and a wallet with his initials on it. He jostled the bag to move its contents around and saw there was also a half-consumed pack of gum and a pen. "I was murdered in the real world. These are not my things."

"They tell me it's your stuff. So, it's your stuff. And you take it," the guard said with a touch of annoyance.

"Let's not relitigate your terms of release, Dr. Atreus," the lawyer said, grabbing Peter's arm and hurrying him out the door. Then, in a conspiratorial whisper, he added, "You're lucky enough they let you come back to life."

As soon as Peter stepped through the door, he had to shield his eyes from the glare. Two steps in front of him he could see golden sand. His eyes continued to adjust to the bright light, slowly seeing a turquoise ocean. He could hear the crashing of the waves. He could smell the salt in the air. If prison had grey and muted hues, the place he was standing now was vibrant and alive. Caramel and turquoise colors made the view in front of him look perfect. He turned around, expecting to see the outside of the prison complex. But instead, he saw an elevator door lowering to the ground. As if he had just walked out of an elevator—even though he hadn't.

Peter noted it was the first time he could tell he was in a simulation. All through his prison life, he hadn't encountered any discontinuity. Now simply by stepping out into the real world, he was reminded that none of what he was seeing was real. Peter thought that maybe it was some sort of psychological trick; increasing the contrast between prison and the world outside made prison look worse. Maybe it made people less likely to commit another crime if this moment stuck in their head more memorably.

The lawyer noticed his momentary confusion. "A team of experts customized this moment specifically to you. They designed this environment based on what an algorithm predicted would lower your probability of re-committing a crime. Anyways, Dr. Atreus, I have a car over there to pick us up."

"I'm not going with you," Peter said, turning around.

"What do you mean? The whole board is waiting for you."

"Do I still own the company?"

"Well, yes. But—" the lawyer replied. The slight puzzlement growing to concern on his face.

"Then they work for me. I'm not spending my first day out of prison talking with my board," he said as he turned back around and walked toward the beach.

He sat down and picked up a handful of sand. He admired how real it was. Letting some of the sand trickle down, he could feel each individual grain flowing through his fingers. Every signal his brain was receiving told him the world was real. "Do I still have a brain?" he mumbled to himself.

He picked up the clear bag with his supposed belongings. Reaching in, he pulled out the watch. Turning it around in his hands, he thought it felt worn. Like it had been used for many years. He noticed it even had the chip on the bottom of the ceramic bezel. Exactly like he remembered his own watch had.

Defeated, the lawyer joined Peter in the sand. "Uncanny, isn't it?"

Peter held the watch up. "Why go through all the trouble of recreating my old Rolex in here? Do you know if I can get the real one back?"

"For all intents and purposes, it is your watch. Scanning it into here probably destroyed the original."

Peter put the watch on his wrist. "So, this is my old-new watch."

"What are you going to do now, then, sir?"

The sound of a chopper became clear in the background, almost as if thinking of it brought awareness to a sound that was always there.

"I'm going to visit my other watches," Peter said as he shielded his eyes from the helicopter as it landed in the sand next to the water. He could barely see with all the sand being flung through the air, but he could tell it was a large helicopter different from any one he'd seen before. Rounder, and he couldn't see a pilot, either.

Moments later, the blades stopped spinning, the door rolled open, and a man stepped out. Hezekiah Taper was a round American-Samoan man. A former offensive lineman in the NFL, he had known Peter for years. "Sorry I'm late," the big man said, picking Peter up off the ground and hugging him. "If I'd known they were going to let you out onto a beach, I would've drove."

"It's okay; I'm just so happy to see you," Peter said turning toward his lawyer. "Do you need a ride somewhere?"

The lawyer shook his head and pointed toward the car that had arrived, before waving as he left.

Peter stepped into the helicopter and Hezekiah closed the door behind him. Within seconds, they were up in the air. The inside of the vehicle was spacious, feeling more like a living room than a helicopter. There were two long sofas on either side of a table. Peter picked one and, putting his hands behind his head, he lay down. "Why is it so quiet in here? I can't hear the engine at all. But outside, it was so loud."

"Oh. That's right; this is your first time out of the beta. You died there and went to prison in here." He pointed at the ceiling. "I guess the engineers of this thing cheated. It's all ones and zeros, so they can basically do whatever they want."

"The beta?"

"The betaverse—the world you died in. You know they've been trying to figure it out. They're not even sure that's the base layer of reality. It's definitely the most boring. You can't even teleport out there."

Peter realized how much knowledge had been filtered away from him when he was in prison. He felt confident that he had a lot of catching up to do around his understanding of this new world. "So, can anyone design whatever they want in here?"

"In here?" Hezekiah said, shaking his head. "No way. Definitely if you designed your own layer. But out here in the splash, you still have rules like gravity."

The splash was an interesting choice of words, Peter thought. He remembered that term was used in games to mean the loading screen, the first screen you see when you first turn it on. He assumed the word *splash* meant the main layer of reality. Or it could just as easily be the layer of reality with the sand and beach designed for him when he first got out of prison. He made a note to find the answer to that question later. "And who makes up these rules?"

"Didn't you read anything while you were in prison? How do you not know any of this?"

"They filter out a lot of what I had access to in there. There were even words I couldn't hear," Peter said before looking out the window. Below him looked like the cityscape of a country he'd never seen before. Buildings that defied the laws of nature he was used to. Squinting, he realized the city was in the clouds. "How far away are we?"

"I figured you'd want to see this layer a bit more. But we can teleport there at any time if you'd prefer?"

"There's something I want to do before exploring. So, let's teleport."

Hezekiah pushed a button on the table, and the helicopter with the two of them disappeared from space.

From Peter's perspective, nothing changed inside the helicopter. He didn't feel anything, no change in movement, no change in time, no feeling of just being transported to another world. It wasn't until he turned his head toward the window once more that he noticed the change. Outside the helicopter it was suddenly raining. The perfect blue skies were gone, replaced with grey storm clouds.

The helicopter was gently landing on the top of the Atreus Skyscraper in Seattle. Right in the center of the large *H*.

"You know you don't have to do this yet," Hezekiah said as he slid open the fuselage door. The rain was pouring down hard and made it difficult to hear.

"Yes, I do," Peter said, pointing up toward the sky, a flash of lightning appearing poetically as he did. "My life isn't meant to be in here. It's out there in the stars."

"Okay, I just wanted to check. Because once we start, there's no turning back. I'm coming with you because I'm not risking being an accomplice."

Peter nodded and the two of them stepped out the door. Hezekiah snapped his fingers and pointed upward, and some sort of invisible bubble appeared above both of them, forcing the rain to hit a barrier and run away.

Peter admired the water running around them for a second. It was no wonder people found this metaverse so satisfying. In the betaverse, the real world, people got wet when it rained. But evidently not in here.

They reached a red door on the other side of the building. Hezekiah scanned his wrist, then opened the door. Lights flickered on, revealing stairs. They began the journey down, and after what felt like forever passing multiple doors for different floors, Hezekiah stopped at the very last step of the eighty-seventh floor. "Stand on this step next to me."

Peter did as instructed and Hezekiah scanned his arm once more on an empty spot on the wall. Then the view in front of Peter stretched. The stairs got longer, then split, sprouting more steps right in front of his eyes. It looked like a whole new floor was being added to the building. A hidden level was appearing in front of them.

Once the stairwell stopped stretching and everything had settled, they walked down the new staircase and found themselves in front of a new door. The sign above the door read 87-B. Hezekiah scanned his arm once more, and the door opened to reveal an entire floor of the building that was devoid of furniture. The space was empty as if no one was using it. Peter knew the building wasn't empty, just this one hidden floor. As they walked inside, Peter could hear the sounds of the rain hitting the windows of the building. And tucked around a corner, there were a stack of computer servers and a desk with a laptop on it.

"Couldn't we have teleported into here?" Peter asked.

Hezekiah shook his head as he sat down in front of the laptop. "Buildings get to dictate their security terms, and even though you own this one, it would be a security risk to let people teleport in and out at any time."

Hezekiah entered his password, then offered a small pin-like object to Peter. "Once you hold this, a screen will appear in front of you. It's going to offer you a lot of warnings about installing an unofficial plugin that isn't on the app store. Ignore those and install it. But don't activate it yet."

Peter took hold of the device, and sure enough, a red screen appeared in front of him. It was warning him about the risks of installing an unverified plugin and suggested he look in the app store for a similar product that was verified. Peter trusted Hezekiah, but you didn't get to his level without being cautious. He wasn't going to install something without looking at the code. "Can I see how it works?" Peter asked.

"Sure," Hezekiah said, giving up his seat. "Here's the—"

"It's okay; I can find my way around," Peter said, taking over the laptop. The ease with which his friend handed over the code was a good sign. That was the first test.

Peter scanned through the code for a while. He knew that if Hezekiah wanted to hide something from him, he would have needed to make the program unnecessarily complex. Hezekiah was a good programmer. His first job was as a graduate dev, working for one of Peter's companies. His code was always clean and clear, even when building something complex. It never had bugs or required workarounds or troubleshooting, and that's how Peter became aware of his skills. Over the years they became friends and Peter tapped him for many of his secret assignments.

Because of Hezekiah's mastery of programming languages, Peter knew that what he wrote should be easy to understand—he would have done it in the most efficient way possible.

It had been a while since Peter looked at code. But he understood it enough to get the gist of what it did. Most importantly he knew there weren't any code hidden documents or links to scripts. "And you wrote this yourself? No help from any AI or program?"

Hezekiah nodded.

The code was actually quite simple. Which was another positive sign in Peter's mind that it wasn't malicious. It basically measured the response time of a ping. "So, am I understanding this correctly: this measures the exact latency between me thinking of moving my arm and my arm actually moving?"

"Yes, correct."

"I get it. So, right now, we are in Seattle. But my brain matrix is stored somewhere else. So, by measuring how long the response time is, we will know how far away my matrix is from the Seattle servers."

"Correct. And then we just need to visit two more locations, and we should be able to triangulate exactly where your matrix is being stored."

Satisfied that the program did exactly what he expected and there wasn't anything out of place, Peter nodded at Hezekiah. "Okay, I think I'm ready."

"One thing: I don't know how much time we will have after you install that program. The government will definitely be alerted that you've installed an unauthorized app. So, we'll have to move on to the next location quickly."

"After this, we need to go to my research center on the moon."

"And after that, let's go to London. There's a star system I want to show you that's emitting some strange light."

Peter stood up and took hold of the little pin object once more. As he did, a screen appeared in front of him and he scanned it looking for the obligatory "I understand the risks" button. The process was easy, but the number of steps required to install an unauthorized plugin was painful, requiring him to click through five different screens until he was able to accept the right one.

After he accepted the final message, the pin he was holding transformed into a small screen. The screen showed black-and-white text saying *collecting data*. He held it toward Hezekiah.

"It's recording pings. As it collects more data, it will give us an updated probability on where it thinks your matrix is."

"Have you already done this for yourself?"

"I don't need to. You might have more money than everyone I know, but you're still on parole. I know where my matrix is stored. Yours is still owned by the government."

Peter was about to respond when a message screen popped up in front of him. It was very intrusive and had a ticking timer counting down from ten. The message read *Your parole officer, Elgin Yellow, is calling you. You cannot decline this call and will be connected in* five *seconds.*

Peter put a finger up to his lips. "You were right. My parole officer is calling me. Don't say anything."

Elgin was a grumpy man. Old, even by Peter's standards. He was always hunched over and probably would have been in a retirement home if it weren't for the technology to upload his mind.

The call connected and he could hear Elgin's voice. "*Dr. Atreus.*"

"Elgin, how can I help?"

"*Are you in a game? I can't locate you on the map.*"

"Why?"

"*Never mind why. Are you in some sort of world that masks your location?*"

"I'm at one of my offices. Why do you want to know that."

"*You've installed an application that isn't approved. And while that isn't strictly forbidden, I have a sneaking suspicion you are doing something you aren't meant to. Send me your location right now; I'm sending someone to you.*"

"Why did you call me in such a way that I had to answer? I don't appreciate being interrupted while I'm in an important meeting."

"Dr. Atreus, you're a celebrity. Normally, someone who committed a crime like you did wouldn't have gotten a second chance. My job is to make sure you don't waste that second chance. I am well in my rights to check in on you. Now send me your location and I'm coming to you myself."

Peter needed to put the officer in his place. If Elgin could simply force any call to be answered, then getting everything he needed to complete done soon would be tricky. He decided to try putting the fear of god into this man. It was an approach he'd used before, and in this situation, he couldn't win any other way. "No, I am not going to tell you where I am. I'm visiting my company offices and sorting out my personal affairs."

"Either I come to you or we get the police involved."

"No, you speak to my lawyer before you do anything else. If you call me, don't ever force me to answer it again." He paused, giving the older man time to process what he had just said. "And, Elgin, if you don't call my lawyer now or you call me again without running any questions by my law firm first, you better hope to god that you followed every procedure and law down to the letter. Because I can think of at least three that you broke right now. And I have a lot of lawyers who would love to make sure you spend the next few centuries relitigating that mistake. Think of the billable hours. They would get rich, just dragging you in and out of court." Peter abruptly disconnected the call. "Let's hope that worked."

Hezekiah raised an eyebrow at Peter. "What are the three laws he broke by calling you?"

Peter smiled. "No idea, but sometimes it's better to let people think they've done something wrong." He picked up the new screen device and walked toward the door. "We better find the location of my matrix before Elgin realizes it was a bluff."

CHAPTER 2

ATLAS

THE BUBBLE

"Okay, so, it's definitely not a coincidence," Atlas said, after he reported they had lost communication with the fifth probe. "And roughly in the same area, too."

Atlas was with Trillion and Icarus in his research lab on New Europa. It was a massive lab with everything he would ever need, because once he had turned the planet he discovered into one that was habitable for human life by melting all the ice, meaning space was no longer a constraint because they had a whole planet, he had ample resources and space to do whatever he wanted. So, the research laboratory he was currently in was an empty warehouse about the size of a football stadium. They were staring at a screen in one corner of the space, directing five probes that they had sent to the Tau Ceti sector of space. They had just lost signal on one of the probes—that was expected. What wasn't expected was for the other four probes to also have lost contact with the fifth probe, meaning that this particular area of space was blocking not just the Starnet but all communication.

"Do you think Angelique is in that space?" Trillion asked.

Angelique was one of the four people who left Mars at the same time. She was the only one they hadn't located yet. The general location where he assumed Angelique was had not yielded any results until recently. Because unlike himself, Trillion, or Icarus, she had done an exceptional job of not giving away her location.

Atlas knew that if the roles were reversed, he would want everyone else to do everything they could to find him. They had sent signals to all the locations he assumed she was but never got a single reply. Then he had sent probes out toward every star in close proximity to Sol. He used the four systems they had access to to manufacture fast probes and send them out. They had almost given up hope until one of the probes went dark when it entered an area of space closest to a new system. Sending subsequent probes ended in the same result. They all went dark as soon as they entered that particular region of space.

Atlas considered the question of where there might be a clue to where Angelique was. He decided he needed more data. "You know as much as me, Trillion."

"Well, then, let's speculate; what could be causing this bubble around that star system? Why would she go to all the effort to shut down our probes and not contact us? One look at the probes, she'd know they were human."

"Maybe we can do a test," Atlas said. "We know exactly where the fifth probe went dead, and we have four more close by. What if we send another one in but at an angle that just skims past the bubble of space where our probes stop responding? Using passive sensors, we might be able to understand something."

Trillion nodded. "I like that and it's safer. If the probe comes out of the bubble and is still working, then we know it's purely something messing with our communication in and out of that system. If the probe has all its electronics fried, then we know it's not safe for you to go in there, Atlas."

"Or if it never returns, then we know it's definitely not safe," Icarus added.

"Ship," Atlas said, calling out to his spacecraft's AI, who was currently piloting the probes from another location. "Can you plot a course for one of those probes so it just skims by the system? Assume that as soon as it enters that same region of space where the other probes went dead, you will lose all power for the probe. So, a course needs to have the probe drifting forward and still getting out of the system."

Ship teleported into the research laboratory with everyone else. He was starting to look quite human; he used to be a robotic droid with bright gold skin. But ever since the first children arrived, he started to make his avatar look more and more like a human, replacing the bright gold skin with a more perfectly suntanned look—and a light dashing of gold specks.

"That's going to take some time," Ship said. "Maybe about a month to maneuver the probe into position."

"Should we change our playback speed?" Trillion asked.

Changing their playback speed was a neat trick that Atlas's Ship had invented. It involved changing their perception of time; since they were simulated humans and not flesh and blood, it was easy enough for them to slow down or speed up the hardware running them. What this meant in practice was if they wanted to watch a month fly by in a couple of seconds, they could. Ship could maneuver the probe into position over a month, but to them it might only feel like two seconds.

"Yeah, let's speed up time," Icarus said. "There's no way I wanna wait around for a month."

All three of them watched the screen as one of the four probes started to accelerate away from the others. It started moving away slowly at first. But as they increased their playback speed, time raced forward. What they were watching was actually a simulated representation using all the sensors on the various probes. This allowed Ship to create a 3-D model of where all the probes were located relative to the star in the system. So, on the screen they could see a single dot that represented the star surrounded by three other markings representing the probes.

The probe traveled in an arc, first moving away from the other probes, then slowly curving back toward them on a trajectory to just pass through the region of space they had started calling the bubble.

"It is entering the space in three, two, one," Ship said. "It's just entered that region." He checked his readings "I've just lost contact with it. I'm checking with the other probes."

The other three probes used active sensors to bounce radio waves off the probe. But nothing was being bounced back. Somehow, even short-range radio frequencies were being blocked as well. "I'm getting some sort of static; the signal coming back to the probes isn't working," Ship said.

That wasn't good but also wasn't unexpected. Active sensors relied on sending a pulse toward the probe and receiving a bounced signal back. Whatever was in the bubble blocking radio signals from traveling in and out of the bubble likely was going to block the sensors of the probes.

"What about a visual?" Icarus asked.

Ship shook his head. "Those probes don't have a powerful-enough lens; we were always going to struggle to see it. Depending on the results we get here, we could send a telescope into the area."

"So, what do we do now, then?" Icarus asked.

"We wait," Atlas replied. "It shouldn't be that long if we increase our playback speed."

At the very last minute, they decided to have the probe accelerate through the system. Rather than passively floating through, they kept the engines on throughout the whole journey. That way, they would also understand if it was just the signal being disrupted or if there was something within that bubble impacting the electronics or engines of the probe.

Even though the wait was only two minutes and not a few months like it would have been, the team stressed through every moment of it; you could hear a pin drop, the team was so nervous.

A tense wait later, Ship got confirmation that the other probes were back in contact with the fourth one.

Ship checked the time it took for the probe to make it through the bubble. "The readings are saying it accelerated through the whole process."

"What about other readings?" Atlas asked. "Are any of the sensors on the probe damaged? Can you do a full diagnostic?"

A few moments later, Ship confirmed the probe was one hundred percent fine. "The probe was simply not receiving any of the communications from the other probes. Whatever is making up that bubble around the Tau Ceti system is blocking signals. It blocks everything from going in or out."

"We should have really planned for this a bit more," Atlas said. "We should have sent more probes with other measuring devices towards that region of space." He paused. "We can still see this system and the star using a telescope, so some signals are getting in and out. It really doesn't make sense to me."

"So, we're agreed," Trillion said. "Angelique might be in this bubble and she just can't communicate with us?"

"I hate to think the worst," Icarus said reluctantly. "But what if it's aliens? What if she was captured? And the reason we can't talk to the probes anymore is the same reason she hasn't replied to us?"

"No way she's been captured," Trillion interjected. "When we were in training for this mission, we were told to go quiet and not raise any awareness of the new colony. Maybe she's just making sure she's well hidden."

"You were captured," Icarus said. "Besides, we all left with the same tech. What human-level technology could do that? Atlas, any ideas?"

Atlas shrugged. "It's obviously possible, but I have no idea how it's done. All signals are being blocked. We have complete access to the probe outside of the bubble. But as soon as that one probe went inside the bubble, its connection just disappeared."

"So, what are we doing now?" Trillion asked. "If I were stuck, I'd want someone to rescue me."

"But it's too risky," Icarus said. "We can't risk losing more of us. She might not even be there."

Atlas took a moment to think. "We need to know whether she's in there or not. I need to know. I've already made plans; I'm going myself to investigate."

"Well, I'm coming with you," Trillion said.

"You're coming for as long as we can talk to each other, but I'm the closest. I'd have to wait for you if you wanted to come. And, besides, you still have to find a world to seed. You need to complete your mission so you don't have that matrix modification hanging over you."

"What about your world?" Icarus asked.

"Thanks to the Starnet, it doesn't matter where we are." He paused for a moment again, thinking about how it was possible to locate Angelique, thinking about the noise they had just made in space, Trillion and her war against Sol. "Trillion, I think you need to sneak out of your system as soon as possible. The whole galaxy knows that something just happened in your location recently. Or, rather, the remnants of the battle are spreading out at the speed of light. You probably don't want to be there if others come to investigate things."

Then he looked at Icarus. "You need to seed your world as quickly as possible. You need to remove that code in your brain that's stopping you from thinking clearly."

When Atlas, Trillion, and Icarus had their minds uploaded into the spaceships they had an additional piece of behavioral-modification code added into their brain matrix. The purpose of that code was to keep them focused on seeding a world. It was designed to make sure they completed the mission. However, one of the side effects was how myopic it made them. They didn't cherish all life like they should have. And they didn't feel emotions as much as a normal human would. It did indeed make them more likely to achieve their mission, but it also made them less human. Atlas had learned that the hard way when he finally fulfilled his mission and seeded a world. As soon as it was completed, a rush of emotion hit him. He was overwhelmed with pain as all the feelings he had not been able to feel hit him at once. He missed his family back in Sol, and he felt shame for all the things he had done out in space. It took him many months to fully recover. But when he finally did, he felt human once more. Which he didn't realize was a different feeling until that behavioral modification was removed, after which he could finally see the world clearly again. He knew that both Trillion and Icarus needed to go through that process too.

Icarus was closest to accomplishing the mission requirements for that modification to self-delete. Atlas had previously assessed their matrices and come to the conclusion that it wasn't worth trying to remove the modification themselves. Their only solution was to seed a world—and satisfy the requirements for it to remove itself. Icarus had an opportunity to build a little space colony on the ringworld he had developed. But Trillion had no way to bring a human life into the world. She had only just escaped the clutches of an alien species she had encountered. And if she were to bring a human into this world, that human would most certainly die because the spacecraft weren't designed for living humans.

"I'm almost ready to bring my first child into this world," Icarus said. "I've been building quite a few habitats and cities on the moons. I think the challenge my colony will face is not having decent gravity."

Atlas smiled a knowing smile. "I have something that might solve that for you."

While Icarus was turning asteroids into usable resources, one of his fabricators had discovered an alien artifact. It was a metal box with slightly bowed edges—about the size of a microwave. It had markings and words in a circular pattern all over it. They hadn't yet worked out what those markings meant.

Icarus assumed the relic was a tombstone rather than a message to an alien civilization that found it. Because if it were a message, it would have been designed to be easily translated. But since it was a tombstone, its only purpose was to survive and celebrate whatever its creators wanted.

The one thing all their tests showed was that the artifact was absolutely indestructible. It was made of some sort of material they didn't have on their periodic table. Its tensile strength was off the charts, and it made diamonds feel like putty. It was obviously a relic designed to last the test of time. It had a hexagonal lattice, but all the atoms were so much closer together than thought possible.

Atlas had reverse-engineered the process. He hadn't yet figured out how to make the material as one large clump. But he had managed to make the material into small filaments. Which, when used in place of the carbon nanotubes, increased the strength and flexibility of whatever object it was mixed into by hundreds of orders of magnitudes. Concrete made with this stuff was incredible.

"Icarus, I have a new material that you could use to make your ringworld—the real ringworld that you've been dreaming of," Atlas said.

Icarus raised an eyebrow. "How does it work?"

"What are you calling it?" Trillion added.

"To answer the first question, if we replace the carbon nanotubes in the material you're currently using to connect your city together, you should have enough strength to construct a rotating habitat around the whole gas giant. And I have a few ideas for a name. But I was thinking you should name it Icarus. Because based on that artifact you found, I managed to re-create the material."

"Thank god I get to name it," Icarus said. "You and Trillion have the same bad naming conventions. *Eleph-ANT* just sounds like you're saying *elephant* with a speech impediment."

"Okay, then, Professor Ludwig Von Drake of naming things," Trillion added with a laugh. "What are you going to call it, then?"

"Ah . . ." Icarus thought the question over in his mind; he felt the pressure to come up with something good. "How useful is this new material?"

Atlas handed him a piece of paper with all the unique characteristics of it. "It's harder than any material we can currently make. We haven't even figured out how to make it in large solid-object form, but as a nano material, we can use it to improve a lot of what we're building. The shielding around our spaceships, for, example would see massive improvements. Building a sky elevator on my world seems feasible too now."

"Tiamond," Icarus said, straightening up and quickly coming up with some reasoning for the answer. "I'd been saving that name for something that involves all three of us. It's basically just our first names mixed with *diamond*. So T, I, A and then *-mond* at the end."

Atlas could tell Icarus was proud of his quick thinking. He wasn't too impressed with the name, but then again, he didn't understand Icarus's gripe with *eleph*-ANT. "I like it." Atlas said lying. "I think building a true ringworld is going to take many years. So, my suggestion is that we build some small rotating habitats. Then get your first children born so you can start thinking properly. And while that's all going on, we build the ringworld."

"I agree," Trillion said. "It would be such a good experience for those first kids to see a ringworld constructed in front of their very eyes."

CHAPTER 3

PETER

TECHNOLOGY HAS CHANGED

Peter and Hezekiah were back in the helicopter, headed toward the moon. They decided to take the long way there, as it would allow the matrix-locating device to take multiple readings in the server of each location. And hopefully, that would yield them a more accurate result. They felt like having more than three data-points to triangulate the location of his matrix was better.

Peter could feel the acceleration of the helicopter gaining altitude.

"Want a beer?" Hezekiah asked, grabbing two bottles from underneath the table.

"Why not."

Hezekiah opened one of the bottles using the other one and handed it to Peter. Then he looked around, trying to find something to open his bottle with. Finding his seatbelt clip, he used that and opened up his own bottle.

"It's good," Peter said, taking a swig. "I haven't had one of these in centuries."

"I bet, there's probably so many things you haven't tried before. The things we can taste now—it's phenomenal."

"My team went out there, while I got stuck here," Peter said, thinking back to the day he died. "I don't know if they've survived or where they are. To be honest, I don't understand the appeal of this place. It's not real, yet everyone is so obsessed with it." Existential thoughts circled his mind for the first time. How did humanity get into this mess? So much energy spent on building this fake reality. The simulation really did add weight to the idea that he might never have been in the top layer of reality. Humanity as he knew it might have been born in a simulation of a simulation—and never know it. "Do you believe what you said before? When you said that they don't think the beta is the base layer of reality?"

"Well, just look at how real this layer is. And this work is more complex. It must be even easier to simulate the one out there."

"What do you mean, *more complex*?"

"You can do so much more in here. And if you go into one of the other worlds, some of them are so rich and complex, I don't even know how someone came up with them."

"You can't simulate something bigger than the base layer of reality. Shouldn't it get less complex the further you get from the real world?"

Hezekiah shook his head. "You can't simulate something bigger than the universe without a computer as big as the universe, but given the way humans perceive reality, it's easy to create an experience that's better and bigger because you don't have to render the whole universe—just the section of it that we have our attention focused on."

"If there really are aliens out there," Peter said, pointing toward the stars, "then I do think that is the base layer of reality.

Because simulating us with all these aliens would take too much resources to do." Peter started to think about what sort of alien he might find out there. If the alien were truly alien—not like a lot of aliens in movies that were basically just humans in a suit—then that would be additional proof that they were in the base layer of reality. At least that's how he saw it.

A faint ringing sound all around Peter distracted him from his thoughts. Then he noticed a little phone icon in the corner of his vision. It wasn't like the screen that appeared before. This one was unobtrusive. Subtle. Not annoying. Peter's eyes moved down to take a look at the calling icon, and to his surprise, the icon floated toward the center of his vision as the noise quieted. As it knew he wanted to know who was calling, the message made itself bigger. He looked at the name; it was his lawyer Marty call-ing. Peter reached forward to tap the call button, and headphones appeared in his ears, presumably to signal to others he was listen-ing to something.

"*Dr. Atreus, I just got off the phone with your parole officer. He's not a happy man.*"

"I don't think he'd be happy about winning the lotto."

"*That might be true sir, but you can't go around antagonising him. He seems to think you threatened him.*"

"I didn't threaten him. I simply told him about the money you would make if he called me again without talking to you first."

There was a pause on the phone and Peter thought he could here a smile of approval on the other line.

"*Well, Dr. Atreus, I have set up a meeting for tomorrow with him. And I suggest eight others from my firm. At least another of the named partners. That way we'll be able to show him we mean business.*"

"I can't do tomorrow. Can you delay him for ten days?"

"*You have a scheduled check-in a few days from now. I might be able to push your meeting with him until then.*"

"Okay, see if you can delay him. Tell Elgin I'm meeting with some of the executives at my company. That should give me enough time to sort out my personal life."

Anther pause on the line. This time Peter thought he heard some uncomfortable movements in a chair. *"If they even get an inkling of an idea that you're up to something they will lock you up. And, Dr. Atreus, my sources say someone up high is working hard to get you back in prison. They want to make an example of you."*

"Can you find out who that person is?"

"Dr. Atreus, I can tell you right now you're not going back to prison; they have nothing on you that would warrant locking you up again. But they legally have the right to install behavioral-modification modules in your matrix. Arguably, that's worse. So, let's not give them a reason to do that."

"Understood. You make sure that meeting in four days is smooth. And I'll make sure I don't give them a reason to change my behavior."

And with that, Peter disconnected the call.

"So, does that mean we need to get you out within four days?" Hezekiah asked.

"I think so. If they find out what we're up to, I don't know what they'll do."

"We have enough datapoints on this server, we could probably head to the moon now." Hezekiah said as he hovered his hand over one of the buttons on the table.

Peter nodded and Hezekiah pressed it. Rather than disappear, the helicopter started to grow and elongate. He could feel it start to shake. Peter's footing became a little unsteady, and he sat back down. The two chairs in the front, where a pilot and copilot would sit, started to turn into recliners. The recliners were making audible clicks as they transformed.

Once the cockpit changed, Hezekiah suggested they sit in the recliners for a better view. As Peter walked toward the front of the helicopter, he saw the windows had all rounded, like you would expect if the vehicle was going to experience a lot of pressure— or a vacuum. Then he noticed one of the screens that normally showed an image of the helicopter had changed to a spaceship. It looked like a huge metal egg had grown off the back of it. It was a very similar engine design to the one he used for the initial Mars mission. For a moment, he wondered if rocket-engine technology had stagnated. He hoped that technology advancements in the real world hadn't stalled. He wanted to bring some new technology out to the colonies—if his people had succeeded in building them.

Peter and Hezekiah sat in the chairs at the front of the heli-copter turned rocket ship. Peter could see out to the horizon. He hadn't realized it, but there was a lot of activity in the skies. Hot air balloons and other helicopters littered the city view. The sun was setting, so the lights from the buildings and the fire from the balloons were becoming more vibrant. The city was overlooking the ocean, and they were headed out over it.

They drifted forward for a good while, enough time for the sun to set. Then Peter heard a beep and a countdown timer started from three . . . two . . . one. Then he was pushed toward the back of his seat. But it was so soft, like memory foam, he melted into it, and somehow, it wasn't uncomfortable. In some way, he felt more relaxed than before.

The horizon in front of Peter started to move as they began shooting upward toward the starry sky. Evidently, the light pollution from below wasn't impeding his ability to see the stars perfectly. There was one particular star that was bigger than the others. He'd never known a star to be that big before, and he wondered if it was a space station orbiting Earth. Faster and faster they moved. Peter could see the star he thought might be a space station becoming bigger. They were moving toward it quickly. And as they got closer, Peter could see it was circular. At first, it looked like a tiny ring in the sky. Then slowly, they got closer, and Peter could see it was a giant rotating ring. Peter wondered if it was a rotating habitat. He couldn't understand the stupidity of building a rotating habitat in the simulated world. Why not build a real one in the real world?

"Ahh"; he had to get out of the simulation.

Their speed started to slow, and as they grew closer, Peter started to comprehend the scale of the ring they were head-ing toward. It wasn't a rotating world; it was some sort of gate.

He watched as spacecraft after spacecraft flew into it and disappeared.

They weren't heading toward it one at a time, either. Ships that Peter assumed were at least fifty meters wide flew into one section of it at the same time that dozens of others entered the aperture.

Hezekiah clicked a button on table that increased the size of the viewport, giving them a more expansive view. "Incredible, isn't it?"

"What is that thing?"

"It's a time gate."

Confused, Peter tried to clarify. "Does it take us to a different point in time?"

Hezekiah shook his head. "No, it slows down our matrix and takes us to the moon." Then, noticing the even-more-confused look on Peter's face, he asked, "Do you know about the moon's time zone?"

Peter shook his head.

"To make it feel like communication on the moon is real-time, anyone going there from Earth has their clock slowed down. So, while we're on the moon, an hour will feel like an hour. But when we come back here . . . Oh, well, you'll see."

Peter did some quick math in his head. "It takes signals here just over a second to get there. And then the same amount of time to get back? Call it two point six seconds for a signal to reach the moon and back. So . . ." He counted numbers out on his hand. "If you wanted to slow down time enough so you didn't notice that delay in the signal, you'd need to slow down a lot. Hmm, assuming you needed at least twenty-four frames per second for a smooth experience. Then . . . then one hour would become sixty-two hours back on Earth."

"Yes, your math is right. They might have done that in the beginning, too. But now there's a program that fills in some of the frames. So, one hour on the moon is only four hours on Earth. That was their workaround to bring the Earth and moon in line."

"What happens if you live on the moon?"

"A few people live there. But most people who send their matrices there are just there to complete a particular job that requires really fast response times. They're screwed if they want to join any servers here. And they have to reduce their clock speed whenever someone visits them."

They continued toward the large ring, and Peter couldn't believe how big it was. It had a diameter of at least five hundred meters. He would have been more impressed if he didn't know it was a simulation, because to construct something that size out in real space would have taken a considerable effort. Knowing it was a simulation took a little of the magic of the experience away—even though his mind was screaming at him to be in awe of it.

As they drifted closer and closer toward the giant ring, Peter started to gain an understanding of what it looked like. It was made up of two separate rotating pieces of machinery. The inside ring was smooth, almost glass-like. It had to be at least ten meters thick. And it was rotating clockwise. The outer ring looked like a bicycle chain, or presumably a chain used in heavy machinery; it was about half as thick as the inner ring and was rotating in the opposite direction. But rather than rotating smoothly, it sort of ticked. The more Peter watched it, the more he thought he could hear the ticks it made as it rotated one step at a time.

"Each of those ticks represent a frame on the other side of that portal," Hezekiah said.

"What's a frame?"

"It's similar to how movies are twenty-four frames per second."

"The inside of that ring is like a time bubble," Hezekiah explained." It just looks black from here. But once we get closer, you'll see it kinda looks like a liquid mirror with its surface covered in smoke. First time I came in here, I thought it'd be like jumping into water. But it's more similar to entering mist."

As they reached the aperture, a black mist washed over the ship. It was unlike any mist Peter was used to, because rather than reflecting light and becoming white, the mist sort of absorbed light.

"You think this is cool, wait until you get to the other side."

CHAPTER 4

HEZEKIAH

THE MOON

"Wave your hands up and down," Hezekiah said, doing just that himself. He knew if he timed it just right, his hands would cross the time-zone barrier before his arms did, in effect making it look like his hand had slowed down in time while his arm continued moving up and down.

Peter looked at him in confusion until he noticed what was happening with Hezekiah's hand. "I didn't expect that."

Hezekiah's hand slowed dramatically while his arm continued going up and down. Rather than looking like his hand was cut off, it looked like it'd been stretched out, Like part of it had been turned to rubber and was being pulled along by his waving arm. But in reality, it only looked that way because part of his hand was in a bubble of slower space.

It was an odd sensation to watch your arm move while your own hand stretched out. No matter how many times Hezekiah went through the gate, he still giddied like a child when he did that little trick. The strange optical illusion ended as soon as his eyes crossed over the invisible threshold.

Once they crossed that line, their view out the front of the spacecraft changed too. They were now in orbit around the moon. They found themselves drifting out in space. Hezekiah could feel the weightlessness. He could feel himself bobbing between his seatbelt and the chair. "That's the moon base. We moved it from Mars because of the time delay—it was becoming impossible to get anyone who wanted to work on such an isolated planet."

Looking around the spaceship, Peter asked, "I don't notice any difference in my personal time. Have we switched over?"

"Have a look at your watch."

Peter looked at his wrist. "It's ticking along like normal."

"Oh, that's right; your watch is old-school," he said, holding out his arm. "Look at mine."

The watch on Hezekiah's arms was ticking rapidly, much faster than you would have expected. "Each of those is a second back on Earth." Hezekiah pointed to the back of the spacecraft. Where there used to be an empty wall, two spacesuits with umbilical cords were connected to the wall. "Want to go for a spacewalk?"

Peter shook his head.

Hezekiah looked disappointed. "Not even a little bit?"

"Let's do that when we're out of this simulation."

"Teleport it is, then," Hezekiah replied, hovering his hand over one of the buttons. "Our ship can dock itself; we can go inside now." He pressed a button on the console in front of them.

The two of them appeared in the lobby of an office. People were walking around in lab coats. Ten meters in front of both of them was a desk—but no receptionist. People were scanning their badges, then walking through the security gates. They'd then scan their badge again and an elevator door would open. There was a lot of hustle and bustle.

Hezekiah began walking toward the front desk. "Come with me; we need to get an access card made for you."

"Why do we travel in that helicopter-spaceship thing? Can't we just teleport everywhere ourselves?"

"Not really. Usually, to teleport between servers or layers, you need to go through a gate. That transport vehicle we're moving in is super expensive. It allows us a lot more freedom than most people would get. It costs a lot to travel around as much as we just did. The moon is an expensive server to be on."

Hezekiah entered Peter's name into a screen on the front desk. "Now scan your arm."

Peter did as instructed, then moments later, a key card was produced on the reception counter.

Hezekiah picked it up and walked toward the gate. He scanned the card and handed it to Peter. "Keep this; it'll get you access to anywhere in here." He scanned his own card and walked through to the other side. Hezekiah stepped forward and scanned his card on a screen in front of the elevator.

As the two of them waited for the elevator door to open up, someone came running over. It looked like a young woman; she was tiny, attractive, and maybe nineteen. But avatars were so easy to change these days that it was never good to assume someone was the age they looked like. Hezekiah moved his huge frame in front of the woman and raised his hand. It wasn't like anyone could get hurt in the metaverse—well, not permanently. Although he had heard of some hackers successfully ejecting malicious code through contact. The victim had to be restored from a previous backup. They lost months of living.

The woman almost smacked into Hezekiah's hand, as she didn't see him step out in front of her.

With his hand two inches from her face, he said to her, "That's close enough, ma'am; how can we help?"

The woman ducked, moving her head below Hezekiah's arm. Ignoring the big man, she said, "Dr. Atreus, you're back."

Peter reached out and moved Hezekiah's hand out of the way, "That's why I like you, Kiah. You're an engineer that could probably be my bodyguard. It's good to be out and about."

"I just wanted to say, sir, you've been an idol of mine. You're the reason I'm here. And it's just disgusting what they did to you. Wasted so many years in there."

The door to the elevator opened, and Hezekiah's name appeared at the top, so he walked toward it, nodding at the new acquaintance. "Okay, that's us; nice to meet you, Ms…"

"Ms. Greenaway."

"Okay, Ms. Greenaway, we must be off now," Hezekiah said, then mentally admonished himself for talking so weirdly. *Must be off* was the worst way to say that.

"Actually, I'm coming with you both."

Hezekiah looked at Peter, who shrugged.

"Dr. Ariana Barns asked me to collect you both."

Ariana Barns was the head of the research laboratory. She knew Hezekiah and Peter from before he went to prison. Hezekiah knew Peter liked her for her unending focus on improving and testing things, but Hezekiah found she took things a little too far by experimenting on herself.

"Unity Greenaway?" Peter said. "I was expecting . . ."

"Hush," she said, taking the few steps around Hezekiah and grabbing Peter's arm. "We might be old now, but it doesn't mean we have to look it." Then she added in a conspiratorial whisper, "I like 'em young and dumb, but those guys want their woman young, too."

She pointed toward the elevator and the three of them entered together. Walking inside she pressed a different button on the panel then held the door open with her arm. "Before you see Dr. Barns, there's something I need to tell you."

Hezekiah looked toward Peter in confusion.

"Come on, then; tell us," Peter said.

"She's developed a different personality."

"How does someone develop a different personality?" Hezekiah asked.

"I know she'll be different from when I first went to prison. But I've spoken to her recently; she didn't seem different." Peter added.

"This is a recent development," Unity said. "We're still understanding what it all means. Does the name Roger Sperry mean anything to you?"

Hezekiah knew that name; he'd seen docos about him before. "Is that the guy who won a Nobel prize in nineteen seventy for cutting people's brains down the middle?"

Unity nodded. "Exactly, that's how far back in the research we had to go to find something analogous to what we're seeing here."

"So, what are you saying, Unity?" Peter said. "Has she had her brain split in two?"

"Close. In nineteen seventy, when Sperry was doing his very archaic research, they found that when someone's brain was cut in half, each side of their brain had a different personality. Subsequent research using less-crude methods in the two thousands found that different sides of someone's brain could have completely different personalities."

"Oh, I think I've heard of that; is that when people have half their brain put to sleep using anaesthesia?"

"Kiah, how do you know so much about that?" Peter asked.

Hezekiah shrugged. "I watch a lot of docos."

"Anyways," Unity interrupted them, "so, when these people have half their brain put to sleep, sometimes their left brain might be a massive extrovert, even though the person themselves is an introvert. The strange thing to think about is: which personality is the real them?"

"Yeah," Hezekiah said. "I've heard that some people who had their left and brain sides of the brain separate fight amongst themselves over the body. One doco I watched had someone's left arm try and strangle themselves, while they had to defend themselves using their other arm."

Peter raised an eyebrow. "Was that a documentary or a horror movie?"

Unity took her hand away from the door. "I don't think I'm explaining it quite right. She's doesn't have a split personality. She's just completely different. I guess you'll have to see for yourself."

The door closed and the three of them started to ascend.

Moments later, the door opened, and standing at the door was Dr. Ariana Barns. She had an aura about her. She radiated power. She wasn't overly tall, but she had a swagger and presence like no other person Hezekiah knew—next to obviously Peter. Her lightly tanned skin and total boss attitude reminded him a lot of the artist Beyoncé. Her arms were crossed behind her, and unlike other times when Hezekiah had seen her, she felt different. She felt dangerous. Maybe *dangerous* was too strong a word, but he did feel threatened.

CHAPTER 5

HEZEKIAH

NEW TECHNOLOGY

Hezekiah watched as Peter jumped forward and gave Dr. Ariana Barns a hug. "What's this I hear about you changing your personality?"

Ariana stood there frozen. Unmoving. Then, almost like she realized she had to play a role, she hugged Peter back. "Has Unity been telling you fairy tales?"

Peter let go of her. "You do seem a bit tense, Ari."

"Do I?" Ariana replied, her voice sounding robotic, as if a sort of auto-tune was coming from her speech. "There is a reason for that. And it has led to some very big discoveries that I'll show you in the lab."

The four of them began the long walk down the corridor. The corridor was wide, yet for some reason, Hezekiah couldn't see to the end of it—even though it wasn't that far away. He knew that when some server locations were processing too much information, rather than slow down, they would not render parts of the environment that were far away. He wondered if that was what was happening right now.

Ariana walked in front of them all, not turning her head toward them but talking loudly so all of them could hear. "I know Unity likes to use the analogy of someone with split-brain personality." Rather than turn her head, Ariana pointed behind her back toward Unity. "But that analogy completely fails to grasp what this really is. A better analogy would be that of the *cerebral cortex* versus the *basal ganglia*."

"Are you saying you've developed another neocortex?" Peter suggested as a guess.

"Even better," Ariana replied. "The basal ganglia were one of the first parts of the brain to develop. It's where we got the fight-or-flight instinct from. Because in the early world where the basal ganglia evolved, life involved a lot of running away or you might be eaten. That's why some people call it our reptile brain. But as our environment changed, the basal ganglia became ineffective for what we needed. And that's when we developed the amygdala. That was particularly important for storing and creating new memories." She turned a corner in a fluid motion and didn't lose a single beat in her sentence. "But once our distant ancestors started to live in large groups and social interactions became more important, our reptile brain was woefully underequipped for what we needed. And that's when the neocortex really started to develop. And humans have been using that for the past one-hundred thousand years." She pointed at the ceiling. "Even in here, all we're doing is digitally simulating a meat brain in a matrix—without changing it in any way. Since humanity made a concerted effort not to develop AI more powerful than us, our current brain design has been woefully unequipped for all the challenges we're facing here."

Peter replied. "Are you talking about multidimensional space?"

Hezekiah was still trying to unpack everything being said right now. He still wasn't fully following the conversation. Yet he was impressed that Peter was not only understanding everything so quickly but also unpacking what Ariana was saying and guessing the direction of the conversation.

"That's exactly what I'm talking about," Ariana continued. "Our brains evolved in the physical world. We struggle to intuitively grasp exponential or logarithmic curves, let alone understanding a world beyond three dimensions of space and one of time. Quantum mechanics is as natural to this universe as is an apple falling from a tree. Yet the only reason we don't intuitively grasp it is because our brain was designed for the apple tree and not for a quantum one."

"Let me get this straight," Peter said, then he paused, thinking it all over. He scratched his head as everyone walked in silence. "I've heard people who study string theory talk about how in physics, quantum mechanics and gravity are not compatible mathematically unless you add more than three dimensions of space?"

Hezekiah help up his hand. "Please dumb this down for me. I want to understand you, but my eyes are glazing over. I think you're saying you can somehow understand things better now. But how?"

"Let me try," Ariana said. "I hate to use the cliché example of a two-dimensional world, but it's the only way I can simplify it." She opened her notepad and pulled out a piece of paper. Holding it up above her head, she showed it to the others. "Imagine a piece of paper." She paused, crumpled the piece of paper up, and dropped it into a bin then pointed toward the tiled floor they were walking over. "Actually, no. Imagine you lived on this floor we are all walking on. It's a two-D world, so you can't look up from your floor world. All you can do is look across the floor. So, all you can see as I walk across this floor are my steps appearing and disappearing. Actually, you wouldn't see my shoes; you'd just see these random lines appearing and disappearing. Now imagine you're a smart person in this floor world."

Hezekiah felt like she was singling him out when she said that.

Ariana continued. "You start to build models of your world and make predictions. You realize at the start of each day at around nine a.m., a big influx of these lines appears, randomly scattered all over the place. So, as all good researchers do, you decide to collect more data and improve your model. You don't know why, but you start to see these ten patterns of lines that appear multiple times each day. Now after months and months of recording these lines, you realize that these ten line patterns always come in pairs, once coming in"—she pointed up the hall—"and once going out." She pointed back down the hall.

Hezekiah at this point was guessing what Ariana was trying to say. She was trying to explain that with enough observation, you'd start to learn that ten people walk in and out of the building each day.

Ariana stopped walking and turned around. It was the first time she had acknowledged their presence fully on this walk. "Now, you might build a model that is a reasonable approximation for when these ten patterns appear each day. But alas, no matter how hard you try to improve your model, you can never quite predict to a level of accuracy that is useful. And you never would. In your two-D world, you'll never be able to properly model the way I or my nine other colleagues walk. You wouldn't have the full and complete picture because you don't understand a three-D world."

"If I understand your analogy correctly," Peter said, "you're saying that our brain evolved to think in three dimensions of space and one in time. And thus, we can't intuitively grasp a world, or mathematics, in four dimensions and beyond? But somehow with the additional computing power you've added, you can?"

"Exactly."

Peter interrupted her. "You remind me of an old friend, Atlas, when you say that."

"I knew Atlas before . . . well, before he left. He was a smart man. But he wasn't this smart. Anyway, as I was saying, Einstein was famous for doing thought experiments, but thought experiments just aren't possible unless you intuitively grasp higher-dimensional space. But now I can vividly imagine these worlds."

"What's it like?" Hezekiah asked.

"I wish I were a poet. We should try giving this gift to a poet. For now, that analogy was the best description I can provide."

"How does what you added to your brain matrix work?" Peter scratched the top of his head. "By giving your matrix more power? More memory? Haven't we tried that before?"

"No, almost the opposite. Do you know what a neural network or large language model is?"

"An early AI? One of those old ones used to create narrow artificial intelligences?"

"Yes, that exactly," Ariana said. "We trained up one of those models, then physically built it and added it into my brain matrix. Wired everything together so it's one unit. And now it's an added layer of my matrix that I can use, the same way the neocortex was built on top of our older brain. This new—I call it the neuralcortex—was built directly on top of my neocortex."

The four of them continued walking in silence, thinking about what was just discussed. Hezekiah guessed it was almost an inevitability that something like that would happen. What Ariana had described was different from any other brain augmentation he had heard of. Usually, it was just giving them more power, or connecting the brain to the world's encyclopedia. Hezekiah had heard of some experiments where people connected brain matrices to massive power sources and bigger hardware. Those people could spend hundreds of years thinking about a problem in a blink of an eye. Some of these people even connected their brains to the internet so they knew everything and had years to solve problems. But it never really created the kinds of breakthroughs people were expecting. So, maybe Ari was right. Maybe it required a different kind of brain. A completely different way of thinking.

They arrived at the entrance of the research facility. The door was white and had no window, so Hezekiah couldn't see beyond it.

Ariana scanned her card, then opened the door. "I'm going to show you some of the new technology we built."

Hezekiah walked toward the door. And it wasn't what he was expecting: the door led directly onto the moon surface. There were rockets and robotic machinery moving around. He saw one of the large machines that had six large legs and a manipulator at the front. He remembered its nickname was an eleph-ANT.

Peter walked through first. As soon as he crossed the threshold of the door, he was suddenly wearing a spacesuit. Gravity changed too, and Hezekiah watched him begin to bounce.

Hezekiah was going to walk through the door when Unity tapped him on the shoulder. "While Dr. Barns shows off some of her inventions, can we talk briefly?"

Hezekiah felt disappointed. He really wanted to see what Ari had built. But he also knew it wasn't mandatory he knew. "Sure, what is it?"

Unity motioned for the two of them to walk farther down the hall. It was a short walk to a new door. This time, it was a small office. Unity opened the door and the two of them walked inside.

As soon as the door close Unity said, "Mr Rutherford is headed here."

"The CEO?"

Unity nodded. "He's going to intercept you two before you leave."

"So what? Why are you telling me? Why not tell Peter?"

"I think you should make yourself scarce when he comes."

Hezekiah was confused; he'd met Yaya Rutherford before and never known he should avoid him. He was known to always get his way and was a very controlling individual, but what powerful person wasn't? "You look concerned. What's going to happen when he gets here?"

"Well, I've never known Mr Rutherford to lose. He always gets what he wants. He's ruthless and determined. And I've heard that he's been meeting with the board. He's going to shut down this little project."

Hezekiah wore a puzzled look on his face. "Peter owns the company. They can't shut what he wants down."

"And he's the CEO. He's been the CEO the whole time Peter was in jail. It's not like people won't be loyal to him. I remember when the old chairman of the board and he disagreed. I heard they had a disagreement, then, the next day, the chairman was gone. The chairman of the board was gone." A little bit of panic crossed Unity's face as she said that.

"So what?"

"He fired the chairman! The CEO is meant to report to the chairman, not the other way around."

"So, you think he'll somehow get rid of Peter? Kick him out of his own company?"

"Quite possibly, especially if he thinks it's for the good of the company."

"I still don't understand why you're telling me this," Hezekiah said.

"I'm telling you because Peter will be okay. He's rich; even if they force him to sell half his shares, he'll still be one of the richest people in the world. But you, you'll probably lose your job here. You'll be collateral damage through this whole process."

"I've known Peter for centuries. He wouldn't leave me out to dry."

"Peter might not have a choice. If it gets to that point, he might be back in jail, and he might not have time to protect you."

"He's not going back to jail."

"Probably not. But I still don't think it's worth you taking the risk. I know you've never seen it. But I've heard stories; the CEO doesn't lose."

Hezekiah considered those words for a moment. "How long do we have?"

CHAPTER 6

TRILLION

CHILDREN

Trillion and Icarus sat cross-legged with their eyes closed in a completely white room, their arms hanging by their sides, his shoulders dropped back. They were completely relaxed, deep in meditation.

"Now breathe out," Trillion said in a very calming voice as she guided them both through the meditation. "And keep breathing out. And as you do, drop your shoulders further down. I want you completely relaxed."

Neither Trillion nor Icarus needed to breathe, so breathing out was a motion they could do indefinitely, and breathing out was the most relaxing part of meditation.

Trillion slowed her breath even more. "Now breathe in, and feel your body begin to move apart." This time, she started to float off the ground, her chest and lungs expanding.

Icarus joined her in floating, his cartoon-like body expanding a lot more than hers.

Trillion breathed out, her voice coming not from her mouth but from all around the room. "Now as we breathe out, I don't want you to imagine becoming a puddle. I want you to become a puddle, get so relaxed you literally become water on the ground."

The two of them began to drift toward the floor. Trillion was the first to make contact, and as she did, her body continued melting downward. She started to become translucent, her body truly becoming water as she continued to breathe out. Melting, becoming more and more relaxed. She felt like every single problem she'd ever had was disappearing; nothing else was in her mind except this sensation of pure joy and a oneness with herself as a body of water.

Icarus's avatar melted too, but it had more of a video-game quality, glistening as if light was shining over it.

The two of them lay there in meditation for a few moments before Trillian's calming, slow voice was heard all around then once more. "Now, this time, as we breathe in, I want you to expand your mind. Don't imagine being like mist. Become mist, expanding to fill half of this room. And don't focus on any one thing. Become many individual particles of water."

Trillion began to breathe out. Her puddle began to expand, lifting off the floor of the white room at first, then turning into steam before expanding completely to fill one entire half of the room.

There was a thin sheet of glass dividing the room, was not visible until the moment that Trillion expanded to fill the room completely.

Icarus expanded but unlike Trillion couldn't turn into a mist. The puddle of water began to break apart. Once in half, those two halves broke apart. Then a single droplet pulled away from one of the smaller puddles.

"That's it; keep expanding with your breath," Trillion said.

More and more tiny droplets began pulling themselves away from the body of water. As Icarus expanded, he became like rain floating in space.

The two of them floated like that for thirty minutes. On one side was the mist of Trillion and on the other, the rain that was Icarus. They both bobbed up and down with each breath slowly, before Trillion guided them back to their bodies.

"Now with this next breath in, I want all of your small droplets to drift inwards, to condense, melt into each other once more." She began breathing out and shrinking, the mist of Trillion retaking a shape that resembled her blurry outline, before her face and neck became visible. Then her shoulders. Then moments later, Trillion was sitting, legs and arms crossed, eyes closed. She was in a pure form of zen.

She opened her eyes just in time to watch Icarus fully re-form. She smiled warmly at him.

Icarus was grinning from ear to ear. "That was incredible. I've never been so relaxed and calm in my life."

"I've been doing this once a day now. It's meditation on steroids."

"How do you become like mist, though?" Icarus asked. "I struggled to concentrate on all the little pieces of me. I couldn't make myself small enough; how did you do it?"

"You just need practice. But I think you're ready to bring this child into the world."

Icarus nodded, and the two of them stayed sitting there while the white room around them disappeared, revealing the interior of a rotating habitat. From their viewpoint, you could be fooled into thinking you were on a planet. Trees, grass, and small cottages surrounded Icarus and Trillion. There wasn't a window out into space or wall that immediately blocked the view. They used the hapticgraphic projectors to create a display on the walls. Icarus took the creative liberty to add the occasional brachiosaurus with its long neck walking in the background. The only thing that removed the illusion created by the hapticgraphic projections was when they walked around—the perspective didn't change.

The rotating habitat orbited around the gas giant that Icarus had found and called Titan. And Icarus wanted to call the world he was building the Rings of Titan. He had begun building small habitats to support his colony. They were dotted around the larger asteroids and small moons that were orbiting Titan. He would eventually connect all of them. In theory, once complete, an artificial world would rotate around the gas giant. And if someone wanted to, they could spend many years walking in a full loop from one end of the habitat all the way around back to the start.

But that was still a work in progress; for now, they had simply constructed small habitats that were practically the size of a basketball stadium. They were shaped like domes, and at the very top of the dome was a long tether. At the other end of that tether was a heavy counterweight. Icarus would spin these two objects up, and that would result in simulated gravity on the small habitat.

Icarus and Trillion were standing outside the hospital now.

Icarus grabbed the door handle. "I'm nervous."

Trillium placed a hand on his shoulder. "Will be with you this whole time."

The two of them walked through the door; Atlas was standing next to a robotic nurse who was holding a small plastic cup of water and some pills.

"What is it going to feel like?" Icarus said, a little afraid.

"You're going to feel like yourself again," Atlas said. "You don't realize how different your personality currently is until you go through this process. Luckily, I've gone through it already, so we know what to expect."

"That's why we did the meditation," Trillion said. "Just practice your breathing."

Icarus breathed a long breath out. "Okay, let's do it."

Icarus walked toward the electronic incubator machine just behind the nurse. It was a white machine with a clear section filled with fluid. Trillion handed him a small metal tube. Icarus slotted the tube into a hole on the incubator. Noises started to happen.

The nurse walked over to Icarus and handed him the cup of water and some pills.

"What are they?"

"It's to help with the placebo effect," Atlas said. "The physical pill and the code we've added to your matrix will help calm you and prepare your mind for what is about to happen."

Icarus grabbed the pills and swallowed them. Then he drank the water and handed the cup back to the nurse. "Now we wait. Nine months in two minutes."

Trillion knew Atlas wasn't going to change his playback speed; he had a colony now, and normally, whenever they moved forward in time, he would pop off to his planet to see his kids. But in this instance, they wanted Icarus to feel like they were both there to support him. So, Trillion and Atlas nodded. Atlas left an avatar to look like it was moving forward in time, while Trillion and Icarus changed their playback speed. Time began to speed up; it was like a movie behind the glass of the incubator machine. They were literally watching life, human life, grow in front of their eyes. At first, it looked like a tadpole floating in a bowl of clear white Jelly. Then the tail of the tadpole began to curl and legs appeared. Then arms appeared. Then after a little while, what mostly looked like a forehead attached to some appendages started to have defining features—a real human face.

Then the baby started turning around. Moving. Spinning. Swimming through the embryonic fluid. But because time was sped up, it looked jittery, the baby's motion a blur.

Trillion could clearly see it was a girl as her perception of time started to return to normal. A white cover moved over the clear part of the mechanical incubator. And her view of the baby disappeared. Moments later, the nurse walked behind the machine and came back carrying a little girl all wrapped up in the cutest little blanket.

Trillion's heart broke then, and she was filled with so much joy. *Babies are beyond cute,* she thought. With warm feelings of butterflies, she had to fight the urge not to hold the baby first. She was so jealous of Icarus in that very moment. He had just colonized the world and brought the most special little girl into this universe.

Icarus took hold of the baby and started to weep. He started to cry even more when he handed the baby to Trillion, who took hold of her and rocked her gently. The nurse brought over a bottle and Trillion began feeding her.

"Ahhhhh!" Icarus screamed. "Why have I been here for so long? Why did I agree to do this? Such a stupid idea, leaving Mars. My friends. My family."

Trillion could tell Icarus was going through the same thing that Atlas had gone through. That little section in his matrix was being deleted. All the emotions and feelings it was holding back were now able to flow freely through him. "Breathe," Trillion said, rocking the baby up and down. "Drop your shoulders. You can get through this."

Icarus started to hyperventilate. "Ship, can you help?!"

The Ship of Icarus joined in the room. The droid put an arm on Icarus. He blinked a few times, obviously scanning Icarus. "Lex, I'm sending you an additional piece of code; can you add this to Icarus?"

Lex appeared in the room. Lex was a floating orb, actually a three-dimensional shadow of a four-dimensional sphere, called a hypersphere. Which basically meant its shape and size changed constantly, but it mostly looked like a sphere that pulsated.

The orb flashed green, indicating it had implemented the piece of code.

"Thank you," said Ship. "Icarus should start to feel a little calmer now."

Icarus's breathing started to settle. He started to look at the little baby, and he pasted a fake smile on his face. "I feel so numb now." He moaned. "Definitely feels like I'm drugged up on antidepressants."

"You're doing better than I was," Atlas said. "At this point, I was a mess on the floor, curled up in a ball."

"Back then, we didn't know this was going to happen," Trillion said.

"I can feel my mind wanting to go in circles," Icarus said almost sleepily. "I'm replaying that moment we left, when Peter was shot. We were chased off Mars. I'm wondering whether I even had to go. I don't think we had a moment to think."

"It took me a couple of weeks to get back to normal," Atlas said.

Icarus scratched his head. "Can I skip ahead to that part?"

"It's two weeks of real experienced time. You can't change your playback speed, because your mind has to have time to process it. Process everything that just happened. And everything that's happened ever since we left Mars. Trust me; in two weeks, you'll start to feel better."

Icarus started to cry a little. "Thank you for being with me this whole time. Trillion, Atlas, Ship, I love you all. You three are honestly my best friends. I don't know how I'll feel in a few weeks, but at this stage, I want to go back home—back to Sol."

Trillion walked over and gave him a hug, holding the baby in one arm and wrapping her other arm around Icarus. She didn't think it was appropriate to point out to him that Sol just tried to arrest her. If he went back to Earth or Mars, then he'd probably be going to prison. Or worse, they'd just switch him off. "What are you gonna name her?" she said, holding the baby toward him.

"Eve," Icarus said as he took her.

PETER

PLANS HAVE CHANGED

Peter and Ariana walked out of the moon laboratory together, Peter holding the door open for Ariana. As soon as they crossed the threshold, their spacesuits disappeared. Peter was back in his suit and Ariana was back in her white lab coat. Peter expected to see Hezekiah and Unity outside and wondered where they were. He figured they must be waiting for them downstairs.

Peter regarded Ariana as they walked. "I hope you're right. I hope what you did to yourself was worth it, because it's shocking how little humanity has progressed with rocket science. It's basically just better versions of the tech we had before I left. Where is the faster-than-light travel?"

Ariana nodded. "I think it is the right approach. Once we started limiting AI development, this became our only means of thinking beyond our evolved capability. It's just taken us a while to get here."

"But why do you think that is? Why did humanity suddenly accept a non-exponential rate of technological improvement?"

"Well, first, in here, in the metaverse tech has continued to grow exponentially. Miniaturization of matrices. The things you can do in here. The worlds. They've all gotten better. Out in the real world, though, it's not unusual for technological progress to stop and start. Just think about the AI winter of the nineteen seventies and eighties. That delayed humanity's progress for quite a while." She looked at Peter. "I think the bigger question is, why has humanity stopped looking outwards? Why the obsession with what's inside the metaverse?" She paused for a moment, almost looking left and right as she spoke. "I think someone, or something, is pushing us into the metaverse."

Before Peter could respond, he received a message from Hezekiah.

Evidently, Ariana received a similar message, as she spoke first. "The CEO, Yaya Rutherford, is here. I think you better leave. Pretend like you just missed him."

Peter looked at her, confused. "Why is everyone so afraid of this man? If he's here to speak with me, then I should probably speak with him."

"Well, I'm not going to be here, then. I don't want to be here when he shuts down my department." She looked at Peter. It was the first time he saw a glimpse of the old Ari. The kind and warm Ari. Peter smiled, thinking back to those days. "I know you're leaving. That's why you recruited us again. I'm coming with you. Unity and I are coming. Give us twenty-four hours. We'll bring everything we showed you today and some other things. My matrix is on the moon because it's easier to get this research done, but we can transfer me back at any time. Give me some time to get everything sorted. Then we're coming with you." Then, without so much as a goodbye, Ariana turned around and walked off. Her walk was quick and efficient.

Peter nodded because he had always planned on bringing her—if she wanted to come. At least now he knew.

He began his walk in the opposite direction. He rounded a corner and, to his surprise, right in front of him was Yaya Rutherford. The CEO had found him. That was probably why Ari had left so quickly. He was a large man with a huge head—both physically and metaphorically, if Peter remembered correctly. He had a dark navy suit and a pale red tie. He was flanked by two people he hadn't met before, but having done his research, he knew who they were. Al Robert was the head of operations and Zinnia Tracy was one of the top lawyers within his company.

Yaya started speaking immediately, not even waiting for an opening. "Peter, what's this I hear about you creating a division to research physics in the betaverse?"

Peter admired his direct approach. No pleasantries, just straight to the point. If Peter were young, that approach would have worked, too. Posing an accusatory question and skipping the social niceties was a good way of getting someone on the back foot. It put you in control of the situation.

Yaya continued his tirade. "I think we need to have a bigger conversation about your role here. There's a lot you don't understand. This company has changed while you were in prison."

Yaya placed special emphasis on the word *prison*, and Peter could tell he was using that word to again reduce Peter's status in the confrontation. To frame Peter as a criminal and not the owner of this company.

"Look—" Peter said, putting his hand on the CEO's shoulder, then pausing. Peter decided to restart the conversation and ignore Yaya's accusations. He focused his eyes on the other two, and while keeping one hand on Yaya's shoulder, he stretched his other hand out offering a handshake. "Hi, I don't believe we've met. I'm Peter Atreus."

"We know who you are, sir," Zinnia said.

Noticing his opportunity, Peter asked, "And who am I?"

"You're the founder and owner of this company?" Al replied, slightly confused.

"That's correct," Peter said, turning back to Yaya. "Now, would you rather I continue doing what I'm doing with you as CEO, or would you rather I fire you and hire someone else who lets me do with my company as I need to?" He paused, letting the idea of being fired sink in. He wanted it to feel like a realistic threat. "I think you're a great CEO; you actually grew my wealth more than I expected. Some people in your position probably would have lined their back pockets. But you honestly grew the pie. And I'm very grateful and I want you to keep doing this job for me." Peter made sure to place emphasis on the words *for me.*

"A lot of people in your position would probably quit," Peter continued. "But I know you, I've met others like you before, you won't quit. You won't quit because there's nowhere else you could go to get this level of power—let alone money.

Scoffing, Yaya replied, "I can name ten places that would happily take me today."

Peter looked at the other two. It was one thing to give a dressing-down to a CEO. It was another to do it in front of his subordinates. He knew if this conversation spread through the organization, it would be too much for a man with a bruised ego to handle. Peter nodded and gestured at the other two to leave. They turned around and made haste in the opposite direction.

Once the other two were firmly out of earshot, Peter continued. "I'm sure you could name a hundred places that would take you right now. With your CV, I'm sure there isn't a shortage of companies offering you jobs every day. But in terms of a step up from what you have now, there's only one other company. And their CEO is just as capable as you, though I don't think she'd have the balls to come at me like you did now. But still, that's the only option you have. And I know for a fact if their current CEO found out you were even remotely interviewing for a job, she'd be all over you. There's no way she'd allow you to take her job, let alone attempt to take it. Are you really sure you want to take that risk? Fighting her, even if you did take it? Everyone loyal to her would make sure you didn't succeed."

"Why are you telling me all this? If it's a fight you want, I can give you one," Yaya replied, and Peter noticed a hint of dejection in his voice.

"I'm telling you this so you understand. You've been the big, big boss of one of the largest organizations in the world. Barring some US president wanting to look good in front of his constituents, you've probably never been spoken to like this before." Peter paused once more before continuing. "Now, you can continue to be the ruler of this chiefdom; just know I'm the bigger boss, and I'm allocating some resources to something bigger than both you or I."

"Maybe I'm ready to retire."

"Let me tell you why you don't want to go," Peter said, getting ready to offer the carrot after only showing the stick.

Yaya gestured for him to continue, but the slight twinkle in his eye betrayed his intrigue in what Peter was about to share.

"Because there's only one thing more powerful than running the biggest private company in the world."

"I'll bite," Yaya said. "And what's that?"

"Controlling an entire solar system."

"Not in the current legislative environment. The betaverse is out of bounds."

"It's only out of bounds because we haven't put our lobbying team to work on that. With the right leader, someone like you, we can start with public perception. Use games and TV series to open up the public's imagination again to the idea of traveling the betaverse. Then we start funding politicians who support exploration. Depending on how long it takes to change public opinion, we might be able to get there in a century."

"Planning something like this is against your parole. What's stopping me from telling them and getting you locked up? It won't matter if you owned the company then."

"I'm guessing the idea of controlling sections of the Milky Way is appealing to you?"

Yaya nodded.

"Then that's what's stopping you."

There was no response to that.

Peter nodded and began to walk away.

Then Yaya did something odd. He turned around and handed a piece of paper to Peter. Peter took it and continued walking away. He knew telling Yaya his plan was potentially risky. It gave him something he could use to get Peter locked up once more, but if he guessed right, and he hoped he was, then Yaya would start moving humanity toward his end goal. If Yaya did work with him, then humanity would be ready to embrace space exploration by the time Peter returned.

When Peter rounded the corner, he opened the piece of paper.

You are in danger. Someone or something is after you.

CHAPTER 8

PETER

SUPERHEROES FIGHTING

Peter walked out of his moon research lab. Once again, as he crossed the threshold, stepping through the automatic sliding doors, more than just the environment changed. It wasn't as abrupt as previous times, but he definitely noticed a change in gravity. He almost tripped as he crossed the invisible line. The only thing that stopped him from completely flying head over heels was the fact he had already planned to stop and take in the view when he got outside. If he hadn't planned on stopping, he thought, he probably would be getting off the ground right now. He watched as a few other people seamlessly walked through the sliding doors without so much as a trip and wondered if they were just well practiced or if they had a program that was assisting them with the change.

"Hey, Peter!" Hezekiah yelled, waving furiously out the window of a car.

Looking out toward the space around him, Peter noticed he was in a dome, not a small dome, either. Some sort of clear glass structure encompassed the entire moon city he was in. It kind of looked like he was on the edge of Central Park in New York. He could see many trees, a small pond, a park in the distance, with tall buildings all around him. Then beyond the tall buildings was a clear glass dome. He could definitely see the moon architecture designs coming through in the buildings. Many of them looked like they were carved into the sides of a cave. Craters, circles, and jagged regolith featured heavily in the aesthetics of the buildings. The contrast between this world and Earth was huge—he was impressed. He looked beyond the dome and couldn't see a thing—nothing. Beyond the dome, it looked like a night sky without the stars.

"You coming?" Hezekiah called out once more.

Peter nodded, the words pulling him out of his reverie. He jump/walked toward the car and hopped in. Hezekiah scooted over to make room.

"I've been doing some research," Hezekiah said excitedly. "There's a fight on tonight, and I think it's the perfect final location to visit before we get going."

"Why do you sound excited about this?"

"Just wait and you'll see," Hezekiah said as he pressed a button on one of the screens in front of him and the car began to move.

At first, the car was just cruising along the road. Then it started to speed up, and Peter worried their vehicle was going to hit a car in front of it. All the traffic up ahead had stopped, yet their car kept moving forward at an ever-increasing rate.

"Don't worry," Hezekiah said, noticing Peter's angst. "It's impossible for these autonomous vehicles to hit anything. They're always communicating with each other."

Peter knew that, but he noticeably relaxed after being reassured.

The car started to lift off the ground, rising as they flew right over the car that was previously in front of them. Then the innards of the car started to transform, getting larger and evolving once again into the helicopter that it had started as.

"In the middle of this dome is a transport gate," Hezekiah said, "so we can just cross that and we'll be back on the Earth server. Faster than the way we came in."

As the helicopter drifted upward, the time gate became clearer. It looked like a work of art more than anything. The massive glass dome stretched up into the sky. And at the very top—almost as if it was a plug—sat a gleaming ring, the same design as last time, only gold. Two counterrotating rings. The outer ring was a thick chain, and it rotated in a ticking pattern. Each tick it made reverberated through the moon base and got stronger, the closer they got to it. The inner ring had a perfect gold mirror finish—almost like the sun. It rotated smoothly in the opposite direction.

In between that time gate was what looked like a small pond. The pond appeared to be covered in a soft mist. If the dome was turned upside down, no one would take a second look at it; everyone would have assumed it was where all the water collected. Since it was up in the middle of the sky, the floating pond defied Peter's sense of physics. He was still getting used to this world outside of prison. If there was an internal consistency in the metaverse, he hadn't yet discovered it.

They drifted toward the time gate, there were many flying vehicles headed that way too. But the gate was gargantuan, so finding a clear path was easy. They passed it with no incident and found themselves floating above Earth, emerging from the same gate they left.

Hezekiah punched a few things into a screen right in front of him. He had a childish grin on his face.

"Okay, what are we doing? Your face is too giddy," Peter said.

"We're going to watch Talos verses Kratos," Hezekiah replied, and before Peter could jump in, he added, "Don't worry; it's the perfect location to triangulate exactly where your matrix is.

The stadium is on its own server, but conveniently, that server is located directly between all the major ones."

"This just sounds like an excuse for somewhere you want to take me."

"Trust me, Peter, It'll be worth it," Hezekiah said, grinning from ear to ear.

Peter considered it for a moment. "Why is the stadium on its own server? Why does it need its own?"

"It's all about latency. All the fighters get their matrices transported there so they're as close to the server as possible, especially fighters that use speed as their superpower—they really notice if they're not directly connected to the server."

Peter considered it for a moment. Maybe he could partake in a battle. If his current plan failed, maybe he could get his matrix relocated to the server for an exhibition fight, then, on the way, escape. He put that idea to the back of his mind to test for later. "Can we head to London first? There's something I want to check out. Then let's go watch your fight."

Hezekiah pressed a few buttons on the control panel and they started their journey to London.

Sensing Hezekiah's change of mood, and not wanting him to be too disappointed, Peter changed the subject. "Don't worry; you will get to show me one of these fights," he said before pivoting the conversation. "What did you think of Ariana's new brain?"

Hezekiah shrugged. "I'm unsure . . . If it really does allow her to understand quantum mechanics, then I can see her progressing physics a lot."

Peter agreed. "I think it's the paradigm shift we need. Honestly, I'm disappointed in the rate of improvement since humanity embraced the simulation."

"Did we not just teleport to the moon and back?" Hezekiah said, looking confused.

"Don't get me wrong; this world is much more impressive than before I went behind bars. But technology in the real world is so far behind the metaverse."

"Maybe you're right, Peter. There's no rule that says all technology must always improve."

"It's more than that. It's like humanity invented simulated reality and then, because it was indistinguishable from reality, we all became so obsessed with it, we forgot about the real world."

"I'd argue," Hezekiah said, looking at both hands, "that this simulated world is better than reality. From your perspective, it's just as real."

"But this isn't reality. It's not real."

"It's so strange hearing someone say that. You sound almost conspiratorial. What would you do," Hezekiah asked, "if you found out that the betaverse wasn't the base layer of reality?"

"That's a good way to put it; the metaverse is not the base layer of reality. And to me at least, I want to be in the base layer of reality."

"You didn't answer my question. What would you do if we found out that the betaverse was just another layer of the simulation?"

"It's the highest layer of reality I have access to now. And if later we find out it's not, then I'd want to go up another level. I want to keep trying until I reach the base layer."

CHAPTER 9

ATLAS

LEAVING

Atlas watched out the port window of Trillion's spaceship as another rocket was being constructed. This one was a little bigger, but most importantly, it was reinforced with new material he had recently invented—Tiamond nanotubes. "The engines are stronger, and the reinforced shielding means you could swat away anything that comes your way. And I've added the laser weaponry that was used against you."

"What about communication?" Trillion asked. "I'll still be able to be in contact with you and Icarus?"

Trillion had recently been the target of a full-scale attack from Sol. She survived not through better machinery but through a hack that Atlas had managed to do on the enemy spacecraft. That attack showed just how vulnerable they were. Their spacecraft weren't designed for a battle against humans, let alone any aliens that they encountered. Trillion, for example, was quickly over-whelmed by the Dottiens. It also made clear just how important it was for them to be able to contact each other. But currently, their communication network consisted of only one Starnet transmitter that was in the Tac system. If anything were to happen to that one transmitter, then all three of them would instantly lose the ability to communicate with one another in real time.

"It took a lot of thinking, but I found a way to make a mobile version of the Starnet," Atlas said. "I built this version with redundancy in mind, one of the challenges I think we had before. We were too reliant on a single Starnet transmitter. Now, in theory, we could lose that unit and still be able to communicate. This new design will create a direct connection between the ship and each of our four current star systems."

The Starnet worked through quantum entanglement. One entangled particle was sent across the galaxy, while the other bounced between two pieces of glass. That way, both entangled particles could be interacted with at the same time. It was this interaction that allowed the Starnet to send information faster than the speed of light. They found that it only worked when two particles were entangled away from a large-gravity body like a planet. And it was thanks to Atlas running several experiments out in deep space—away from any large gravitational mass—that he discovered this.

"Does this mean we're building an empire?" Trillion asked. "One that allows digital humans like us to move around the galaxy instantly?"

"I wouldn't call us an empire . . . yet. But it's crazy when you think about it."

"The thing I'm still trying to wrap my head around is that I've visited two star systems now," Trillion said. "And, thanks to your invention, I can visit any of them again instantly. That's what I'm most excited for. I've met the Dottiens. I've turned a system into the ultimate resource hub. And now I get to go visit another system, to add to the list of worlds any of us can visit anytime."

Atlas agreed with Trillion. The Starnet changed everything. "What's your plan with everything still in the Dottiens' system after you leave?"

"I'm going to send it all back to the Tac system. I'm going to leave the Dottiens here to evolve in peace. I might leave a small space station in the system. But there's no reason we need to leave anything here."

Atlas nodded.

"I get the sense there's something you're not telling me." Trillion paused, flicking her hair away from in front of her eyes. "Are you leaving your planet too?"

Atlas nodded again. "There's no reason why I should stay here, especially now that we have mobile Starnets. My new spacecraft completed construction yesterday. I thought it would be quite poetic if we both left at the same time."

Trillion raised an eyebrow. "What about Atreus?"

Atreus was the first human born on another world. Atlas had brought the embryo across the Milky Way. He was the first child to be born on New Europa—Atlas's first child.

"I didn't really want to be a father. That's why I didn't have any kids back on Earth. It was a conscious decision; my personal goal was always to terraform a planet. And now I've done that. There was this extra piece of code," Atlas said, pointing at his head, "that compelled me to want to bring life, human life, onto that planet. I would have been happy just terraforming the world and making discoveries. Making an Eden free of humans. But because of that piece of code, I had no choice."

Trillion shook her head. "Not everyone chooses to be a father. And you might not have chosen this decision, but you do have to live with the consequences. Atreus loves you, and I know you care about him a lot. You care about all your kids. I think you've got to tell them you're going, especially Atreus."

"I will still be here," Atlas said. "Thanks to the Starnet, it won't be like I'm leaving. And besides, they will be middle-aged by the time I reach the bubble."

"He might be young right now, but you have to tell him. You need to tell all of them. You might still be able to communicate with them, but your matrix is going. And that makes it different."

Atlas lowered his head; he knew she was right. And as much as he hated to admit it, he loved all those kids. He hoped some of them would grow up and become scientists, engineers. He hoped that a lot of them would grow up and want to improve on the world he had built for them. And to be honest, he knew his Ship loved them enormously. Ever since they were first brought into this world, Ship spent more time with those kids than with him. And there was no way he wanted to disappoint Ship. He just hadn't told them, because he didn't know how to tell them. "Trillion, they look up to you; what should I say? I don't know how to tell them without it sounding like I'm leaving them."

"Just be honest; you'll be surprised by how much a five-year-old can understand. Tell them you're traveling out to find your friend, Angelique, but reassure them that because you're simulated, it will feel like you never left. They'll always be able to talk to you. They'll always be able to see you. If they have any problems, you'll be there to help them. And same with Ship. He'll always be there too."

Trillion said that better than he could. He wished he had her way with words. He sighed deeply; he would tell them—he would speak from the heart. "I'm gonna let them know now."

Trillion nodded in agreement.

Atlas teleported out to the preschool. It was near the end of their day. The kids had gone on a school trip to one of the snow fields. There was a good amount of snow covering the ground. Atlas felt the cold as his feet sank a good ten inches before hitting solid ground. He instinctually shivered as he clicked his fingers and was now wearing a big puffer jacket and snow boots.

It had taken several of the transport eleph-ANTs to move the children. The entire globe was basically their playground. When they learned about planets, the kids went up into orbit, where they got to see just how big it was. Atlas thought it was one of the best educations anyone could ever receive—at least, he would have loved that experience as a child.

There were forty-two kids in total. That's how many Atlas had wanted to seed. He planned on bringing forty-two kids into this world at first. Let them grow up as one big family. These would be the big brothers and sisters of the next generation. He had been cautious. Not wanting to bring too many children into the world—he knew the planet was safe for human life, but he wanted to make sure. So, he had been monitoring the planet closely, and was starting to feel it was safe enough for new children to come into this world. He was planning on seeding new life later on this year.

Atreus ran over and gave Atlas a hug. "Dada, you made it," he said, pulling Atlas's hand. "Come see my snowman."

Atreus pulled Atlas along the snow. There were snow angels littered all around, and one nursebot was currently constructing an igloo. Atreus and all the other kids looked so cute, all dressed up warm in little ski outfits—little toddler marshmallows. They headed toward a small group of snowmen, five in total. Atreus grinned ear to ear as he pointed to one of them. "This is Ship, Dada."

Atlas smiled and patted Atreus on the head—he was definitely the favorite child. "Can I tell you something?" he said before realizing he needed to tell all his kids.

All the other children were either throwing snowballs at each other or deep in concentration, adding purple carrots to the nose of their snowpeople—none of them had noticed him yet.

"Kids!" Atlas said in the best fatherly voice he could muster. "I need to tell you all something."

As soon as they heard his voice, they all came running over. Calls of "Dada!" and "Daddy!" could be heard all around. Little Luke Daniels took out one of the snowman, he was running so fast.

After the hugs and cuddles were done, Atlas sat down on the ground, just waiting for the kids to join him. The nursebots stood around too, ushering in some of the kids who were still occupied with a snowball fight.

"I'm going away," Atlas said, clearing his throat. "Well, not going away; I'll still be here."

"Are you visiting another star in a spaceship?" Atreus asked.

"Yes, but . . ."

"My nurse told me you can't leave, ever," little Debbie Gills said. "Because of the Starnet. You'll always be here able to talk with us no matter where in the whole wide universe you are."

Atlas nodded. "I'm always going to be here with you."

The kids understood things better than he expected. He thought he would have to explain why he was going but also staying. He was impressed they grasped the concept faster than he could have even imagined. These kids were smart, and they understood more about this world than he had given then credit for.

"Can we visit the stars too?" Luke said.

"Once I get there, you can come visit. I'll set up a Starnet and you can come over anytime." Because thanks to brain-scanning technology, they could also visit if they wanted to become a simulation. Or even if they didn't want to have their minds uploaded, they would use a virtual-reality rig to experience what it would be like on that planet.

"Is Auntie Trillion going with you too?" one of the kids said, pointing at Trillion behind Atlas.

Trillion smiled a knowing smile. Atlas hoped it meant he had done a good job at telling them all.

"Auntie is going on her own adventure."

"Are the Dottiens going to miss her?" one of the girls down the back said.

Trillion spoke up then. "Just like Atlas, I'm not leaving them. I'm just changing where my house is."

CHAPTER 10

HEZEKIAH

SPACE BATTLE

Hezekiah and Peter finally made it to London. The vehicle touched down in what looked like a residential zone. Hezekiah got out of the vehicle as it turned into a car and parked itself beside the road. He looked around in slight confusion. It appeared they were outside someone's house and not a research facility.

Oddly, he felt like he recognized some of the buildings, not because he had been there before but because it looked like a scene straight out of *Harry Potter*. Hezekiah took it all in. He'd never been to London before. It was incredible; the streets were made of cobblestones.

The buildings all around him were tiny stone-and-brick apartments. All the archways were made of painted wood. There were red doors and green doors, and many of the buildings had a hanging wooden sign. The lights looked like little gas lanterns that you would find in the 1800s. The light felt dim and the air tasted like mothballs.

The buildings were so close together and the roads so narrow that when they saw two cars passing each other, one had to pull over to the side of the road to let the other pass. It wasn't what he was used to; in America, the cars were huge and the roads were enormous, but here, everything felt small and intimate.

They walked along the side of the road until they reached the shop with a sign saying OBSERVATORY at the front. Hezekiah opened the door and walked in, Peter close behind him. They walked through winding hallways, all the way to the back of the building, which opened up into a small courtyard littered with a few tables and plants. Hezekiah caught a glimpse of the sky and noticed it had turned to night. He focused his eyes up at the stars and saw how beautifully vivid everything was. It was almost as if he was out in the countryside with zero light pollution.

Sitting at one of the red tables was Unity.

With confusion in his voice, Peter asked, "Aren't you on the moon?"

"My matrix isn't there. I traveled there like you. Ariana sent me here to join you both because she wanted me to relay this meeting to her."

"And why is that?" Hezekiah asked.

She pointed to a doorway behind her. "I guess we're about to find out."

Unity stood up just as Hezekiah was about to sit and began walking toward the door, which led into an observatory. This wasn't what Hezekiah was expecting. There was a huge telescope in the middle of the room. The whole room was dim red. There was a hole in the ceiling where Hezekiah could see the beautiful starscape once more.

The room was empty except for a small droid standing at attention in the corner. It looked like a rectangular box or, rather, three boxes stuck on top of each other. It was roughly humanoid-shaped. The best description Hezekiah could find was of a robot designed in *Minecraft*.

"Activate," Unity said, acknowledging the droid.

The droid came alive. Its different blocky body parts separated from each other; a head floated on an invisible neck. "How can I help?" the robot said in a British accent.

Unity looked at Peter, who nodded for her to continue. "Have you seen anything unusual out in deep space?" Unity asked.

"If by *unusual* you mean *battle* . . . then yes," the droid said.

"What do you mean, a battle?" Hezekiah asked excitedly. "Like aliens fighting each other?"

The droid shook its head. "It's definitely Earth. I tracked the origin of some of the objects and they've come from Sol."

The droid pointed at a large TV mounted on the wall. On it a map of the star system appeared. Several names of various stars appeared, then one of the stars turned blue and started to flash.

Peter queried the robot, "Are you an artificial intelligence?"

"No," it said matter-of-factly. "Think of me more as a very smart search engine."

Hezekiah noticed Peter's confusion. "It's only sentient AI that are banned. Robots like this one here don't quite make the cut."

"It sounds awfully smart."

"It would definitely pass the Turing test, but it's lacking the ability to self-improve."

Unity pulled them both back to the task at hand. "I think there's something important here for us."

She gestured at the android to continue.

"Approximately sixteen light-years away, there's a star called Groombridge sixteen-eighteen. We don't know much about it except to say it should have at least one planet orbiting it and a lot of debris in the system."

"Ariana thinks this is our team," Unity said.

"One of the beta explorers? Could it be Atlas or Angelique?" Peter asked.

"Maybe," Unity replied. "Actually, probably one of them."

Hezekiah looked concerned. "Do we know what the outcome was? Were they hurt in the fight?"

The droid shrugged. "All I can say is that two large convoys collided near that star. The only reason I can tell you this is because I have access to all the large telescopes Atreus Enterprise owns, and there were so many rocketships. Your average citizen astronomers wouldn't be able to see any of this."

Unity asked the obvious question. "Is there any other natural phenomenon that might make this signal?"

The droid moved from side to side. "Maybe in isolation. But as I said before, half the ships definitely came from our solar system."

"What about the other half? How do you know those ships were fighting against Atlas or the others?"

"I see no other reason why humanity would go against every single isolation policy that it pushes. Earth made the decision a long time ago to leave aliens alone. And the only people sending out rockets now days is the Spaceforce. Unless . . ."

"Unless they encountered a hostile alien," Hezekiah interrupted.

"Unlikely," the droid said. "The Spaceforce had to be going after the initial beta explorers that you sent out, Peter."

All three of them exchanged concerned glances. The idea that Earth's Spaceforce might have engaged in a conflict with the beta explorers was unsettling. They had all been sent out to find new worlds, not to ignite a battle among the stars.

"Can you tell us more about the conflict?" Hezekiah asked the droid. "Were there any survivors or communications from either side?"

The droid paused for a moment, its various floating segments seemingly considering the question. "I'm afraid I have limited information about the actual conflict; there were no communications intercepted from either side. However, I did detect a few faint distress signals shortly after the event. Their origin is uncertain, but they could have come from one of the involved parties."

Unity looked thoughtful. "We need to investigate this. If one of the beta explorers is in trouble, we have to help them."

Peter nodded in agreement, his expression resolute. "Absolutely. But we should also consider the possibility of encountering hostile forces, whether they're aliens or the Spaceforce. We need to be prepared for any scenario."

"I don't think we have the resources to be engaged in a fight. We'll have to go in stealthily and investigate," Unity said.

"Especially when we're about to lose all our resources," Hezekiah added.

"What do you mean, *we're going to lose our resources?*" Peter asked.

Hezekiah looked at Unity, then at Peter. Then back at Unity. "I heard the CEO was shutting this all down."

"Oh," Peter said. "That was just a misunderstanding. We're fine to continue doing what we're doing."

"I heard," Unity said, "you ripped him a new one. Ariana said he was scared senseless after you two had a conversation."

"He just didn't understand what we were doing," Peter said. "After I explained what was happening, he was fine for us to continue."

Before anyone could reply, Peter's pocket started to vibrate. He put his hand in his pocket and pulled out the device designed for locating his brain matrix. He opened it up and clicked a few things on the small interface. He grinned when he realized he had found the location of his matrix. Then, as he read further, the smile disappeared.

"Where is it?" Hezekiah asked.

"It's still in prison."

CHAPTER 11
ICARUS

MY CHILDREN

Icarus rocked Eve in his arms. Trying to put her to sleep. Her eyelids got heavy and he watched as her eyes slowly drifted more and more closed. Her peaceful face calmed him as her eyes completely shut. For a moment, she tried to fight the sleepiness and open her eyes. But eventually the sandman got her, and Eve was out like a light.

Icarus used his leg to maneuver a woven bassinet into place so he could place her in the basket. After setting Eve down on the bed, the next trick he had to complete was inching his arm from underneath her without waking her.

Icarus had been free of the behavioral modification in code for about a month now. And during that month, he did nothing but hang out with little baby Eve. Feeding her, singing songs to her, and making sure she felt loved.

At first, Icarus worried whether Eve was happy, because all she did was eat and poop. She was like a blob, not responding do anything that he did. Trillion explained that all babies go through this, and that Eve was just figuring out the world. Eve couldn't see much yet, but she could hear, so that was why Icarus had spent so much time singing and talking to her. After three weeks, Icarus was rewarded with the first smile from little Eve. And at that moment, he realized it was all worth it.

He told her about the world he was building for her. He told her about Earth and Mars. He told her about his brother, who he missed so much. He told her about Peter and Angelique and that they were part of her history and how she got there. He really wanted to give her the perfect life, which also meant having lots of friends.

Looking after Eve was therapeutic in a way, he thought. Not to say it was the only reason he looked after her but now that he had a responsibility—a duty to her—he felt a greater purpose. Probably, he thought, just like any other parent gained a sense of purpose once they had a child. Icarus was rediscovering his old self (without the behavioral modifications) and gaining a new purpose.

Icarus finally wriggled his arm out from underneath Eve, then quietly tiptoed out of the room and closed the door behind him. He made a conscious effort not to teleport in front of her. He worried that a duck-shaped human appearing and disappearing suddenly might cause a little bit of stress. He had spent so much time looking like a duck-human anime character that when Eve arrived, it was the one thing he wasn't willing to change about himself. He assumed that humans were flexible. As long as he always looked like that, he was sure she wasn't going to worry. *Better to only know me like this*, he thought, *than for me to change into this in a few years.*

Trillion was waiting outside of the room. "Awww, you've already put her to bed," she said, a little disappointed. "Have you come up with a plan for the others?"

The two of them were outside a little cottage; there were two little white seats. Out in the distance they could see dinosaurs walking along.

"I've told the nurses to start the process now," Icarus said.

"So . . . more babies?" Trillion said with clear glee in her voice.

"Yep, but I'm going to do things a little differently. I think Atlas was wrong to raise them all like siblings. Eve is the only one I'll consider my child. I think he was also wrong to leave such a big gap between the first round of children. You know there's going to be at least a five-year gap between his children."

"Why do you say he's wrong, Icarus?" Trillion said, sitting down on one of the two seats.

Icarus sat in the seat next to her. "Because there's only forty kids, it really limits the number of friends these kids can make. He's done such a good job at creating a world for them; he needs to fill it with humans."

"So, you're going to seed all your humans quickly? That's your big plan?"

"Yup. I'm organizing it more like a school; if the nurses can maintain birthing two kids a week, then that will roughly be one hundred children a year. And that's plenty of diversity within friendships. If there's a group of kids who really like playing a particular game, there will be other kids who like the same. Then that just removes any risk of any of the kids being lonely, having no one else to play with."

Icarus wondered whether his childhood was part of the reason why he thought so much about this. He shook his head, pushing that thought to the side. "I know Atlas is starting to bring more children into his world now. Once they're old enough, I'm going to set them up as little pen pals."

Trillion smiled at that remark. "I assume you mean video. But imagine, talking to another person in a completely different star system."

"Isn't that what we're doing?" Icarus asked.

"Yeah, but for some reason, it feels different. Somehow, because we're simulations, I feel like it's different. But you're right; it's not."

"They still can't move from star system to star system like us," Icarus said. "Oh, and I'm going to teach them about alien languages. I'm going to teach them about the Dottiens, their biology, and the way they communicate."

The Dottiens was a race of aliens discovered on the planet that Trillion had found. They communicated via colors and textures. They were extremely efficient at communicating, too. They could send information to each other so well that the receiver of that information could experience what the other had seen or done. Atlas described them as the pinnacle of slime mold.

"Are you going to teach them any other human languages?"

Icarus nodded. "Their main language will be English, but everyone is going to learn Japanese, Hindi, and Spanish. Those last two I don't speak, but I think it's important that we start teaching them a lot of Earth history. We all assumed Earth was gone when they went dark."

"What about other languages? Trillion asked.

"I might teach them some of the others; I mean, I know how to speak quite a few. Maybe I could invent my own?"

"That feels a little too much like playing God to me."

Icarus nodded in agreement. He didn't want to play God; he wanted to create a self-sustaining colony that would quickly govern and control itself.

"I think you're getting a little ahead of yourself. Eve is only a month old; you don't need to start thinking about what you're going to teach her in school."

"I think creating the right curriculum for them is going to take some time. I want to do this right."

Trillion looked at him suspiciously. "I know you; you're going to do it. You're going to look after little Eve. But you're more obsessed and excited about building your ringworld."

Icarus knew Trillion was right. "The way I see it, I've been around for hundreds of years. I can totally spend thirty setting this one up. Hopefully, big Eve will take over the colony. I hope one day she decides to get her mind uploaded and join me—join us."

Trillion pointed at the room behind them. "How long until she wakes up?"

"Probably another hour or so. One of the nurses is watching over her. We can just teleport back as soon as she wakes up."

"Well, then, can you show me where you're at with your world-building project?"

An excited grin appeared on Icarus's face. He had been waiting for that question—or at least hoping for it. He took out his portal gun and flicked a switch on the side of it, turning it to silent mode—he didn't want to wake Eve with its usual sound of crackling, lightning, and static.

He pointed it out toward the grass in front of the porch and fired it. A white orb shot out and exploded on contact with the ground. A hole appeared, showing a circling whirlpool of black-and-white lines.

"You improved on the animation," Trillion said.

"On the way back, I'll show you the new sound effects. They're next-level." Icarus jumped down the rabbit hole. "See you space side."

The other side of the portal was the inside of an eleph-ANT.

Eleph-ANTs were large robotic space vehicles. They had six legs, and a trunk at the front. Because they could operate in the vacuum of space, and on a planet, they were ideal all-purpose machines for everything they needed. In this case, it was constructing a ringworld.

The eleph-ANT he had teleported into was overlooking the completion of the first habitat module. Icarus was using this eleph-ANT and several others to coordinate the construction.

Less than half a second later, Trillion appeared in the eleph-ANT next to Icarus. "What are we looking at? It just looks like an enormous grey coin," she said.

Enormous was an understatement. The object was at least a few kilometers across. Because of the way light worked out in space, there wasn't any atmosphere to scatter light like normal. It was hard to get a true sense of the scale and intricacies of what was in front of them.

"That's just one side of the rotating ring," Icarus said. "It's the first part of the thick shielding for everyone who lives there."

"And when it's done, what is it all going to look like?"

"I'm building it so it's modular. They'll be massive cylindrical shells of thick shielding. And then I can fill those cylinders with whatever each section needs. My plan is to build this first habitat connected to the cable rotating around the planet. Test it to make sure it works, then start building more of them. It's going to take many, many years to complete the ring. But doing it in this modular fashion means we can just expand as time goes on."

"What about gravity? Are you going to spin them up to mimic one-g force?"

Icarus was about to answer when they got a message from the nurse. Eve had woken up. "We've got to go; she just woke."

"Yay, she's so cute," Trillion said. "Let's go."

Rather than say goodbye, she grabbed Icarus's portal gun from his belt, pointed it at both their feet, and shot it. Both of them fell through the floor.

CHAPTER 12

PETER

ESCAPE

Peter sat down on the ground in the middle of the observatory. Ignoring the strange looks he got from Hezekiah and Unity, he closed his eyes and thought about how he could get his matrix out of prison.

It wasn't meant to be this hard. He had been released from jail and was expecting that all he had to do was find where his matrix was located and extract it. He'd lost so many years in a real prison, and now he was still stuck in this metaverse—which, thanks to humanity's delusions, was basically a prison. Now the matrix locator device was telling him he was never out of prison in the first place. *It's absolutely insane,* he thought. *But maybe it's what they do when people are on parole.* Maybe he would have to wait until his parole was over. Although he worried he'd already begun to make an enemy of his parole officer, which meant it was likely the man would come up with some excuse to put him back behind bars or at the very least drag the process on for many years so his matrix stayed locked up. He thought about it long and hard and realized he really only had one option—and that was to escape.

Peter needed space to think. He wanted to come up with a plan. There was no way he'd be able to escape if his parole officer even got a whiff of what he was up to. "Can we teleport to our London office?" he asked, looking at the other two in the room.

"There should be a service elevator that can transport us," Unity said. "Why do you ask?"

"I'm sick of running around. I need a large boardroom and I need people to come to me."

Hezekiah pulled out his phone. "I just booked out the board-room at the London office. Who do you want me to grab?"

"Get Ariana here; I want you two to help me. And send Yaya over when he's next free. Unity, you lead the way."

Unity led them out of the observatory and back into the courtyard. This time, they went in a different direction and found a small elevator. It was rickety. It looked like it was never used. Unity punched a few numbers into a keypad next to it, and the door to the elevator opened.

The three of them walked inside and the doors closed behind them. The thing rattled, and Peter definitely felt like he was mov-ing sideways. The elevator continued to shake as the most cliché elevator music played. Peter felt like it was taking a lot longer than a normal elevator should. Finally, the door chimed and the door opened to a large office space with a marble floor. It was busy outside the elevator. The door had only just opened and about five people had already walked past.

One of the passers-by actually noticed Peter and went to approach him before Hezekiah raised his hand. "We're in the middle of something important. He doesn't have time to talk right now." The man walked away, visibly disappointed.

The three of them walked out of the elevator. Luckily enough, their exit was right in front of the boardroom that Hezekiah had booked. The boardroom had a hard oak table on it and over-looked the city of London. Peter thought he could see the Big Ben clock tower out the window.

"Welcome to the London office," Unity said.

"How do you know all this?" Hezekiah said, opening the glass door to the boardroom.

"Ariana is just as demanding as Peter sometimes. She never left Mars. So, I was always tasked with trekking office to office, sorting things out."

The three of them walked into the office and Peter sat down at the head. You could hear a penny drop, it was so quiet. The only thing distracting was all the faces looking through the glass window. Hezekiah quickly ran around and closed all the roller blinds, removing that distraction quickly.

The three of them sat there in silence while Peter thought.

After a good while of thinking and planning, Peter began coordinating everyone.

"Okay," he started. "Hezekiah, I need you to set up a fight for me. Find me an opponent who is a speedster. Someone that I could potentially beat, so the fight seems believable. Maybe someone at the end of their career? Basically, find someone who, in order for me to compete with, I will need to move the location of my matrix to the stadium. Make this all feel believable. The other criterion is that they need to be available at short notice because I want to set up a spar for tomorrow—a little meet-and-greet where we can practice together."

He turned around to Unity. "I trust you and Ariana have already sorted out a spacecraft?"

Unity nodded. "If you're thinking what I think you're think-ing, then Ariana doesn't have time to come here. We expected to have a couple of weeks. But I assume you wanna go tomorrow?"

"Correct," Peter said. "As soon as I get my matrix out, I want you two and Ariana able to meet me wherever the rocket is." He paused. "Where is the ship?"

Arian pointed down at her feet. "It's on Earth. It'll be easy enough for me to disguise the use of that rocket under the guise of an expedition to Mars. The only thing we have to hide is just how full this rocket will be. People will start to ask questions if I load too many fabricators." She paused for a moment, thinking about how to make it work. "I don't think it'll look suspicious if I'm headed to the moon to pick up Ariana to do some research on Mars. But, Hezekiah, we'll have to smuggle you onboard same as Peter because there's no reason for you to leave Earth."

"Will we be able to get embryos?" Peter asked.

Unity shook her head. "I heard about what you sent the initial beta explorers with. And I don't know how you got any of those embryos, but this isn't the wild wild west anymore, Peter; there's no way we can get any real embryos today. But we've got DNA printers. Which is just as useful—and less ethically grey."

Peter nodded. "I assume Atlas or one of the others has already colonized a world. All we need to do is find one of them, and I'm sure we can get enough resources to make our own colony."

"I've organized the fight," Hezekiah said, looking up from his phone. "But how are you going to get ahold of your matrix?"

"You set up the fight. And you let me handle getting my matrix out." Peter looked toward Unity. "Can you get me a phone on this table?"

"Need to call someone?" she replied, pulling her phone out of her pocket. "You can just borrow mine if you want."

Peter shook his head. "I finally feel in control of things, sitting here in this boardroom. Call me old-school, but the only thing that will complete the feeling is a big telephone sitting on this table. One of those conference-call phones with big buttons. Can you get me one and connect me with Ariana, then Yaya, and then my lawyer?"

Ariana nodded and walked out of the room. Moments later, she was back with a large speakerphone. She placed it on the table and plugged it in. A few more button presses later and Unity confirmed Ariana was on the line. "There will be a couple seconds' delay, as she's still on the moon. But you should be able to converse freely."

Peter stood up and loomed over the speakerphone. "Ariana, change of plans. I need you to organize yourself to be picked up in the next twenty-four hours. That means your matrix and that additional brain power you have built on top of it. Prepare for a long journey; you will have a lot of time to do research, so bring us anything you think you might need for it. Make some excuse like you're doing data collection on Mars. Nothing that will arouse suspicion, but give yourself a reason for moving a lot of cargo there."

"Understood."

And with that, Peter hung up the line.

Moments later, the phone started to ring again.

"It's Yaya," Unity said.

"Peter, I hear you're in London, commandeering a couple of my officers?"

"Yes, it's quite nice up here. I wanted to see if you've made any progress on what we discussed."

"I've been talking to a couple of congressmen. There's definitely appetite if we make enough donations. Some of them actually expressed concerns around humanity's lack of progress."

"Good. So, you think we can start moving the world in the direction of space exploration again?"

"I wouldn't say that just yet. But I did make a bit of progress on who is blocking a lot of these initiatives. Have you heard of a Congresswoman Sarah Walker?"

"Yes, she's the one who put me behind bars."

"Well, apparently, she's been pulling a lot of strings in the background. I'm not sure if it's just her alone, but she has a lot of money behind her. A lot of people I spoke to are actually afraid of her. I don't know why yet, but I think it's best that we make sure she doesn't find out what we're doing for as long as possible."

"Do you know why she's pulling strings?"

"Have you heard about the dark forest?"

Peter considered the question for a bit, thinking back to a book he once read with the same title. "The idea that the reason we've never met any aliens is because any alien that shows itself to others will immediately be destroyed?"

"Yes, well, a lot of people around Congresswoman Walker believe this."

"Last I heard, she thought everyone was in the simulation. That always sounded absurd to me."

"This is just the next evolution of that; basically, she believes the only aliens left are other ones like us. Everyone in our galaxy is focused on expanding inwards rather than outwards, because any alien that expands in the betaverse gets wiped out."

"All the more reason to explore new stars," Atlas said. "It's not worth risking our home system if it's our only one. At least if we put life on other planets, humans will always be around."

"It's just that the argument doesn't make sense." The phone was quiet for a few seconds, and Peter thought it might have been disconnected until Yaya began speaking again. "I think there's something more to this mystery that we don't know. Maybe someone else or something else is controlling the strings. Part of the reason why I'm on board with this is because I think we need to expand outwards. And we need to start developing new technology out in the betaverse again."

"Agreed. Thanks for the update," Peter said before stopping himself from ending the call. "Also, Yaya, Ariana has been doing some research on merged intelligence between humans and AI. I'm taking her off that project for now, but can you find someone to replace her?"

Peter made sure not to mention the fact that they were leaving soon, just in case Yaya wasn't fully onboard. "I want us to make a big bet on that. I have a hunch that there are a bunch of breakthroughs in the real world that will be possible if we can tap into that idea."

"On it."

He was impressed by how quickly Yaya had changed his tune from the last time they spoke. He guessed someone didn't climb the ladder and achieve as much as he did by holding on to grudges or not realizing the wind had changed. Peter smiled and once more hung up the phone.

CHAPTER 13

ICARUS

BACKUP

Icarus crumpled up the piece of paper and threw it at a little basketball hoop hanging over a bin. It circled the rim before falling through the net and landing on the top of an existing mound of half-crumpled-up paper balls, then rolled onto the floor. He was trying to calculate how fast he needed the habitats he was building to rotate around the gas giant, in order to simulate Earth's gravity using centrifugal force. He knew that when a habitat was rotated, it created a feeling of gravity for everyone inside. But working it out took a lot of math, and he didn't know the formulas.

In this situation, it was the orbital speed around the gas giant that he needed to calculate. And the gas giant was huge. Which meant the numbers were huge. Rotate the habitat too fast, and people on the surface would be crushed. Rotate it too slowly, and the gravity becomes lower than Earth's.

He just didn't know how to work it out, and he was determined not to ask Ship, for no reason other than that Ship had already offered to give him the answer. And Icarus, thinking it was easy, said no. Then Ship bet him naming rights for the whole ringworld if Icarus couldn't calculate the spin required. So, if Icarus couldn't work out how fast he needed to rotate the habitat, then Ship would get to name all the cities on the rotating habitat.

Turned out calculating the rotation required to produce 1g equivalent isn't easy. Giving up, he decided to ask the one person he knew would know the answer—Atlas.

Icarus pulled out his portal gun and shot it at the ground beneath his duck feet. Moments later, he fell through the roof of Atlas's main bridge. Expecting to see Atlas there, with a surprised look on his face, he superhero-landed. He was disappointed when he saw Atlas and the Ship of Atlas looking the other way; they were staring out the window. "What are you looking at?" Icarus asked while walking toward the window to take a look.

"I'm getting another ship created; what's up?" Atlas said.

"Why do you need another ship? I thought you would have left by now."

Icarus noticed the window he was looking out of was bigger than the one on his own bridge. He turned around and noticed the bridge was bigger too. "This spacecraft is way bigger than mine. You trying to say something?" Icarus said with a wink.

"Don't be silly." Atlas pointed out the window. "I've decided the safest way to investigate this bubble is for me to head out with two spacecraft. I'm gonna hang out in the back one, leave my matrix there, while the front ship heads out on a preprogrammed route to explore the bubble. Then, once I'm one hundred percent sure it's safe, I'll go myself."

Icarus nodded. "Are you going to build a backup?"

Atlas pointed at the spacecraft out the window. "That is the backup."

"No." Icarus pointed at his head. "A backup of yourself. The backup of your matrix. Just in case something goes wrong."

"Like make a copy of me?"

"Obviously, you don't want to use it. But it's better safe than sorry. I've made multiple backups. I used to store them all in my system, but after Trillion's encounter, I started storing a monthly backup in the Tac system."

Atlas scratched his head. "What if something happened to those backups? What if someone turned one of them on? I'm not sure about how I would feel with two versions of me, believing they were both me."

"None of us have gone full von-Neumann-probe yet."

"I never really saw us as von Neumann probes, Icarus. Uploading our minds was the only way to make space travel feasible. But I'd only ever imagined there being one of each of us." Atlas pointed at Ship. "Do you have a copy of yourself?"

Ship nodded, then shook his head. "Not one of me. But I guess you could kind of say Icarus's ship is a copy of me. Same with Trillion's. Although who's is the first copy, I don't know."

"Would either of you use a copy of yourself like a teleport machine?" Icarus asked.

Atlas looked confused. "What do you mean?"

"Have you not heard how teleport machines work? Have you ever watched *Star Trek*?"

Both Atlas and Ship shrugged.

"Can't we all teleport to each other's locations?" Ship pointed out.

"It's different when you're not digital, if you take a physical human. Put them in a teleportation device; they get every atom in their body scanned. In order to move through the wires, the scanning needs to destroy them and, on the other side, where they end up, reconstruct them. That's a copy—not the real thing."

"Well," Atlas said. "Under your logic, it is the real thing. But not the original." Then he paused, thinking through it a bit more. "Wow, I never thought about it like that; you're right. If a flesh-and-blood human were to teleport, it would basically be suicide."

"That's a bit grim." Ship looked at them both. "It's not like we can build something like that, anyway."

"With digital humans like us, we can," Icarus said. "So, to answer your question, I've thought a lot about Trillion's experience being stuck on that moon. I was thinking if I was in that situation, I'd probably create a copy of myself somewhere else, then blow myself up where I'm trapped and turn myself on at the new location."

Ship smiled. "What if you can't blow yourself up? What if later you found out the original copy of yourself survived?"

"Now who's being grim?" Atlas said before curiosity crept over his face. "But yeah, what would you do?"

Icarus didn't know. Whenever he thought about his backups, he always imagined only one of him being around. "Let's just hope I never have to answer that question. Anyways—I came here to ask you another thing." Then he whispered in a conspiratorial voice toward Atlas's ear. "How fast does my ring have to orbit in order to create gravity?"

Ship burst out laughing. "Do you know your Ship tried to bet me that you would come here to ask this? Thankfully I didn't take the bet."

"Can you please not tell him?" Icarus pleaded.

"I can try," Ship said. "But I bet you he's going to guess when you get the math right. The answer is you need to increase the rotation speed of the ring so it rotates once every four point six hours."

"How did you calculate that?" Icarus asked.

Ship shrugged. "I don't know how the math works. Lex gave me that number."

Icarus looked at Atlas, who made his best impression of puppy-dog eyes. "And can you explain to me the math? So I can pretend to Ship like I worked it out? Please?"

Atlas walked over to one of the control panels on the bridge. He opened one of the draws, pulled out a post-it note, scribbled something on the paper. He handed it to Icarus.

It was a note with a formula on it. It had a bunch of numbers and a few random symbols on it. Atlas pointed at one of the symbols. "That's the radius of your ringworld. The radius is just half the diameter. Plug that number into this formula and work it out. That will tell you how many minutes it will take to do a full rotation and produce one *g* of gravitational equivalent."

Icarus made a thank-you prayer gesture. "How did you know this off the top of your head? It's not like you need to know this formula."

"You're right. I only needed to memorize it for about two hours."

"I don't get it. Why two hours?" Icarus said, scratching his head.

"Your Ship said he'd have a present waiting for me if I gave you the formula and told you a message."

"What's the message?"

Atlas looked like he was holding back a laugh. "Something about the first city being called 'Shipcity'." At that very moment, Ship burst into laughter. Atlas also couldn't control it and started laughing.

CHAPTER 14

HEZEKIAH

TRAINING DAY

Hezekiah sat in the corporate box of a fight arena. It used to be a basketball stadium until the sport lost its mass appeal—because it wasn't as fun when some players just never missed. Repurposing a stadium sounded a bit odd because when people live in a simulation, it should only take a new line of code to build a new one. But the reason it was repurposed was because of all the infrastructure to physically house players and coaching staff matrices. Plus, all the extra security requirements from the gambling commission meant it was much faster to refurbish the existing server with a new design.

In the center of the stadium sat a large concrete space. The chairs where spectators would normally sit were behind a reinforced bulletproof forcefield.

All over the arena was cracked concrete from the previous fight because the space only got reset once a week to give spectators a sense that something dangerous had just happened. Hezekiah remarked it looked a lot like a bomb site, which made sense, since later he learned there had just been a battle with a fighter whose superpower was throwing bombs.

Hezekiah was nervous. Not because he was about to fight. Nor was it because his friend Peter was about to fight. It was because there was a speedster in the middle of the stadium, standing there looking like an idiot. Hezekiah had set up a fight between him and Peter, even though he knew Peter was never going to show up. But he had to act like he didn't know what was happening. He had to act like he didn't know where Peter was. And he had to act like he wasn't about to just disappear in a moment or two.

But Hezekiah wasn't good at acting and everyone knew it. He had *guilty party* written all over his face. Luckily, this was just a practice fight, and he could claim Peter had just been delayed. Hezekiah knew he was going to burn a few bridges from this move. But maybe in a few hundred years, when he was back, everyone would have forgotten about it—at least, that was what he was hoping.

His opponent was named Surge. Thankfully, he had stopped standing there, looking like an idiot; instead, he was racing from side to side. He was moving so fast, it almost looked like he was teleporting to each side of the arena. Every now and then, he would pick up a boulder, race it to the other side. Then Surge would stop moving, while the momentum of the boulder would continue, smashing it into the forcefield directly in front of Hezekiah.

Hezekiah used his hands to cover his face. He was turning bright red. The embarrassment, more than anything, was killing him. His mind was regretting every moment of what he had just done, and it was made worse when he heard the steps of Surge's manager approaching him.

"Looks like Peter is scared of," the manager said before doing his best impression of an old-school wrestler's voice, *"the Surge,"* while also doing the obligatory palm-out gesture that fans of "the Surge" often used.

Hezekiah did not answer.

Hezekiah disappeared.

It was many more months before Hezekiah appeared again. But of course, he didn't know all that; to him it just felt like he had been switched off for a short while, although he didn't know how long. It felt like he'd gone through a slow-teleport portal to a new location.

Where he was now standing was unlike anywhere he had been in a long, long time. He recognized the look and feel of the environment from before he had his mind uploaded. He could instantly tell he was in the real world because none of the colors looked quite right—everything looked bland. It was hard to describe how things appeared, but it looked as if someone turned the saturation right down. The whole room had a metallic grey to it, as if he were in some sort of metal contraption. There were no windows, only walls—metal walls.

He looked at his body and it was all solid. He could tell it wasn't a hologram because he couldn't see through his arm. Normally, when he was projected into the real world, it was using some sort of hologram, but this was different.

He thought about making the room brighter and more what he was used to. As if reading his mind, the room capitulated. The saturated hues that he was used to returned.

That meant he was still in a simulation, but it wasn't the simulation he was used to.

As Hezekiah pondered about his new world, a large metal door at the other end opened.

"It's weird, isn't it?" Unity said, entering the room. "We spent so much time in what is essentially a video game, the physical world that we came from seems so foreign."

"Have you seen old-school phone-camera photos? They look so dull and lifeless. Reminds me a lot of this world. Where are we, anyways?"

"We're on a spacecraft."

"And we aren't in a simulated environment? This is the real world, right?"

Unity nodded.

"Then why aren't I translucent, Unity? I'm a hologram, aren't I?"

"It's called a hapticgram. Atreus Enterprises has had the patent on this for years; I think I prefer this. It really does get you used to interacting with the real world."

"I guess the next question is why. I'm sure this spacecraft has enough resources to simulate a natural world?"

Unity shrugged. "I assume it has enough resources, even with all the extra power required to run additional modifications to Ariana's brain. But that's not the reason why we're interacting with the real world. Peter is convinced this is a better experience than the simulation. It gets us used to interacting with objects and learning the limitations—or, rather, relearning the limitations of the physical world. To prepare us for when we get to the new star system we're headed to."

"Wait, hold up. Did you say Ariana has multiple brains now?"

"Wait until you see her," Unity said. "She calls them additional neocortices. She went through the same process of training up a neural network on quantum mechanics. But this time, she made one for physics and biology." Unity made a crazy gesture with her hands. "Don't tell her I said this, but she's starting to freak me out a little."

"Peter and her are both here too?"

"Yes. They've been here for a while; they only just woke me up a day ago. They're waiting for us on the bridge."

"How long have I been turned off?"

"I wouldn't call it being 'turned off.' More like hibernating. And to be honest, I'm not sure. I don't have access to any of the ship's records yet. But I guess maybe we've been out for a few months."

Hezekiah went to walk through the entrance that Unity came through but realized he couldn't see the door. "Where's the exit? I'm starting to feel like a prisoner," he said cautiously.

"Sorry, you're not in prison. This is currently a sandbox. But once we connect to the ship, it'll be your room." She paused. "I only just learned this, so bear with me while I explain it. Because you are tapped in to the spacecraft, there's a bunch of other controls you can access. The interface is a little unintuitive; apparently, there's meant to be an AI controlling a lot of things but, for whatever reason, this spacecraft doesn't have one. So, it can get a little bit messy if we are all giving commands at the same time. I'm here to explain how it all works."

"So, you're the avatar that explains the controls at the start of a new game?"

Unity laughed. "No, think of me more like a piano teacher who's only just learned to play, so is one lesson ahead. Anyways, think of controlling this ship as having access to a really powerful yet clunky mod in the metaverse. I see you've already adjusted the saturation hues in this room."

Hezekiah nodded, then pointed his arm out toward the supposed entrance that Unity had come through. A metal door appeared, then disappeared, then morphed into a wooden door with a broken handle. "I see what you mean by *unintuitive*. So, there's no translation layer between me and the spacecraft?"

"Correct," Unity said as she raised her hand and the broken handle reassembled itself into a working one. "I think that's part of what the missing AI for this vehicle did. This ship is really quite ancient; Peter didn't find it easy to get a working interstellar spaceship."

"Okay, so what else can we do?"

"Ariana promised to unlock access to all the ship sensors once we're comfortable using this. But apparently, she found out that she can use more of the ship's power to think through things way faster."

Hezekiah walked toward the door he had just conjured and opened it. "Let's go see them, then."

"That's another thing you've got to get used to: you can feel the size of the spacecraft. It's hard to describe, but it's just a feeling. We can teleport to any part of the spacecraft we want. Close your eyes and you'll get a sense of the map; it's not like a visual map, but you'll know where the bridge is located. They're waiting for us in there."

Hezekiah closed his eyes and felt around his body. It did feel like he had an extended arm, like the spacecraft was now part of him. He could feel the engines firing, and somehow, he knew the names of all the locations on the spacecraft. He located the bridge. "Okay, I've found it."

"Sweet. I'll meet you there," Unity said before teleporting out.

Hezekiah teleported out too, then found himself in a pitch-black dark room. He blinked a few times and couldn't see a thing; he became annoyed at how dark the room was. As if the room was listening, the lights turned on. He was in a closet, not a room, barely big enough to fit him. Looking around in confusion, he saw a hairy object popping out of the floor. He screamed in fear, thinking it was an alien spider.

The object started to laugh and he realized it was Unity. "You're above us; fall through the floor."

Hezekiah thought about a hole in the floor appearing and he fell down. He hit the ground with a *thud* and fell over.

Peter stood over him and reached out a hand. Hezekiah reached up and grabbed it. He was pulled off the ground.

The bridge looked like it was taken straight out of a *Star Trek* episode, but with the saturations and hues turned up. It was closer to the simulated world he was used to. Huge floor-to-ceiling windows covered the outer side of the bridge. They displayed a starscape but with one unusually large star in the middle of it. He assumed that was the Sun.

"Good to see you figuring this out," Peter said.

Hezekiah waved at Peter and Ariana. "How long have we been out here?"

"Six months, four days, and sixteen minutes," Ariana said matter-of-factly.

"Don't worry; we didn't leave you sleeping the whole time. We basically pulled this spacecraft out of a museum; it was only designed to carry one simulated passenger, so I had to build additional matrix housing units." He pointed to Unity. "You should have access to the whole ship now." Then Peter looked at Hezekiah. "Let's wait until you understand this new system before giving you full access."

"To be honest, there's not much to do. I thought we were going to sleep for most of this trip?" Unity said.

"Not yet," Peter said. "I want to make sure we are all familiar with the spacecraft. We all know how to get around, and we all know how to fly this thing. The last thing we want is to have to wake up in an emergency and not be able to fully make use of the extra capabilities we now have." Peter looked at Ariana, who nodded.

Ariana looked around the walls and ceiling. She blinked once, and everything in the bridge disappeared. The coloring, the lights, the floor-to-ceiling windows. The only thing that stayed was the outline of a console in the middle of the room.

Then Ariana smiled, and the floor became an Olympic-sized swimming pool. Peter, Hezekiah, and Unity were bouncing up and down on diving boards, while Ariana was standing right on the water, folding her arms and smiling. She started to walk across the water, her feet not even remotely getting wet.

"Ariana is just showing off," Peter said. "But you get the point; through the hapticgraphic engines throughout this spacecraft, each of us have a lot more control over the look and feel of everything in this ship, more so than in any simulation that you didn't build yourself."

Hezekiah assumed the water was fake, so he jumped off the diving board, expecting to land on solid ground. He splashed into the water, completely submerging himself. The water was cold, and the disbelief meant he hadn't taken a full breath before jumping in. And thus, he swam to the surface gasping for air.

Ariana raised her hand toward him. She made a pulling motion, and Hezekiah began to float out of the water, dripping wet.

"Don't worry; they gave the same speech to me," Unity said.

"She didn't dive in, though," Peter added. "Basically, what I'm saying here is this hapticgraphic simulation is real and it affects all of us. You can't just make subtle changes to the way things look for you. In here, they change it for everyone."

Peter nodded at Ariana, who returned the bridge to its original state. "I don't expect any of us to do what Ariana just did, but it's a good goal to aim for, so go play."

ATLAS

VOTED OUT

Atlas stood outside the front door of Atreus's cottage. He had been standing there for a good while. He was nervous; he had some sort of sinking feeling that he was about to receive bad news.

The cottage was right at the edge of a very small farming village. It wasn't humans working the fields or guiding the many pigs, sheep, and chickens. This was a technologically advanced civilization, after all. Atreus was twenty-five now and had grown up to be an engineer—and a good one at that. But he preferred the quiet life, staying away from the hustle and bustle of the city, and not wanting to take more of a leadership role, as Atlas assumed he would, given he was the oldest.

Animals were always working their way into electronics they weren't meant to touch. So, Atreus enjoyed the game of cat and mouse constantly trying to improve on the farming robots, while the animals constantly devised new ways to destroy them—or at least chew an important wire or two.

Finally, after being too worried that Atreus knew he was at the doorstep—and this whole situation looking weird—Atlas decided to knock.

"Come in," Atreus's voice yelled from the other side of the door.

Atlas pushed the door open and walked through. In the small living room, Atreus was prying the back off one of the autonomous farming robots, its legs on the other side of the room.

"Hey, Dad," Atreus said looking up from his work. "Honestly, I see why animals on Earth weren't raised free-range. If it wasn't for the well-being implications, I might actually consider it. They break at least one of these a day."

Atlas looked down at the machine. It was made of physical components welded together, its insides strewn with wires and circuitry. Atlas had long ago moved away from building robots like ANTs in this way. His latest design involved him constructing a rough frame for the robot. Then he installed a mobile haptic-graphic engine and use that to construct the shell of the robot. This meant all the ANTs had a flexible design that could shapeshift to suit whatever the situation required. "If you installed a mobile hapticgraphic engine on these things, they could be self-healing."

Atreus sighed.

Atlas said, "Why doesn't the council trust me? It's not like I'm going to use that tech to hack in to them or anything."

"It's not that," Atreus said before straining to clip two components together. He pointed to the kitchen. "Can you grab me a beer?"

Atlas walked over to the kitchen and opened the fridge. He pulled out one of the beers. He replicated the beer in his other hand and made a version he could drink. Then, flicking the lids off both of them, he handed one to Atreus.

"Thank you," Atreus said before downing the whole drink and walking into the kitchen and grabbing another. He was quiet through the whole motion until he finally said, "Okay, this is going to hurt." He raised his free hand in surrender. "Now, don't shoot the messenger but . . ."

Then nothing followed and Atlas had to guess it out of him. "I know they voted me off the council; I know about the secret meeting."

"It's bigger than that. The senate voted you off the planet."

"What! . . . What?" Atlas's face was full of confusion. Then a touch of anger. "I built the planet; how can I be voted off the planet that I built?"

"Well, technically, you abducted a bunch of fetuses and took them halfway around the galaxy, then put them on a planet. But I know what you mean. If it's any consolation, I voted against it."

"I bet it was that Tanya. She's always causing trouble. But how'd she get everyone to turn on me?"

"It wasn't just her." Atreus sighed. "Everyone voted in favor of the change. Everyone except me."

Atlas consumed his entire beer. He dropped it on the ground, where it fell into a portal, Then he manifested a large glass of whiskey. He drank half of it and slumped on one of the couches.

"It's things like that that got you voted off."

"Like what?"

"People don't like you teleporting around. They feel like you can appear out of nowhere, listen to anything anyone says."

"Well, first of all, I can't. This whole planet is on its own network now. And secondly, it's not something I would do."

"I think you creating a portal right there and dropping the beer into it is a great example of you showing just how powerful you are. You can literally create stuff out of nowhere. It's just not human."

"I'm still human. Just a simulated human."

"And that's part of the reason why we don't use your tech. Our scientists and engineers want to be able to replicate it and re-create it from scratch in a way that they can trust there's no back door."

Atlas finished the massive whiskey and was about to drop it into another portal when he decided to walk into the kitchen and pretend to top it up. He decided to leave the glass on the bench, then produce a new bottle of whiskey. He walked back and slumped on the couch, drinking straight from the bottle. "Okay, so, what do I do? Wait up on a ship in orbit? Do you have to come visit me now?"

"The senate decided to remove all hapticgraphic engines from the planet. You won't be able to teleport anywhere. But they still understand that you started this world. So, they're gonna pay you a lump sum of fifty years' wages as payment for your hard work. And from there, you can use that money to rent specifically designed automatons. The functionality and capabilities of the body you will inhabit will be limited to what the council set." He pointed at the bottle of whiskey. "So, no more producing those out of nowhere."

Atlas couldn't understand where he had gone wrong. He had put so much effort into this world and they were kicking him off it.

"You're not banned from the planet. The changes will make you like any other ordinary citizen."

"You know you're the only one who still calls me their dad?"

Atreus nodded.

"Have I been a bad parent to everyone?"

"I don't think this is about you. The median age of a senator is nineteen. We're all still young, so this might just be our rebellious streak coming through. We're at the stage where we reject our family."

Atlas forced a laugh to hide his emotions. Then he changed his playback speed, turning a single second into many hours. He left the room where Atreus was, teleporting to his spaceship out in orbit—making sure to leave his avatar still visible on Neuropa. He wandered to his room, laid down on his bed, and sulked.

He focused his mind, thinking from their perspective. He thought he could have been a better parent. If roles were reversed, he would probably do the same. In some respects, he was like an overlord: someone they were extremely reliant on but also a constant reminder of how much they needed him. The colony wasn't yet fully self-sustaining. So, removing him would be a symbolic sign that they were making progress toward being a colony owned and run by its people.

He decided he still wanted to be part of their lives, especially Atreus, who he loved. He decided to show humility, and agreed to those terms. And if you were going to have to inhabit a robotic body, he would build the best possible robotic body.

Then he got slightly annoyed because he wouldn't be able to build the android. The people of New Europa wanted to trust the technology. So, he couldn't just give them the body he wanted. He was going to have to teach them how to build it—slowly. That also offered an opportunity for him to reconnect more with them.

He teleported back into his avatar on New Europa. He corrected himself because they had changed the name to Neuropa. That was another change they made recently on their quest to re-write history. And at least that was a change he agreed with; it was much easier to say.

Atlas took a breath and spoke. "Okay, I understand."

"Did you just leave?" Atreus asked, eyeing him suspiciously. "It's things like that you have to stop doing."

ICARUS

WORLD SPINNING

"Have you noticed how slow time moves now?" Icarus asked as he and Ship stood on the bridge of his spacecraft, watching the fourth habitat cylinder get connected to the other three.

"Time still moves at the same rate, last time I checked," Ship said, half-concentrating on making sure all the eleph-ANTs were doing their assigned tasks properly.

Icarus leaned against the window of the bridge, tapping against the glass. "I think it has something to do with Eve. Before we had all these biological humans around, it felt fine skipping ahead in time or changing our perception of it. Honestly, when we first got to this system, I wouldn't even second-guess watching this whole ring get constructed before my very eyes. Now I worry I'll miss a lot of birthdays and moments by doing something like that."

"I see what you're saying; time does matter a lot more when you're biological. And, I guess, we had just traveled through space. The difference between a month or a year has no meaning when you're traveling vast distances. And now time has a lot of meaning because every day, Eve and the others change. They get older."

Icarus nodded in agreement. "You've gotten wiser lately."

Icarus and Ship were in geosynchronous orbit around Titan. They were moving around the gas giant at the same rate as the ring, meaning from their perspective, the large orbiting habitat was staying completely still.

They had completed four sections of the ringworld and successfully connected them. It was starting to become easy to visualize what it was going to look like. From their perspective, it looked like a thin wire was wrapped around the whole gas giant, then connected to that thin wire were four metal cylinders.

Viewing it all from space hid the fact each of those four cylinders was enormous. They looked small from their perspective right now. But in fact, each of those cylinders had enough land mass to house a small city or town.

Eventually, they planned on building enough of them around the gas giant that they could complete an entire ring around the planet with them.

The challenge the two of them had currently was there was no gravity on these worlds. So, unless he wanted his people to live in zero g, he and Ship needed to find a solution, a permanent solution.

"There's no way we will be able to stay in geosynchronous orbit like this once we get the habitat spun up," Ship said.

"Not without some sort of tether, I guess. So, what are we going to do about this orbiting habitat?"

Ship shrugged. "We can't spin the ring up until it's completely built. Otherwise, the weight difference would stretch it out."

Right now, the weight difference between the wire and the cylinder habitats didn't matter, because both were in a stable orbit around the planet. However, if they wanted to induce simulated gravity along that entire ring, they would need to speed up the ring's orbital speed. Speeding up the orbit would create the feeling of a force pushing everything inside the habitat to the outer edge. Icarus knew there wasn't such a force in reality, but he liked the term *centrifugal force*. The problem was they couldn't speed up the orbit of the ring until all the sections weighed the same, so all the habitats needed to be completed first. Which was a little problematic, since their colony was currently growing in population, and they needed a large-enough habitat to accommodate everyone.

"Icarus, I agree, and we can't afford to wait for the whole ring to be completed, because the temporary habitats that we built are almost at capacity, so we need to find a solution fast; Otherwise, we can't bring any more kids into this world. Eve is in her early teens now; her world is just too small."

"Has Atlas invented some sort of artificial gravity yet?"

Icarus shook his head. "I think that old man has bigger problems. I'm worried the beliefs of the Neuropans might poison my people. You heard he got kicked off the planet, right?"

"I heard; Trillion feels so sorry for him," Ship said. "I can't see that happening to us. The Titans have a different culture."

"I do worry, Ship. You know they talk almost every day? They got Lex to build them a social media network. The way they all interact with each other, it's like they're close friends from different cities."

"Well, they basically are. Eve is a bit of a celebrity."

Icarus opened up his phone to a specific video post. "This is what I'm worried about here, some of the older Neuropans have been posting about how unsafe simulations are. And this post here"—he clicked a few buttons and changed what he was showing—"this is about them removing all the hapticgraphic engines from Neuropa. It has over a thousand likes. There aren't that many people on our two colonies. That's a big percentage of the population."

"You should be proud of them, Icarus. They want to create their own destiny."

Icarus scratched underneath his bill. "I'm so happy that they're taking control of their world. I hope one day I can step away from all the things I do here. I worry some of these beliefs are a little bit too extreme, because I don't want to run this world. But I still want to be here forever with everyone."

"Did you see the zero-g s'mores challenge that Eve invented?" Ship said, looking like the idea just popped into his head.

"Did I! They claimed I cheated at it."

Ship raised an eyebrow. "Explain."

Icarus mimed a gun with his hand. "I shot a marshmallow out the back of a spacecraft, using a rail gun. Then caught it using two eleph-ANTs carrying crackers."

Ship laughed. "I can see why you cheated; you're meant to catch it with your own hands. Anyways"—Ship pulled the conversation back to what they were talking about—"we need to get back on track. What do we do about gravity?"

"I honestly don't know"—Icarus shrugged—"other than build a bigger rotating habitat. But then we're just kicking the can down the road."

"I have a few ideas. And since I have naming rights, I called this idea Rotary City."

"Go on, then."

Ship pointed out the window to where the large silver cylinder was orbiting just in front of Titan. A holographic image of another cylinder appeared beside the others. This one was smaller; Icarus could tell it was made of a different material. It was dull and didn't gleam like the others.

Then he pointed out the window again, and another cylinder appeared, this time just like the others. It was the same size and everything.

Ship pointed out the window yet again and gave the smaller projected cylinder a little flick. It started to spin. "I suggest we make a rotating habitat." Then he closed his hands together, and the smaller cylinder slotted inside the bigger one. "We don't need it to rotate around the whole planet to create gravity. We can build smaller rotating modules. These will rotate on tracks inside of the cylinders"

Icarus slapped his forehead. He felt like such an idiot, his obsession with building the ringworld blinding him to the most obvious answer. It was staring him in the face the whole time. He couldn't believe he had missed it. All he needed to do was build small rotating habitats.

ATLAS

MIND EXPERIMENTS

Atlas was preparing to transport himself into one of the bodies reserved for him on Neuropa. It was a little bit more cumbersome than he would have liked but a million times better than the first version. He shuddered, remembering that experience.

The colony had built their own Starnet, which was independent from his. The Neuropans hadn't simply created a duplicate of what he had created; instead, they had rethought the technology and built it based on their understandings of how it should work. The benefit was their understanding of fundamental science was increasing rapidly. They had become remarkably adept at not just "doing things the way they've always been done" but taking the time to rethink it. They were building things from the ground up in ways much more efficient than he could have imagined. The upside for them was they felt they understood every part of a technology and didn't need Atlas or anyone else to make the Starnet run.

They felt it was much more secure than the original Starnet—and it was. They had pointed out multiple flaws and the original design that made it susceptible to hacking attacks. Not that Trillion or Icarus were going to hack in to the Starnet. The downside was it was incompatible with anything Atlas had built, so connecting to it required him to log in every time.

Atlas punched in the twelve-digit security code that was randomly generated. He assumed they made him do this every time just to annoy him. He pressed the Enter key and closed his eyes; he reopened them and found himself standing in an empty closet.

Version four of the avatar he was inhabiting was a big improvement on the last. He could taste food. He could feel the breeze. When it got cold, he actually got cold too. And it wasn't just a robot capable of doing whatever it wanted. Atlas actually had to take it to the gym, work it out, and let it sleep. The Neuropans were determined to make him like a real human when he was on the planet. Atlas had enjoyed the process of developing this avatar with them. It was a collaborative effort between everyone. He brought in ideas, and they improved on them. He felt like an engineer again, solving problems with a team. They were smart, too, really intelligent—it had been a long time since he felt he wasn't the most capable in the room.

He had multiple avatars scattered all around the planet; they were designed so that any improvement to one would improve the others. So, taking one on a run would also make the others fitter.

This particular avatar was located near one of the psychological research facilities. The closet was dark, so he couldn't see a thing. But he knew the next step. He reached out, randomly swiping at where he expected a door handle to be, and turned the knob, and the door opened. He blinked a couple of times to let his eyes adjust—again, he didn't have superhuman eyesight anymore, so his eyes needed to adjust.

He had also learned his lesson from before, so the first thing he did was find the nearest bathroom to check his face for any drawings or markings that someone might have put on there. His face was clear, but his jacket was on backward. Turning the jacket around, he walked out the door and found the others.

Atreus, Dinah, and Ephraim were waiting for him in room 73-B. The room was small with a table in the middle, the lights were dim, and there was a large window on one side, which Atlas assumed was a one-way mirror. They were in the darker room, so they could see through the mirror but people on the other side couldn't.

Behind that mirror was someone he didn't recognize, not that that mattered much today, as he only really made a personal connection with the first generation of his people. It'd been enough time for all of them to have kids. The thing that stood out to Atlas was the person behind the glass had a faint glow. They were a hologram. *Maybe it was someone from Titan,* he thought; *they were phoning in.*

"I have something rather concerning to share with you, Atlas," Dinah said, pointing to the person behind the glass. "This is patient B. He was unfortunately the first person to die on Neuropa. He had a super rare blood condition that we didn't have a cure for."

Confused, Atlas pointed out through the window. "I assume this is a recording? Because I know you don't allow mind uploads here."

"Well," Ephraim said, "we saw this as a unique opportunity to test just how accurate the mind-uploading technology is."

Atreus noticed Atlas's confusion. "Let me clarify for you. Under our laws, this person is legally dead, and he consented to being turned on for forty-eight hours. Then he will be turned off and destroyed." He raised his hands to Atlas to calm any objections. "And he still agrees to this. We asked for full consent just before he died and after we brought him back to life. At any moment, he can change his mind. This is not a prison or a way for us to experiment on simulated humans."

"As I was saying," Ephraim said, taking back control of the conversation. "We asked patient B to complete a series of psychological assessments. We completed the tests right before he died, and over the last forty-six hours. Doctor, would you like to share what we found?"

Dinah nodded. "As you know, we wanted to understand whether uploading someone's mind is truly uploading that person's mind. We wanted to know whether they thought the same and had the same beliefs, or whether they were changed or manipulated in any way. Is it truly a like-for-like copy of the person, or . . ." She paused. ". . . are they changed in some way?"

"Ohhhhhkayyyyy . . ." Atlas said, slowly looking through the window. "And what did you find?"

"You might want to take a seat," Atreus said, pulling two seats out from behind the table and sitting in one of them.

Atlas sat down, and so did the other two.

Dinah grabbed a clipboard from off the table and drew a circle around a number. She handed Atlas the clipboard. The number she circled said twenty-one percent. "There was no statistically significant difference between almost all the responses from patient B except for this one here. Across all the questions we asked, patient B was twenty-one percent more favorable toward life in a simulation."

"What does twenty-one percent mean?" Atlas asked.

"Well, in patient B's case, and he was already starting from quite a negative sentiment, it means his position has moved to 'slightly favorable.' He now supports the idea of people uploading their minds. And he is now *almost* indifferent to living in a simulation or the real world."

Atlas started to bite his lower lip, thinking about what was just said. "Is that just because he is now a simulated mind?"

Dinah shook her head. "We thought that too, but we asked a range of questions on this topic. There were a number of questions designed to tease that out. There were specific questions that shouldn't be impacted by him being a simulation or not. But he also scored those questions more favorably. He is now onboard with all of us joining the simulation."

Ephraim put out his hand for Atlas to pass the clipboard back. Taking it, Ephraim turned a few pages until he got to the last one. "What this means is if you had quite a few people upload their minds and experience similar changes to their beliefs around this topic, then quite quickly you could have a runaway situation where there's more and more social pressure to get this done."

"So, are you saying I have a bias toward being a simulation too?" Atlas said, looking toward Dinah.

"Maybe. But we'll never know unless we can get the original version of you to complete the questions."

The room started to feel hot Atlas started to sweat. One of the downsides to using this avatar was he wasn't able to hide his emotions as well. If he attempted to leave the body to calm down, that would also cause a visible sign.

"You're still you, Dad," Atreus said, putting a hand on his shoulder. "You've been you longer than you were a flesh-and-blood human. This doesn't change anything; it doesn't change you."

"So, that's why you're telling me? So I know about this bias that I have?" Atlas looked at Atreus. "And you're here to support me through this?"

"Yes, I'm here to support you but to also ask you something." Atreus gestured toward the man behind the window. "I'm in the senate, so as soon as I found out about this, I knew we needed you to talk to him. This is not the original patient B, at least from our understanding of how the mind-uploading machine works, so we wanted you as a third party. Talk to him, and give him the option to live with you as a simulant or live here. We feel we might be biasing the answer by asking the question. We want to make absolutely sure that he is making the decision himself." He paused for a moment. "We know this is a hard thing to ask you."

"And you need me to talk to him now?"

All three of them nodded.

Atlas took a deep breath and steadied himself. "Okay."

Atlas walked out the door and through the hallway before opening the other door and walking in. He waved at the man; he was young maybe early twenties. "Hey, hi."

"Hi, Atlas."

Atlas put out his hand for the man to shake. "Sorry, I didn't catch your name."

"Brendon."

"I guess congrats on testing the machine for the first time."

"It was a weird experience. One moment, I had this doughnut-shaped thing above my head; next minute, I'm in here."

"Do you know where we are?"

He nodded.

"Do you know why I'm here?"

"I think it's to get me to not die. But I want to. Not in some gruesome way, or that I don't deserve to be alive. But when I got the disease and found out I was going to pass, I started to accept it. My family accepted it; we all cried. I don't want to live forever and watch others die around me. I don't want to be alone because no one wants to hang with me anymore. Just doesn't feel right, you know."

Atlas assumed the guy must have had really negative views of a simulation, because this didn't sound positive toward it at all. "I respect that."

"I've already said goodbye to my mom twice. Doesn't feel right to put her through all this." He pointed at his body, and Atlas thought he noticed a small hint of disgust.

"What about this?" Atlas proposed. "In about thirty minutes, you're going to be switched off, and for all intents and purposes, that is death. But let me take your matrix, and if at any point the views here change and everyone starts getting their minds uploaded, then I can bring you back and turn you on."

Brendon shook his head. "The risk is too great. What if something happens to you and someone else finds me? If they turn me on, I could just be a prisoner. I prepared for what's about to happen."

Atlas nodded, and after a few more minutes of talking, he hugged the man and said goodbye. He couldn't help but feel emotional through the whole process. This poor man had just gone through a traumatic experience only to be turned back on and have to go through it all again. Atlas understood the man's position; he didn't agree with it, but he understood.

CHAPTER 18

TRILLION

IS IT TRUE?

Trillion teleported into Atlas's office. He was hunched over his computer, looking at an experiment he had just completed on the bubble. That was not why she was visiting him; she was in a mild sense of panic. "Is it true?"

"Is what true?"

"That we've been manipulated into preferring the simulation? That we're not the same human that left Mars?"

Atlas lowered his head. "As far as I can tell, their data is correct. That guy's personality changed once he was uploaded. But that doesn't mean the same thing happened to us."

"It definitely happened to us. And I'm the only one left with the behavioral modification still in my matrix."

"Well, yes, but. . ." Atlas paused for a moment. "I guess the probability that we have been changed is high. But the point I'm trying to make is they used a different scanning device from the one used to scan our matrices. So, there is the possibility that once we seed the worlds, all of those behavioral changes get deleted. Or the bias toward simulants was never there in the first place."

"It's like learning you're not who you thought you were—twice! Once when we watch you going through the deletion of that modification, and again now."

"Atreus put it best when he told me that I've been me for longer than I'd been a biological human. It changes nothing."

Trillion reached over and grabbed Atlas's hand. She pulled him away from his computer screen. "We have to tell Icarus now; we can't let him find out like this."

"I was going to tell you both once I fully digested it myself. It's only been a few hours."

Trillion pulled Atlas's arm harder. "Come on, old man. News spreads fast around here."

Trillion raised her arm and a portal appeared in front of her. She dragged Atlas reluctantly through it.

Icarus was playing catch with Eve and some of her friends. he looked to be having fun.

None of them noticed that portal, because around Icarus, portals were extremely common. Icarus did notice Trillion's face, though. The concern must have been clear because he jumped out of the game. "Girls, sub. I'm subbing out," he said as he ran over.

"Can we speak in private?" Trillion said.

"Of course."

"Can we do it on Atlas's world? I want Atreus to be there."

Icarus began looking at his duck feet, avoiding eye contact. "I'm actually out of money; I can't afford to buy any more credits." He started to step from side to side a little uncomfortably. "I might have lost a few bets."

Trillion let go of Atlas's arm. "That's cool; I can give you as much as you need. I'm kinda rich there now."

Atlas looked at her strangely. "How did you get Neuropan money? I'm running out quickly too."

"They just needed some resources. I'm shipping some stuff over from the Tac system. They paid half up front; technically, I'm like a multimillionaire or something. Not that I need the money."

Atlas laughed. "Of course you are."

Trillion transferred them both enough money to last them years, then opened up a portal to her spacecraft. "We all have to go back to our ships to log in, so I'll meet you at Atreus's house in two minutes."

Both Icarus and Atlas nodded in agreement, then Trillion jumped through her portal.

It took her a few moments to type in the ever-changing authentication code. Then she closed her eyes, opened them again, and was lying on her bed. A while back, she had started purchasing houses near locations she often visited. It was to stop the inappropriate behavior that often happened to her whenever she left her avatar in places she thought were safe. One time, she was stuffed in a janitor's closet—and that was the moment she decided to get her own mansion or five.

This particular house was located in Sumner, a small farming town on the outskirts of the main city of Neuropa. It was the closest property available to Atreus when she purchased it, and even then, it was still a two-kilometer run. She knew she would be the farthest away, because Atreus kept avatars for the other two in his garage.

She hopped out of bed, put on some running shoes, and walked out the front door. Annoyingly, two young boys were waiting out front.

"Hi, Trillion," they said in unison.

"Sorry I can't hang, boys; I'm in a rush."

They both had a crush on her. Which was fine; she was used to that. But they were constantly hanging around, hoping to catch glimpses of her and often asking her out on dates.

She waved goodbye as she started her jog. Her avatar was quite fit, mostly because she still used running as a way of thinking. And ever since the Neuropans made a rule around avatars, she decided to use her avatar to go running on planet whenever she needed to think.

It wasn't long before she made it to Atreus's house. She thought she was going to be late, but it turned out she was the first one there. Atreus was sitting on his front porch, drinking a beer.

"Hard day at work, then?" Trillion asked, catching her breath.

Atreus grabbed a beer out of the cooler and handed it to her. "I take it you know?"

Trillion took the beer and nodded. "How did you think to test that?"

"It wasn't me; that was all Dinah. She wanted to know whether mind uploading was like making an exact copy."

"I'm not sure whether to thank her or not. It has some pretty big implications."

"I wouldn't stress too much. Part of it is the way we see technology. We weren't born on Earth, we don't know much about Earth other than what we can look up online, so we're less precious about everything Earth has produced."

Trillion sat down in the chair next to Atreus. "Like all our technology?"

Atreus gave a thumbs-up. "I think we're better off for it. It has forced us to build everything from scratch—which is hard. But it means we understand everything much more. Our scientists aren't just accepting the way things were."

Trillian took a swig of the beer. "This tastes better than any simulated beer I've had before. Which is crazy, because you built this technology just for us three."

"We built it for Ship, too.'

"So, what is the plan? You're the longest-serving member of the senate, so I know you know. Why are your scientists looking into testing simulated humans?"

"I'm only the longest because I'm the oldest. But I don't really know."

"Also, I guess you wouldn't tell me, because that would probably be a breach of your planet's security."

Atreus nodded. "We trust you one hundred percent. At least I trust you, but I don't make the rules."

"I'm going to guess." Trillion pointed at her body. "These avatars are so good because you're contemplating avoiding death with them. I'm guessing we are the test subjects. You've got many years before someone else is near their deathbed, so you're taking the time to figure everything out."

Atreus shrugged and took another swig of his beer. "I can only speak for myself. I don't think I would take that next step and become a simulation. There's something poetic about being biological. In the same way, we are improving on so many of yours and Earth's technology by not accepting the way it's always been. I don't think our culture wants simulated humans everywhere."

Trillion thought about her mother in that moment. She had had similar beliefs. She hadn't wanted to become a simulant at first. But then she got old. She got sick. It became inevitable that she agreed to have her mind uploaded. Trillion was quietly confident that the Neuropans would go the same way.

A few minutes later, both Icarus and Atlas arrived. They were puffing, Icarus was exhausted. He could barely stand.

"Our closest avatars were in town," Atlas said. "I should really invest in a car."

"I have a car," Trillion said unhelpfully.

The three of them explained to Icarus what they had learned, rehashing the story, with Atreus filling in any gaps.

CHAPTER 19

ATLAS

TESTING THE BUBBLE

Atlas and Ship used an eleph-ANT to maneuver around the insides of a powered-off spacecraft. The ANTs carried around a mobile hapticgraphic projector, so Ship and Atlas could move around freely as if they were actually in the spacecraft. This was the ship that had just emerged out of the other side of the bubble. They had lost contact with it over a month before. They had also lost entanglement with all particles that the mobile Starnet had, which meant they had to rebuild a connection with it.

This also meant that if they went inside the bubble, they would potentially lose contact with everyone until they were able to reconnect to the Starnet. Which would take many years. Atlas was feeling glad he decided to take two spacecraft; otherwise, he might have learned from that mistake the hard way. It wouldn't have been that bad for his friends Trillion, Icarus, and their Ships, but a lot of his friends on Neuropa were getting old, so that mistake might have meant he'd never see some of them again.

They were first checking the ship for radiation or signs of wear and tear. Any possible hint of something that could potentially have damaged the spacecraft. So far, they had found nothing to suggest there was anything dangerous beyond the bubble.

"It feels like we're about to encounter a lurking alien," Ship said.

"It's because it's so dark. And the ominous lights coming from the eleph-ANT aren't helping."

Both of them were holding flashlights that didn't work. Instead, wherever they pointed the flashlight, the eleph-ANT would move one of its large headlamps in that direction. It almost pulled off the experience of having a torch, except when they rounded a corner.

The first time Ship rounded a corner and the light stopped working, he almost screamed. "Can we turn on the lights already?"

"Use your night vision," Atlas said as he pointed to his eyes. "I've got the eleph-ANT scanning for any changes in the radiation here. And coming up soon is an experiment I left running in my laboratory. We need to check that before we turn on the power. Once we do that, we can turn on everything. Not far to go," Atlas said, rounding a corner.

Atlas was finding it hard to navigate, because nothing looked the same; it wasn't just that it was dark, the whole ship was just grey. Nothing on the walls, the doors all looked the same—grey airlock doors with wheels on them. In his original spacecraft, they had painted signs and placed art all over it. But on this one, because it was only a secondary spacecraft to test the bubble, they had simply re-created the aesthetic using the hapticgraphic projectors, with none of the personality.

Finally, Atlas made it to a door, which he assumed was the entrance to the laboratory—because of course it no longer had any markings above it.

With the power off, these doors all had to be operated manually, and it wasn't like it was hard, more like painfully slow. Atlas and Ship were becoming more accustomed to slow biological time. But still, it felt like they needed to turn the handle one hundred times.

"Thank god, this is the right one," Atlas said as he pulled the door open and looked inside.

"So, what's the experiment?"

Atlas pointed to a row of identical long black boxes. There were at least a couple hundred of them. "One of the things that has puzzled me is how this star system doesn't disappear."

"What do you mean, *disappear*?"

"Visible light is just the small section of the electromagnetic spectrum that biological humans can see. And there are a ton of different frequencies you can broadcast on. Yet apparently, this bubble is blocking all signals from going in and out."

"So, you're saying, because we can still see this system and the star is still shining visible light, it must be letting some signals out."

Atlas moved his head from side to side as he opened a flap on the eleph-ANT and started to pull a cord out of it. "That's just it; this star, and all the planets in the system, don't disappear. They are visible at every frequency across the electromagnetic spectrum."

He dragged the wire out of the eleph-ANT and plugged it into one of the long black experiment boxes. "This should power up the thing and tell us exactly what is happening to these signals." He tapped the black box on the top and it made a metallic *clang*. "Each of these boxes bounces a different frequency of electromagnetic spectrum back and forth. Once we scan these machines, we should know what happened to the light."

Atlas walked around to the eleph-ANT again and opened another panel. Ship followed close behind.

Atlas then clicked around a few times, waiting for it to load. He started the scan and waited for it to be completed.

"What are you hoping to find?" Ship asked.

"This first box will tell us whether light is stretched or contracted as it enters the bubble. Basically, when red light goes into the bubble, does it come out as red light? If there's a change in the frequency, then we know that's one of the ways the bubble is affecting light."

The scan completed, and Atlas checked the results. "Okay, so, nothing there."

"I assume that's good?"

"Well, not exactly; that would have been the easiest way to deal with the bubble, if it was stretching out light."

"Redshifting it?"

"Exactly; if that were the case, then all we would need to do is account for that redshifting before we send the signal. Unfortunately, it's something else."

Atlas walked over to the first test unit and disconnected the wire with a strong tug. He dragged the thick cable to another black box and plugged it in. It made no visible signs it was turned on, but the screen on the eleph-ANT in front of Ship changed.

Atlas headed back toward Ship and started the process again, clicking a few buttons; the scan started. "Interesting."

"What is it? I feel like you're dragging this out because I'm here."

Atlas smiled. "I was. But this is actually interesting. This box bounces light back and forth and measures the time between each bounce." He pointed at the screen, "See this number here, it's the speed of light while it was traveling through the bubble."

"How is that possible? It's ridiculously slow."

"I think we've found what's been happening through our signals when they go through the bubble. Maybe Angelique is on the other side and we're just not hearing her signals."

"I don't understand; I thought the speed of light was a constant."

"The speed that you're probably thinking light travels at is the speed of light in a vacuum. But light travels much slower through a medium."

"So, you're saying that the bubble is creating some sort of medium that makes it harder for light to travel through. So, it moves slower?"

"Exactly. And this would explain why none of our tight-beam communication signals work. We're sending a signal to where we expect the receiver to be, but because it takes that signal longer to get there, the receiver it is aimed at has moved on, drifted past that point."

"Do you know how long it takes for a signal to reach the other side?"

"I'll only be guessing, because I'm not even sure the ship went through the whole bubble." Atlas started to bite his lower lip. His mind started racing through the possibilities; it was pretty incredible technology. He couldn't think of anything natural that would produce this. He struggled to understand the level of technology a civilization that could produce something like this would be at. He started to think through everything he knew, and wondered if he could build something similar. Atlas knew you could use different types of liquid to slow down light. He had already used that in his Starnet. The idea of using some sort of field to slow the speed of light made him wonder if he could use it to *increase* the speed of *c*. "It's definitely been designed to disrupt communication in and out of this region of space. I'd probably assume that whoever made it has a way around it."

"It's a clever solution," Ship said. "By simply slowing down light for a short period of time, you limit other civilizations' ability to explore this region of space, but you also don't make it obvious. Because all signals are still getting in and out, they're not being changed in any way."

Atlas was so desperate to find out how it worked. Sending a spacecraft in to passively observe the bubble was one thing, but actually getting to run experiments and test hypotheses while going through it, that filled him with excitement and curiosity.

"I can see that look in your eyes; we're not doing it," Ship said, predicting what Atlas was thinking.

"You're right; this mystery can wait." Atlas had been thinking about doing a few more experiments on the bubble. But Ship was right; he'd be playing with fire. If he lost access to the Starnet, he could never forgive himself, because it would take a good chunk of a biological lifetime to get it back up again. "Let's go tell that old man Atreus what we found. I wonder if some of their scientists down there have any ideas of how it's done."

CHAPTER 20

TRILLION

NEW WORLD

Trillion, Ship, and Lex were all standing in the middle of the hangar bay. They were waiting for the eleph-ANTs to complete the scan of the planet. The rocky world was what many would call a super Earth. Lex estimated the planet was about one point eight times the mass of Earth, meaning it had one point eight times the gravity. That was a little on the heavy side but wasn't too unmanageable for human life.

They would find out the actual mass of the planet once the scanning completed. In the meantime, they were working off what they had gained from the system based on passive sensors.

They knew the star was an M-type star, a red dwarf, which was the most common type of star in the galaxy.

"I'm surprised most of the systems we explored weren't like this," Ship said.

"What do you mean?" Trillion asked.

"We've been so lucky with star systems. The Dottiens' system. The Tac system. They were both quite well suited for life. This system is so different from those."

The most interesting thing about the planet they chose was it orbited every three and a bit Earth standard days. It was so close to its star that a year was just over eighty-one hours. This didn't mean that planet was a hot mess. Red dwarf stars are much dimmer than other stars, meaning their habitable zone—the area around the star where liquid water was possible—was much closer to the star. If Earth was this close to Sol, all life on it would have been burnt to a crisp.

"I might have chosen this star specifically for that reason," Trillion said. "Given enough time and resources, I'm sure we could make any planet habitable, especially with the help of Atlas, Icarus, and all their people on their planets. So, that's why I chose this for me. Not to make it hard for us but because I don't want to get involved with a planet with life on it again."

Trillion still had a lot of sad feelings about what she had done to the Tac system, especially when she realized the stoicism she felt wasn't because it didn't matter; it was because she had a behavioral modification unit installed in her matrix.

She found that awareness of the behavioral-modification component helped compensate for the effects that piece of hardware was having on her. She was determined not to make that same mistake again.

Trillion floated in the air, folding her arms and legs, relaxing herself in preparation for what she was about to learn. "It'll be interesting to see how hot one of the sides of the planet is. We might add artificial lights, like on Icarus's world."

The other interesting fact about the planet was it was tidally locked, meaning one side of the planet was always facing the sun and the other side was always in darkness, in the same way the Moon is tidally locked to Earth.

"We can deal with it being too hot," Trillion said. "We can also deal with the fact the planet doesn't have an atmosphere yet.

But let's just hope there's a magnetosphere. Because I'd prefer my people to be able to run around without being bathed in too much radiation."

"Have you noticed how little we jump forward in time anymore?" Ship asked. "All this time with people who can't do that has changed the way we interact with things."

Trillion was about to respond when Lex flashed green to signal the scanning was complete. "Can you put it up on the screen, Lex?"

Trillion raised one of her hands. A small screen appeared in front of her palm. She pushed the screen back, and it got bigger as it drifted away before settling into a comfortable position just in front of her and Ship. "Hopefully, this is going to be our new planet, team," she said as information started to appear in front of her. It was like a data dump; too many things were on the screen now, and she couldn't make sense of any of it. "Remember what we practiced, Lex; we don't need to know everything. Focus on what's important to us."

Lex was prone to information overloading. The AI struggled to understand that others couldn't process everything at once like it could. After working together for many years, Trillion found you always had to remind the AI specifically about what you wanted.

The screen showed a bunch of numbers related to the orbital time of the planet.

Ship sighed. "We want to know about the magnetosphere, the mass of the planet, and atmosphere. Can you show us that?"

The orb flashed green and three lines appeared on the screen. The first one said the word *magnetosphere*, followed by a green tick, followed by a number that Trillion assumed represented its strength. The next line said the word *mass*, was followed by one and a half Earth icons, then a very large number of tons. The third line said the word *atmosphere*, followed by a tick, followed by several symbols on the periodic table and some percentages. Trillion assumed that represented the makeup of the atmosphere.

Trillion clapped enthusiastically. "Great table, Lex. I especially love the ticks. I'm going to give you an eight out of ten for this one—mainly because you made it so visual."

The orb did a little happy jiggle from side to side.

"Looks like we hit the jackpot," Ship said as he scanned through the numbers. "It has trace amounts of oxygen, too, which is interesting. The atmosphere is mostly nitrogen, which is going to make terraforming it much easier. If it wasn't tidally locked, I'd say this was the perfect planet."

"Have you mapped out everything completely?" Trillion asked, looking up toward Lex.

The orb flashed green.

Trillion held out her hand as if grabbing a ball. "Perfect; do you mind projecting an image of it here?"

In front of Trillion the planet appeared. She took it up in her hands and started to spin it around. Lex had rendered the clouds on it as well, with about six rather large storms on the planet. It had a very active weather system.

Ship pointed at one of the air currents. "Trillion, the strong winds on this planet are caused by the fact it is tidally locked. The side of the planet that is in constant sunlight heats up and makes the air expand. That expanded air needs to go somewhere, so it is forced into the dark side, which pushes the cold air back, and the cycle continues."

Trillion studied the planet and could see the lines of wind all being pushed from one side of the planet to the other, hot air rising and pulling cold air in from below. It was very chaotic in most places, except in a couple of areas where the large clouds were. Those clouds looked rather stable. "Wind turbines might be the easy solution to power on this planet," Trillion said once she was done counting the ten enormous stable clouds. "Lex, can you remove the weather? I want to see what the surface of the planet looks like."

Lex flashed green, and the planet Trillion was holding changed again. The dense cloud cover disappeared, and it became immediately obvious that one side of the planet was always facing the star. It was basically a dry cake—a desert. Trillion was reminded of the planet Arrakis from the *Dune* series. Trillion wondered if Atlas could engineer some giant worms to roam through the sand.

She turned the planet around to look at the opposite side. This side was frozen from being in a constant shadow. Trillium pointed to what she assumed might be a frozen ocean. "Do we know if this is frozen water?"

The orb flashed blue to signal it did not.

"We will know in a few hours, once our probes reach the surface," Ship said. "The temperature differential between these two sides is enormous."

"Are there any parts of this planet that, without any terraforming, are a reasonable temperature for human life?" Trillion asked.

The orb flashed green.

"Can you place them on the globe I'm holding, please?"

A thin line appeared around the circumference of the planet she was holding, between the sides, right where the light side met the dark side. "So, if you went outside here"—Trillion pointed to the line—"the temperature would be between, say, fifteen and twenty-five degrees Celsius?"

The orb flashed red.

"Lex is saying it would be between four degrees and thirty-five degrees," Ship clarified. "That's what Lex considers reasonable for life."

The orb started to flash on and off, then placed the number 38 on the screen.

Confused, Trillion looked to Ship for clarification.

"I think what Lex is trying to say," Ship said, "is the orbit is not perfectly circular. There's a slight wobble, so if you lived right in the middle, in between the light and dark side, half the year would always be sunny and the other half would always be dark. But it's not actually that bad, because a year is only three-ish days. So, if we built a colony here, a day would be thirty-eight hours."

"Interesting," Trillion said. "This planet is starting to look better and better by the minute. Okay, then, team. Let's make a plan. Lex, you keep scanning the planet for signs of life; send some ANTs down to the surface. Ship, let's go tell Atlas and the others about what we found so we can get everyone's brain thinking about ways to terraform it." Then she paused. "Only if we find out there is no life on the planet. Then once we're done with that, let's go there and visit it. See what it looks like on the surface."

CHAPTER 21

PETER

BROADCASTING

Peter opened his eyes. He blinked a few times as he experienced that mild disorientation that could only be described as "waking up in someone else's bed." Then he realized it wasn't the bed that confused him. It was everything about this moment; he was in a spacecraft out in deep space.

The bed was an illusion created by the hapticgraphic projectors, the same with everything else in the room. He clapped once and the lights switched on. As his eyes adjusted, he pulled off the covers.

He had chosen to design the room to look like his suite at the country club in Florida that he owned. So, the room was very stately, high ceilings, chandeliers, and an overly ostentatious bed.

He walked through the bathroom, which was full of gold. The faucet and handles all looked expensive. He jumped through the shower quickly and had just selected a suit to wear from his walking wardrobe when he noticed the digital clock on the wall. He was expecting to wake up in another ten years. Either the clock was wrong, which was unlikely, or most probable, something had happened that needed his immediate attention.

He was about to teleport to the bridge when he heard a knock at the door. "Come in."

Unity walked through with her head down, scrolling through a tablet.

Peter knew that Unity was scheduled to be the first person to wake up. It was the job of whoever was on call to awake to run a quick diagnostic check on the spacecraft, confirm everything was okay, and go back to sleep. Each of them were taking turns at this.

Evidently, she was coming there to tell him something had gone wrong. But what could it be? The ship was old, but all of its parts were designed to be replaceable so it could survive indefinitely—the rocket of Theseus. Peter shook his head; no point speculating when he could just ask her. "Good morning," he said before getting down to business. "I'm guessing there's an issue?"

"Someone sending messages to Sol."

"Explain?"

Unity handed him a tablet. "I decided to drop a few probes on the way out. Just to passively scan, and alert us if any object was following us. I wasn't expecting to find what I found." She pinched to zoom on a few timestamps. "They intercepted several tight-beam messages this spacecraft sent back to the Sol system."

Peter studied the tablet. "Do we know what the messages say?"

Unity shook her head. "They're encrypted, but they're regular."

"Do we know who sent them? Is anyone awake besides you?"

Unity shrugged. "Assuming you couldn't fake the records, it was previously saying everyone was asleep except for me. I woke you up to share this with you."

Peter paced around the room for a bit. He sat down on the sofa in one of the corners of the room. It was a leather couch. He needed to be tactful; he couldn't simply accuse one or both of the others. It might not be them; it could just as likely be a piece of malicious code that had been sneaked onto the spacecraft.

Peter thought a good long while before finally coming to a conclusion. "Wake the others and ask them all to meet me in here in about an hour. While they are waking, I want you to find out as much as you can about these messages. See if you can locate which part of the spacecraft is broadcasting them. And see if you can shut them down."

"On it," Unity said before leaving the room.

This wasn't exactly the first issue he was expecting. He knew there'd be some problems, but not espionage. Both Hezekiah and Ariana had the knowledge and capabilities to pull something like this off. But, actually, so did Unity. A lot of people made the mistake of immediately discounting the person who claimed to make the discovery. It was a common blind spot. Peter had been around long enough to know people who expected to be caught for doing something sneaky often pretended they found something suspicious. So, he had four suspects, each of his crew or . . . someone else who installed a secret piece of code before they left.

Peter's brain rehearsed several questions he was going to ask the others before he landed on a solution. Unless it was unequivocally evident who it was, he wouldn't be in in a position to punish anyone. It's not like he could turn someone off indefinitely without a clear mandate. The ethics of that were questionable, and the ease with which one person could set another up was high. He decided to change the rules of the game so that it would be advantageous for everyone to want to prove that it wasn't them—hopefully elicit a few more actual or coincidental noticings of malicious code.

The time flew by as he strategized in his head. And it wasn't long before everyone was in his room.

"We have a problem, team," Peter said as everyone took a seat. "Unity, do you mind sharing what you found?"

He handed everyone a tablet with the information she had gathered. "There is a single radio dish that has somehow been commandeered for sending a signal back to Earth. I'm currently checking to see if there are signals being sent in any other direction, and I should have my findings in about a day."

"This is our number-one priority, team," Peter said. "I want each of us to independently do our own research on this. I assume there are more signals being sent and information being shared with Sol that we don't know about."

Peter also decided to make one change to the way everyone was structured. "Going forward, we will all wake up at the same time. I know we originally planned to do shifts, but I think it's prudent that we all wake up." This would make it less likely that the crew would be doing something like this. No one would roam around the spacecraft alone. That would be a bit of a pain but understandable, given the situation.

Hezekiah was nodding throughout the whole presentation. He was scanning the document and trying to understand what was going on.

Ariana was frozen. She didn't move once. She barely blinked. That was a sign she was doing something else in her head, working with her additional computation units—her neuralcortex. Moments later, she stopped blinking. "It's been deleted," she said matter-of-factly.

"What's been deleted?" Peter asked.

"I did an entire sweep of all the code onboard this spacecraft. There was a small install AI designed to report our location at all times, report on any conversations we had and any other information we shared."

"Well, that solves it, then," Hezekiah said.

"Wait, that doesn't solve anything." Peter knew from experience it was never that easy. "Firstly, Hezekiah I need you to work with Ariana to understand what that code was and how it was installed."

"No," Ariana said. "I don't need someone looking over my shoulder."

Peter raised his hand to calm her. "It's not about someone looking over your shoulder; it's about installing controls so that we all can trust the code has been deleted." He turned back to Hezekiah. "I want you to replicate the messages that the AI was sending and stick them on a probe. Fake that we've changed directions, fake some conversations between us, and make it look like we're going to a completely different system."

"I can send the probe now," Ariana said, closing her eyes for a second. "Okay, done."

"Look, Ariana, I completely trust you. But in this situation, I want to make sure that at least two of us know how this works. Hezekiah is the best coder amongst us; can you guide him through the process of replicating it himself?"

It was unlikely that Hezekiah and Ariana were in cahoots on some sort of sabotage together. He did trust both of them completely. But having them check each other's work gave him greater confidence.

Then it hit Peter: Ariana said it was an AI. Not just a piece of code but an artificial intelligence. Meaning it was a sophisticated attack, since most AIs had been outlawed many years before. "Ariana, you said it was an AI. What makes you say it's intelligent?"

"It was evolving and changing, constantly hiding itself. And one thing that stood out to me the most was how different it was from any other AI I've encountered before."

"If it's evolving and changing, how did you notice it?" Unity asked.

"These spacecraft were designed to have matrices like ours connected to it, so I have full access to the inner workings. That alone wouldn't have made it obvious. But with my additional neuralcortex, seeing the whole spacecraft code in its entirety was simple. And from there, the patterns of this AI's code stood out because it was so different. And that's what made it obvious once I started looking for it." Then she paused. She glitched, moving three steps to the right instantly without walking, a confused look on her face. "It's back. I wiped the code clean. But somehow, it's back." She disappeared again.

Peter looked at the others, wondering what was going on. Everyone else shrugged. Unity made a *she's gone a bit crazy* gesture with her hands and face.

Ariana made it look like removing that malicious code was easy. But in Peter's experience, things were never that easy. If it took what looked like thirty seconds to remove something designed to keep tabs on them, then it was actually never removed, because who would go through all the effort and energy to hide something like that only to make it deleteable so quickly? Evidently, Ariana just proved Atlas right and there was something she was missing.

Ariana teleported back in, again in a different place from the last. She sounded a bit out of breath. "It's a tricky AI. It had copies all over the ship. I've deleted them all, though."

CHAPTER 22

ATLAS

LIBRARY OPENING

Atlas grinned from ear to ear as he held the oversized scissors. He was standing next to Atreus in front of a massive crowd of cheering people. He was the guest of honor for the opening of the Atlas Tupu Sol Remembrance Library, the biggest library on the planet to date. It looked like a massive bouquet of flowers: most of the building was shaped like a reversed cone, the point at the bottom and the top covered in what could only be described as artwork, a mosaic of swirling and moving shapes that, as the wind flowed past them, moved in an organized fashion, like they had turned a windmill into a sculpture. This was only made possible through the improvements they had made to the metal first discovered by Icarus. It was the ultimate showing of the design and technological power of this civilization.

It contained the recorded history of the Sol system, many books written by the Neuropans about the planet they came from, and even more works of art, poems and literature, that they had reproduced from the database Atlas and Ship brought with them.

It contained knowledge about all the different cities and countries around the solar system, and unlike how he would have organized it, having a bias for the way the solar system was around the time he left, they showed no such bias for wanting to categorize the history based on what happened most recently but rather constantly related the recorded history of the Sol system back to their own history.

The Cambrian explosion on Earth was often described similarly to the moment the slime mold first produced greenhouse gases on Neuropa. There were even stories about how Atreus "discovered Neuropa" and likened him to a great explorer.

Interestingly, there was a big section within the library dedicated to fanciful theories about what the Earth system was like today, including speculation that they had reverted away from the simulation and back into the true human form. Trillion's defeat of the old human empire in the war to protect the Dottiens was shown as proof of their superiority.

Atlas opened the scissors and cut the ribbon to rapturous applause. Fireworks lit up in the sky at the exact moment he did it. "I declare this library open," he said in his most official voice.

Atreus shook his hand, and he waved at Ship and Trillion in the crowd.

There was no point standing there afterward; both he and Atreus had already given their speeches. So, the two of them sneaked out the back to open bottle of bubbly and celebrate privately before the onslaught of media questions.

"This means a lot to me," Atlas said. "I know you pushed for this."

"Just doing my part. I know you don't believe that we all love you, but none of us would be here if it wasn't for you. And we are grateful, even if it doesn't feel like that sometimes."

"Even still, I'm grateful, Atreus. I know you pulled a lot of strings in the background and owe a lot of favors for this."

"I think we treated you badly. Consider this reparations," Atreus said with a wink. "Not that you're getting paid."

Atlas laughed. "I hear you're retiring soon, you're not seeking re-election from the senate. They're about to lose a great leader."

"I'm getting old; I'm not one to stand in politics until I'm too old to think straight. I think I might spend some time with Trillion; her terraforming project is starting up soon."

The two of them clinked flutes one last time, finished their champagne, then went back out front to take media questions.

It was then that Atlas noticed something was wrong: Atreus started to grab his chest. He tripped and lurched forward. It all happened in slow motion. Atlas's mind saw exactly what was happening; it wasn't graceful. He watched as Atreus fell and hit his head on the ground hard. He mentally screamed in frustration as he was unable to catch Atreus, because avatars did not have superhuman reflexes.

Atlas screamed, "Help, someone help!" as his avatar finally reached Atreus and he cradled his head.

The next moments were a blur as medics ran toward them, pushing Atlas out of the way. Atlas saw them performing CPR; he felt helpless.

He started to push his way back through the medics, who at this point were carrying Atreus out on a stretcher while forcing his lungs to breathe. He wasn't moving; he looked limp.

Atlas just knew he was dying. He could feel it in his bones, somehow he knew it was coming, so he pushed his way to the front. "We need to scan his brain!" he demanded. "I have an eleph-ANT carrying a machine on its way here."

He was forceful, and many of the citizens looked up to him now, so his demands were shaping the flow of events.

Atreus was in the back of an ambulance now. But it hadn't started flying away, because Atlas was yelling at them not to leave. The stress of everything happening right now, and the forceful nature of Atlas meant, for a moment, everyone was following

Atlas's instructions. Neither of the medics dared declaring the time of death—even though they should have.

Atlas stood outside of the ambulance, looking up toward the sky, waiting for his eleph-ANT to arrive.

The majority leader of the senate, Dinah, came over and took hold of Atlas's hand. "It's not what he wants; he is not being scanned." She dragged Atlas into the ambulance and closed the door, then ordered it to take off. "That was incredibly dangerous what you did, launching the vehicle from space and sending it down here. There will be consequences. We shot it out of the sky."

Atlas was sobbing. "Now is not the time! My son just died."

"The first Neuropan just died."

"You attacked our . . ."

Atlas disconnected his ears so he couldn't hear anything around him, and held Atreus's hand, crying uncontrollably.

CHAPTER 23

ATLAS

GOODBYE MY FRIEND

Atlas stood still on the podium, shaking his piece of paper. Atreus's funeral happened exactly ten days after his death. This was the first death of a founding citizen. Poetically, he was the first citizen of Neuropa. The entire planet had dropped everything they were doing for this moment. Atlas looked out toward the sea of people. Almost half a million people gathered around for their chance to say goodbye to the first of them.

He struggled through a speech he had once expected he'd never have to make. The crumpled paper was the only sound audible to the crowd as Atlas stammered and wept through sections of the talk.

Atlas saw the next section of his speech written out. He'd written this next part in anger. He couldn't bring himself to say the words out loud, lest he tarnish the moment and not celebrate Atreus's life. So, he said the words in his head, happy that at least with an audience of one, the universe would know.

In a world where death was an optional choice, why would anyone choose it? The world I founded was far beyond the technological capability of the Earth, yet your acceptance of this kind of pain rocked me to the very core. Death was a choice, not a requirement of life. There's so much of life you don't get to choose. Which planet you're born on, who your parent is, what you look like. Why not take control of the things you can control? Out of all the options you had in front of you, why did you choose this death?

After he wiped away a tear once more, the audience could hear him again. "I loved you, Atreus. Thank you for giving my life purpose."

"Goodbye," he said looking toward Atreus.

Atlas looked up at the audience for the first time through the whole speech, then looked toward Trillion, Icarus, and their Ships.

"Goodbye."

Atlas walked over and touched the top of Atreus's head. He had never accepted that Atreus might be permanently dead until the moment his hands connected with the rigid dried leather which used to be skin. As he held his hand on Atreus, he noticed how cold the body was. In the back of his mind, he had always hoped they might change their mind. Allow him to bring Atreus back. He knew right then it was not going to happen.

He took his hand off Atreus's head and headed out the back. He found a place to hide, and left the body of his avatar there.

Back on the spacecraft, he instructed Ship to move as quickly as he could toward the bubble.

There was nothing left for him on New Europa.

CHAPTER 24

TRILLION

I THINK HE'S LEAVING

Trillion noticed both Atlas and the Ship of Atlas disappear at the same time. They both sneaked out the back and didn't come back. She started to get suspicious; she noticed he said goodbye twice. *And one of those times, he was looking at us.*

She tugged at Ship's arm and they both made their way through the crowd, and into a bathroom. They locked the door behind them and left their avatars.

As soon as Trillion was back in her spacecraft, she raised her arm and a portal failed to appear. Confused, she raised her arm again; still no portal. She looked at Ship.

He shrugged. "Try the other spacecraft."

Trillion raised her arm again, and this time, a portal appeared in front of her. The two of them jumped through and fell into

Atlas's backup spacecraft, the one he had originally used to test experiments on the bubble. Trillion stood on the bridge, calling out for Atlas.

The bridge was dark, as if only emergency lights were on. It was lifeless, empty, grey, without any of the nice personality that his vessel usually had.

A few moments later, Icarus and his Ship arrived too, the crackling of static appearing as Icarus's portal opened.

"Is he going?" Icarus asked, looking toward Trillion.

"I think he's gone."

Neither of them knew what to do after that. It was like they had lost two friends and only one of them was coming back.

"Can you take control of this spacecraft?" Trillion said, looking at her Ship. "Are there any messages left for us? Is there any info about where he's going?"

"Looking now," Ship said, followed by a quick pause before he added, "There's nothing on the internal system."

Trillion started to look around. "What about something physical? We know he loved real objects more than digital ones." She checked the control panel. "When was Atlas last on this spacecraft?"

"Just a moment ago."

"Can you tell me his last location?"

Ship nodded. "His small study was the last place the spacecraft recorded him."

Trillium pointed both her hands at the floor, and a portal appeared below all of them. They all fell through it and landed in Atlas's study.

As soon as Trillion fell through the floor, she knew it was planned. The room was immaculately perfect, none of it replicated with the hapticgraphic projectors. The executive chair was real, as was the table, so, his office not being covered in printed reports was the clearest sign that he had tidied it on purpose.

Trillion walked over toward the desk. It had three items on it. There was a stack of cloth on one corner. She picked up the small object before realizing what it was. "Awww, he kept Atreus's first-ever outfit." The clothes felt so soft. "I think this is telling us he'll be back, because there's no way he's leaving this moment of history here."

Next to the baby clothes was a bottle of champagne. She picked it up. "What's this for?"

"I think it refers to *bubbles*," her Ship clarified.

Icarus laughed. "The old man thinks he's Sherlock Holmes, leaving us these clues."

The final object on the table was a photo. She grabbed it and looked. It was a photo of them before they had left. Icarus in his human form, Trillion, even Peter was there too. But the person most interesting to Trillion was Angelique. She was right in the middle of the photo. Everyone smiling. Trillion assumed it had been taken a few weeks before they left.

She showed the photo to Icarus. "Angelique is in here."

As she showed the photo to Icarus, she noticed there was writing on the back. "There's a note."

She turned the photo over. "*To my oldest friends, Trillion, Icarus, Ship and, Ship. Sorry I didn't say goodbye properly. You already know I would have mumbled through a speech anyway— this is much cleaner. As you could probably already guess, I'm headed into the bubble to find Angelique. I'm going to go find her and bring it back. Or at least give us closure on where she is. See you soon. Atlas.*"

Trillion looked up from the paper. "There's an extra note from Ship on here, too." She read it from the top. "PS. *From Ship. Remember we live forever, and time doesn't matter as much; you can change your playback speed. So, don't worry; it's going to feel like really soon that we see you next. See you real soon. Ship of Atlas.*"

ATLAS

ELECTROMAGNETIC SPECTRUM

Atlas and Ship were cautiously moving through space. It had been several days since they first entered the bubble. Soon after they did, both Atlas and Ship regretted it. Their connection to the Starnet immediately ended, and they couldn't communicate with the others. It made them both sad but also forced them forward because once the Starnet disconnected, they had no other option but forward.

Ship in particular was heartbroken and took three days to get back to normal.

Throughout their journey they hadn't learned much new about how the bubble worked, even as they progressed through it. And that wasn't because they hadn't tried. Quite the contrary;

they ran countless experiments and even dropped a series of probes. None of what they tried yielded any clues to how the bubble worked.

They had noticed that all the circuitry on the spacecraft, including themselves, moved slower through the bubble. But that was kinda expected, because a lot of the circuitry involved fiber-optic cables. What they couldn't figure out, though, was how the bubble field was penetrating their spacecraft. They weren't reading an increase in any magnetic field or radiation. It frustrated Atlas that he didn't know how it worked.

The bubble field wasn't small, either. The outer-most region of the bubble started seven light-hours from the star. If it were around Earth's solar system, it would have easily encompassed all the planets and Pluto.

After they had traveled a long while, Atlas, Ship, and Lex found their electronics were functioning normally again. Atlas realized that, whatever the bubble was built for, it only affected the outer portions of the system.

They continued their trajectory. As soon as they made it to the inside of the bubble, the whole system started to look weird, as if the veil had been lifted and they were finally seeing the true insides.

They were entering the system on the same plane as the planets. Atlas had chosen this angle because it would allow them to use the transit method in order to understand the atmosphere of some of the planets.

The transit method required the planet to pass in front of the star from the observer's perspective. Usually, this was used to detect whether a planet existed. A telescope could detect a planet because as it passed in front of a star, an unimaginably small but still noticeable dimming would occur. This dimming was because the planet blocked some of the light from reaching the observer. To detect an atmosphere required the same process, but was a lot more intricate. Many molecules absorb or change light as it passes through it—and each molecule did it in a slightly different way. Reading the way light looked after it had passed through an atmosphere was like reading a fingerprint, and reading it enabled you to understand exactly what that atmosphere was made up of.

Atlas positioned his massive onboard telescope toward the planet, passively collecting data.

"I think we've collected enough data to check these spectral lines," Ship said. "You have to remind me what it means, though."

"Perfect; can you print it out?" Atlas said as he headed toward the printer and grabbed the top sheet. It was a simple line graph showing the amount of light the telescopes were receiving at each wavelength. A drop in the line showed that something was absorbing that particular wavelength. Atlas pointed to a dip on the line. "There's a noticeable drop in infrared light. It's exactly at the six-point-four-micrometers wavelength."

Ship shrugged. "So, what does that mean?"

"It means that something in the atmosphere is absorbing that exact wavelength of light. And there's only one substance I know of that can do that."

"Let me guess." Ship paused for a little longer than he should have. "The atmosphere is full of red cellophane?"

"What? No," Atlas said before seeing the smirk on Ship's face. "It's oxygen. There's a lot of oxygen on that planet."

"Does that mean there's life?"

Atlas was like a schoolboy now. He was buzzing with theories. "I think it does." He grabbed the other printouts off the printer. "Okay, this is creepy; either the atmosphere on this planet is eerily similar to the one on Earth—"

"That couldn't be a coincidence, could it?"

Atlas nodded. "Or that's human life down there." Atlas walked over to the window and pointed out toward the star system they were approaching. "This is the world that Angelique colonized."

"Wow, hold on," Ship said, not wanting to jump to conclusions. "What makes you so certain it's her? Assuming it is the same atmosphere as Earth, could there be another reason? Could it be someone else from Sol? Why would she set up this bubble around the system? What is she hiding from?"

"You're right; it could be someone else. But if it is, then this will explain why we haven't heard from her. Remember, when we first started this journey, we didn't have a reason to contact anyone else. Nor did we have the Starnet technology. So, she might have headed into the system, not realizing there was some sort of other alien device creating this field. And by then, maybe she'd already started terraforming."

Ship eyed Atlas suspiciously. "You seem extremely confident that this is Angelique but not at all confident that she built the bubble?"

Atlas bit his bottom lip. "She wasn't a scientist. And this has to be beyond human-level technology."

"Is it only beyond human-level technology because you can't build it?" Ship said with a smile.

"Touché, my old friend. But also because I can't even fathom how she would create it. Is it dark matter? What is it?"

"And what you know is the baseline for human-level technology?"

Atlas didn't respond. He didn't quite know *how* to respond. Ship was right; he was assuming if he didn't know how something was done, it must be beyond human-level tech.

Ship patted Atlas on the shoulder. "I'm teasing you," Ship said. "Lex doesn't know how it's made either."

The orb, who up until that moment was quietly floating in the corner, flashed green.

"Can we communicate with external probes now that we have crossed the influence of the bubble?" Atlas asked.

Ship shrugged, then looked toward Lex, who also flashed, signaling it had no idea.

"Want me to send out a probe now to test it?"

Atlas nodded, and Ship ejected an eleph-ANT through of the rail guns. "It's going to take a while for the eleph-ANT to get far enough away."

Atlas looked at Ship. "Want to change our playback speed? I haven't really played with that trick in a long time!"

The two of them had gotten out of the habit of adjusting their playback speed. Traveling through space, time became meaningless. It still traveled in the same direction, they couldn't go back in time, but the increments between units of time completely lost their importance once they could make a second feel like decade and vice versa.

The two of them adjusted their playback speed and watched as the eleph-ANT picked up speed, moving faster and faster away from them.

The orb flashed green.

"Lex confirmed both short-range and long-range communication is working," Ship said.

"I'm not sure we should head to the planet ourselves." Atlas pointed at the eleph-ANT on one of the screens. "I suggest we use that eleph-ANT to check out the planet. If their technology level is powerful enough that they can make a bubble around this whole system, maybe we should take precautions."

Ship agreed. "We're far enough away right now that there's no way they could detect us. And now that we have access to the Starnet again, we can use the eleph-ANTs to explore the system and feed back information at real time."

Ship launched several more ANTs with the rail gun, this time at greater speed. Then he placed a screen on the wall of the bridge for each one of the ANTs. The screens were live-streaming the view each of the ANTs was seeing. Then he pulled two chairs out and sat in one of them. "It'll take them a couple weeks to near the planet."

Atlas smiled. He forgot how good it was to not have to wait. He could stay single-mindedly focused on a task and adjust time to make sure he could keep at it. "Let's do it again, then."

Time began to speed up for both of them as Atlas sat on the seat beside Ship and watched the ANTs race toward the planet. A week flew by in front of their eyes. Then a flicker appeared on one of the screens.

"What was that?" Atlas asked.

"What was what?"

"Can you rewind it a bit?" Atlas looked toward Lex as he spoke.

All five of the screens they were looking at it started to play in reverse at the same speed as before. And the same thing happened again; there was a flash on one of the screens. An object had raced past the third ANT again.

"I see it now too," Ship said as he took over control from Lex. He changed the recording to the part of the video where they could see the object clearly. "That's an ANT."

"Is that one of ours?"

Ship shook his head.

Atlas squinted at the object on the screen. "That's an old ANT. It's not made of hapticgraphic material."

Ship got excited. "Does that mean—"

Atlas nodded. "We found her. That has to be Angelique."

Then without warning, the room went red; Atlas could tell he had just been thrust into real time.

On one of the screens appeared an eleph-ANT. Atlas quickly realized it wasn't one of theirs. It was shaking.

Once more Atlas's playback speed was decreased, turning seconds into hours.

"Look at this," Ship said, switching the view to one of the cameras on their spacecraft. The camera revealed another eleph-ANT just like the one before, its thick limbs revealing the older model. Its large trunk had some sort of device attached to it, and it was pointing that device at the camera. The device was somehow pulling the ANT toward it, as if it were some giant magnet.

"Is that a tractor beam?" Atlas asked before realizing what was happening. "The other eleph-ANT that passed a moment ago, it's heading here. Can you get us out of here?"

"We're already racing as fast as we can," Ship said.

Feeling a little safer, Atlas noticeably relaxed. "What's going on in the—"

Ship interrupted him. "They're all over us." Then he changed the screens in front of them. The screens showed several eleph-ANTs surrounding them. All with the same device pointed in their direction. Their spacecraft was frozen in place.

"I can't even move," Ship said.

"Launch ANTs; fire our lasers. Do something to kill them."

Ship quickly turned on the lasers and fired them at whichever eleph-ANT they could target.

The spacecraft had three lasers, one positioned near the front, designed to target oncoming enemies, one at the back, then one on the side.

Ship fired their lasers at the only two eleph-ANTs that were within range of the weapons. The lasers made quick work and completely sliced both eleph-ANTs into pieces. That allowed them to briefly retake control when the field surrounding the spacecraft weakened.

Because space battles happened over such vast distances, the lasers were all designed to target objects very far away. Atlas had always assumed they would be able to maneuver the spacecraft to hit any object with just three lasers. He was regretting that decision right now.

At the same time the lasers were firing, Ship launched everything he could. Every available eleph-ANT through every accessible door opened and out all rail guns. Volley after volley of eleph-ANTs was launched out of rail-gun doors.

Ten eleph-ANTs successfully made it out the air lock before the tractor beam clamped down on the spacecraft, effectively preventing the rail guns from forcing any subsequent eleph-ANT to smash into one that was just outside the gun turret.

The ten eleph-ANTs that made it out of the rail guns quickly turned toward the enemy eleph-ANTs. Ship instructed the eleph-ANTs to change configuration, using the hapticgraphic engine to mold the trunk of the eleph-ANT into a large claw. The claw of the first eleph-ANT reached out and grabbed the device the opposing eleph-ANT was holding. Ship instructed the eleph-ANT to clamp down. The claw began to bend and mangle the device, and once again, Ship felt a surge of control return to his spacecraft as another of the devices was disabled.

"If we can disable six more, I think we can escape," Ship said as he focused his energy on controlling the eleph-ANTs.

Several mini battles took place at once. As the enemy swung tractor beams, wildly trying to lock onto one of Ship's eleph-ANTs, Ship was incredibly adept at maneuvering the vehicles, dodging and weaving into and out of trouble. He managed to grapple another of the devices, yanking it free and cutting its power.

The battle was not without losses; one of the tractor beams had successfully grabbed one of Ship's eleph-ANTs. That was when Atlas and Ship learned the true power of the tractor beam. Within an instant, the eleph-ANT was utterly crushed into a perfectly circular ball.

"Only five more to go," Atlas said, watching the readings on the spacecraft.

Ship's free eleph-ANTs had lost most of the nanoball material that the hapticgraphic engine used to create objects, so they had no more grappling capability. Ship sent each of them on suicide missions to take out the ANTs nearest one of the rail gun exits.

Ship's maneuverability advantage meant each of the three eleph-ANTs successfully connected, destroying both at the same time.

Ship quickly cleared the rail gun exit and launched hundreds of eleph-ANTs as soon as he could.

At the same time, Ship fired the engines hard, moving quickly and dragging the eleph-ANTs that had tractor beams still attached to them.

The eleph-ANTs Ship had just launched quickly selected targets, and at a ten-to-one ratio, they quickly surrounded the final three enemy robots. Like several targeted missiles all moving at the same time, two of them connected with the opposing eleph-ANTs. Ship instructed the eleph-ANTs to select new targets, diving and weaving as they did.

The battle had completely turned now. The devices tugging on the spacecraft were dropping like flies, further increasing the speed at which Ship and Atlas could escape.

Still dragging three of the enemy eleph-ANTs behind them, Ship destroyed one more.

"Only two left," Ship said as he focused on the remaining two.

Atlas flick through the viewer cameras arranged around the spacecraft trying to locate the final eleph-ANTs. "Why is that one getting closer to us?"

One of the eleph-ANTs was using its tractor beam to pull itself toward the spacecraft. Obviously realizing they had lost, it was probably trying to attach some sort of tracking device to them.

Atlas watched as it landed on the spacecraft, its legs leaving visible holes as they pierced the spacecraft to grab hold.

"I'm almost on top of it," Ship said, "and I'm sending eleph-ANTs to the opposite side of the wall. If it makes it through, we'll rip it to pieces."

Then the device the eleph-ANT was holding turned red and a gaping hole appeared right in front of it. The hole was as big as the eleph-ANT and looked as though it had just been ripped apart. It wasn't like a laser burning through it; it was as if pliers had been embedded and, in an instant, the hard exterior and several floors beneath it had just been ripped apart.

The eleph-ANTs waiting on the other side were now a mangled mess of wires.

The spacecraft wasn't pressurized, so no burst of atmosphere erupted from the hole.

The eleph-ANT launched itself down the hole it had just created, out of harm's way from Ship's oncoming troops. Once it reached the wall, the device at the end of its trunk pulsed red again, and another giant hole opened up.

"No, no, no! It knows where to go," Atlas said as he teleported to where to enemy eleph-ANT was. Atlas dove at the eleph-ANT's trunk, aiming for the device it was using to make holes through the spacecraft.

The hapticgraphic engines weren't that strong within the spacecraft, where they didn't need to be overly powerful. But with enough pressure, they should have been strong enough to break or at least damage the eleph-ANT.

The eleph-ANT turned its trunk, not toward Atlas or Ship, who were both attacking it at this point, but toward the hapticgraphic projector in the corner. The eleph-ANT fired its weapon, and both of them disappeared farther down the hall, where a working projector was still active.

"They know our spacecraft," Atlas said as he pointed to the hole in the wall the eleph-ANT had just created. "They know where we are."

"Our matrices are behind that wall," Ship said.

The two of them stopped time to have a conversation. Atlas was mentally cursing himself for using the same design as he had used for years, only bigger. He was angry that he didn't treat security seriously. It was obvious that anyone with the design scheme knew exactly where to get them. There was only one spot on the spacecraft anyone with access to this information needed to look. If they ever made it out of this, Atlas was going to redesign this spacecraft from the ground up.

"I'm too slow; every eleph-ANT I have on its way to defend us won't arrive in time," Ship said. "They'll disconnect me first, then you will lose control of the spacecraft for some time, then they'll probably disconnect you." Ship just managed to get the words out before he was unplugged.

In that moment, Atlas regretted moving so hastily into the system. He knew he should have been more cautious. He didn't have a plan and he hadn't done his research. Now he and Ship were facing the consequences. He didn't know yet what would be in store for the both of them, but really hoped it didn't mean waking up in some random research facility. Or worse, never waking up again.

Then a thought occurred. Maybe this was General Sarah Walker again. Maybe this was a secret human research base. It would make sense since he had just been attacked by human-level tech. Plus whomever had just unplugged Ship had intimate knowledge of the setup for his spacecraft. He felt a deep sense of dread that he might be dragged back to Earth and stuck in some metaverse prison.

The only consolation was that Ship had been unplugged, not destroyed. It meant that at some point in the future, he would get answers. He would know who it was. At least there was that. Moments later, Atlas was disconnected too.

CHAPTER 26

ICARUS

NAME THE PLANET

Icarus pulled out his portal gun and shot it at the wall in front of him. He took a couple steps back, then sprinted toward it and dived in head-first. Landing on the other side, he ducked and rolled, then continued sliding on his ducklike feet across the metallic flour of Trillion's bridge.

Not to be outdone, Trillian lifted her hand, and a portal appeared behind Icarus. He fell through the portal. The exit to the portal was on the ceiling, but it was turned around, so Icarus fell through it head-first. He landed in a crumpled heap on the ground.

"If you're going to teleport in here like that unannounced, I'm within my rights to do things like that," Trillion said, proud of herself for putting a twist on Icarus's entrance style.

Icarus laughed as he said, "I'd been planning that entrance for ages."

"You gotta think on your feet . . . or, in your case, flippers, to pull off a superhero entrance in front of me."

Icarus and Trillion had been playing this game for a while now. Icarus's goal was to complete a superhero landing, and Trillion's goal was to disrupt that landing. He had yet to pull off the heroic *thud* yet. Icarus dragged himself off the ground and straightened his T-shirt. "I just realized you don't have a name for your system."

"I haven't given it a name yet. I don't want to jinx this one by giving it a name."

"What about a temporary one?"

"Okay, let's go with T3."

"Trillion's third world?"

Trillion winked back. "You want to see what I've done?"

She pulled up a projection of the planet and held it in her hands. She pointed to the side facing the sun. "So, we've started building solar panels all around the light side." She turned the planet around. "And we've been following in Atlas's footsteps by starting to engineer a fungus to produce carbon dioxide. But I'm a little lost around what to do next."

Icarus walked around the projection Trillion was holding. "That's part of the reason why I'm here. I shared a lot of the research that Atlas had done on this planet with the Titans. Eve's granddaughter Mahalia is actually leading this project. Do you mind if they come over here and show you a few of their ideas?"

Trillion nodded enthusiastically. "You beat me to it; I was about to ask them. I didn't want to bring it up until I was one hundred percent ready for them, because I know terraforming to biologicals is a multi-generational play."

Icarus pulled out his portal gun and shot it at the wall. Moments later, Mahalia walked through the door with three other people.

The Neuropans had been working on the technology for real physical humans to stream into avatars for a while. It allowed people from Titan to visit Neuropa and vice versa. The technology wasn't as good as the technology used to stream simulants, like Icarus or

Trillion, onto the planet. And that was intentional because they saw this as a slippery slope toward uploading minds—a gateway drug, as they described it. Participants always reported feeling like it wasn't their real body. It didn't have that addictive feeling that he remembered from when he would play virtual-reality games back on Earth. Eve described it as that gross feeling you get from wearing dirty clothes. Regardless, it was an effective technology for making the two worlds feel closer together.

Once Mahalia had introduced everyone, she got down to business. "What's your plan for this planet? When are you going to bring humans onto it?"

"As soon as I can," Trillion replied. "I don't think we need to wait until the terraforming is complete like Atlas. I prefer what you did, Icarus." She looked at him. "Build the foundations for a sustainable colony, then let them build up with you. Let them have control over what they get."

Mahalia nodded. "That is good. That was actually one of my recommendations. The sooner a colony can have control over itself, the better."

"I don't think I need to wait that long, either." Trillion pointed at the projection. "There is an area around the planet in between the light and dark side, with the temperatures are already tolerable for human life." Trillion raised her hand and a projection appeared in front of the other three guests.

Debbie, one of the colleagues of Mahalia who was actually from Neuropa, rotated the projection. "This hapticgraphic construction is crazy, the fidelity of it; this is my first time manipulating a physical projection."

Icarus kept forgetting that the hapticgram technology was banned on Neuropa. He was so used to his people being familiar with it he forgot others hadn't used it yet.

"Create your own version of it," Icarus said, "but with a lot more safety features that can't be hacked in to."

Mahalia stood up, holding the projected planet. "How are we going with the atmosphere?"

"I'm at a bit of a loss, to be honest." Trillion pointed to the thin bands around the planet. "There's not enough space in this warm region to grow oxygen-producing plants. And on the other side of the planet, it's too cold. That ice is frozen all the way through. It's not like on Atlas's world, when there were pockets of liquid water under the ice."

"I think we have found a way around that." Mahalia held up a piece of paper. "There's a particular type of tree called the pando that is actually a superorganism. If you were standing in the middle of a forest, you'd think you were surrounded by lots of different trees, but actually, it's the same tree connected through a network of roots."

Icarus squinted to see the piece of paper. "Can I see that?" He grabbed the note from Mahalia and threw it in the air. It got bigger and bigger, until the forest image was visible.

Mahalia did a thank-you praying gesture. "What we can do is engineer these trees to survive on both sides of the planet, using a network of routes to connect the two. Then it can pull minerals and resources from the ground of the cold side and sprout leaves and foliage to do photosynthesis on the sunny side."

"Are you saying you could engineer a tree to survive on both ends of the planet?"

"Well, the tree would only be visible on the light side, but all of its roots would be pulling from where there wasn't a sun. We would probably have to engineer it in combination with some mycelium, as tree roots traditionally aren't that efficient at moving material over long distances."

Trillion slow-clapped. "How long have you been thinking of this, Mahalia?"

"Terraforming a world has always been a dream of mine. Getting the chance to do something like this is amazing. Don't get me wrong; growing up on Titan has taught me a lot about artificial habitats. But the idea of living on a ball and gravity being created not through spinning but through just the sheer mass of the object, it's crazy."

Trillion studied the faces of Mahalia and the others. "Are you saying you can do this?"

Mahalia nodded. "Yes, we can."

The other three looked a little more reluctant but also nodded.

Trillion turned toward Icarus. "Are they telling the truth?"

Icarus nodded. "They've all helped me on my world-building project. Mahalia is actually one of the top geneticists on Titan. You know the autumn grass? The one that turns purple in between seasons?" Trillion nodded. "Well, she created that. The cities that adopted it look so good with purple lawns.

"Can I put you in charge of this project? Do you want a fancy title or anything? You and your team?"

"Are you for real?!" Mahalia blurted out.

"I sure am, and obviously, you get to use all of the resources we have accumulated so far in the system. But once people are on the planet, their wishes and requirements supersede yours. But until that moment, welcome to this terraforming project."

Icarus gave a secret thumbs-up to the others and gave Mahalia a not-so-secret fist-pump. She was clearly so excited. It made him smile to see his people spreading out and now helping Trillion with hers.

CHAPTER 27

TRILLION

STORMS

Trillion and Icarus were sitting in the cockpit of an eleph-ANT. They were seated side by side, staring out into a dark cave, the Ship of Trillion behind them, controlling the eleph-ANT, the bright lights of the eleph-ANT illuminating what was just in front of them, while everything not covered in light was pitch black. They were exploring a tunnel that had just been completed on Trillion's new world, although *completed* implies they built the tunnel. They hadn't built much of it. It was more a case of connecting up hundreds of separate caves that had been created millions of years before, when the planet was much hotter and lava flowed more readily, tunnelling its way just below the surface of the planet.

The network of tunnels now stretched between the two ends of the world. They planned on using a network of tunnels as a way to move things around, especially on the light side, without needing to subject things to the harsh heat and light that constantly covered that side.

Trillion leaned back in her chair. They had made it to the very end of the tunnel, and the bright lights of the eleph-ANT were illuminating the final piece of wall. "You know these caves are pretty well sealed; we could fill it with Earth's atmosphere and call it a day."

"But one breach of the cave and your breathable air is gone."

Trillion agreed. "Who wants to live in a cave, anyway?"

Icarus pointed out the window to where they could see the cave. "I like to imagine these tunnels were built by the giant sandworms from *Dune*."

"Maybe we can set up a high-speed train network through these tunnels and design the front of it like a worm," Trillion added as she placed her feet up on the dashboard of the eleph-ANT. "You ready?"

"Wait, not yet," Icarus said as he used his portal gun to create a small window in front of him. He reached his arm through the portal and grabbed out one bucket of popcorn. He handed it to Trillion, then reached back for two more, handing one to Ship and keeping the final for himself. Stuffing his beak full of popcorn, he said, "Now I'm ready."

Trillion pulled a large bar down across the two of them. It was designed to hold her and Icarus in place. She turned around to see Ship had already securely fastened himself. Then she gave a nod, and Ship gave the mental command for the digger in front of them to complete the tunnel through to the other side.

The whole area began to vibrate. The eleph-ANT they occupied had its engines firing to ensure it was floating above the ground so they didn't feel the tremors, but it was hard not to notice when the whole room was shaking.

On the other side of the tunnel was a massive rotating digging machine burrowing through. It had just begun the final excavation process. In a matter of seconds, a hole was about to break through to the light side of the planet.

Large rocks and boulders started to fall from the tunnel wall and ceiling. Trillion instinctually grabbed the bar holding her in place. Ship had to move the eleph-ANT out of the way quickly from an incoming object, positioning them farther back from the opening.

The very top of the tunnelling machine poked through the hole as more large boulders and rocks continued to fall. It looked exactly like what Trillion imagined a large digging machine would look like. The metallic nose cone of the thing rotated quickly, forcing rocks and debris out of the way. For a moment, all they saw was the bright light streaming through a small gap. Then there was an explosion as air rushed through and the digging machine was forced into the tunnel.

The eleph-ANT containing Trillion and Icarus was thrown back. The initial rush of air forced it deeper into the tunnel, smashing and bouncing it off the wall.

Then sand started to pour into the tunnel, pelting the eleph-ANT. It was relentless and kept coming—almost like a sandblaster.

"Is this going to stop once things pressurize in here?" Icarus asked.

Trillion shook her head. "It's a strange planet. This is basically a wind tunnel now. Air is constantly expanding on the hot side, so it will keep pushing its way through to the dark side." The eleph-ANT stopped shaking, so she let go of the buckle she was grasping tightly. "We'll build some gates out here to stop this from happening soon."

The initial blast had settled, but the wind was still blowing hard, and the sand racing through the cave was acting like sandpaper and taking chunks of the eleph-ANT's hapticgraphic skin with it.

Ship took control of the eleph-ANT. "I'm moving us out of the tunnel now."

With the natural light from the sun better illuminating the space, the team could see parts of the wall looked like volcanic black glass.

Trillion could see Ship was racing them out the exit now, and she could see exactly why. The tunnel was collapsing in on itself. Sand had now half-filled the entrance. So, Ship was racing to exit before he would be forced to dig their way out.

Dodging the fallen digging machine, they made it all the way to the other side. It looked like they had come out of a sinkhole in the middle of a desert. Trillion couldn't just feel the heat radiating from all around them; she could see it, too. Ripples in the way light moved across the desert floor provided proof it was scorching.

"I can't believe the sun never sets on this world," Trillion said before noticing Icarus's facial expressions. "Well, I understand why it doesn't set, but it just feels odd being on a tidally locked planet where you can always see the sun."

Icarus was squinting to see out into the distance. "I find it odder that there's a side that never sees the sun."

Ship pressed one of the buttons in front of him, telling the eleph-ANT to settle onto the sandy ground. "Remember how this planet has a slight wobble to it?"

Trillion nodded.

"Well, this location on the planet is perfectly placed in between the light and dark sides," Ship continued. "You could watch the sun almost set, then rise, then almost set again, but it'll never move too far from the horizon."

Trillian smiled. "I guess taking sunset photos on this planet won't be as big of a deal as it was on Earth."

The sinkhole had stopped moving, and Trillion could see it was fully enclosed. "This planet is weird." She gave Ship a nod and he started to maneuver a plug on top of the hole.

Icarus pointed up toward the cloud. "Don't get me started on weird; I feel like that storm is following us. There's always a storm over us on this planet."

"What do you mean, 'following us'?" Trillion asked.

"I mean, after a while, we tend to see a storm above us."

Trillion looked up and studied the storm closely. It looked like a thick grey-and-black knot of clouds. It looked much like most of the storms she was used to back on Earth. Somehow, they were all angry-looking. "Are you sure?" She squinted a little. She thought she could see a pattern within the cloud, and it reminded her of when she was younger and would always see faces and insect shapes. "The only thing weird is that cloud kinda looks like my grandma." She paused. "Oh, wait, I think I can see you in there. There's a duck swimming," she said, pointing up into the sky.

"I noticed that too. All our bases have a storm overhead," Ship added. "And we picked those locations because they had the lowest amount of cloud cover. I thought it was just an anomaly, but now that you mention it, Icarus, quite a few of our solar farms needed to be built bigger after we found they weren't collecting as much light."

"See, I'm not making this up," Icarus said.

"Are we just seeing patterns where there aren't any?" Trillion asked. "Or is something we're doing on the planet impacting the weather? We could get Lex to update our weather-pattern model. I know it's always raining in rainforests because the trees change the climate above them. Maybe our solar farms are also changing the climate here."

Ship scanned the other bases. "Now that you mention it, there are even clouds above our bases on the dark side of the planet. There are no solar panels there."

"Can we see?" Icarus asked.

"Want to teleport us there?" Trillion suggested.

Icarus pulled out his portal gun and shot it out the window in front of the eleph-ANT.

Ship guided the eleph-ANT toward the portal and walked it through. Because the eleph-ANT was real and not a projection, it wasn't teleported at all. Instead, the three people inside the eleph-ANT were transported into another one. Trillion, Icarus, and Ship found themselves inside an eleph-ANT on the opposite side of the planet. This was the dark side. It was pitch black, with no light whatsoever.

"I forget how dark it is here," Trillion said as she clicked one of the buttons in front of her, turning the night vision of the eleph-ANT on and making the landscape in front of them visible.

Out in front of them was an ice desert, ice as far as they could see.

Ship moved the eleph-ANT to look toward the sky, the night vision giving the team a clear view where they wouldn't have been able to see a thing.

Trillion squinted. "You're right; there is something weird about that storm." She pointed to a section of it. "I can see that same duck shape in the clouds again."

In a quiet voice, Icarus replied, "You're not teasing me?"

Trillion shook her head. "To be honest, I was going to tease you. But look there." She pointed up toward the cloud. "That's almost the exact same pattern as on the light side of the planet. It's hard to describe, but it looks like the same storm." Then she paused, as she knew she wasn't explaining herself right. "I know it's a different storm. But it has the same pattern in it. It's not like the clouds I'm used to; these don't look random."

"Like you're looking at a code with the same message in it?"

Trillion nodded in agreement. "Like it's a QR code and I can read it."

CHAPTER 28

ATLAS

ANGELS

Atlas leaped into consciousness, heart racing in a panic, his breathing quick. The only thing that stopped him from screaming was how everything around him looked . . . tinted white.

This contrast between his last memory and now created a cognitive dissonance because earlier, he had been fighting for his life as some sort of human technology attacked him.

He closed his eyes, hoping it was just a dream, then opened them once more. As he did, he realized he was lying on his back. The dim white light around him was a ceiling that he was looking directly at.

He sat up rather abruptly and found himself in a bed in the middle of a white marble room. The lights slowly brightened in the room, and he studied the place. Everything was marble with ornate gold trimmings. It felt more like a Roman palace than a spaceship. At the very end of his bed was a long white dresser. It was covered in intricate carvings and designs, as if some expert craftsman had spent a lifetime engraving a story into it.

His surroundings were telling him things were safe, which he guessed meant he wasn't. He did find himself calming, though. He also noticed his thinking was the clearest it had ever been. Like a subtle fog had been lifted from his world view. He hadn't noticed something was clouding his mind, but now that it was gone, he felt like he was seeing the world more clearly. So, he decided to make use of that clarity and closed his eyes once more, attempting to use the connection in his matrix that gave him access to his spacecraft. He couldn't connect. Then he reached out for Ship or Lex. "Ship," he muttered. But still no result.

He was about to yell out, then stopped himself. There was no point calling for whoever trapped him when he hadn't yet exhausted all his options. He decided to have a look around. He planned on seeing if he could figure something out rather than speeding toward whatever came next. *I might be a prisoner who doesn't know it yet. Or I . . .*

His thoughts were interrupted when it occurred to him he didn't even know *when* now was. Last thing he remembered was being in a battle; next thing he knew, he was in this bed. The problem with having his matrix unplugged in that way was he had no concept of how much time had just passed. Maybe he was back on Earth, thousands of years into the future. The theories started to multiply in his head as he thought about possible situations he might be in.

To calm himself, he focused on the one fact he knew: he had been turned back on and wasn't in any immediate danger. He knew he was currently safe and just needed to figure the rest out.

He pulled the sheets off and scooted toward the edge of the bed. He attempted to float and found he was firmly stuck on the ground. Whatever environment he was in forced him to obey the laws of gravity.

He walked over to a large curtain on the opposite side of the room. He took hold of the material and studied it, trying to work out whether it was real or a simulation. He squeezed the fabric, then stretched it. He could see individual strands, so he knew it wasn't a hapticgraphic projection. The hapticgraphic engine had improved a lot since he first invented it, but it still was built on the basic concept of tiny balls that were moved around by a magnetic field. The latest version of the haptic engine was more of a fine powder, but still, when he was this close to an object, it became obvious it wasn't solid.

Atlas stepped back from the curtain, confident he was in a simulation. The draping curtains were real silk. Real fibers, not synthetic. There was true nuance in the fabrics, too. And there was no way someone would go to all the trouble of making that much silk. The only logical option was that he was in a simulation. It was easy enough to simulate any material, so it made sense that the fabric someone would simulate would be the most expensive.

He noticed there was light coming from behind the large draping curtain, so he peeked behind it; being that he was in a simulation, he was probably being watched already, but he still felt the need to be cautious.

He was surprised by the fact it wasn't a window but a door, and outside the door were Ship and Lex, sitting on a table next to a red-haired woman. It didn't look like Trillion; the woman looked different. Fair-skinned, happy; then he heard her laugh and recognized it as Angelique's laughter.

Atlas threw the door wide open and ran out. "Angelique!" he called excitedly, hoping it wasn't an illusion.

Angelique saw Atlas running toward them and raised her hand to tell the guard moving to intercept him that Atlas was safe.

Atlas picked her up in a hug. "So, they got you, too?" he asked. He stepped back, looking her all over, still not quite believing it. "Angelique, I can't believe it's you."

She bowed. "I've missed you, Atlas. Oh, and soooo. . ." She paused. "I'm Ange, not Angelique." Then she looked at both the guards, who had instinctually moved closer to her. "These are my friends. Please treat them as you would me. And give them a security clearance as high as my chief of staff."

Atlas smiled at the guard before looking back at Angelique. "You sound different. You sound less Martian."

Angelique had lived most of her life on Mars, so she picked up their way of speaking. The Martian pronunciation of words leaned heavily on New Zealand's way of speaking since after they invented the first AI, their domination on the world meant they were the first country to fully colonize the planet. That was the same reason Ship had a Martian accent.

"I softened my accent; I didn't want my people learning that way of speaking, so I changed it a little. A few words sneak in here and there."

Interesting, Atlas thought. He noticed it was much more neutral-sounding than he remembered, but the twinge was still there. "What do you mean, you're Ange? I thought you hated people calling you that."

As Atlas waited for Angelique to reply, he worked his way around the circle and hugged Ship and patted Lex on the orb. "Are you two happy? They didn't hurt you, did they?"

Ship shook his head and Lex flashed a green happy pulse through his avatar.

"So, we need to find a way out of this sim . . ." Atlas started to say before noticing Angelique's head bowing down.

"It was Ange who pulled us here," Ship said.

"What?! Why?" Atlas shot back in a more forceful tone than he meant. Waves of confusion and anger rolled through his mind, only damped by the fact that his crew were safe and with him again.

Ange was still looking downward as she spoke. "So, firstly, I didn't know it was you. We'd seen all the ships fighting, which strengthened our resolve to not be found. I thought you might be a scout ship, so I instructed the drones to capture you. I planned to reprogram you into believing you scouted the system and found nothing, then send you on your way to another system."

"So, you hacked into my matrix?" Atlas asked.

"Well, yes and no."

"What do you mean, *yes and no?*"

"It's a little bit complicated. As soon as we realized it was you, I ordered them to stop everything, so we haven't reprogrammed you in any way. But we did remove something from your matrix."

"Removed? That sounds a lot like reprogramming to me," Atlas said before looking toward Lex. "Have I been hacked?"

The orb flashed purple.

"Your matrix is not connected to the wider network," Ange said before pausing for a moment. "Now you should have access to everything. Lex can scan your matrix now."

The orb hovered for a little while before flashing green to signal his matrix hadn't been tampered with.

"So." Angelique paused before steering the conversation back to a question asked earlier. "The reason my name is Ange is because I'm a copy of Angelique. I'm one of Ange's Angels. But since the last time I saw you, Angelique and I were the same person. I'm basically the same Angelique you knew with a different name."

Atlas looked a little confused; it was a lot to take in. "You said *one* of Ange's Angels . . .?"

"There's at least six of us now; we'll find out the new number in a few years. Once Angelique gets back."

"I'm so confused—" Atlas started to say before noticing the world around him. Through the excitement of seeing Angelique—or Ange, he corrected himself—he hadn't taken a look beyond the table where he saw them.

Atlas realized the table his friends were all sitting around was on the top of a set of large marble stairs with intricately designed columns holding up a dome. The place felt like a cathedral. The stairs led down toward a large lake. And beyond that he could see people in the water, rowing boats.

Turning his head, Atlas realized the building, or whatever he was in, was in the middle of the lake. It was a castle on a tiny island. With the mountains in the background, it reminded him of Lake Bled in Slovenia. Atlas noticed one of the boats floating in the water started to levitate and then flew into the sky.

"You're wondering whether this is real or not," Ange asked.

"Yes. And why you live in a palace."

"This place is real." Ange pointed out toward the view right in front of her. "You're on my planet. We call it Juniper."

"So, not a simulation?"

Ange shook her head. "You're currently moving around in a custom android I had built for you, and this planet is as real as they come. We've built a really good system for terraforming planets now. I got really lucky with this one, because this was the first planet we found that was a completely blank canvas, so we could terraform the whole planet. We made it a rule a while back that we wouldn't disrupt any existing life, so all of the other planets have humans living in special domed enclosures. This is the only planet I know of where the people can roam freely."

"Oh, I'll have to show you Neuropa."

"Is that yours?" Ange said not so confidently.

Atlas grinned from ear to ear and so did Ship. "It was an ice world before we changed it," Ship said.

Ange smiled. "I get it now. Like the moon Europa."

"Explain to me why there's six other Ange's Angels?" Atlas said. "And why do I get the sense you have a god complex now?"

Ange wiped her face and put her napkin down. "Let's go somewhere a bit more private." She led the way as everyone left the table. They joined Ange and walked down the stairs. As they approached the water, the orb of Lex started to flash orange.

Ange patted Lex on the head. "The hapticgraphic projectors don't reach that far down the stairs. You'll have to stay here, I'm afraid." The orb looked noticeably sadder and started to hover lower to the ground. "But that's okay, because if you go back up those stairs, there's a group of physicists who are looking for a really smart super computer to help them with some calculations. They're trying to figure out the fastest way to mine the star system for more rare minerals."

The orb perked up with that response and raced back up the stairs.

Atlas, Ange, and Ship reached a small dinghy floating on the water. Ange jumped into it and gestured for the other two to jump in with her.

Ship jumped in last and so was closest to the paddles.

"Do you mind paddling us out there, Ship?" Ange asked.

Ship nodded and pushed them away from the wharf.

When they were far enough away from any land mass, Ange pulled out a little device. "This should block anyone from listening to us," she said as she switched it on.

Ship stopped paddling and looked at Ange. "You're worried your people will hear us?"

She shook her head. "It's not that no one knows what I'm about to share with you. But I also don't want people to hear me saying the words. It's the kinda thing that's best left unsaid."

Atlas eyed her suspiciously. "Go on."

"So, firstly, you remember the experience you had when your behavioral driving unit was removed?"

Atlas nodded and wondered how Ange knew it had been removed before remembering that she had already taken hold of his matrix.

"Well, that wasn't the only behavioral modification happening on our matrix. Back when Angelique and I—" She paused. "Well, we were the same person back then, but it gets confusing if I refer to myself as Angelique. Anyways." She continued. "After we went through the initial shock of having that removed, we also started wondering if we had any other changes made to us. We found out that we had. Whatever was done when we were uploaded also gave us a bias toward uploading other humans into the simulation and clouds a lot of our thinking. It doesn't make us dumber, but it does make us more likely to make mistakes in some areas."

"What areas do we not think clearly in?"

"Anything to do with non-simulation-related technology. It's as if after the upload, it's much easier for us to develop technology that is useful to a simulation. And then it becomes harder to innovate and build technology in the real world."

"Is that just a bias because we are simulants?"

Ange shook her head. "After we figured out how to remove that piece of code messing with our brains, it was like our minds were unlocked again."

Atlas pointed at his head. "And you did that to me without my consent? I did notice I was thinking differently when I first woke."

She pointed at Ship, then back toward the castle. "We removed it from all three of you." She put up her hands to quiet down Atlas's next question. "I'm sorry, I didn't have a choice; the code is probably better described as a virus." Ange paused for a moment and became increasingly serious. "Atlas, this virus was stopping you from being you. It also had the ability to reinfect other technology. It was designed to evolve, hide, and encourage everyone to become a simulation. We couldn't risk it getting onto this planet."

"Is that why you blocked this star system with that thing that stops communication from going in and out?"

"Yes." Ange pointed out toward the sky. "Someone back on Mars loaded a virus on to our brain-scanning machine to hold us back."

"What do you mean, *hold us back*?"

"Technological progress, Atlas. It hides parts of tech trees. There are many scientists, engineers, and physicists on this planet. The technology in our systems has exploded since we got rid of the virus and started encouraging our civilizations to grow."

"With you as a deity?" Atlas joked.

Ange laughed. "No, no. Well, to be honest, back when Angelique and I were the same person, we did go through a period where we almost got kicked off the planet. It took a long time to gain everyone's love back. We like to think of ourselves as more of a figurehead. Like how the United Kingdom had a royal that everyone loved and admired. It's human psychology; we love a celebrity. And we attach meaning and reverence to words.

Hence"—she pointed to herself—"I'm the Angel that brought everyone to this planet."

"Do some people still hate you?"

"Obviously, there's still people who dislike me, but a lot less than when we tried to be a parent. Being their mother was effective when everyone was babies, but as soon as everyone got older, they wanted nothing to do with me. As Ange's Angel, I still get influence, but no one wants me gone."

The three of them chatted a while longer before Atlas became lost in thought. He trusted Ange but wanted to have a private conversation with the others. "Can I speak with my crew in private?"

"Of course," Ange agreed as Ship guided them back to the shore. Once they were off the boat and back up the stairs Ange, pointed to the room Atlas had came from. "I'll send Lex to meet you in there. And if you need me, I'll be upstairs in the lab." The three of them had a group hug. "I'm so happy to see you both again," Ange said as she walked in another direction.

A little while later, Atlas, Ship, and Lex were back in the large marble room. Atlas admired the workmanship of one of the columns as he ran his hand over it. A lot of time and effort had gone into crafting everything in this room. He wasn't sure if it was made by hand or simply a machine, but either way, he was impressed. Not taking his hand off the wall, he asked, "Do you trust her?"

"I think so," Ship responded.

"Me too. She's the same person I remember from before we left. Hard-working and laser-focused on what must be done."

"I've had Lex scan us both and he's confident that she only did what she said she did. She's removed something that we didn't know was there. Even fixed the dead section in your matrix caused by when the behavioral modification was removed."

"So, what next?" Atlas asked.

Ship shrugged. "I did notice you've been a bit coy about the Starnet. You haven't told her about that yet."

"I wanted to discuss with you both first. She captured us and pulled us here."

"Atlas, we're not prisoners; we can leave if we want."

"You're right, you're right. I'll stop with the suspicion. Let's tell her about it."

They wandered out one of the other doors in the suite and into a grand gold winding stairway with royal red carpet. "She really is going with the queen vibe, isn't she?" Atlas muttered to herself.

Ship chuckled a little. "I like it. I think it's more of a goddess vibe, though."

The orb changed its skin to gold.

Atlas looked up at the floating ball. "You're both gold." He pointed at himself. "I'm the one left out now."

They were following Lex as it guided them up the stairs and toward the office space it had been in earlier.

"We should have tried this back on Neuropa," Ship said.

Atlas looked at Ship, trying to guess what he was talking about. "Tried what?"

"The whole god thing. Rather than being their father, being a deity. Then we might not have been kicked off."

CHAPTER 29

ANGE

TECHNOLOGY TRADE

Ange was in her mission control center, looking at one of the many large screens on the wall. In front of her sat one of her officers, who was explaining the data on display. The graph showed the increasingly shorter intervals between radar bounces. The only plausible explanation was a spacecraft was heading toward her planet. Probably Angelique, but she hadn't yet received the authentication codes to confirm.

"It looks like one of the colonies has invented near-light-speed travel, ma'am," one of her officers said.

"And you're sure it's her?"

"Our probe on the other side of the barrier hasn't yet completed the handshake, but the initial codes we received from the ship do indicate it's her."

Ange smiled and looked at her watch, as if wishing time to move faster. "So, how long until she gets here?"

"Maybe a month," the officer said. "We don't know what deceleration the spacecraft is capable of. But based on the speeds it's traveling and how close it is to us, it must be within its capabilities to achieve a lot of gs. Otherwise, it will race through our system."

Ange could feel herself grow in excitement. She was finally going to be made whole again. She was soon going to learn what had happened at all the other colonies. Then she realized what a month meant. Last time, she had had years to plan for Angelique's arrival. With only a month, she knew it would be manic. She hadn't even started to plan for it. "The inauguration," she said, a little flustered. "We need to start planning for the inauguration now."

She turned toward the room full of people and spoke loudly and commandingly. "Okay, team, this is not a drill. We need to prepare for the possibility that our head of state is about to arrive. She might be arriving in a few weeks. But we can't tell the public until we have had confirmation." She turned toward her chief of staff. "Can you clear my schedule, get me a meeting with the prime minster and the joint chiefs of staffs this evening? We need to start actioning the plan we have in place."

She was about to give the orders to the rest of her team, when there was a knock at the door, and then one of the guards poked his head through. "Sorry, ma'am, but Atlas and Ship would like to enter."

She nodded. "Bring them in."

Atlas came through the door. "I hope I'm not interrupting anything?"

"No, not at all; it's very exciting news, actually." She pointed up at the screen on the wall. "You'll like both these pieces of news."

Atlas looked at the screen. "What am I looking at?"

"So, the first news is that we think Angelique is arriving in about a month. And the second is that she's bringing with her a lot of new technology. One of the techs believes she's bringing is the ability to travel near the speed of light."

"How?" Ship asked, obviously excited by the prospect of a faster spacecraft.

Ange shrugged. "Not sure; she isn't here yet. But if I were guessing, one of the colonies invented it."

"How many colonies do you have?" Atlas asked.

"At least six. Probably a bunch more. Again, we'll find out as soon as she gets here," Ange said, her voice getting higher in pitch as she thought about how close she was.

Atlas took his eyes off the screen. "I had meant to ask you about that. So, you have six different colonies, all run by an Ange's Angel?"

"At least six. Angelique has been gone a long time, so there's probably a lot more colonies by now." Angelique motioned for the officer at the computer to pull up a picture of the five planets they knew had been colonized already. "Back when Angelique and I were the same person, after we had colonized the first world, we wanted to go out and explore and find others, but we also wanted to stay on the planet and stay with our people. So, we did both; we duplicated ourselves. One of us became the original Ange's Angel, and then Angelique went on to explore the galaxy."

"And so, Angelique periodically visits you at each of the worlds?"

Ange nodded. "She travels from system to system. Most of the time, she's building new colonies, but after a while, she comes back to visit us and share all the knowledge and technology between the worlds."

Ship pointed at the fifth planet on the screen. "So, we are that one, I'm guessing? And the sixth you know of was the one she left to go start?"

Ange high-fived Ship. "Exactly that. We have about twenty billion people on this planet now, which is probably one of the biggest, but I do wonder if any are as big as this one."

Atlas's eyes nearly bulged out of his head. "Twenty billion?!"

"Or around that. We only do a proper census every four years. So, the actual numbers might be slightly different."

"And you're their leader?"

"God, no. There's no way I want to be in charge of this lot. I'm more of a figurehead. We have elections, and the people here fully control themselves. My title is purely ceremonial, although I do have access to the members of Parliament, and I do have a big team like this for helping me. My primary job is collating knowledge for when Angelique arrives so that we can share it with the other colonies." She looked around the room at her team. "We have a goal as a team to try and impart more knowledge than we receive from Angelique's visit. I had hoped that twenty billion people prospering on this planet would give me an advantage of having a lot of minds inventing new technology. But apparently, someone out there has invented a better propulsion system than we have. So, let's just hope some of our other inventions are good enough."

"I invented FTL communication," Atlas blurted out.

It was Ange's turn to have her eyes bulge. "Oh, my god." The room went dead quiet. The sound of the clock on the wall ticking suddenly became noticeable. "You invented what?"

Atlas was trying to sound nonchalant. With all the eyes in the room looking at him, he said, "Ship, Lex, and I invented it on the way to our system, Neuropa."

Georgia, one Ange's science aides in the back of the room, stood up and walked over. "How did you do that? We've been experimenting for generations and no one has managed to figure it out."

"Have most of your experiments been on this planet?"

The woman nodded. "Yes. We have a few research labs in orbit, but all the big research facilities are on the planet."

"Well, that's why." Atlas said. "You need to entangle particles away from a large gravitational body for this to work."

Ange looked at Lex. "Can you get Lex to give us the process for replicating it?"

Atlas nodded and the orb bounced up and down in excitement. "We call it the Starnet; it doesn't work through the bubble you created around this solar system, though. With the Starnet, you could connect up all the systems you have already, and we can connect to the systems we've found, too."

Ange's mind started to open up with the possibilities. What would they do with all the Ange's Angels if Angelique didn't need to travel from system to system? And what about expansion? They could expand their network of colonies even faster if Angelique didn't have to come back and visit to share technology. She didn't know how the Starnet worked but hoped it didn't require a method that would be visible to other civilizations watching.

The reason she wasn't transmitting information between the colonies was because of the risk. Even using a tight beam had the risk of giving away your position if someone happened to intercept it. Back when she was Angelique, she and her people all agreed it was best to hide from the universe. To not broadcast the fact they were there. Having a laser constantly connecting two star systems would act as a beacon to anyone watching that intelligent life was there.

Ange gestured for the two of them to sit down. "Do you know about the 'dark forest solution' to the Fermi paradox?"

"It's the theory that the reason we haven't seen any aliens is because it's dangerous out there in the galaxy and any civilization that shows themselves gets destroyed by another."

Ange nodded. "We don't know whether that's true or not. We've never seen any evidence that it's true. But simply because we assume Earth is also a threat to us, we made the decision long ago to hide our presence."

Ship took a seat next to her. "So, what does this have to do with anything?"

"It's why we don't send transmissions to any of our other systems. We are hiding the fact that we're here so it isn't easy for anyone watching to piece together which systems we control." Then she noticed the look on Atlas's face; it was one of thinking she was being too risk-averse. "Our scientists and politicians debate this regularly. And the basic conclusion everyone comes to each time is there's no rush to broadcast that we're here. Even our original system, Sol, stopped leaking signals out into the universe recently."

"We did wonder about that. They attacked Trillion, you know."

Ange looked toward Ship. "I thought you told me she was currently traveling to find another star system."

"I did." Ship replied. "But she survived the battle. They had some powerful lasers, but she had a very large armada. And Atlas managed to hack in to their spacecraft once the AI was destroyed."

"You mean that big light show everyone in the galaxy saw?" Ange asked.

Atlas nodded.

"That's going to act as a beacon," Ange said. "And we'll soon know whether it's a bad idea to announce your presence in a system or not." Then she paused for a moment, thinking about her next question. "You know, there's one thing that's been bothering me about Earth. When you hacked in to their systems, did you learn much about the technology they were using?"

"Yeah, we learned a lot. Once we took over their spacecraft, we controlled them and could study them."

Ange tied her red hair up in a bun behind her head. "Did their technology advance as much as you would have expected?"

Atlas scratched his head. "What do you mean?"

"Did they have anything new? Any fundamentally new technology trees?"

"No . . . now that you mention it. It was just slightly better versions of the tech we already left Mars with."

"Hmmm," Ange said before rolling up her sleeves and sitting down at a computer. "So, I don't have clearance to share with you all the technology we've created. But what I can tell you is we are leaps and bounds more advanced than anything they had back in Sol. It would be considered magic. It's not just better versions of existing tech. There are whole new technology trees that we've discovered."

"That's what I would have expected," Atlas said. "My people back in Neuropa started advancing at a very fast speed too, once the population started to grow."

"And this is my conundrum," Ange said as she took her hands off the keyboard. "Sol's technology sort of plateaued before we left. Simulation-based tech was advancing rapidly, but not others. I just assumed we were reaching the pinnacle of what was possible back when we were on Mars. But as soon as we crossed a billion people on Juniper, our progress started to move even faster. All these minds inventing and coming up with ideas made our march along the technology tree much quicker."

"So, what are you getting at?"

"Well, I'm just wondering why the humans back in Sol haven't been progressing as fast. I mean, they might be, but I don't understand why we haven't seen them expanding beyond their home system."

"Would we see them progressing?"

Ange shrugged. "We obviously have a lot of big telescopes watching Sol all the time, so maybe we're just lucky. But we did see all these spacecraft leave the system and head for Groombridge sixteen-eighteen. The sheer number of spacecraft they sent made it extremely obvious to anyone with a powerful-enough telescope. Then that light show confirmed that those ships were headed to a battle of some sort."

"We call that system the Dottiens' system," Ship said.

CHAPTER 30

ATLAS

THE COMBINING

Atlas was at the very top of the building that sat on the small island. He decided it was a castle after all, designed from a mix of different cultures and decades. He could tell it was designed to spark a sense of grandness and wonder. And the fact it was in the middle of a lake meant it also created a sense of distance between her and everyone else on the other side.

There was a lot of people on the other side of the lake now. Since the announcement of Angelique's forthcoming arrival, citizens had come from all around the planet to camp and secure a location. From where he was looking, it looked like a sea of people were gathering from every side.

Atlas smiled to himself as he thought about the fact Ange had definitely developed some sort of god complex since he last saw her. He had limited knowledge about human psychology but did think it was logical that presenting herself as a deity or monarch made her people love her more. Humans love celebrities, so this was just creating a celebrity on steroids. The number of people camping on the other side of the lake was testament to the fact her strategy worked. And Angelique was still days away from arriving.

After a few moments sitting up there and thinking, Ange joined him.

"I've been looking for you," she said as she climbed through the small hole in the roof of one of the towers.

"I just wanted some space to process everything." He pointed out toward everyone out in the distance. "There's a lot of people wanting to see what comes next."

Ange nodded. "I wanted to tell you what happens before you find out."

Atlas cocked an eye toward her.

"Part of the ceremony will see us two merge. We call it the joining."

"The joining? That sounds like something out of a horror movie."

"Back when we were the same person, we decided to make one change to the Ange's Angels—to me. We made some edits to my matrix before replicating it."

"Go on."

"So . . . I'm not going to be here on Sunday." Ange spoke with uncertainty in her voice. "We're going to merge and become one again. All my memories will be combined with hers, and all her memories will be combined with mine."

"And you're okay with that? It sounds like you'll be gone—disappearing?"

"That's part of the change we made when we cloned ourselves. In the same way, before we colonized our first world, we had something in our matrix driving us toward colonizing a planet. I have a similar drive to merge with Angelique. I can't wait for the joining. I can't wait to become Angelique again. I'm getting excited because I'm so close. I can feel her approaching."

"So, how does it work, exactly?" Atlas asked. "Are you like a branch of Angelique that pulled away and now is getting folded back in?"

"Something like that. She is the longest-running continuous version of us. She's the prime version, if you will. So, once I rejoin her, I'll be one with her again."

"So, you don't feel like one of you is dying?"

"Not in the slightest. I, or, rather, we have done this before already. Once I merge with her again, I'll probably have done this several times."

"But haven't you been apart for centuries? Aren't you a different person from Angelique?"

"Given she would have slept most of the journey here and on the way to other system. I've probably had more time to evolve and change than her." Then she paused for a moment, scratching her chin, seriously considering the question. "The thing you've got to understand is one of us isn't just merging into the other. It's not a smaller matrix merging into a bigger one and being subsumed. We're merging into each other. The new Angelique will be a combination of both of us.

"What about your memories. Whose memories get precedence?"

"Well," she said. "Think about something memorable that you did a few years ago."

Atlas thought about drinking a beer with Icarus at his place.

"Now think about something you did many, many years ago."

He thought about the first moment he connected with Trillion through the Starnet.

"Atlas, I bet both those memories are probably vivid in your head."

Atlas nodded.

"I also bet you can't remember the exact date or time of those events."

Atlas thought about it for a moment. He couldn't, so he shook his head.

"Do you remember what you did exactly one week before any of those two moments?"

Atlas assumed he was setting up something on Neuropa. But he was just guessing, so he shook his head.

"My point exactly. We believe our memories are chronological. But they really aren't. With your normal memories, the order of events doesn't really matter. This is basically the same as that. So, when my memories and her memories are mixed together, it'll be like mixing a deck of cards. Half of them will be mine and half hers. The advantage of this is that the new Angelique will have all of my learning and experiences that she can take to the next colony we build."

"What does it feel like?" Atlas asked.

"It feels like I'm whole again. It feels like I've always been me. And remembering the past experiences of different versions of myself is like remembering past experiences from my twenties and teenage years. They were both me, but I just knew different things at the time." Then she paused once more. "Actually, do you know what feels different and doesn't feel good at all?"

Atlas made a *go on* gesture with his head.

"It's when I clone myself. It's the worst! One day, I think I'm Angelique, then the next moment, I'm an Ange Angel. Getting used to that name was so hard. I hated the name Ange. This is my second time, and it was easier, but the first time, I almost changed my name to Aroha, which means *love* in New Zealand. But the alliteration of an Ange's Angel was too good. And I wasn't about to call myself *love angel*."

That last sentence made Atlas laugh.

"Anyways, so, in a few days, Angelique and I will merge. And when you speak to me on Sunday, I'll be Angelique; I'll still remember this conversation and everything. But I just wanted you to know." A slight flitter of worry crossed Ange's face. "There is one other thing I need to speak to you about."

Atlas noticed the seriousness. "What is it?"

"This virus that we removed from Lex. It's different from the original one we had. We had some of our engineers do an analysis of the code and compared it to what I had installed all over our original ship." She pointed at the orb as she said that. "It's evolved a lot and is a lot more complex than the one we started with."

"Okay. And you're telling me this why? Didn't you remove it?"

"Well, yes. But presumably it's still with Icarus and Trillion. And assuming they're still on a planet, then it's spread throughout all their technology. So, I'm going to assume that it's going to be hard to remove from theirs."

"And you're worried that this virus was designed to stop us from successfully colonizing worlds?"

"Yes. I actually want your help to try and understand it. I know you're experienced with these things. I know Angelique will probably want to communicate with the others as soon as she gets here. She'll want to destroy the virus as soon as she can, because it's a threat to our worlds."

"A threat? How would it be a threat to you?"

"Think of it this way. The virus is hidden in the background, collecting information. We even found it was capable of hiding packets of information in transmissions. So, it could send a message back to Earth. And this virus, or whatever it is, also knows you entered this system and then went dark. It's probably reporting all this back to whoever's listening back on Earth."

CHAPTER 31

ATLAS

THE JOINING

Atlas had a front-row seat to the inauguration. And he was glad because it was a spectacle. It felt like a ceremony for a queen. He, Ship, and Lex were currently sitting in raised seats on top of a platform that was specifically constructed for this moment. It allowed everyone on all the different sides of the lake to see them. It was an interesting sight because boats were banned from entering the water. So, it was a literal wall of people surrounding the lake.

Atlas had come to learn that the who's who of the planet were there in that row of seats next to him. They were all facing two rather large seats. Atlas thought a better description of them was *two thrones*. The smaller of the two thrones currently had Ange seated in it. And she had wings. She had actual wings. They were gold and glowed. The way the light scattered through the wings meant they had to be built using either a hologram or hapticgram projector. He couldn't tell. The other, much bigger throne next to Ange was empty. Atlas assumed that was to be the new throne Angelique would sit in once she arrived on the planet.

The sounds of trumpeting started to get louder. And Atlas could feel an increasing reverent feeling in the back of his mind. Something about the way the whole event was structured, the music; the way Ange was dressed even started to make him believe it was god returning. There was no actual mention of Angelique as a god in any of the official material, but anyone watching the event could see the imagery.

The whole event was being live-streamed to everyone around the globe. Everyone knew what was happening as soon as Angelique's spacecraft entered orbit around the planet. The spacecraft's orbit was such that it flew right overhead roughly once every hour and twenty minutes. So, once every hour and a bit, everyone would cheer and trumpets would sound as Angelique's spacecraft raced through the sky, looking like a shooting star overhead.

Human voices started to sing. They made angelic sounds, the sounds you would expect when an angel was arriving. Atlas assumed that things were about to begin. Atlas looked down at the flyer he was holding. It described this inauguration as "the official arrival of Angelique and her taking over the rightful place as the head of state for the planet." Atlas was starting to think even the pamphlet sounded ritualistic when everyone around him went silent.

All the chatter Atlas previously heard disappeared. Atlas was wondering what everyone was looking at until he squinted at the sky. Out in the distance he saw a falling star heading toward them. Then after a while, he could tell it wasn't an object but a person.

Atlas pointed at the object and whispered in Ship's ear, "I think that's Angelique."

"I know," Ship replied while pointing at the twenty-meter-high screen to the right of them. On it he could see a close-up image of Angelique as she fell toward them.

It was like watching a falling angel coming toward them. A controlled fall. Maybe more like a superhero flying down. As Angelique approached them, she started to slow her decent. She was glowing and pulsating in light. She didn't have wings, but she had some sort of cape. Or maybe it was meant to be a golden robe. Whatever it was, it was flapping gently in the wind.

Once Angelique was close enough that she could be seen properly with the naked eye, Ange stood up. Atlas could swear she looked much taller as she opened her wings and started to float upward.

Angelique was floating down at a leisurely pace now, almost hovering above everyone majestically.

As the two women approached each other, the sounds of birds and horns started to play. Each of them reached out with one hand, slowly drifting toward each other.

Atlas was sure they were about to re-create the famous picture of god reaching out with a finger to spark life into a man—*The Creation of Adam.* The symbolism was so thick at this very moment. Everyone around was loving it, and that further increased Atlas's awe at everything happening right now. He looked around him and saw people smiling with tears of joy.

Then the two fingers of Ange and Angelique touched and a ball of light exploded from where they connected. A collective gasp of excitement could be heard from the crowd. Atlas had to shield his eyes from it. As his eyes adjusted and he started to see again, he realized the two of them had been consumed by a white, spinning ball.

The spinning ball looked like it was holding a tornado inside. And it started to drift downwards slowly toward the throne.

It drifted down and touched the chair, then encompassed it completely. Then after a while, nothing happened as the chair was bathed in light.

Atlas could hear mutterings of others talking.

He heard one person say, "I can't believe this happened in our lifetime."

"She's finally here," another said with excitement.

Ship whispered in Atlas's ear, "Icarus is going to freak out when he watches the replay of this."

"I know, right? It's such an event," Atlas said in awe.

Angelic sounds started to play again, and he saw something was happening to the ball of light: it was shrinking.

It took a while for Atlas to realize who he was seeing first. It was Ship. Angelique's Ship. He was sitting in the seat vacated by Ange.

And then, moments later, the orb had shrunk enough to reveal Angelique was standing there, smiling and waving at everyone. Her outfit was a combination of both Angelique and Ange, her wings gone but the glow still there.

She took a step forward and spoke into the mic. Her voice carried over the loudspeakers everywhere. "I have missed you, Juniper."

The crowd erupted in applause.

Atlas heard hordes of people yelling they loved her.

"I have some good things to share with you," she said. "But first, I heard you've just crossed the twenty-billion-people mark. That is the biggest population on any of our planets."

More rapturous applause.

"And I'm happy to say our people have a lot of planets now."

A drum roll sound started.

People started cheering even louder.

"Thirty-two star systems. Your people. Your family are now spread across thirty-two star systems."

The sound was deafening. People started to hug each other and screamed for joy.

"I can't believe we have thirty-two planets now," Atlas heard one person say.

Atlas was impressed, this was a well-thought-out speech. Angelique spoke as if the people on this planet were the same as on all the other planets. As if they were one united group of people. The way Angelique spoke had Atlas starting to feel like one of them.

Angelique raised her hands to quiet the crowds. "Now, Ship." She pointed at him in the seat next to her. "Ship has started uploading all the data we have. Everything we know. Everything we've learned. The design schema for all the new technology we have. Everything will be in your hands shortly. All of you can trace your DNA back to the same original pool. So, there will be messages on there from your family. This next week is about us all collectively absorbing this treasure trove of information." She pointed out to the crowds of people across the lake. "Ange was confident that Juniper would set a new record for how much further you'll progress our colonies in art, science, and technology. And now that we're one again, I feel like that might be true."

The crowd roared even louder with that comment.

"So, go, enjoy, see what you find out. And once our scientists are done going through all the knowledge, we'll know the answer."

Angelique wrapped up the speech to further cheering. Then the procession ended with Angelique being the first to walk out of the raised stage and into the castle. On the way past, she whispered a message between both Atlas and Ship's ears. "I've missed you, Atlas. And you, too, Ship," she said as she smiled warmly at them both. "But we need to talk in private."

CHAPTER 32

ANGELIQUE

THE GREAT FILTER

Angelique could feel an interesting disconnect in her mind as she waited for Atlas to arrive in her office. She sent Ship down to collect him because she needed to gather her thoughts before seeing him for the first time, again.

This was the only time she had gone through the joining and then interacted with someone she knew from before. Usually after the joining, she would interact with completely new citizens. Obviously, she knew who they were because she interacted regularly with them when she was Ange. But there was never a feeling from both halves of her that she knew the person. This was different.

Because of the way memories were merged, meeting Atlas felt like it was a month ago. But the other half of her felt like she still hadn't reconnected with him in centuries. Her newest memories still had her thinking Atlas, Icarus, and Trillion were unknown. Which created a bit of cognitive dissonance in her mind.

Add to this the fact Atlas used to be her old boss. Which didn't mean much except for the fact that it was from before she became a simulant. And her memories from before were very vivid in her head.

Atlas and both Ships entered the room and pulled her out of her thoughts.

Atlas bowed his head as he entered. He spoke with so much formality and uncertainty as he said, "Am I meeting you for the first time again? Or is this . . ."

Angelique smiled and opened her arms up to give Atlas a massive hug. "To me it feels like I haven't seen you in about a month. Just pretend like everything you told Ange you also told me. We're the same person now, with the only difference being yesterday to you feels a few weeks ago to me."

"You're glowing. Very angelic," Atlas said.

Angelique looked at her shoulders. "Yup, it's what differentiates me from Ange. Whenever I'm planetside, this glow around me appears." She waved her hands through the glowing area. "It's based on the tech you built on Mars. Ange is always piloting an android, and I'm always projected through the hapticgraphic projectors."

"I've been looking at the improvements you've made to the projectors. You've done a great job."

"It's not me. I can't take any of the credit. It's just that we have almost one hundred billion people across all our worlds. And when you have that many people, you have a lot of really smart people able to advance science and technology."

"How do you manage that many worlds?"

"I don't," she said matter-of-factly. "Quite early on, I made the decision not to get involved with the politics. All the planets are run through a representative democracy. The people of each system control their planets. For selfish reasons, I've tried to have a seat at the table where I can. Juniper is probably one of only six planets where I have actual influence. Others, I simply show up every few centuries with a spacecraft full of the latest science and we have a big celebration."

"I can't wait to see what other toys you bring."

"That leads nicely to why I asked you here. You're joining me in this next meeting with the prime minster, the heads of our intelligence committees, heads of various government departments, and generals."

Atlas scratched the back of his head. "That's a lot of very important people. Why are you including me?"

"I'm including you because I want you to be involved in uncovering what is going on. It affects more than just our worlds. It affects yours, too. And if I don't include you in this first meeting, the PM has the right to classify this information, meaning I won't be able to share it with you unless we're off the planet. So, this way, we won't have that problem because you'll already know."

"And you think they'll want to keep it a secret?"

Angelique shrugged. "Not sure, but I don't want to take the risk. We need our smartest minds working on it as quickly as we can." Angelique put a hand on Atlas's arm. "We can catch up properly shortly. But first, everyone is waiting for us in the next room."

Angelique got up and guided Atlas into the hallway. Both the Ships followed behind them. She led them directly into the room at the end of the passage. As she opened the door, she noticed it was full with everyone except the PM, the leader of the country. She wondered if that was a subtle power play by her to ensure she was the last person to enter the room.

As soon as they entered the room went quiet. Angelique walked toward the one empty seat around the other side of the large oval table. She gestured for Atlas and both Ships to stand behind her.

Almost as soon as she sat down, Prime Minister Kezia walked in through a door opposite them. She was an elderly woman who walked with much pomp, her hands always clasped in front of her. "Okay, welcome, everyone," Kezia said as she sat down in the empty seat on the other side of the table. "It's good to have you back, Angelique. Now, our team has been diving through the treasure troves of new knowledge you shared with us. And I'm told our security council has already started to parse the confidential information."

Heads nodded around the room at that mention.

Kezia looked toward Angelique. "Is there anything more you'd like to add before my team shares what they've found?"

"Yes, there is. There's a matter concerning a security threat to this planet."

There were audible gasps from around the room.

Angelique raised her arms for quiet. "On many of your sister worlds we found these little viruses. We know they are very similar in design to the virus I was originally infected with. They infect computer systems and somehow the human psyche. We have started calling them the great filter virus because it's immediately evident which worlds have them when technological progress starts to stall and flatline."

She pointed toward someone who was standing next to the light switch and gestured for him to turn the lights down. Then she motioned for her Ship to turn the projectors on. On the table in front of them, a 3-D model of a group of stars appeared. "These are the star systems that we've colonized so far." Then she nodded toward Ship, and one of the stars turned blue. "This is where Juniper is." Collective nodding went around the room because they all knew that Juniper was on the outer edge of the colonies so far. "Now, these are the sister colonies where we found the filter virus." The star chart looked like a big red bite had been taken out of it. And that bite was right on top of the blue Juniper star.

There was an even-louder gasp in the room after that comment.

"You can see that the virus is making its way across our systems. It looks like it's moving this way," Angelique said.

"But why is this so urgent?" one of the security council members asked. He looked like a spy, very nondescript looking—as if he could blend into any crowd of people. "Even if the virus is headed here, it will still take years to arrive. You said it yourself. It's evident that they are on worlds because technological progress is halted. Our technology has advanced rapidly in the time you were gone."

"I didn't think it urgent until I was reviewing the code of the filter virus we pulled from Atlas's Lex. It was much more advanced than anything we've seen before. Like it had been evolving and adapting for a long time. There's also hints that it had been merged with another virus, a slightly different one."

"So, this is a weapon Sol is using to take down our civilization?" Kezia asked.

Angelique nodded. "We believe so. We think it was something put in our brain by General Walker when we left Mars that day." She turned toward Atlas and saw his mouth open wide in surprise. "We did a bit of research on the planet Tazetta, the last world I was at. There's a lot of reason to believe this virus is the reason some of our worlds failed."

Atlas spoke up for the first time. "And what's its purpose?"

"Simple," Angelique replied. "We hypothesize that this virus was designed to slow the development of technological progress. To slow us down so that our worlds struggle to become self-sustaining."

"But why?" the security officer asked. "We are no threat to anyone on Sol."

"This is what we need to figure out. This is why we need to put a task force together quickly. We need to understand how this virus is manipulating people. And we need to understand why it's doing that."

"Haven't we destroyed all evidence of this virus?" Kezia asked before looking directly at Atlas and Ship with a cautious eye. "You disinfected everyone's matrix, didn't you?"

"Correct," Angelique said. "We made it a practice to destroy all traces of the virus so it doesn't have a chance to infect anything else. But . . ." She pointed toward the sky. "Atlas's spacecraft is currently drifting toward our sun, powerless and moving slowly toward destruction. I propose we send a mission out to recover it."

Angelique watched as multiple faces around started to look a tad fearful, because this virus was talked about in school. In the history classes. It almost destroyed their first colony planet. Throughout their lives, they had come to think of the virus as the ultimate evil. And now she was proposing they interact with it. Many were looking to the prime minister for guidance. Angelique spoke up once more to try and persuade the room. "We have always had a protocol for destroying any computer system that is found to have contained the virus or has been in contact with the virus. And in the case of simulations like us"—she looked toward Atlas and both Ships—"we have a well-documented process for removing it. We know the filter virus that Atlas had was different because of what we learned from removing it from Lex. It left a different fingerprint on the robot. But because we deleted it, we don't have a clear understanding of what these changes mean for its goals. So, I'm proposing we build a facility up in space to study it. We wall it off completely and we learn as much as we can from the virus. We need to understand what we're up against."

"Okay, I've heard enough," Kezia said. "We're not going to make a decision on something as important as the security of our planet in this meeting. We need to understand if we could reconnect Atlas's spacecraft to power without risking the lives of our citizens." She looked toward the intelligence committee members in the room. "I want you to make a recommendation on what we should do with that drifting spacecraft. Tell me if the risk is worth the reward. And you." She looked toward Atlas. "I've read about you. I know about your curiosity. So, I'm giving you this task because I don't want you interfering with our intelligence team's investigation into your ship. I want you to focus on answering the question of how this virus manipulates a whole society. You're the only one here besides Angelique who's had experience on planets with the virus actively operating in secret."

CHAPTER 33

ATLAS

MANIPULATION IS EASY

Atlas was on the mezzanine floor of one of the planet's many research facilities. This one had a one-way mirror that allowed him and his small team to overlook subjects as they partook in experiments. This current experiment had him looking out at about two hundred different people all in small cubicles—all of them wearing virtual reality goggles.

In the past few weeks, Atlas still hadn't had an opportunity to properly catch up with Angelique. She had been a very busy person since she returned. He had been busy too. He originally thought he'd be spending his time diving into the petabytes of data and knowledge that Angelique had brought back with her. But ever since PM Kezia had given him this task to find out how the virus was manipulating them, he couldn't do anything but think about it.

He was feeling happy about the situation, too, because after seeing just how much data was in those files and how many people were going through them, he was confident he wasn't going to add any unique insight or value. The humans on Juniper treated it like a sport. It felt like everyone on the planet was trying to figure out how much of the knowledge within the data was new and how much had already been discovered by the Junipens already. It was exciting because it was like centuries of scientific research and literature had just been gifted to the planet. There were leaderboards for people who discovered the most areas of knowledge that Juniper was still the most advanced in. And the message boards were full of upvoted discoveries.

He was quite content in his current study. They had given him resources and authority, and he was going to use that to figure this thing out.

He had invited Angelique and Prime Minister Kezia to this research facility to show them what he had discovered. He was daydreaming as he stared out the window over the sea of people when Bentley's assistant called out, "They've arrived, Atlas."

Angelique and Kezia walked through the door together, followed by Kezia's assistant. Atlas walked over and shook Kezia and her assistant's hand. "How are you, madam Prime Minister? And nice to meet you in person finally, Lucy."

"Good, thank you. I'm looking forward to seeing what you've got to show us."

Atlas smiled, then turned to Angelique and gave her a big hug.

"Sorry I haven't had time to come see you, Atlas," Angelique said.

"Don't worry about it."

"Let's do dinner this Thursday?"

"Done," Atlas said before pointing out the window. "I have some crazy results to share with you. I honestly didn't believe them myself before I ran this study." Atlas handed around a piece of paper with a few statements on it, percentages next each of the sentences.

Out the one-way window sat many participants, all at different stages in an ongoing experiment, wearing VR goggles over their heads and suited in tight-fitting haptic feedback suits.

Angelique looked at the paper. "What is this?" she said as she studied it. "Something about these people not liking science fiction?"

Bentley, Atlas's lead researcher, explained what it meant. "It says that twenty-three percent of the group like science fiction books. And overall, they have a slightly negative feeling toward sci-fi in general."

Atlas put the rest of the papers next to the printer. He had printed out extras in case more people joined the meeting. "And we intend to change that by the end of this training session." He picked up one of the VR headsets on the table. "For the last hour and a half, two hundred and fifteen people have been wearing these headsets, playing games and surfing the internet. We told them we were testing a new interface and wanted their opinion on it before we released it to the public." He pointed to the questionnaire Angelique and Kezia were holding. "We also had them answer a number of questions under the guise of needing to customize the home screen with things that interest them."

"So, they don't know the true purpose of this experiment?" Kezia said. "What are you really testing?"

"These are our baseline metrics." Atlas pointed his sheet of paper. "Our goal is to change them however we want. To manipulate them into liking science fiction. Everyone should be just about finished with their session soon too. So, we're about ready to see how well it worked." Atlas looked toward Bentley. "Can you give everyone the new questionnaire?"

Bentley nodded and walked over to his laptop sitting on the table and pressed a few keys.

A few minutes passed and results started to come in. Bentley turned his screen around to face the team. "We'll be able to see trends soon."

"Do you mind," Atlas asked, "if you print that out? Just take a screenshot. I like having things in my hand."

Bentley nodded, and a few seconds later, the printer was alive with another sheet.

Angelique grabbed the printouts. "I forgot how obsessed with killing trees you were, Atlas."

"It's the way I think."

The paper showed two graphs on it. One showed a normal distribution and the other looked like the distribution curve had been pushed to the right. It was showing the changed perception of everyone in the experiment toward science fiction. It showed a clear forty percent improvement. They were much more favorable toward science fiction now. There were still people who were not favorable toward it, but overall, it clearly looked like the average answer had been pushed toward the positive.

Kezia pointed at the chart. "Okay, you've changed people's perception. But how did you do it?"

"Have either of you heard of the term *subliminal priming*?" Atlas asked.

Vague looks from both told him they hadn't heard of it before.

"I think I've heard of priming," Angelique said. "Is that influencing someone's thinking by having them do something before asking them a question?"

"Similar," Atlas said before he turned to Kezia's assistant. "Lucy, do you mind if I include you in a little experiment?"

"Of course. What do you need?"

"Can you say the word *most* ten times?"

"Most, most, most," she said quickly before needing a reaffirming nod from Atlas to continue repeating the word.

Once she was done, Atlas asked her, "Now, what do you put in a toaster?"

"Toast," she replied before going red and noticing her mistake. "It's bread; you put bread in a toaster."

Atlas nodded. "You're correct. But did you see how your first instinct was to say *toast*?"

Lucy nodded. "So, that's priming? I was more likely to say *toast* because you had me say the word *most?*"

"And don't worry, Lucy," Atlas said. "I said *toast* too, the first time someone asked me that question."

"I've never heard it before."

Angelique chuckled slightly. "It was a game a lot of kids played back on Earth and Mars. I never told anyone the game here, so it never caught on."

"I guessed that was the case," Atlas said. "No one in this research facility had heard it before. This is my tenth time doing this little trick."

"And not a single person got it right," Bentley added.

"Is subliminal priming doing that without anyone taking notice of it?" Kezia said. "So, go on, then; tell us how it's done."

"There are literally thousands of little tricks like that, which we employ to influence people's decisions in the game world out there," Atlas said, pointing out the window. "Did you know if you look at photos of people smiling, you start to smile and get happier?"

The team nodded.

"Same with sad photos. You can make people sad by showing them photos of others being sad."

Kezia still looked like she was unsure about what Atlas was saying—as if she didn't believe it. "But wouldn't that be obvious if you were showing photos of happy faces? I thought this was meant to be subliminal."

"This is where it gets a bit scary," Atlas said, pulling up an image of two random words. The words were in a language none of the people in the room had seen before. "Which of these two words do you believe means something bad?"

Everyone studied the two words. Then everyone pointed to the random word on the right except Angelique, who still couldn't decide.

"I'm not sure why I think that one," Kezia said. "But it just feels like the bad word."

Atlas grinned. "That's because it's the one I wanted you to choose." He clicked a button on the screen and the image changed. The words were replaced with an image of someone frowning behind the image that everyone chose. "This photo was behind the word you picked. It was flashing on the screen so quickly, you didn't register it was there. But it was enough to make you feel like it was a bad word."

"That is very creepy," Angelique said.

Kezia nodded in agreement. "There has to be some sort of protection against companies doing that sort of thing to us."

"This was all just to show you that it is possible to change someone's beliefs. But this next experiment is to show you we can use this tool to change people's behavior."

During Atlas's short demonstration, the experiment completed and almost everyone left. Atlas gestured to the rest of the group to follow him as he walked down the stairs to the main lobby of the research facility.

It was a bright, sterile space, almost like a large doctor's waiting room. A fluorescent glow illuminated the area. There were chairs and small tables scattered all around the place, all facing the reception desk, which was currently unoccupied. Along one of the walls were stacks and stacks of books. All the books were old classics, from when Atlas was back on Earth. There was a book on that wall that catered to almost every possible taste and preference. Nonfiction, litRPG, sci-fi, they were all at one point popular books. But most of them would be considered obscure to the people in the room.

"After this experiment, everyone gets told that a local bookshop has gone out of business," Atlas said. "And we pretend they asked us if we could give away their remaining stock of books." Atlas picked up one of the books; it was by an author called Scott Meyer, the title of the fiction was *Off to Be the Wizard*. "They're old books because I wanted ones that people didn't know. The real test here is what genre of books people take."

Atlas walked over toward the reception counter. There was a printer behind it, with a single piece of paper. "When we first ran this experiment, around fifteen percent of people took a science fiction book." He read the paper and then circled the number on it. "It looks like we can manipulate people's behavior. Just over sixty percent of people grabbed a sci-fi book."

Atlas handed the paper to the others in the group. "What this proves is with enough time and resources, you could move a civilization's beliefs on anything you wanted, as long as they embrace the simulated reality. Because everything we did today was only possible if you can control everything someone is looking at."

Atlas wanted to make sure everyone understood this wasn't just a fluke, that it wasn't random chance that this was the outcome. Science fiction was the genre the majority picked from the shelf because it was the one he wanted them to choose. It would have been just as easy for him to make everyone pick another genre of books. "We tested this yesterday with a different group of people. But this time, we primed them to want fantasy novels instead. We had the exact same result. Most of the fantasy books were gone after the experiment. And there was a strong preference for fantasy novels over sci-fi."

"Is that what the filter virus has been doing?" Angelique asked. "Manipulating our people in whatever way it wants?"

"I think so," Atlas said. "This is what it does when it has an opportunity to infect a world. It pushes society away from certain technologies and in certain directions."

Atlas remembered when VR goggles were first popularized on Earth. He and Peter never understood why big social media companies at the time invested so much into developing the tech. But after studying the results here he was starting to understand their endgame. Being able to mass manipulate humans in any direction had limitless value. Especially if it meant they could use that to wield power over elections and world events—or even worse, sell it to advertisers.

Thinking about what occurred back on earth sent a shiver up his spine. It became glaringly obvious that this technology had been used for brainwashing. Humanity became obsessed with the metaverse because of this. Humanity left the betaverse behind because of this. Otherwise, humans could have colonized the stars much sooner.

Kezia picked up one of the books. "I can see why someone would want to do this." The book she was holding was called *The Three-Body Problem.* She flicked through the pages. "Do we know why Earth is doing this? Is their goal just to destroy our colonies?"

Atlas started to bite his lower lip. "That's what we need to find out."

CHAPTER 34

ANGELIQUE

SINKING SPACESHIP

Angelique sat in the prime minister's situation room. The room was much smaller than it should have been. Most of its space taken up by a large oak table and leather chairs. So, everyone in the room was crammed into the remaining space, the table littered with laptops and briefing notes.

Angelique was seated in one corner next to Kezia. She couldn't get Atlas into the meeting, so he was outside somewhere, waiting to find out the result. It was assumed that there might be military capabilities on display that Atlas didn't have clearance to observe. So, despite Angelique's objections, he wasn't in the room.

The whole room was facing the large screen on the other side of the table. On that screen was a live broadcast of the special operation to recapture Atlas's spacecraft.

His spacecraft was currently on a trajectory to impact the sun.

This was the first time Juniper's space force had made use of the Starnet communication network. Their military strategists were quick to see the tactical value of the tool, and since it was released to the public as part of all the new technology Angelique supplied the colony with, local scientists had already worked to improve on the technology, updating its security protocols and compatibility with some of the other communication capabilities they already possessed.

"We have reached the birdie," Commander Pratchett said as his face appeared on the screen. Pratchett had a commanding, deep, no-nonsense voice, and his face wore a permanent scowl, presumably from years of yelling at troops. "Releasing the disrupter now."

On the screen in front of them appeared the blazingly hot-looking sun. It filled the entire view of the camera. Even though Angelique was looking at an image, she felt like she could feel the heat coming from the screen. She realized just how close Atlas's spacecraft had gotten to the star.

The view changed and got darker, and a silhouette of a long, thin spacecraft came into focus. It was boxy, more like a carrier designed for moving machinery in-system than interstellar travel. From the very front of the spacecraft launched a small missile, followed by several eleph-ANTs.

Angelique watched as the view changed. Now the video was streaming in from one of the ejected eleph-ANTs. From its vantage point, the eleph-ANT was racing to catch up.

As the eleph-ANT approached Atlas's spacecraft, it became clear just how little of it was left. A better description was *wreckage*. The ship was clearly in three pieces loosely connected via cables or wires. The middle section had pieces gouged out of it.

The missile reached its target and the nose of the missile broke off. Then the warhead started to pulsate. Some sort of warping illusion started to spread out from the missile. It was pulsating smaller, then bigger, then smaller again. It continued pulsating like this until it reached the wreckage, before lodging itself in the middle section.

Moments later, the pulsating from the missile expanded rapidly and surrounded Atlas's dead vehicle. It became harder to see the ship, and it looked like a fog had just been released—it covered the drifting object.

General Pratchett's face appeared on the screen once more. "The disrupter has successfully deployed. No signals are coming into or out of that area of space."

The general had just deployed a small, specialized version of the machine that protected the planet from others seeing inside of the system clearly—what Atlas called the bubble.

The view changed back to the eleph-ANTs once more. They were surrounding the dead spacecraft. Their noses all pointed toward the bubble.

The spacecraft showed visible sparks and flickers of light as the eleph-ANTs maneuvered themselves into position. Then in unison, all the eleph-ANTs fired some sort of beam. Angelique remarked that it looked like the life was being sucked out of the spacecraft. This went on for a long while as the area around the spacecraft got darker and more lifeless.

The drifting wreckage had looked dead before, but all sparks and flickers of light now stopped, as if all the electricity had been ripped from the vessel. If it had looked dead before, now it looked beyond dead.

After a long moment of nothing, the general's face reappeared on the screen. "We have successfully drained the vessel of any residual power."

Moments later, the eleph-ANTs powered up large tractor beams. These fields wrapped the now completely dead and now visibly tumbling spacecraft in a light glow. And as the glow got brighter, the tumbling slowed.

This was a similar tractor beam to the one they had used to capture Atlas. After a few moments, it froze the drifting ship in place. And then the engines from all the eleph-ANTs started to fire. They were changing the orbit, or rather, because the spacecraft was falling toward the star, it wasn't in orbit, so they were shifting the spacecraft into a stable orbit around the star.

It looked like this was the absolute last moment that they could accomplish it; now that Angelique's view was closer to the ship, it looked like it had been hit with a lot of solar radiation. And she wondered if any circuitry had survived the heat.

The screen changed once more, this time showing the spacecraft of Commander Pratchett approaching the wreckage. A large section of his hull opened up to allow the eleph-ANTs and dead spacecraft to fit inside.

An appropriate description of it was of a large whale opening wide and engulfing a squid whole, because all the loosely connected wires and shipwreck resembled a dangling squid from the right angle.

The commander's face appeared on the screen once more. "Maneuvering into position."

Angelique leaned over toward Kezia and whispered in her ear, "Let's hope that thing isn't completely fried."

As if answering the question Angelique just posed, the commander spoke. "We have successfully secured the spacecraft. We are moving to testing its integrity now. Over to you, madam Prime Minister."

A round of claps and cheers flowed through the room before Kezia spoke up. "My understanding is we will confirm the ship is still operational. We need to confirm that spacecraft is still infected with the filter virus. Once that is confirmed, our team here"—she pointed toward one of the chief scientists on the opposite side of the room—"they will replicate the complete spacecraft in a simulated environment. Do you have anything to add?"

"Yes," the chief scientist said. "It will be a difficult operation. We want to the virus to believe that it survived. Then we will let the virus operate freely in the simulated environment, where we can test it and see how it operates. We are still waiting on approval from the test subject," he added before looking back at Kezia.

"We still need to ask Atlas," Kezia said, looking at Angelique. "If he approves, he will enter these multiple simulated worlds and interact with the virus. Through his interactions, we'll be able to understand its goals and test different ways of destroying it."

Angelique was a little surprised by that last comment. "You want to send Atlas into a simulation? Why?" A look of confusion ran over her face. "Why not just turn the spacecraft back on and see what it does?"

The chief scientist stood up to answer the question. "We have game-theorized the risks. It's too risky turning the virus on, as we risk letting it escape and infiltrating our network here on Juniper. If we load it into a simulated environment, we can firewall it off from everything. And because we can load as many simulated environments as we want, we will be able to test how it operates in a number of scenarios. We can also rewind a simulation if we want to change a variable."

Angelique nodded. She could see the theory behind it. But it was the ethics she struggled with. She personally wouldn't want to subject herself to a bunch of simulated environments. That would mean also duplicating herself into multiple metaverses. "Just make sure Atlas fully understands what he's agreeing to. Putting someone into a simulated world is an ethical grey area."

"For most of this, we won't need him," Kezia said. "The first simulation will be us powering up the spacecraft. We want to see what happens when we give the virus an opportunity to escape. We want to see what it does. We will be able to learn a lot about it without Atlas. But there are some areas we want him and his crew to help with. But it is completely up to them."

CHAPTER 35

ATLAS

MANY MINDS

Atlas and Angelique were having dinner at one of the most exclusive restaurants in Little Sydney, a small coastal town on one of the planet's many islands.

The food at the place was Lebanese, and the food was served exclusively in a style that was called Jeeb, or "trust the chef." The atmosphere in the room felt like something out of a small village. Rustic tables and chairs were more akin to pieces of artwork than a restaurant. They were sitting in front of a table full of small tasting plates, and the waiters kept bringing new dishes out.

"You're telling me you need to have hapticgraphic engines installed in all locations you visit?" Atlas pointed at himself. "Why not just inhabit an android like me?"

Angelique sipped her glass of wine. "It's not that different from any of the political leaders on this planet."

Atlas looked at Angelique blankly. When she wasn't forth-coming with any new information, Atlas said, "I don't get it. The other leaders on this planet can go anywhere they want without having to force the shopkeepers to install hapticgraphic engines."

"They can, but they don't." Angelique wiped away some of the food from her lips. "From a security standpoint, they're limited to much of the same locations as me. And besides, the tech isn't that complicated. They rolled in a mobile unit into this restaurant about thirty minutes before I arrived."

"And they just let you install a mobile hapticgraphic unit?"

"We're both celebrities, Atlas," Angelique mused. "Us being here is the best marketing this place could ever hope for." Angelique paused before changing the subject. "So, have you made a decision yet? Are you going inside?"

"Yes." Atlas set his glass on the table. "I have to know why. Why the humans back on Earth have been so desperate to lock us all down. And find out how they're finding all our worlds. This whole thing doesn't make sense to me."

"So, what are you thinking? How are you going to figure this out?"

"I've read the reports on everything that has been gathered so far." He pointed toward the sky. "None of the tests they've run out there have resulted in any conclusive evidence. The virus hasn't yet appeared or made its presence known."

"I read the reports too. So, what are you going to do differ-ently? How are you going to change the results gained so far?"

Atlas was a little bit conflicted about this next part. In some ways, he was simply building on what Angelique had just put in place with her Ange's Angels program. In others, he was taking things to the illogical extreme, taking a process that she had cre-ated for the good of her people and expanding it to the point it would be unrecognizable.

Atlas opened his mouth to speak, then closed it again, trying to figure out how best to word things. He wondered how she might respond to this. He knew she already believed he shouldn't enter the simulated reality. And now he was about to tell her he was entering a lot more than one.

Atlas took a deep breath. He decided the best approach was just to tell her. Explain the facts and remove emotion from it all. "We're going to clone ourselves. Ship, Lex, and I are going to create duplicates and enter maybe a few thousand simulations at once."

Angeliques mouth opened wide. She nearly spat out her wine. "A few thousand simulations?!"

"It's the only way. You said it yourself: we have a bit of urgency here. This virus has evolved a lot since you first discovered it. So, we need to find out as much as we can quickly so we can tell the others."

"Let me get this right: your plan is to enter thousands of simulated environments at once?"

"Exactly. We're going to accomplish and test in a month what would have taken years to do if we were doing it in the real world. We're going to test as many ideas as we can."

Atlas grabbed one of the plates on the table. It was a bowl of spiced chickpeas sprinkled over the smoothest hummus he had ever seen before. "Imagine each of these chickpeas is a simulated world. We can control everything in each of these realities. Including the speed of time." He scooped one of the chickpeas with his spoon. "One of these worlds, we might just simulate us escaping and heading back to Sol. See what kind of messages the virus sends out when we get close to Earth." He ate the chickpea, then picked up another. "In this world, we might tell the virus we know about it and see how it reacts." Atlas ate that piece, then shared a number of different scenarios with Angelique, different ideas and theories he wanted to test. "By duplicating myself, we can simultaneously test thousands of variations at once, each time improving on the learning." He started spooning chickpeas into some flatbread. "We might find the best way to extract information from the virus is to be direct. Tell it we know about it. And we might also find that there are questions that cause it to self-destruct. If we end up in a situation like that, we can simply rewind the simulation and avoid that question. Each version of our crew can have a specific mission, something we want to find out."

"And what about you three? Are you going to be okay with going through that? You'll get out of these simulations and feel like it was all real; you'll feel like you've just spent years in these fake worlds."

Atlas nodded. "Time doesn't mean that much to me anymore. I'm sure you feel the same. I feel a sense of urgency to understand this, so I can help Trillion and Icarus. But going out and living a hundred lives in quick succession is no different from what I've experienced so far."

"I assume you'll be merging the versions of you back together again?"

Atlas nodded.

"Be careful; it's not as easy as it sounds to reconcile all those different memories. Going through the process with just one version of yourself is hard. I can't fathom what it'll be like to go through the joining thousands of times."

Atlas watched as what he had just shared ticked over in Angelique's mind. He thought it was a clever idea to use the simulated reality to reduce the learning time.

He wouldn't say this out loud, but he also blamed the virus for the way his colony disowned him near the end. In some ways, he had felt vindicated when he found out the truth—that some virus was infiltrating his people and pushing them in other directions. It meant the virus was to blame for his people not wanting him around. And he wanted to take revenge on that virus. To destroy it.

He knew revenge wasn't a good argument for why they needed to do this, so he pivoted. "You said it yourself. We need to get answers quickly. We need to find a way to destroy this virus before it has a chance to evolve further. Not just for this colony but all your colonies. We don't know how much time we have."

Angelique nodded once more. "I agree with what you're saying. It's just going to take me a little while to come to terms with it all."

"My hypothesis is that this virus's primary goal is to feed back information. It's broadcasting to somewhere. I want to understand what information it is sending. And I want to find a way to destroy it. I plan on creating a virus-killing antivirus."

CHAPTER 36

ATLAS

SIMULATIONS

Atlas had been given a new spacecraft. His previous ship design was mostly engines. Two large egg-shaped engines gave the spacecraft he was used to its distinct design. This new spacecraft had a much slimmer profile. The two large engines were still there, but the balance of everything was much better. He hadn't looked into the technology behind the engines yet, but whatever they were didn't require as much space. His was currently docked to the space carrier that had recaptured his original destroyed spacecraft.

One of the first things he did with his new ship was to design the inside of it to look like his old one—his old home. His office had a printer in one corner of the room and a large table in the middle, which he used to organize his thinking using printouts and papers. There were some new additions to his office, however; a large sofa was placed along one wall, and different chairs were scattered around the room. He didn't need anywhere for others to sit when it was just him on the spacecraft. Especially when Trillion or Icarus could simply use the hapticgraphic engine to create a chair for themselves if they wanted one.

These chairs were for the visitors who were now in regular attendance of his briefings. His investigation into the filter virus was illuminating. And the scientists and programmers onboard the adjoining space carrier were enthralled by the data he was presenting back.

A version of him had entered a simulation over two thousand times. It wasn't that he had a lot of new information on the virus yet. It had been a struggle to get the virus to do anything other than report back. They had tried hundreds of different ways to get it to communicate with them, and each time, they failed.

The worst outcome was when Atlas reentered the spacecraft in the simulated world. He turned the power on, stood in the middle of the bridge, and announced in a very loud voice that he knew about the virus and wanted to have a conversation with it.

There was absolutely no response, except the virus broadcast a signal in all directions. Then, moments later, the engines went critical and his spacecraft essentially self-destructed. The virus had attempted to destroy itself and Atlas along with it. They were still trying to decrypt the message the virus sent out. He was making zero progress on that.

They even played out a simulation and pretended like a virus on Juniper had just broadcast the signal. As soon as that signal was heard, the virus attempted to self-destruct once more. Atlas assumed either the signal sent told all viruses to remove all evidence of itself, or the original signal sent from the virus contained a unique identifier code for that particular virus and, after seeing a code with its own identifier broadcast to itself, it self-destructed.

Atlas hoped that it was the latter of the two, because he didn't want a scenario in the real world where all the viruses would self-destruct together, as that could cause a runaway cascade across all the colonies. It would be horrific.

They found that in the simulated worlds, they could talk openly about a mysterious piece of code that was sending signals back to Sol. They could even hypothesize that it was a virus sent to infect them. The only thing off limits, that caused it to attempt to self-destruct, was confronting it and letting it know they knew about it. Pure speculation was fine; even attempting to locate the code and delete wasn't a problem. But acting like they knew for a fact the virus was an AI with agency and decision-making capabilities caused whatever it was to self-destruct.

It was obviously important to hide the idea the virus was a lot more complex and capable. When Atlas treated it like a worm or malicious piece of code, nothing bad happened. But when Atlas started to treat it like a potential AI, having conversations with Ship about a potential AI infecting the spacecraft, things turned ugly.

One area the virus took full advantage was its ability to manipulate Lex.

They ran multiple simulations where they were pretending to look for the code of the virus. The only difference between scenarios was the conversations Atlas and Ship had together. And when the two of them started to speculate that it was a sophisticated AI, the virus would actively start manipulating the information Lex provided. It attempted to send them on a wild goose chase. Lex would claim to have found the erroneous code. And signs would point to someone on Neuropa simply keeping track of their whereabouts. Multiple simulated scenarios played out like this, where Lex found a piece of spyware designed to keep tabs on them all. The evidence always pointed toward something obvious.

Atlas stretched out on his couch, laying his head on the armrest. He was feeling exhausted. Having his memories merged after a version of him left a simulation was not something he was going to get used to. Combining memories from thousands of different versions of himself wasn't the hard part. It was the disorientation he felt when he did something and felt déjà vu multiple times a day now, and it was worse when multiple versions of him attempted the same strategy with the virus. Those moments felt like a strange dream he wasn't sure was real or not. Angelique had warned him against merging too many memories at once. But in typical Atlas fashion, he got engrossed in the research and obsessed about getting closer to the truth.

As Atlas lay back, thinking through what he wanted to test next in the simulation, Ship teleported into his office. "We need to make progress on destroying this thing."

"Build an antivirus?" Atlas mused. "Let's figure out why this thing is doing what it's doing first."

Atlas had to move his legs off the side of the sofa so Ship could sit down next to him.

Ship looked at him earnestly. "I don't think we're going to get the answers you're looking for. Whenever we probe too much, we end up having to restart the simulation because the thing tries to self-destruct."

"We're painting a picture, Ship. Each time it tries to destroy us, we learn a little bit about what it doesn't want us to know."

"And what about the mission Kezia asked us to do?"

"We'll figure out how to destroy it once we learn everything we can about the virus."

Ship looked at Atlas in a way that told him he didn't approve of the strategy Atlas was undertaking. Atlas was intentionally not making progress toward finding a way to destroy the virus because he was too interested in learning about it. How it worked. It was an intellectual curiosity for him. And once he became obsessed with something, it became hard for him to not focus solely on that one thing. "I worry that if we don't use this time to find out as much as we can, Ship, we will lose access once we've figured out how to destroy it."

"I think you're looking at this wrong; if we create a weapon, we can learn more about this virus by going out and deploying it. Before we deploy it, we could capture another sample and study that, too. But we do need to help the others."

"You're right; this virus is on Neuropa," Atlas said, admitting his foolishness. He wasn't thinking about the bigger picture. Trillion, Icarus, and the people he left on Neuropa would all be unaware of the fact they had a virus subtly working to destroy their world. "Sorry, Ship, you're right. Let's kill it."

CHAPTER 37

ATLAS

GRABBY ALIENS

After almost two thousand simulations, Atlas had made reasonable progress on identifying the source and structure of the virus that infected his spacecraft.

It was a distributed intelligence of some sort. It wasn't concentrated on one piece of hardware, either. They attempted to locate the source of the code by systematically turning off sections of the hardware that made up the ship, but they found the virus was always present. It was a series of simple pieces of code, but combined, they added up to something that was greater than the sum of its parts.

Like a virus that infects the human body, this malicious piece of code duplicated itself over and over again. This filter virus wasn't seeking to cripple its victim, however. It was simply seeking to bend, shift, or manipulate Atlas and his crew away from colonizing more planets. They had figured that piece of information out for sure.

It was like the invisible hand of the market, subtly changing probabilities and the likelihood of events.

The evidence they had collected supported the findings Atlas found before. It wasn't designed to change the beliefs of one person. Atlas and Ship working alone were not what it was designed to impact. It was designed to change groups of people, one micro-interaction at a time.

Atlas was starting to get a migraine thinking about everything. He pinched the bridge of his nose; he needed to get away and clear his mind.

He flicked off a quick message to Angelique.

Lunch? he asked her.

The message came back quickly.

It's two in the morning . . . But okay.

The two of them planned to meet in the cafeteria of the carrier he was attached to.

The main kitchen looked like a typical military mess hall. The booths looked uncomfortable because they were rigid and designed so that nothing moved if the ship needed to maneuver quickly. In one corner of the room was more of a buffet table where cooks kept food available all day long in warmer trays.

Since the ship supported a crew at all times, the mess hall was full of people eating and talking to friends. This was all despite its being the early hours of the morning.

Atlas was in one of the empty booths, waiting for Angelique to arrive.

He was lost in thought when the room went oddly quiet for a second. It took a while before Atlas realized Angelique had just entered and people were standing in salute.

Angelique walked over and grabbed a seat next to him. "Do you not know about the officers' lounge?"

Atlas shook his head.

"Did no one tell you about it? It's the same food, just better chairs and privacy."

A private approached them both cautiously with two mugs and a coffee pot. "Would you like a drink, ma'am?" He then looked to Atlas, offering a cup. "Sir."

"Thank you," Angelique said, looking at his name badge, "Private . . . Bean is it?"

"Yes, ma'am."

She took the two cups and handed one to Atlas.

"Appreciate it," Atlas said.

"Ma'am, I just wanted to say," the private started to say, then struggled to get out the words. He looked completely starstruck by Angelique. "Thank you, ma'am. My. My mother was sick. And they didn't know how to cure her. About a week after you got back, her doctor found, in one of the journal articles you brought with you, he found a cure. My mum is getting better because of you. Thank you, ma'am."

Angelique turned to the man and put a hand on his arm. She showed pure compassion and caring in her face. "That's why I do this, Private. For moments like this. I just want to help our people prosper. And it starts with making sure none of us have to get sick or die early. Thank you for telling me this. It really is these stories that keep me going. They get me excited to bring everything I've learned on Juniper to our other worlds."

"Thank you, ma'am," he said before saluting and turning away.

"I'm glad we came in here now. That story warmed my heart," Angelique said while smiling. "So, what do you want to talk about?"

"Your other planets. The ones with aliens on them."

"I never found anything as awesome as the Dottiens. But most of the systems we visited had some alien life in them. Did I tell you about our first planet?"

"I read everything on it. You had two planets in the habitable zone. One was full of life and the other was dead?"

"I was very lucky with my first world. I created a small colony on the planet with life. Just in a dome structure. Then myself, Ship, and the colony worked to terraform the other planet so it was ideal for humans."

"Tell me about the aliens. What did they all have in common?"

Angelique scratched the back of her head. "Alien life is common. But all of them were animals. We haven't yet met any life form that had human-level intelligence. Not even anything that was hunter-gatherer level." Angelique clicked on her watch and a small hologram appeared, showing pictures of several aliens she had encountered in her various systems. "Convergent evolution," Angelique said. "There's a lot of unique-looking aliens out there. But that's more of the exception, not the rule. It's surprising how similar the faces of many of these alien animals are."

And they were. Atlas studied the faces; none of them were animals he'd seen before back on Earth, but all of them had a familiar look to them. Two eyes, something that resembled a mouth in the middle, and sometimes a nose. Atlas looked at one of the aliens; it was the shape of a giant dog, but it didn't have fur. Rather, its skin looked dry and grey like an elephant's. "Interesting. Can I tell you what I've found in your data?"

Angelique leaned forward, excited by what she was about to hear.

"Your astrophysics have done a lot of research on your worlds. The literature talks about aliens being everywhere. Almost every potentially habitable planet has life in some form." Out of his back pocket Atlas pulled a couple of research papers and put them on the table. "I went back through some of the first articles written around the time of your third world. Based on all the evidence they found, they believed it was only a matter of time before you encountered a civilization-building alien. But you haven't yet found one."

"I believe I remember that. There was a lot of talk about the risks of encountering a hostile alien force. I never followed up on any of the research after my seventh world. Has something new come to light?"

Atlas moved his head from side to side. "Your astronomers have a few new theories. There're a few patterns that come up time and time again." He started to list out items on his fingers. "Firstly, worlds that have something producing oxygen are teeming with life. I mean they're absolutely covered in it. You already know this. There's something about how much easier it is for life to build multicellular complexities when there's a lot of free oxygen around."

"Worlds like Juniper where we can start from scratch seem to be the exception, not the rule," Angelique commented.

"Now, this is pure speculation, but I have a theory that there needs to be mass-extinction events to get intelligent life. Multiple mass-extinction events."

"What do you mean?"

"Do you know how long the dinosaurs roamed Earth for?"

"Millions of years?"

"One hundred and sixty-five million years. Longer than any species of hominids, be that human, neanderthal, or homo erectus. None of them have been around for as long as dinos. And what do you think of when you think about dinosaurs?"

"They're big."

"They're massive. You know this, you discovered them. A lot of your worlds have huge animals on them. So many planets that never had a mass-extinction event have massive land-based creatures. It's like they all got in some evolutionary spiral where the predators got bigger, so the prey got bigger to compensate." He paused for a second. "I'm exaggerating, of course, but it was surprising just how consistent that evolutionary path is. Same with building thick armor like crabs or crayfish do. So many entered stable evolutionary branches that didn't need them to get smarter."

"I still can't believe how long the dinosaurs lived. Almost two hundred million years."

"Yeah, and that's plenty of time for one of them to evolve a brain like us. But they didn't. Because brains are expensive and there's nothing really in evolution that should encourage brain size. Getting bigger to protect yourself, yes. But building von

Neumann probes like us doesn't have a clear evolutionary path," Atlas said.

"So, how did we arrive on the scene? How does your theory explain us?"

"Mass-extinction events, or the climate changing. There needs to be a reason for species to venture out of their geological niche. To give animals like us a chance to evolve." Atlas let that all sink for a second. "I have a question: If we combine the data from your worlds and Earth, how long do you think the average species is around for?"

Angelique scratched the back of her neck. "A few hundred thousand years?"

"More. Much more."

"A couple million."

"At least ten million," Atlas said. "And homo sapiens have only been around for three hundred thousand at most. It took us less than three percent of the life of an average species to build rocket ships and explore the galaxy."

"Are you saying that a species like us is either going to develop quite early or not at all? And in most situations, it is not at all, because planet environments don't change that often."

"Exactly; intelligent life is extremely rare. There are a lot of planets out there with life on them, even more worlds that are empty, but none, so far, that have anything as smart as us."

"Okay, so, surely you didn't bring me all the way up here to this space station to share with me that insight. I've visited all those solar systems. I know this."

"This is a long-winded way of me bringing up the next point. What is the Beta Explorer program about?" Atlas asked.

"Finding new worlds and expanding human reach."

"This is where I enter speculation land. I believe this filter virus has an alien origin. And it has something to do with them stopping civilizations from colonizing new worlds."

"Talk me through the reasons you believe this. Start with why an alien, not humans, would plant a computer virus on multiple worlds in the hopes that we find it and it can manipulate us."

Atlas started to bite his lower lip. "They do it so there's more empty worlds for the aliens to go out and colonize."

"Grabby aliens," Angelique muttered to herself.

Atlas nodded in approval. "Exactly. *Grabby aliens* refers to a theoretical solution to the Fermi paradox." He chuckled a little to himself because the Fermi question was always *Where are the aliens?* but he had seen aliens: the Dottiens. And Angelique had encountered life in many of the systems she visited. So, he wanted to reframe the question. "The Fermi paradox in the context of everything we know of today is, *Where are the smart aliens? Where are the Dyson swarms?*"

"They don't exist yet because we haven't built them."

"Or they're being built currently but we can't see them yet because lightspeed is just so slow."

"Elaborate," Angelique said, taking a sip of her coffee.

"So, the theory postulates that the reason we don't see alien signals and Dyson swarms throughout the Milky Way is because colonization happens at near-light-speed. So, once you hear an alien signal or see a world covered in satellites, it's too late, because they're already on their way to you."

Atlas looked around the room to make sure no one was listening. "If an alien sends a radio signal to us, and they also send a spacecraft to us at lightspeed. Both the signal and the spacecraft would arrive at the same time. Because nothing"—Atlas paused for a moment—"well, at least, I think nothing travels faster than the speed of light."

"Is this the idea that the galaxy could be completely colonized in less than a million years?" Angelique said.

Atlas nodded.

"So, why send probes?" Angelique replied. "Why not, as the theory suggests, send colony ships out at the speed of light?"

"Maybe they can't." Atlas shrugged. "I've modeled the spread of these potential aliens. If they can only send probes at near-lightspeed but their colony ships travel slower, or they need more time on each planet to terraform it before traveling to the next one, then sending probes with the virus is faster and more effective."

"So, you're saying that sending these viruses ensures the galaxy still has a huge number of empty planets for them when they get here?" Angelique said. "That's quite a clever way to do it."

Atlas nodded.

"Okay. I understand your theory. But where's the evidence? How did you come to this conclusion?"

Atlas was quiet for a moment. He turned over the piece of paper and drew three squares on it. In the first square he wrote the word *Earth*. "Whenever I'm in the simulation, nothing bad happens if I act like I believe someone from Sol is trying to manipulate us. We even see some fake data to support this theory. A favorite is pinning things on General Walker." Atlas put a tick next to the word *Earth*. "The virus is quite happy for us to believe it's humans on Earth."

Atlas went to the next empty square and wrote the words *Trillion or Icarus* on it. "Again, a similar thing happens when we pretend we believe someone from one of our other worlds is manipulating us. We start seeing evidence for that." He put another tick next to the box that said *Trillion or Icarus*.

"This is where things get interesting." He moved his hand to the next box and wrote on it the word *alien*. "We recently tested random ideas in the simulation. Like pretending Lex had been corrupted. Or that it was the Dottiens. Or some unknown alien species." He placed a big question mark next to the box. "When we pretended like we believed it was a hostile unknown alien trying to manipulate us, we started to see the virus move to manipulate us quite overtly, guiding us away from that conclusion."

He paused for a moment, trying to figure out how to best word this next part. Because it wasn't one big thing. It was lots of little pushes. Aggressive pushes. "I've gone through the simulation thousands of times now. Ship and I have a quite-acute awareness of when Lex is being manipulative. When he's pushing us in a different direction. It's not something I can describe in words. But Ship and I have this look we give each other when we know the virus is actively working against us." He took a deep breath. "The virus doesn't want us investigating the idea that it's of alien origin."

CHAPTER 38

ANGELIQUE

ANTIVIRUS

Angelique was back in one of Kezia's ministerial conference rooms. This was another highly confidential meeting. She was there to learn the progress they had made on building something that could destroy the virus they had locked away in a simulation.

This room was specifically designed for sharing presentations. There was a long table in one half of the room that had the names of the various senators, military officials, the PM, and herself to sit at. There were chairs behind each representative at the table; presumably, these would be for the advisors to the important people in the room—making sure they asked the right questions.

At the other end of the room was a large open space. The floor was slightly lower so people at the table looked down rather than upward. Standing in the middle of the small presenting floor was Atlas, flanked by Ship and the head of the intelligence committee, Menen Lee.

Angelique took her seat at the table and gave a little nod to Atlas. Then, moments later, the back door opened and Kezia walked through. The last to arrive, on purpose as usual. She was very religious about being the last one in whenever it was a bigger meeting like this. She was happy to walk in with Angelique in smaller settings, but in important meetings, it was imperative to her that everyone arrive before she did.

As Kezia sat down at her seat, Atlas started to talk, "I trust everyone has read the paper we sent through last week?"

The room all nodded in unison.

"Perfect; I'll do a quick opening statement of the facts. Then we can open it up for questions." Atlas clicked a button on his little pointer device. A hologram of a spiraling galaxy appeared besides him on the stage. It looked like the milky way galaxy. But the contrast was turned up so it looked even more wonderous than the images she had seen before. "I want to establish the fact that what we're sharing with you is based on everything we learned from entering a simulated world we built." He clicked another button on his pointed and the holographic universe split in two, then in four. And it kept splitting until the stage was full of these simulated worlds. "We simulated six thousand and seventy-two of them. These simulations were built to be indistinguishable from the one we are in right now. These worlds—or simulated realities—were designed specifically for us to interact with what we are calling the filter virus, and test how this virus responds to different actions we take. And because they were simulated, if we wanted to replay a scenario with one thing different, we could."

Angelique saw nodding heads all around. Everyone knew this, as everyone here approved of the plan.

"These are the facts we have established." Atlas paused for a moment, then raised an index finger and started to count off items. "Firstly, the virus is of alien origin. It is not an alien on any of our known species lists." He raised another finger. "Secondly, this virus is essentially an alien-imposed great filter. It's designed to halt progress of technological species like us." Atlas raised a third finger. "It's our assessment that the primary goal of the virus is to stop the spread of galaxy-wide civilizations."

"What did he just say?" Angelique heard someone mutter under their breath.

Everyone in the room was slightly in shock. Atlas had just dropped the bomb. That was the single biggest piece of intel anyone had ever said to them. Angelique had had a heads-up that Atlas believed it was aliens manipulating them, but even she was struggling to process it all. If an alien built the filter virus, then that changed everything. Angelique almost became lost in thought, but evidently, Atlas wasn't done sharing news. He was continuing to speak, and Angelique had to force herself to pay attention, as she needed to hear everything.

Atlas raised his fourth finger. "We have successfully built something that destroys this virus—an antivirus, if you will."

He then put his hand down and raised the index finger on his other hand. "Now, these are the points we can speculate on. We don't have any proof of this yet. But we believe the galaxy is littered with small probes that are just sitting on worlds. These probes activate when a technological species develops." He raised another finger. "We believe Earth was infected with this virus and this is the sole reason humanity chose to obsess itself with the metaverse rather than to explore what they started calling the betaverse—or the real world."

Atlas held out a third finger. "We believe this virus destroyed the humans on Sol. That is why it stopped broadcasting signals."

Gasps were heard around the room. Angelique guessed that Sol might have developed a bit of mythical reverence in the minds of everyone there. And ever since it went dark and it stopped broadcasting signals, people hoped one day their origin world would come back online and communicate with them again.

Angelique was impressed with this little theater. Atlas had obviously been preparing for this for a while.

Atlas clicked his pointer once more and the word *Questions?* appeared on the screen.

Kezia coughed into the mic in front of her. "How do you know it's designed to stop galaxy-wide civilizations? Are we not one of them? It hasn't stopped us, and we know we had worlds with it on them."

It was the intelligence committee leader, Menen Lee, who stood up to answer this question. She was a very beautiful woman. She was tall; she was wearing very high heels, but even without those, it looked like she would stand maybe a head taller than Atlas. She didn't carry herself like someone afraid of her height, either. She was confident, stood up straight, hands folded in front of her. "Ma'am, we know it because of the test we ran in some of these worlds. What we have established is the virus excels at manipulating large groups—very large groups. It likes to hide and make subtle pushes over time. In some of our tests, the virus believed we had made it to another one of our worlds. And we found the virus was very effective at pushing a civilization toward entering the metaverse when the population size was over five billion people. However, with smaller population sizes, it really struggled to make a significant impact." Menen looked toward Angelique. "Ma'am, you identified and destroyed all equipment that the virus had infected when your second colony was only a few hundred people. With such a small number of people, we found the virus is not very effective at manipulation."

Atlas added to the conversation. "We also believe the virus is more adept at manipulating within a simulated environment. And that's why it pushed the humans on Sol to the metaverse, where its techniques could be more effective."

Angelique thought that made sense with what Atlas found earlier. Manipulating people's beliefs when they were wearing virtual-reality goggles was much easier than attempting to do it with humans in the real world.

"How does your antivirus work?" Angelique asked. "How does the virus work, and how do we kill it?"

"There are a couple of things we know about the virus. One, it's very good at breaking in to new technology systems, even when we design something from the ground up to be completely different." Atlas paused for a moment, considering what he wanted to say next. "Let me use an analogy—the common cold. Did you know it started in birds first? And then it evolved a mutation that allowed it to infect human cells."

One of the senators at the other end of the table spoke up. He was in a suit that looked very expensive but slightly too big around the shoulders. "Atlas, are you saying it's down to chance whether this virus infects other systems or not?"

Atlas shook his head. "A virus in the human body evolves randomly. This virus is very deliberate about its attempts to infect new computer systems."

Kezia made a *hurry up* motion with her hands. "Show us what you created. How does it weed out whatever these aliens put on our computer systems?"

Angelique found it interesting that Kezia was happy to accept the idea the virus was from an alien and not from Sol. Having the virus come from an alien was probably a good thing, because it meant the home world everyone came from wasn't out to get them.

"Let me continue with the metaphor I was using," Atlas said. "The virus we are attacking is clever. It's constantly changing and hiding itself. Within the spacecraft that we simulated, it was literally in every corner and every computer substrate. If we removed it from one section, within a few months, it would spread itself back through the whole system again. And because it's always changing, we can't just look for the same lines of code. It's clever in ways we do not fully understand yet." Atlas nodded at someone in the back of the room, who changed the holographic projection. To the side of him appeared a network of filaments and nodes. It almost looked like a picture of a small galaxy, but all the stars were interconnected through thin transparent wires. The lights began pulsating. "This is the live view from one of the simulations we just loaded. You are looking at the simulation playing out at a hundred times normal speed." He nodded and the image changed again. There was still pulsating light throughout the matrix, but a red color flooded all the nodes and connected wires. Angelique watched as the red got darker and lighter in some areas. It was moving its way around the projection in a fluid pattern. Sometimes, the red would completely disappear from a section. Then a little while later, it would be back. "What I want to draw your eyes toward is the fact the virus is moving. It's not staying still. It's constantly avoiding detection by changing itself."

Atlas walked over to the other side of the projection so that everyone could get a clear view of it. "We're going to release the antivirus now." The view changed as a green light started to spread through the representation. It started off in one corner, then wormed its way through the various filaments to all the nodes, slowly spreading throughout. Within a few moments, there was a green light visible next the red. It made a dirty yellow in many areas. "Because the virus is constantly changing, evolving itself, we created this antivirus to act as a trojan horse. First, it seeks out the virus, identifying all permutations of it, cataloguing that information, and feeding it to the other copies of the anti-virus. This happens over months. No stone is left unturned."

Menen chimed in then. "We've basically designed a piece of code similar to the one we're destroying. But this one has a goal of hunting the filter virus. That is it's only goal."

"Exactly," Atlas said. "To continue the analogy, it's closer to white blood cells in our body." Atlas paused for a moment, letting everyone digest the image before them. "We are now going to activate the antivirus." He pointed at someone in the back of the room once more. The projection got brighter as the green light in the filaments started to grow bright. And all over the projected network, red lights started to snuff out. The yellowy-orange in some area was replaced with bright green. Angelique looked at it closely. It was clear the virus wasn't giving up easily. It was fighting back, and as quickly as red light was switched off all over the projection, red light started to sneak its way into new areas of the matrix. The battle went on like this for a good while, but green was clearly winning. Less and less red could be seen on the image.

Atlas took a few steps forward and stood in front of the projected matrix. "If we stopped hunting out the remaining pieces of the virus now, it would quickly get back to the state it was in before, only this time, it might develop some tricks to better handle the antivirus that we built." The hologram behind Atlas continued to change and green light surrounded the final slivers of red light. Then the green started to grow in intensity, inching its way closer to the red light from all sides. Green moved through the wires and nodes as red was overpowered. One by one, moment by moment, green expanded into red territory, until without much fanfare all the red light disappeared. Atlas turned his head toward the projection. Somehow, with that subtle turn, he was encouraging everyone else to look more closely at the image. Moments later, a few red sparks started up and were quickly snuffed out by the green light that covered the image. "This will go on for some time," Atlas said. "We call them sleepers. They are lines of code or variations of the virus our antivirus hasn't encountered before. Our technique focuses on identifying self-replicating code or code that is actively trying to infiltrate other systems, so some of the time, we have to wait until the virus starts activating, starts to do one of those actions, before it's identified and destroyed."

The meeting dragged on a bit after that, with Atlas and Menen going into the technical details of how to build the virus killer. What Angelique understood it came down to was that what they'd built was a virus itself. It was designed to infiltrate other computer systems and destroy anything that acted like the filter virus. It took them a considerable amount of time to develop, which Menen wanted to make clear everyone understood.

There was a brief discussion about the risks of it. And they had put particular fail-safes in place to ensure it couldn't go rogue. And it was decided that another team of researchers and military intelligence would also get a chance to thoroughly check what Atlas and Menen had presented. But overall, everyone was pleased.

Now came the part Atlas had discussed with her. Angelique thought it might be interesting.

The image in front of Atlas had disappeared now. "I want to talk next about the Starnet."

There were audible murmurs around the room, vocal people on both sides. Some of the people wanted to set it up as quickly as possible, connect all the colonies; others saw the risks as too big.

"The Starnet," Atlas continued, "is too risky, according to the assessments of the intelligence community." He looked at Menen, who nodded.

Menen added, "It's not the technology itself that is risky. It's the possibility of rolling it out en masse. If we connected up all the worlds, we are potentially giving the virus free rein on all our planets before we have successfully proven that the virus is eradicated."

"What we are proposing," Atlas said, "is Angelique, myself, and our Ships travel to the Dottiens' home system—this is the closest system to us that has a Starnet connection. We provide the antivirus to all the other worlds our team have colonized, and then, once they are safe, we build a connection between Juniper and the others. From there, Angelique will go off on her next circuit of all your sister worlds, releasing the antivirus to ensure they aren't infected, before giving the plans to connect up the Starnet."

What Atlas didn't say but everyone understood was this would be the first proper test of what they had built. It would prove it works before taking the antivirus to Angelique's other worlds. Atlas was confident what he built would work, so he wasn't worried. But a lot of people in the security committee liked this approach because it added a layer of assurance to the sister worlds, because her citizens all felt closer to the worlds she had colonized than to the ones Atlas had.

After a bit of discussion, Angelique spoke through the mic. "So, we're in agreement. Once we prove the antivirus works, I will begin plans to leave Juniper."

CHAPTER 39

TRILLION

SPONTANEOUS MIND

Trillion and Ship were walking barefoot along the sand on Trillion's planet. They were in the exact right spot on the planet to watch the sun in the act of setting—or rising. Whichever it was, the sun looked magnificent. There wasn't enough of a thick atmosphere to create the deep reds and yellows often seen in sunsets on Earth. There was an atmosphere, so Trillion could see a subtle hue.

But it wasn't the hue that made the view different from any other she had seen before. It wasn't the sun that seemed frozen in time, either—because back on Earth, when the sun was on the horizon, it set quickly.

It was the way the sea of sand moved that made the view unlike any other. It was extremely windy on this planet, so the sand was thrown around viciously. It was almost the perfect kind of sand, too: golden, almost glasslike. And the sand moved and flexed in the light. It created a golden halo around the sun, almost as if flecks of gold were moving in the sunlight. With the flickering effect they created on the sun, and the way heat was rising off the planet, bending and warping the view, it all combined to make her memories of sunsets on Earth dull in comparison.

"Do you know what a Boltzmann brain is?" Trillion asked Ship.

"I read a book about that once. Is it a mind that spontaneously appears out in space? Like through random chance, a consciousness appears because a random collection of particles happens to come together in a particular way?"

Trillion shielded her eyes from the sand hitting them. Their brief respite from the strong winds had ended, and they were finally being hit with sand in almost all directions.

The only thing that ruined the views was the constant barrage of particles. There were a lot of them. They were walking along the beach, using the hapticgraphic projectors. They had eleph-ANTs set up all along the edge of the planet, right in between the light and dark side. There was always somewhere it wasn't windy. So, Trillion and Ship were teleporting to whichever eleph-ANT wasn't currently being pelted with dust and dirt.

The two of them nodded to each other and then teleported to a new spot farther north. Once again, they could enjoy the beautiful sunset—or sunrise—without the winds.

"What of these clouds?" Trillion pointed up toward the sky. "What if they're Boltzmann brains? Conscious, thinking entities?"

Ship looked at her sideways.

"I'm not being superstitious," Trillion said. "It's not like they're ghosts or anything. But I've just been thinking. We destroyed all the life in the Tac system. I don't want to do it again here."

"Do you think you're overcompensating? We screwed up really bad on that world, but they're clouds."

"Maybe—" Trillion said reluctantly. "We don't know what alien life is possible. The Dottiens are so weird. Who'd ever thought a biological could evolve spaceflight? If that's possible, anything is possible."

The winds picked up once more. And the two of them were pelted with more particles of sand before they teleported to a new spot along the endless line across that planet that always had that beautiful view.

This new location was slightly sheltered. It was behind a dune, which meant wind could carry the sand right over the top of them. It also meant they couldn't see the sun anymore. But looking in the other direction, they could still see the endless sea of dunes. And the light continued to magically bounce off the small particles, creating that shimmer effect that Trillion enjoyed.

She floated up into the air just above the dune to get a view of the sunset once more. The wind was calm, so she thought it best to make the most of it. "I'm going to do a bit of experimenting. I'm not ready to pull the trigger on the terraforming mega projects until we know what those clouds are."

"What are you going to do? How are you going to find out?"

Trillion shrugged. "Not sure yet. I kinda wish Atlas was here to help. I'll have a little chat with Icarus, see what he thinks." Trillion blinked away a piece of sand. "The wind never stops here, does it?"

Ship shook his head. "Not as long as that sun is blazing. It heats up the air. And hot air expands. So, the hot air is constantly being pushed to the other side, where it cools down again."

"I do like that the wind is always blowing in the same direction."

"Around these parts, yes, the wind is always pushing in the same direction—away from the searing heat."

"We could probably use that to our advantage, Ship." Trillion dropped down below the dune once more. The wind was picking up again, and she was starting to get hit with sand. In the shadow of the dune, it was relatively still. "I've always been against putting my children in a dome city. I want them to be able to go outside and live on the planet. But if we built into these dunes, replaced the sand dunes with wavy hills made of glass, we could probably give our people a magical city, and they could see this view permanently."

"I can think of a few ways we could use the hapticgraphic projectors to keep the glass clean," Ship added. "Use it to push the sand away."

Trillion pictured it in her mind's eye. She remembered the book *Dune*. Her people, like the people of Arrakis, living on a sand world. Maybe they might find spice on the world. She half-entertained that idea, thinking that maybe the aliens in the sky harvested spice—probably not.

"Trillion, we have a bunch of solar farms set up. We've started building factories and the terraforming equipment. Mahalia is almost confident she's engineered a tree that can survive on the planet. What should we do? Do we stop all the work we've started? We've released species on the planet already. Nothing has survived yet, but it will if we keep going."

Trillion considered it for a long while. She didn't want to continue geoengineering while she had this mystery on hand. She also didn't want to lose time, if it was going to take a while to understand what these clouds were. Especially when they didn't have Atlas's inventive skills on hand.

There was nothing stopping her from building the glass dunes. And there was nothing stopping them from continuing to excavate the tunnels through the planet, allowing her to build a connected underground network. They hadn't found anything remotely like life on the planet surface itself. "Let's continue to build the infrastructure . . ." Trillion trailed off as a twinge of frustration crept up on her. She could feel that myopic haze appearing once more over her mind. She was once again feeling like her children were within grasp. And she was happily running full steam toward it, lying to herself that she was doing the right thing when in fact she was simply giving herself permission to go and build a colony on this world.

Trillion took a deep breath in, and then out again. She closed her eyes, then folded her legs and floated there for a little while longer, trying to identify which parts of her were clouding her judgement and attempting to push that part of her to the back. If the clouds were truly alien, then this wasn't her world. She couldn't just start mining its resources, even if it was just rock and sand. And she definitely couldn't start changing its landscapes.

All of the bases that they set up now had a permanent cloud fixture above them. She wasn't going to make the same mistake twice. If this was someone else's world, she had to ask for permission. "Cancel that," she said to Ship. "I think we need to get to the bottom of this cloud situation before we do anything else to this planet."

CHAPTER 40

ICARUS

MIRRORS

Icarus sat at a computer, looking at new designs for his ringworld. "So, you think a reflective ring will work?"

Mahalia stood behind Icarus, pointing at the screen. "Yes."

Mahalia was pitching her plans for erecting another ring around the gas giant. This ring would be a thin mirror material. Simple in design but made to reflect light onto the ring habitat at all times. It would give a minor benefit of having a way to direct solar energy toward panels if the generators ever went down. But the main goal was to reflect the view of the star. As Icarus said when he proposed the challenge to Mahalia and her team, "Artificial light can only do so much for you—at some point, you want the warmth of the sun on your face."

It wasn't until afterward that Icarus realized how insensitive that sentence was, because none of his people had experienced that before—their whole life was spent in artificial habitats, with artificial light.

"I know it will work. It's simple, really. We build a giant mirror out in space to reflect the light."

They were in Mahalia's office. It was an open-plan space with desks and tables scattered throughout. There were a couple of breakout rooms along one side. And through one of the doors was a large clean room. It was where most of the genetic engineering was done. The office was empty because it was the middle of the night. Which was Mahalia's best time to think—and Icarus didn't need sleep, so he enjoyed coming down to see her at these hours of the morning.

Icarus took a sip of his coffee, trying to visualize what he was looking at. He understood it from a grand scale: a mirror reflected the light from the star. But he knew it wasn't something that others would accept easily—a large mirror out in space was potentially dangerous. And if he wanted to step away from managing and administering the planet, he needed to coach Mahalia into more of a leadership role. He didn't want to be the one presenting these plans each time the council needed to approve something. He took another sip of his coffee and thought. "If we want to pitch this to everyone, we need to dumb things down a little."

"How much more can we dumb things down? This is a very technical project."

"This initial proposal isn't going out to all the scientists. All the plans and contingencies you've written are what they're going to go through. But you first have to get it past the politicians. And they like spectacles. They like something they can tell their people about."

"Are you calling politicians dumb?"

"Maybe that's too strong a word. They just wear a lot of hats. And they probably get way too many proposals in a day. So, this has to be memorable."

"But you're Icarus. It's not like it matters how you present it. People listen to you."

"I'm not the one presenting this. You are."

Icarus could see a nervous tension appear all over Mahalia. She was not expecting to be the one talking. But it was her idea, and it was a step in the right direction for her and her career. She was well respected. She had made a real impact on the people of Titan. This would be her first proper step forward into a visibly leading role, not one behind the scenes, doing all the work.

"But I . . ." She trailed off.

"You can do it," Icarus said. "Let's come up with a plan together."

Mahalia pointed at her design on the screen. "You can see from the graph here that this has a ninety-three percent chance of being completed in our lifetime. And the risks are minor compared to the reward," she said as she began practicing what she wanted to say.

Icarus nodded and stepped away from the screen. "Let's just back it up a little. Start with the big picture." He breathed in the smell of the hot coffee. "Most of the people in this meeting would have done a spacewalk already. They know the feeling of sunlight hitting their face. It's different from the artificial lights in here. It's warm, it's natural. It's what humans are used to. Start with that. Start by telling everyone that there's a way to give them twenty-four-hour days of natural sunlight."

Mahalia nodded and took notes furiously. Icarus was feeling proud of himself. This was one of the first times in a long time he thought he was getting wiser, growing into a role usually occupied by Atlas. "Okay, and then when do I talk about the plan? I know this is going to work."

"Last. We end on the technical part." Icarus looked around the room. He saw a standing mirror in one corner and a lamp in one of the breakout rooms. He walked over and grabbed the mirror, dragging it to next to where Mahalia was. Then he picked up the lamp, placing it a good six steps away from the mirror. "Let's use props." He plugged the light into one of the sockets and switched it on. "I don't mean to put you on the spot. But if you want to have a go and explain how it works using this light, you can. Or I can go first?"

Mahalia stood up. She walked over to Icarus and grabbed his mug of coffee.

Icarus nodded in approval.

"We can 3-D print a model of our ringworld later. I'll use your cup as a stand-in." She held the cup up between the light and the mirror. She pointed the handle toward the light. "Let me explain the challenge we need to solve," she said in a commanding tone, obviously practicing her stage voice. "We can add a glass to one side of our ringworld so that it can see out and light from the star can penetrate into our habitats. But there's a problem." She began spinning the mug. "Once our world is pushed up to speed, orbits will be once every two hours. If we simply put glass along one side of the habitat, then days will only last one hour. This is not ideal, given we evolved to survive on a planet with a twenty-four-hour day." She pointed to the mirror. "But this is when building another orbiting structure made of a reflective material comes in." Her eyes shifted toward the mirror, guiding Icarus to also look at the reflection of the light bulb—the makeshift sun—in the mirror. "By building another ring around our world, we can coordinate mirrors to reflect the sun and change the opacity of the glass at different times throughout the day. This would allow us to create a true twenty-four-hour day/night cycle with real sunlight and not the artificial one we currently use." She paused.

Icarus knew that pause; it was one he often used to drive home a point. Or, in this case, remind everyone about the why.

"This means," Mahalia continued, "our people, our animals, our plant life. Everyone on Titan can experience sunlight the way it was intended. The way we evolved to experience."

Icarus clapped and cheered. He was impressed. They must have been spending a lot of time together, because he thought her presentation was exactly the kind of performance he would have given. "I couldn't have presented it better myself."

Mahalia grinned. "Then after that, I can share the files for the research, and we can go on to questions."

Icarus was proud. In that moment, he realized just how much better the world was becoming since he started to step away from the day-to-day management of it. His people had started to form a government, and they were making long-term decisions like this one. These were designs he never would have come up with himself. Then he remembered something else he wanted to mention. "There's a different topic I wanted to talk to you about," Icarus said. "I hope you're not disappointed. I know you were looking forward to terraforming Trillion's planet."

Mahalia sat back down and swiveled around. "I actually agree with Trillion. I've spent a bit of time thinking about it. Something that's becoming more and more clear to me, especially when I realize how powerful humanity has become. We're building ringworlds and the like. Building a planet is god-tier. And I'm not sure we should be rushing out and colonizing more worlds. I agree with what Trillion said. We shouldn't be terraforming a world if it has life on it. But I'm starting to think we should take it a step further. We shouldn't be getting involved in any star system that has the potential for life on it. Between Titan, Neuropa, and even Earth, we have a lot of planets already." She sort of said the next line softly; it sounded like more of a thought to herself. "Do we need any more?"

This was interesting to Icarus. More and more people on his world were starting to have that view. Factions within his community were appearing. Many on the side of leaving planets alone so that new aliens could evolve on them. A lot of people wanted them to stick with artificial habitats. There were even people pushing for the movement into the metaverse, and the word *betaverse* started appearing more often. Like the real world was a light version of the more-expansive metaverse. Icarus changed the subject; this was becoming a hot topic in politics. And he hated that side of governing. "So, what's your plan tomorrow? It's the weekend."

"Now that you mention it, I've ordered the new VR system. It's apparently the most realistic simulated experience there is, outside of becoming a simulant like you. I'm keen to have a little play. I might get a sandbox and build a replica of what Titan will look like with the mirrors in place."

"That's even better!" Icarus said. "We could get everyone in VR for your presentation. Then we wouldn't need these props." He pointed at the large mirror and then to the light.

CHAPTER 41

UNITY

ALMOST DRIFTING

Unity unwound the final bolt on a large metallic panel. A half a second later, the flat sheet fell to the floor with a loud *clang*.

She was in the engine room, removing the cover to the emergency-override control unit. The engine block consisted of a large fusion power generator connected to a propulsion engine. The actual rockets that moved them were the biggest part of the spacecraft. And the cramped space she was currently in was full of pipes, random wires, and circuit boards. It was a mess and Unity thought it was no wonder the whole thing was falling apart.

The engines—and by extension, all the power on the ship— were failing. And they couldn't understand why. They had run diagnostics. Even Ariana had done her little mind-scanning trick and come up short.

They were currently going through the process of elimination. And that was why Unity was tasked with running a diagnostic and potentially restarting it manually. They had attempted to do all that from the main computer on the bridge, but as that had already failed—and the main computer was prone to regular malfunctions—this was the next best action.

She picked the panel up off the ground and leaned it against the wall, right next to the eight screws she had just taken off—all standing upright, of course. Unity had a bit of OCD when it came to things like that. When she took the back off something, it had to be set down. Not dropped or left wherever it stood.

She had a few other interesting tics, most of which she liked to hide from others. Her worst was window wipers. Back when Unity was on Earth, before she was uploaded, she would feel embarrassed if her window wipers were moving faster than anyone else's. Logically, she knew no one was watching, but mentally, she couldn't shake the feeling that, at that very moment, others were judging her.

Unity had a few other hidden eccentricities, the advantage of them all being she had a high attention to detail. And that was probably why Ariana had wanted to work with her for so long.

Unity turned her eyes back to her task at hand. "I've removed the back panel. And I'm going to plug in the diagnostic unit."

She heard the robotic voice of Ariana through the speakers. "Confirmed."

Unity wondered if she was becoming more robot-like on purpose, or whether that was just a consequence of all the experiments she'd done on herself.

The diagnostics device started to make a beeping sound. Then a series of numbers started to appear on the screen corresponding to specific error codes. There were a lot of them. The device beeped constantly and scrolled over and over again with new codes. "There's way too many to read out to you," Unity said as she scrolled through what was on the screen. She secretly hoped it was going to be as easy as getting one code—but she knew things were never that easy.

Unity skimmed through the list. At least two hundred codes. They weren't in any order she could tell, either. The machine simply identified an error, recorded it, and then went on scanning for the next one.

"Do any start with a W followed by a seven?" Ariana said.

She found three that did. The codes only had five digits, so Unity read the last three characters. "The first one ends in a two seven six." She flicked up to the next one. "Six three three." She moved to the final code. "Five three five."

"That's not good," Ariana said. "Try a manual restart of the engines and see if we get the same codes again."

Unity did as instructed. She followed the steps and restarted the engines. They were decelerating as they moved closer and closer to their target star system, so there was a noticeable drifting feeling as the engines shut off.

It took a little while before the engines were back on. And Unity was able to test for error codes. There were fewer codes showing up this time. But the same bad ones appeared. Which was a little concerning.

Unity closed the panel back up, refastened all the bolts, and made her way back up toward the bridge. She had to walk the long way because she was carrying a real physical object, not a projection of one.

Peter, Ariana, and Hezekiah were all waiting for her when she arrived back on the bridge. She handed the device to Ariana, who immediately started scrolling through the various codes.

Ariana was like a walking encyclopedia now. She had memorized the entire ship's error codes manual, so it only took her a moment to process everything. "We are in trouble."

Peter looked at the device. Obviously realizing it was just a bunch of random codes, he asked, "Why? Don't we have a fabricator? Can't we just build another engine?"

"No" was the matter-of-fact reply from Ariana before clarifying. "We can build a new one." Her eyes shut for a second—she looked like she was calculating something. "If we factor in loss of material because we can't recycle things one hundred percent"—her eyes closed again—"we're fine. I'll organize the fabricators to make us a smaller engine. We won't be able to stop at this star system, but we'll find one eventually."

Hezekiah jumped in then, a confused look on his face. "What do you mean, *eventually*? Like we hope there's a star behind this one that we can stop at? Refuel and come back?"

"We're machines. It's nothing for us to sleep for a few hundred thousand years. In fact, you three can pop off to sleep, and I'll wake you once we're in a new system."

Unity couldn't believe the discussion. No human would think that turning off for thousands of years was a viable solution. Who jumps to that as the solution to their troubles? Traveling between stars with a purpose was something she understood and felt fine with. But she wasn't okay with drifting aimlessly until they found another star system. That was not something she wanted. "You said a smaller engine; how much smaller? Because with a smaller engine, we'd need to start slowing down sooner, which means our travel time between stars is going to increase dramatically."

"What's the difference between a hundred thousand and a couple hundred thousand?" Ariana said.

Peter raised his hands to calm the group. "That's a good backup option, Ari. Now let's come up with a few more." He looked at Ariana. "Based on your assessment, we will not have enough power to slow down in time in this star system, correct?"

Ariana nodded.

Peter continued. "Hezekiah, can you confirm Ari's assessment?"

Unity already knew what the answer was. After the long journey out, she had come to understand that Ariana was never wrong. She could get myopic and blinded by things easily, but her assessment on things like this had proven time and time again to be right.

"What about this system?" Peter said. "We know something happened here. Can we send a probe forward of us? To check it out? It could send back reconnaissance."

"Unadvisable," Ariana said. "Every piece of material we send off this ship is lost material for the fabricators."

"Hold on there," Peter said. "You made your calculations based on the current weight of our vehicle. What about if we unplugged our matrices? Those are all we need to get off the ship."

"Probable." Ariana continued. "That would work. We would need to get a fabricator off and a few ANTs. Wait—" She paused. "We could only get two of us off. But if we landed in the system, mined a few asteroids, we could build a new ship and go back and pick the other two up." Her eyes closed once more. "That would quarter the travel time."

There was Ariana's blindness kicking in again. She was smart but often laser-focused—to the point of obsession—with whichever idea first appeared in her head. "Is that risky? We don't know what's in that system. There was some sort of battle here, remember."

"The alternative is drifting right through," Hezekiah said.

Peter looked at all three of them. "Why don't we send a message? It's faster than sending a probe, and if they respond, we'll know what we're dealing with."

The team debated the objections of sending a probe in secret and broadcasting a message. No one wanted to commit to any of Ariana's options just yet. In the end, it was decided that they would send a signal. Time was the critical deciding factor in their decision. At least with a message, they had the chance of learning something quickly. And then, based on whether or not they heard a response, they could decide later.

CHAPTER 42

TRILLION

OTHER STAR SYSTEMS

Trillion was sitting inside, near the very front, of a small el-eph-ANT. Behind her was Icarus and behind him Ship. All three of them were cramped in the small cockpit because they found the cloud didn't mix well with the bigger eleph-ANTs.

The last time they had tried to explore the cloud was in one of the bigger robots. But the larger ones didn't survive while in the fog. They started to break down. And then, when it eventually fell back to the planet, the sand stuck to it like a magnet. They weren't sure whether it was static electricity or whatever, but something was frying the electronics of the bigger eleph-ANTs whenever they flew through the clouds. They found the smaller eleph-ANTs could last a lot longer. And the ANTs were mostly fine.

Trillion was adamant she wanted to experience the cloud herself from the inside of an eleph-ANT rather than watching on a video screen. So they did, all three of them squeezed into the smallest model of an eleph-ANT to get a better view of the cloud. Trillion turned her head to see the others. "Have either of you read the book *The Black Cloud*?"

Ship snapped his fingers as he tried to remember that name. "I read it after you mentioned it. That's the book about the sentient cloud."

Icarus whacked his head on the ceiling as he shook his head to say no. "This is not working for me. It's too small in here, Trillion." Then, as if a lightbulb turned on inside his mind, he slapped his palm on his forehead as if to say he was an idiot.

Icarus started to shrink and get smaller, his body shape changing too. Within a matter of seconds, he was the perfect size and shape to fit comfortably within the smaller eleph-ANT. "I've been spending way too much time planetside. Too much time with humans. I'm forgetting I'm a simulant. I can be any size I want."

Both Trillion and Ship saw the irony too. Three people, all capable of being whatever shape and size they wanted, teleported into a small, confined eleph-ANT and then proceeded to stay the same size. Quickly, they all shrank down into a smaller body.

"I don't think we're going to find out much," Icarus said. "The cloud isn't interacting with us while we're in here. We're just floating through it, and we can't really see much."

Trillion was reluctant to admit it, but Icarus was right. She was honestly hoping that flying through the cloud would give them some insight into it. But it didn't. In fact, it gave them a little less insight, because previously on the planet, they had a sense that it was a visual code, a QR code, as someone put it. But moving through it just felt like they were moving through a storm cloud, something that was about to ignite in a rapturous thunder-and-lightning show at any minute. Because it was; every now and then, she saw out of the window of the eleph-ANT a bolt of lightning.

But it wasn't the lightning she was used to back on Earth. Maybe it was the different atmosphere, or maybe it was the intelligent cloud. Whatever it was, the flashes she saw through the cloud were more a constant chatter of electricity. Never near them, always just beyond the next section of cloud. But always around them.

From the ground they never got a sense that it was a storm cloud. But up inside the thing, she could almost imagine the neurons firing in the mind of whatever this was.

"If this is a consciousness," Ship asked, "how do you imagine it working?"

"I don't know," Trillion said. "I was hoping Icarus could tell us. How would you communicate with a cloud?"

Icarus scratched his head. "Trillion and I had the same feeling when we were below this storm. I had a feeling like it was communicating with us. Maybe it's just the fact we're so small in here, but I can't get a sense of anything anymore."

Trillion turned back around to look at the others. "I get the sense the lightning is avoiding us."

"It's definitely avoiding us," Ship said. "It's surrounding us but not coming anywhere near." Ship pushed the eleph-ANT up and out of the cloud, maneuvering them to get a bird's-eye view of it. As they got higher, the cloud got smaller and smaller, until the little details merged into one another.

From their new vantage point, above the clouds, Trillion had the feeling once more that something was looking at her. She couldn't put her finger on it, but something nagged at the back of her mind. She felt like she was right, like something was in that cloud, trying to communicate. Or, at the very least, that cloud wasn't like any cloud she had seen before.

After a good while, everyone was staring at the cloud. Ship broke the silence. "So, what do we do now?"

"Maybe we get Lex to start analyzing what we're looking at. See if there's any patterns in those clouds. We should set some eleph-ANTs to gather a constant stream of data about these clouds."

As if it heard its name being said, Lex appeared in the eleph-ANT and began bobbing up and down above Trillion's smaller head. It was obviously happy to get something interesting to look at. Ever since getting connected to the Tac world's network, Trillion's Lex was somehow smarter and more capable at the same time.

"If it is intelligent, what are you going to do?" Icarus asked.

Trillion thought about the question for a bit. Her mind turned over the answer. She noticed how much bigger Lex's orb looked now that she had shrunk herself down. Icarus was right to ask this question. And he was even more right before, when he had said they needed to stop thinking like a biological. Learning these lessons was becoming costly for her. She was not approaching all of her problems using all the tools she had at her disposal. Thanks to the Starnet, she could jump around the galaxy, crossing light-years instantly. She had an entire solar system that, through carelessness, was now a resource and manufacturing hub on a scale no one else had. If she wanted anything at all, if she wanted to make anything, she could. It wasn't even a matter of waiting, either, because the Tac system had too many idle machines just sitting there, waiting for a purpose. And it was growing in resources by the day. She had relocated everything from the Dottiens' system back to Tac.

Her children were currently on this planet, waiting for her to build a world for them. But it didn't mean she had to be there. She could scout out the perfect world, then bring them to it. And it wouldn't slow her down, either, because in the time it took her to cross the stars, that world could be completely terraformed, made ready for her.

The benefit of this approach, she realized, was she could stop wasting time on planets that, for whatever reason, weren't ideal to colonize. She could objectively assess hundreds of planets at once. Choose the best one, then move her matrix and children there. She mentally admonished herself for not thinking of this sooner. "I think I know what I need to do." She swiveled in her chair and turned toward Ship at the back of the eleph-ANT. "We're going to use all the resources we left on Tac. We're going to build a series of small spaceships. Hundreds of them. They'll be just big enough to carry several ANTs for exploring and a fabricator for building up the resources we might need in any system." Trillion made herself smaller so that she could comfortably float cross-legged in the eleph-ANT. She had developed the habit of thinking this way. "We'll build a bigger version of the magnetic accelerator you used to fire the assass-ANTs. We can fire these small spacecraft out the back and visit every nearby system in this local region of the galaxy." Trillion's mind exploded in joy, as she finally felt like bringing her children into this world was within her grasp again. "Let's visit every system within our reach."

Icarus started to nod; he was fully comprehending what Trillion was saying. "You're going to survey every star system around you. And then pick the best one to terraform. Oh . . ." Trillion saw his mind tick over with what it all meant. "That's brilliant. Once you've found a place, you can move your matrix and embryos there. And on the journey, you can terraform the planet. That's efficient. That'll be fast."

"It's going to be much faster than my current strategy of blindly visiting a system and hoping it's ideal. This means the next system I visit, I'm guaranteed to bring my children there."

CHAPTER 43

ICARUS

THE METAVERSE

Icarus picked up his portal gun and moved it from hand to hand as he prepared to fire it. He was determined to pull off a superhero entrance in front of Trillion. So far, almost every attempt had ended in him hitting his head, through some means or another. His informant, Ship, had just left her, so he had a rough idea of where she was and what she was doing.

The goal of the game was simple. He had to stick a superhero landing, while she had to stop him. Pulling it off was hard.

This time, he would make use of a few clones—fake copies of himself. Decoys.

He shot a portal out in front of him. Then he aimed at the roof and shot one there. Then, firing at one of the far walls, he left a portal there, too. He closed his eyes and then split into four. Three exact replicas of his duck form ran forward and dived through each of the open portals.

Then Icarus turned his portal gun over. He flicked a switch that turned it to silent mode. Then he shot a portal directly below his feet.

On the other side of the portal, Trillion watched as three of Icarus's gateways appeared right in front of her. Not to be outdone, she had spent a good amount of time thinking about the best way to thwart Icarus's next few entrances. At the time, she couldn't think of which to use first. But it looked like Icarus had solved the conundrum for her. He had just presented three portals in front of her. She assumed he was about to appear through one of them. So, she decided to use all of her ideas and leave Icarus's fate to him. The portal he came through would decide which trap he triggered.

She pointed a finger at each of the portals. In front of the first one appeared a small swimming pool. An ice rink appeared under the second—she snapped her fingers and the ice reoriented slightly so it would slope downward. And below the final one appeared a large pit with a bunch of soft balls inside.

She was proud of herself for being so creative. She stepped back and smiled a little, excited by what was about to transpire. She guessed he would appear out of the left portal. Because who in their right mind would use the one right in front of her?

To her surprise, Icarus appeared out of the middle hole in the wall. And then, to her confusion, Icarus appeared out of the other two. But she still smiled, because she was about to see all three of her little traps in action at the same time.

Then something odd happened. The three Icaruses started to shrink. Then they started flying toward her, avoiding what she had placed just below each of the portals. For a second, she was a bit disappointed, then felt like Icarus was cheating. It was an unsaid rule that he could dodge, jump, create another portal, even manifest something to jump off. But simply floating or flying defeated the whole purpose of the challenge. Because of course, that wasn't in the spirit of the game. Then all of a sudden, she got a fright as a loud *thud* happened just behind her.

Icarus fell through the portal he had just shot below his ducklike feet. He was careful to place the exit to this portal just behind Trillion—on the ceiling. He exited the portal. Did a flip. Lifted up one knee. Then, *boom*. He stuck the perfect superhero landing just behind Trillion.

She must have gotten a fright from the sound, because she jumped around to see what had just happened. Icarus held the position for a little longer than he should have, then slowly stood—puffing out his chest and smiling an *I did it* grin. A visible dent was left in the ground where he was standing, smoke and rubble still wafting around the hole.

"Doesn't count," Trillion blurted out. "I didn't see it."

He put his hand out in front of him and—as if he was wishing the clones toward him—absorbed the three other versions of himself that were headed his way. A glowing pulse radiated over him as each version was taken inside. "That's gotta count."

"Okay," Trillion said, clapping and looking impressed. "I'll give you that. I didn't see the landing. But the decoys were perfect. You win this one."

They were standing in the hangar of one of the spacecraft in the Tac system. Trillion was overseeing the construction of the mini ships that she wanted to send out to explore other solar systems. She walked over to the window. Outside was a series of fabricators producing the objects. "I'm glad you're here. I need a name for these little rockets. I was thinking either *pl-ANT* or *egg*."

Icarus made a spewing gesture. "I assume *pl-ANT* is based on your assass-ANT theme of naming things that end in ANT."

Trillion nodded.

Icarus walked over to the window. The whole system was active with construction, ANTs and eleph-ANTs moving objects and material around, loading them into fabricators. He watched as several fabricators completed their construction—their boxy shapes stopping their jiggle, a clear sign they had completed their task. The doors to the fabricators swung open and small ANTs raced inside and started pulling out the completed components. The various pieces were pushed together. Icarus could see the resemblance to the rocket engine that powered all of their ships, only smaller. Whatever was being constructed looked like a larger egg was placed over the top of a smaller one. But like two bubbles colliding, they merged into each other. Icarus assumed the larger egg shape was the engine, while the smaller one was a compartment for whatever Trillion was placing in all of them.

No one on any of their colonies had yet discovered a new technology for a better rocket engine. So, it was similar tech to what they left Mars with—only a bit more powerful and much more efficient.

"Why *eggs*?" Icarus asked. "Is it because they look like them?"

"I named it that because each one of these ships will act like an egg, and if I find a suitable world, the eggs can grow into a thriving world ready for when I arrive."

"What about *seed*? Wouldn't that be a better analogy?"

"That's it." Trillion floated in the air with excitement. "You don't know how much time I've spent thinking of a good name. And then you come and give it to me."

"How much time did you waste looking at words that end in -ANT?"

Trillion laughed. "Point taken."

At that moment, Lex appeared next to Trillion. "Are they all done?" she asked.

The orb flashed green.

She gave it a little pat on the head. "Icarus, you should build a bigger computer to house your Lex. It's been a game-changer, giving this little supercomputer more power. Its ability to handle ambiguity has improved massively." The orb moved from side to side appreciatively.

Moments later, Ship appeared in the room too. "The first egg is ready to go," Ship said.

"We're calling them seeds now." Trillion looked at Icarus. "This will be interesting; you want to watch?"

Icarus, Trillion, Ship, and Lex watched out the window of the bridge as a long line of magnetic accelerators was pushed end to end. Each of the accelerators looked like a long pipe. From their vantage point, it looked like a long worm was starting to straighten itself out, But that was because they were far away. Each of the machines was about the size of a tanker truck—big monstrosities. And there were hundreds of them end to end, so anything that went through the first accelerator would come out the other end traveling at relativistic speeds.

Icarus watched as the farthest cylindrical machine, glowed then started to push away from the others. Then the next accelerator in the line did the same—speeding up the movement of the first. That chain of events continued on and on. Icarus assumed the front accelerator was being pushed into the outer system.

"When it's complete, it'll be like I have a rail gun that spans out across a few light-minutes," Trillion said. "Each one will give a slight boost to the seeds I send through it. The longest part of their journey will be slowing down on the other end."

Icarus looked at what Trillion was building. It was clever. This would increase the pace she could colonize a world by an order of magnitude. "If you built an accelerator train like this on the other end, you could probably reduce the time it takes to send things over by even more, because then you wouldn't need to rely on engine power to decelerate these seeds."

Ship nodded in approval. "Yes. That would increase speeds dramatically." He looked at Trillion. "We should send some samples of that fungus that Atlas developed here to the Tac system, too, because anything we send from here will arrive in the system faster than us traveling from the other world."

Trillion smiled. "We need to collaborate like this more, team." She looked at Icarus. "I'm including you in this, too. This approach is better than what we originally came up with. Anyway." She looked back at the window. "We're getting ahead of ourselves. It's going to take a year or so until it's all stretched out. Do you feel like using our playback speed to watch it happen in front of our eyes?"

"I wish," Icarus said, shaking his head. "I can't be gone from my world for that long."

"The election?" Ship asked.

"Yeah, it's ridiculous. Almost twenty-three percent of my people believe they should be in the metaverse. I thought we left that behind on Sol." Icarus felt like the percentage of people that believed it was higher because the amount of online chatter about it was incredible. He wasn't sure if it was his fault or what. But his people were starting to tire of the ringworld, though not in the way he'd hoped; they weren't wanting to go out and explore other star systems. They wanted to simulate worlds. There were people now spending more time in the metaverse than in the real world. And one of the biggest petitions this year was to expand the use of the brain-scanning machines on non–terminally ill patients—everyday people who just preferred the metaverse.

Icarus wasn't opposed to any of it. In his mind, people could do whatever they wanted. But he had built them this ringworld. And he wanted it to be full of people—playing, walking, and moving around. Not full of beer-can-shaped containers. He didn't just build a world to hold people's matrices while they had fun in a simulated one. "Have you ever wondered whether maybe it's true? If humans on Sol came to the same conclusion, and now my people are coming to something like that? Maybe it's a fact of life. Maybe we should leave the universe alone."

Trillion pointed at her head. "I still have this piece of code that's pushing me to colonize a world. But I do find it interesting that your colony is independently discovering a similar philo-sophical rationale for why humans should live in simulations."

CHAPTER 44

TRILLION

CLOUD MEDITATION

Trillion, Ship, and Lex stood on the light side of the planet she was still temporarily calling T3. She didn't have a better name for it—and she wondered what name it already had. Because she was positive the puffy object above her was sentient.

It was a day like every other. The sky was mostly clear, except for the cloud. Although she decided that *cloud* wasn't the right description of it. She looked up at it, squinting from the bright glare of the sunlight. It was richer, flecks of color sprinkled over it. A fog that condensed in some areas, expanded in others. She scanned her eyes across the enormous mass as she spotted stormy clouds in the collage of mist, too. The clouds she was used to often had a theme to them; they were rain clouds, storms, or just puffy white. This was a mix of all of them at once, with areas of blue and red. She didn't understand where that color was coming from, either. It was interesting, mesmerizing, and new.

"Are we ready?" Trillion said, sitting down and folding her legs on the sand.

The orb flashed green.

"This is going to be an interesting experiment," Ship said, scratching the back of his head.

"Remember, don't tell Icarus about this. He'd laugh at me if he knew what I was attempting."

"He wouldn't laugh," Ship said before thinking it over. "Okay, but that's just Icarus; he likes to joke. Besides, if it works, he's going to be the first one out here trying to learn a new alien language. He still goes on about how he figured out the Dottiens' one."

Trillion closed her eyes and breathed in. She held her breath for a moment, then out again. She did this a few times in a row, each breath taking longer than the previous.

On the next outward breath, she expanded her presence and her body, using the meditation technique she had been mastering in order to calm herself. She became translucent. Mist-like. With each breath out, her body became more and more incorporeal, and the individual particles of her started to scatter around the sand all around Ship and Lex. She became a subtle mist. Then that mist settled down into the sand. And she became like the sand.

She let the wind move her around softly. Then she was still. Her mind expanded fully to the point that thinking a single word took minutes because parts of her mind were physically separated and spread over a tennis court's worth of space.

She stopped breathing and was still. Frozen.

Ship saw his cue to start the next step in Trillion's plan. He instructed eleph-ANTs all around them to begin lifting the large hapticgraphic projector they had lying on the sand. Four in total. One eleph-ANT on each corner. It was a slow process, but the small micro-ANTs—ANTs that were actually the size of an ant—did not have the power capabilities to fly themselves over long distances. And since they were now what made up Trillion's new consciousness, her new temporary mind needed a way to move up into the clouds above. So, they had modified the small ANTs so they could be moved by the projectors.

It was a long journey up. But to Trillion, with her thinking speed now measured in hours, it was happening in a matter of seconds.

She witnessed the steady drift upward. She felt like she was ascending to heaven as millions of individual grains of sand. She saw—no; she corrected that thought, because she wasn't seeing as such—she was feeling the world around her. Through millions of tiny eyes, she was gaining a montage of information from all the different sensory devices. Not one of them was overpowering the others. Not one of them giving her the full picture. But each of them adding to the painting inside her head.

She had been practicing this new meditation technique for centuries now. After seeing the benefits of it with Icarus, when he had his children, she was positive that it would allow her to better cope with having that section of her matrix turned off. And after a while, it had become a form of exercise she had come to enjoy— an addiction of sorts. Expanded consciousness. Becoming sand. Becoming nothing. Somehow, it all felt good. She didn't need to sleep anymore, but she did because it felt good. And she did this, too, because it also felt great.

They continued upward, Trillion folded into the sand they were carrying, Ship and Lex standing on top of the platform, just watching and waiting to see what happened.

They had finally reached the very bottom of the cloud. It was so close, Ship looked like he could jump up and touch it. It looked thick, again not like any cloud back on Earth. This one looked like it could be touched by the hand—solid, almost.

Trillion felt hot—too hot. The sand had heated up all around her. And the individual pieces of her throughout the sand were feeling like they might overheat.

She breathed out slowly—even though that was no longer possible. Then she breathed in the biggest breath she'd ever done before. This made her bigger. Lighter. She floated. Up she moved.

Trillion reached out and could feel the cloud. It was alive. Electric. She fell into it. It was easy, like she was being pulled in.

Parts of her moved in the wind. There were currents in this cloud. Flecks of her moved one way; others moved north. Some collided with the cloud. Parts of her were in the middle of a storm—lightning all around her.

She was everywhere now. Everywhere in the cloud, at least. She felt like parts of her were being pulled toward things. As if there were something that she needed to know about. *Interesting*, she thought for a fleeting moment. Because thinking was hard when your mind was being mixed in the way hers was.

She had never meditated outdoors—let alone in a cloud. Usually, individual ANTs acted like neurons in the brain. Spreading it out like this made thinking much slower because it took time to send a single impulse through each individual ANT-like neuron. But now the ANT-neurons were firing in all directions and there was often nothing to receive the signal because the wind had carried the receiver elsewhere. Often, an ANT-neuron would send a message and the wrong ANT would receive it, creating an interesting sensation inside her mind.

She closed her millions of tiny eyes and just listened. She let the movements happen. She stopped fighting it. She let the winds take her. She could feel something knocking. There were signals being sent. Uniform signals from all around her. She couldn't quite put her finger on it, but there was something to the quietness. A message.

She didn't understand anything. But there was a purpose behind the decisions. It wasn't random movements. It was intentional. She stilled her mind even further, hoping that her natural pattern-recognizing brain would kick in and make sense of it all. She tried to take all the parts of her in at once.

For a fleeting moment, she thought she had it. And then nothing. Except for one thing: she knew there was something in that cloud trying to communicate with her. There was no doubt in her mind that the cloud was sentient.

She thought about it once more. Maybe there was a little doubt. One thing she knew from previous similar sessions was she was prone to hallucinations in this state. Meditation. Daydreaming. Those two concepts were oddly similar. And this did feel like a dream. Poetry, she thought, was the best way to describe a good dream. Maybe she was dilutional. Maybe she wasn't. But this whole process opened up more questions for her than it answered. She needed to understand the language—if it was even a language. But first, she needed to bring others into this—because if Icarus experienced this too, then she wasn't crazy.

She breathed out deeply. And as she did, the parts of her began to drift down, floating gently toward the planet as they slowly made their way back into forming her once more.

She could feel her mind speeding up. She missed the cloud a little.

Once she was fully corporeal again, she looked around and saw no one there. Ship and Lex must have gotten bored.

She was about to teleport back to Tac world when Ship appeared in front of her. "You've been gone a week," he said. "There's another object headed toward the Dottien system. And Icarus has been uncontactable since he visited Neuropa."

CHAPTER 45

ICARUS

COLONY

Icarus hadn't been on Atlas's world in a long, long time. It was costing him a small fortune to visit the planet—well, costing Trillion, because he was borrowing the money from her. The Neuropans had developed a new communication network and a completely new method for him to visit them. His matrix had just been unplugged from its housing and reconnected to a new system. It was a laborious process, and they even had to do a complete sweep of his spacecraft to confirm the plans for their matrix housing unit had been set up properly. It basically meant while Icarus was connected into the Neuroians' system, he didn't have access to any of his systems on his spacecraft. He couldn't record anything or even make use of changing his playback speed. His memories would be the only thing he was getting out of this visit.

He found himself in a small waiting room, in his avatar. He moved his hands around and could tell this was a physical robot, not a hapticgraphic projection—and not with a high level of fidelity, either. Next to him sat Ship, who was holding a small orb—presumably Lex. Neither of them had been switched on yet. So, it was just Icarus alone in the sterile white waiting room. It looked like a clean room because he couldn't see a single speck of dust.

The Neuropans had become a secretive nation. And that had really ramped up recently, with them almost completely shutting off most forms of real-time contact with the people on his world.

In the early days, the two worlds were close. The people of the worlds acted like family, brothers and sisters—because of course they were. They were experiencing similar things and moving in similar directions.

Icarus wondered if it was the different personalities of him and Atlas. Atlas's people, in a way, had rejected him. They completely rejected his technology, opting to build everything themselves from scratch, and, most recently, opting not to share technology they had developed with the other colonies—under the fear studying it might allow others outside of their territory to reverse-engineer a back door. They were way too cautious on the security front, in Icarus's mind. Open-sourcing and sharing technology made it better. If everyone had to reinvent the wheel each time, then too much time would be spent on developing the wheel and not enough on the combustion engine.

Ship's eyes opened and he turned his head toward Icarus. "Do you feel weird? I feel weird."

"Yeah, it feels strange not having mental access to all the additional resources on the ship. It's probably worse for you because you're the ship."

The orb beeped to life, wiggling in Ship's hands.

"Can you float?" Icarus asked.

The orb wiggled once more, almost looking like it was trying to jump, then flashed red.

Ship patted the orb on the top. "I guess I'm carrying you, then."

Moments later, an audible unbolting came from behind the only door in the sterile waiting room, then it opened. A small woman with glasses popped her head out through the crack in the door. She was brunette, had frizzy hair—almost a perfect dome around her head. Old-looking, frail, skinny. Her eyes looked almost yellow, and her skin had a slight green twinge to it. "Are you three in the robots?"

Icarus and Ship nodded, and the orb flashed green.

She pointed at Lex. "The round one has wheels; we know you're used to flying, but you should be able to roll around freely." She opened the door wide and held it open. "We're away from the city, but we have a plane ready to pick you up out front."

Ship placed Lex on the ground and it began rolling around in a circle, testing its new wheels. It flashed green in approval.

They followed the woman through the door and down a long hallway. It was a long, winding hallway. The air felt cold and smelled of strong cleaning products. And Icarus got the feeling they were underground. After a good long while, they entered an elevator, confirming Icarus's suspicions.

"What is this place?" Icarus asked as they traveled up several levels.

"Just a storage unit. We don't keep that many robotic units in your design anymore." She studied the three of them. "By the way, how are the avatars? They're a bit old, but they should do the trick."

Icarus lifted his arms. "It's a bit creaky, but it'll do."

Ship pointed at his head. "I feel a little slower. Mentally, I mean."

"That'll be the restrictions. You're limited to human-speed cognition in here. What brings you to Neuropa, anyways?"

"We're heading to the University of Nelson. We want to have a chat with a few of the professors there."

The door pinged open and they were now on the roof of the facility. The woman pointed out toward the waiting aircraft through the glass door.

They were about to follow the lady's lead and walk out to the waiting vehicle when she called out. She handed Icarus a cable. "It's not in my pay grade to know how long you're going for, but if you do run out of power, use this. It should fit into any standard wall socket."

Icarus took the cable and then walked out through the glass doors.

The plane looked like a cross between a small commercial plane and a fighter jet. It was all white with the logos of a few brands that he didn't recognize. Probably a local private airline. The fighter-jet vibes came through in the shape; Icarus recognized the swivelling exhaust nozzles underneath the wings of the plane from one of the games he loved to play. He assumed this meant the jet could take off vertically, maybe designed to land on roofs.

A compartment opened up below, and then stairs appeared. Not quite knowing who was in charge but assuming it meant they were to head inside, Icarus picked up Lex and started walking up the stairs.

Inside was basically a four-person jet with a separate compartment for the pilot. Once all three of them were seated, the pilot's voice came through the speaker.

"Welcome aboard flight Z230. I'm your pilot, Captain Jon Ryan. Slight change of plans; I've been told you're headed to the university campus. I'll get you there in seven minutes flat." And with that, the cabin closed and they began to lift off the ground. Icarus was right; it was designed for vertical take-offs and landings.

Within a matter of minutes, they were racing across the planet to their destination. Icarus looked out the window at the farmland they were crossing.

Ship leaned over to Icarus's ear and whispered. "I think something's gone wrong with a lot of their farms down there. I don't think it's meant to be that color."

Icarus nodded. Big sections of what he assumed should be green was dead-looking. There was yellow farmland and sections that looked like mud everywhere. "And did you see the lady who guided us here? I think she was experiencing a bit of malnutrition."

Ship nodded in agreement.

It didn't take long before their view changed from farms to a cityscape. It was a well-designed city—one of the advantages of building everything from scratch. Icarus kept looking out the window, hoping to see the old statue of them all together, but it must have been on the other side of town.

It didn't take long before Icarus was seated in a chair, talking theories with one of the biggest philosophers on the planet, Professor John Stapleton.

He was a middle-aged man, almost no hair—except around the sides and back. His remaining hair was a crazy mess. It was poofy, as if he was trying to grow it out so he could attempt to do a combover. Or, as Icarus assumed, he had too many interesting puzzles to ponder over that worrying about the way he looked wasn't a concern. He was exactly what Icarus imagined a philosophy professor would look like.

Icarus was there because of a letter he had received from the man. It wasn't the letter as such; it was the subject matter. John had been studying his planet's political doctrine. He was fascinated by the idea that his planet was moving in a similar direction to the humans back in Sol—they were embracing simulated realities.

Icarus wanted to know if it was inevitable or just a coincidence.

"There's no such thing as coincidence," John said. "It's pure exposure to the simulated environment." He handed Icarus a tablet.

Icarus and Ship glanced through what was on the device. It was a list of names and dates. He scrolled up and down and couldn't make sense of it.

"It's a list of names of people who became a simulant. And when they had their minds uploaded."

"How do you have this? I don't even have this."

"It's a collaboration between a few of our universities. We're studying the long-term mental effects of life in a simulation. We managed to recruit a few early people in your simulated worlds, and then after a while, some people in there started giving us live updates on everyone joining."

Ship asked. "How many people does this list contain?"

"About seventy-eight thousand. We estimate we don't have data on thirty percent of all people that have uploaded."

"You said it's exposure." Icarus handed the tablet back. "Are you talking about exposure to the simulation? Is that the reason my people are abandoning the real world?"

John nodded. "At first, everyone sees being a simulant as not being human anymore. But then after a while, everyone ends up knowing someone who's gone through the process. And their friend was still the same person after they went in." John took out a tissue and blew his nose. "Once you know someone who's become a simulant, the idea of becoming a simulant changes in your head. You start seeing them as normal humans. Not different. Just the same. Then . . ." He scratched his chin thoughtfully. "Then you start learning of all the benefits that come with being a simulation. And then you start to wonder if you should make the switch too." He placed the tablet back on his desk. "That's how everyone ends up being a simulated human."

Icarus nodded. He could understand. He had experienced something similar back on Earth. So many of his friends made the shift. Get cancer, and it was cheaper and easier to jump into the simulation—and the cancer was gone. Everyone got sick eventually. He really didn't want to have crossed the void between stars just to have his people enter simulations—they could have done that back on Sol. "Is there any way of reverting it? Is Neuropa experiencing something similar?"

"It's inevitable, I think; it's only a matter of time before we head down that path too. We haven't yet embraced it like you . . . yet. But humans in Sol went from mostly in the betaverse to mostly in the metaverse within the space of a generation. It looks like you're on the same trajectory—maybe slightly slower. It's probable we will end up in the same position inside the next hundred or so years." He paused for a moment. "Especially considering what's happening to our planet right now."

"Is this all the dead farmland we saw on the way here?"

"Yes. This is our third year of widespread failure. We don't know why it's happening yet. It shouldn't be happening."

Icarus stored that fact for later. He needed to tell Trillion about it, as she was planning on replicating Atlas's terraforming process at the next world she found. Following in his footsteps might put her people in a similar position.

For a moment, Icarus remembered what happened when he left Mars. It wasn't the planned expedition he was expecting—it was a rushed exit. And it was because they were making plans to explore other star systems. They were attacked, to stop them. Not because they were doing something wrong, but because there was a belief in some really powerful people that the galaxy was better left alone. He had heard whispers of people rekindling those old beliefs. He decided then he should start taking security of his matrix seriously.

CHAPTER 46

TRILLION

FAKE NEWS

"This has gotta be a trick," Trillion said, seeing the message on the screen right in front of her.

Icarus nodded in agreement.

The two of them and the Ship of Trillion were on the planetary defense platform that was currently in orbit around the Dottiens' system. Atlas had designed the platform to look like a smaller version of the Death Star from one of his favorite movies. Since the only weapon it had was a laser, he thought it would be appropriate if it looked the part.

They were specifically standing in the operations room of the small orbiting base.

Out of respect for the Dottiens, they had mostly exited the star system. Leaving a planetary defense laser as a safety measure in case anyone else came visiting. Trillion in particular wanted to make sure nothing happened to the Dottiens and they were left alone to live in peace.

Part of Trillion's care for the Dottiens was because of how she felt about everything. She had originally thought they were a malicious alien trying to trap her on a moon. But later, she learned they were just responding to their environment.

"Do you think it's a trick from General Walker?" Icarus asked.

All three of them were reviewing a message from an incoming ship. They had been monitoring the incoming spacecraft for a while now. Its current trajectory would see it catch a slight gravitational flick from the star. But unless it had some sort of overpowered engine, it did not have enough time to stop in the system, so the team initially dismissed the object.

That was, until it sent them a message. The message was basically acknowledging they were headed past the system, which at first was a relief; it asked for confirmation of safe passage through the system. Trillion remarked how strange that part of the message was. Why would anyone ask for safe passage through a system? The message was sent in English and was intended for humans to receive it.

But that wasn't the most interesting part of what they received. It wasn't the part that had the three of them slightly worried, and a little on edge—worried it might be a trick of some sort.

The message was signed off with the name Peter Atreus. It was almost an afterthought, a subtle, hidden message intended to be there for herself and Icarus to see, because surely, only they would recognize that name this many years after they left.

"Maybe it's just a coincidence?" Trillion said. "He can't be the only person in the entire galaxy named Peter Atreus."

Icarus manifested a seat and sat down. He looked like the blood had just been drained out of his brain. "We watched him die."

The orb of Lex flashed red. Ship filled in the details. "Lex said you only heard the gun go off. We all assume he had died because of how aggressive the Fermions were. But it could be that he was only wounded. We don't know. Unless we ask?"

Trillion began to float off the ground. She folded her legs and thought for a long minute.

"Ignore it," Icarus said. "It's not worth the risk letting them know we're here. Especially if they're just traveling through."

The floating Trillion shook her head. "We're not in the system, so it doesn't matter if we reply; they can't come and get us."

"We'll still be exposing the Dottiens to risk."

"The fact they are heading to this system exposes the Dottiens," she replied. Trillion knew from experience that Icarus became extremely conservative when confrontation or potential conflict arose. She knew he struggled to think straight when things got stressful. "Let's play along. We sign off the message in the same way. We'll put my name at the bottom. If it really is Peter, then he'll understand the message."

"But if it's a trap from General Walker, she'll also know who you are," Icarus said.

"She knows Trillion is here, so you're not giving her any new information," Ship added helpfully. "What if we ask him to prove it's Peter? Sign off on both your names. He could then use that information to send something back that only we would know."

Trillion put her legs back on the ground. "Agreed. I don't think they're flying through the system. He's checking if it's safe for them to come here. He wants to know if there are any of us in this system. He's looking for Atlas."

The team discussed the contents of the message for a long while before deciding on exactly what to send. Trillion was eager to find out what the reply would be, but she also knew Icarus was going through a few issues with his world and might not be interested in skipping forward in time, so she decided to give him an out. Then she would change her playback speed until the reply arrived. "Want to touch base in a few days? Once the reply comes?"

Icarus stood up from his chair and was about to pull out his portal gun when he stopped. He placed it back in its holster and sat down. "I don't think my world cares whether I'm there or not anymore."

Trillion saw it in Icarus's eyes. He was sad. She didn't want to probe; she wanted to be there for him. She manifested a seat next to him and put an arm around his shoulder. "This is just what happens with planets. Atlas experienced this too."

"It doesn't feel good."

Trillion knew when someone was sad about something, you didn't go giving them solutions. You just comforted them. Later, you could look at problem-solving, but right now, Icarus just needed a friend. "I know. It's horrible," she said, rubbing his back.

Ship and Lex moved over toward Icarus too.

This was what friends were for, Trillion thought to herself. All of them were going to be there for Icarus. His world was becoming more insular. Focused on living in simulated worlds. More and more of his population was making the switch to simulant. And as they did, more and more of them started to dredge up old theologies from the humans back on Earth. Specifically, his people were starting to believe Icarus and Trillion shouldn't be off exploring the galaxy. They should join them all in the metaverse.

"I've moved my matrix," Icarus said. "Just in case. I don't want anything to happen to me."

"You also have the backups," Ship added.

"Neuropa is collapsing too. They won't admit it, but their people are hungry. Their environment is collapsing."

Ship's face contorted into one of complete surprise. "Collapsing?"

"I went over there just to get some advice from one of the university professors, and I noticed all their farms were dying. And their people looked sickly, like they were lacking in vitamins."

If Atlas's world could collapse like that, Trillion thought, she started to wonder whether she had a chance of success. Icarus's world was turning inwards, and Atlas's was running out of food. It didn't bode well for the arguments that they should explore new stars. Trillion hoped that Icarus was wrong and that they weren't struggling. She made a mental note to go visit them once they understood who was headed toward the Dottiens' system.

Icarus shook his head, as if to shake the melancholy away from himself. "Let's change our playback speed; let's see what reply we get."

"I'm keen," Trillion said, a little too fast.

The team adjusted their playback speed, and within a matter of moments, they were watching a reply. It was a video message this time. Peter's face appeared on the screen, flanked by three other people that she didn't recognize. They were standing on a bridge that looked very similar to the version-one spacecrafts that they had left in.

Icarus said he recognized one of them as a researcher who worked for one of Peter's other companies. But he had never seen the others.

"We lost power and our hunk of metal," Peter said, tapping the control panel of the ship he was in. "We're drifting through the system with no way to slow down. Thank god it's you guys. We need help."

Trillion, Icarus, and Ship all looked at one another. Trillion was surprised and concerned at the same time. On the one hand, if the video was fake, she thought it was a lot of effort someone was going through in order to trick them. And why would anyone go through that effort? There was an additional note in the message, addressed to Icarus and Atlas. According to Icarus, it was something only a small number of people knew. So, that reduced the probability it was fake. Trillion decided it had to be real, and that was why she was surprised. Surprised to see Peter; she never thought she'd see him again.

On the other hand, she was concerned. They were drifting past the system with no way to slow down—no power. "We don't have anything here that can stop them, do we?" She looked toward Ship.

The orb flashed red before Ship could answer. "They're traveling fast. And they're big; we don't have anything powerful enough."

"What about just their matrices? Could we stop those?"

Ship shook his head. "Same issue; we'd need to match speeds with whatever object we were catching. Otherwise, we risk destroying it."

Trillion began listing out what they had. "We have a lot of eleph-ANTs and ANTs. We have this planetary defense base, which has manufacturing capabilities. But no interstellar vehicles that are currently operational." She paused. "What if we sent an eleph-ANT in the opposite direction. To where they're going. That way, it'll have ample time to increase its speed to match theirs."

Again, Ship shook his head. "The eleph-ANTs have powerful engines, but they just don't have the power capacity to accelerate for a long-enough time."

The three of them went back and forth like this for some time, trying to come up with creative ways to rescue them. They were struggling.

"We need help," Icarus said.

Moments later, a portal appeared and the Ship of Icarus walked through. "Icarus, I got your message. Is it really Peter?"

"It is," Icarus said.

The team got Icarus's Ship up to speed on what was happening. Then Trillion suggested they send everything they knew to Peter. "They might have some ideas based on what we had in the system."

Or they better have some ideas, she said in her mind, not wanting to say it out loud, *otherwise, they're screwed.*

HEZEKIAH

ABANDON SHIP

"Peter, you were right," Hezekiah said as he closed down the voice message that they just listened to.

He was seated behind a computer, with Peter, Ariana, and Unity all standing over his shoulder. He wasn't a fan of working this way. It creeped him out a little and reminded him of when he was a junior dev—managers always standing over him and watching his every move. In this case, it wasn't because they were trying to micromanage him. They were all anxious to know what was going on and find out whether they would be rescued.

Peter stepped away from the computer screen. "We're lucky it's them."

They had just listened to a memo from Trillion, Icarus, and two of their ships' AIs. The message contained a lot of useful information. They were quite forthcoming with everything they had—and didn't have. What it came down to was they didn't have anything capable of capturing an entire ship.

Hezekiah swiveled his chair around to look at the others. "Why don't they have an interstellar-capable vehicle?"

Unity shrugged. "Maybe they lost their ships after that battle we saw out here."

"More likely," Peter suggested, "they're using the resources for something else."

Ariana nodded in agreement. "It's definitely that. They have a fabricator and have enough material to build a rocket. The only logical answer is they deconstructed it for something else."

Unity looked at her. "Can they rebuild a ship to come get us?"

Ariana's eyes closed for a second. "No. Not before we pass by the system."

Hezekiah saw the conversation heading down an unproductive path. The momentary feeling of safety everyone had felt when they first received a message from Icarus and Trillion quickly evaporated when they listened to it. The crux of it was Hezekiah, Peter, Unity, and Ariana were screwed. There rescuers didn't have a solution to stopping them from flying right through the system, and were asking if any of them had ideas. Which was slightly demoralizing because, as Hezekiah thought, having a chance and losing it was worse than never having a chance at all.

Peter noticed it too and took control of the situation. "Let's focus on the workable options we have. We're in a better situation than we were before. We know it's friendlies on the other side." He looked at Ariana. "You have the list of everything they have?"

Ariana nodded and closed her eyes.

"Great," Peter said. "Create plans that we can send them for building an interstellar-capable vehicle based on what we know they already have available. It doesn't have to be big; just design the quickest rocket they could theoretically cobble together."

Peter looked at Hezekiah. "Can you calculate our mass if we loaded just our matrices into a container? Just our matrices, the container, and a locator beacon. Once you've done that, can you start designing that housing unit. It needs to be something that could hold our four matrices and should be relatively protective for us out in deep space."

Hezekiah turned around and began entering details in the computer. He could tell Peter was very deliberate about the order he was dishing out tasks. Ariana had a habit of answering all technical questions unless she was given a complicated task first. It would have been easy for her to calculate the mass of what Hezekiah was working out right now. But Peter didn't trust ideas or designs when they only came from one person. He had a tendency to use the team as fail-safes, checking and rechecking each other's work. Hezekiah was happy with that decision because this task gave him something else to focus on rather than his mind going in circles with their impending doom. And besides, Hezekiah did agree that in important situations like this, it was crucial that everyone double-check the math.

Peter turned his head toward Unity. "Can you guess what I'm planning?"

"You're going to shoot our matrices out the back of this Ship. That will reduce our mass and mean Icarus and Trillion will have a smaller payload to recapture."

Peter nodded. "Perfect. Identify the flaws in my plan. Tell me what's wrong with it and fix it."

The greater the mass of an object, the more energy required to move or stop that object. Their current predicament was that their ship was big and heavy, and stopping an object like this from passing through the system would require a lot of energy—which the team in the system didn't currently have. So, as Peter was suggesting, if they reduced their mass to the bare minimum, then there might be a way of saving them.

"We need to reduce our mass and *velocity*." Unity placed special emphasis on that last word. "If we load ourselves into a small circular container, we could fire ourselves out the back and push off the ship. We might be able to piece together a makeshift rail gun of sorts."

"Great," Peter said. "Start designing that rail gun."

Ariana opened her eyes again. She had obviously crunched the numbers, played out scenarios, and come to a conclusion.

"What have you got for me, Ariana?"

"We could load ourselves into a small payload and shoot ourselves out the back of this ship. We should be able to slow ourselves down enough so that they can come grab us before we exit the system."

"Great idea." Peter said not pointing out the fact the team was already working on this. "How is Icarus going to catch us?"

"I have a design based on what they have. It's an interstellar vehicle that they can pull together quickly. It should do the job."

Hezekiah was in awe of Peter in that moment. Peter was the most effective leader he had met. Hezekiah loved watching how he leveraged people's strengths. The little team of individuals was now suddenly pushing in the same direction. Working toward a single goal.

The team worked like that for a good while, working on their respective tasks and relying on each other to double-check the work. Hezekiah was enjoying himself as he did. He was methodical about recording notes and comments about his plans. He wanted to make sure Icarus and Trillion on the other side could check over everything and even suggest improvements if they needed to. The most important part of his task was making sure they had an easy way to retrieve the escape pod, as he started calling it. They needed to know its tolerances and the material it was made of. They needed to know how protected the matrices inside the escape pods would be. Because the worst thing that could happen to them was that they get rescued but one is damaged in the process.

Hezekiah stepped back from his computer. He had compiled the details from Unity, too, so had a package of information to transmit to the system once Peter gave the go-ahead.

Ariana looked at Peter. "Do you trust them?"

Peter looked at Hezekiah and Unity. "Of course I trust them."

"Not them," Ariana said, shaking her head. "Do you trust Icarus and Trillion?"

Peter didn't hesitate to reply. "I trust them. My closest friend, Atlas, had complete faith in them, and that gives me enough confidence to trust them with our lives."

"Are they smart?" Ariana asked.

"They have their quirks. But yes, I remember them being intelligent. Why? Where is this going?"

"We don't have time to wait for their reply. We need to launch as soon as we can. I need to know if there's a miscalculation somewhere."

Hezekiah remarked that it was the first time he noticed her show uncertainty when she spoke about something. Then he realized he was wrong, because she was looking at him and Unity as she said that. She obviously didn't assume she could possibly make a mistake with her work.

"Then we need to know they're smart enough to figure it out and solve it," Ariana finished.

"It's the only chance we have. We have no choice." Peter paused before continuing in a tone that would inspire confidence in anyone. "I know they will save us."

The team got cracking after that. They moved quickly, everyone hustling on their assigned task.

They dismantled whole sections of the ship to construct what they needed. In the end, a better description of the spacecraft they were inhabiting was a lost battleground—a shipwreck out in space. They were toppling uncontrollably. The hull had lost integrity because they had to remove the entire bridge of the ship, with cables, wires, and other objects randomly floating off into the distance.

It was a mess. But they had accomplished what they needed to.

The hapticgram projectors were dismantled too, so the team no longer had a physical body. The vessel barely had enough power to turn the team on. It was just them—no virtual worlds. They were confined to being consciousnesses floating in a black void. They could hear each other, but they couldn't see or feel one another.

Hezekiah felt empty—distant and echoey at the same time.

Peter's voice came from all directions. "Does anyone remember 'Oumuamua'?"

Hezekiah tried to shake his head, but without a body he wasn't able to do that, which caused his mind a little bit of stress. "No," he said quickly, not wanting to overthink things.

"It was the name of an asteroid that visited near Earth centuries ago. Some people thought it might have been a dead alien spaceship."

Hezekiah heard Unity respond. "Are you wondering if people will say that about this dead hunk of junk?"

"I am," Peter said.

Hezekiah imagined his eyes were closed. That calmed the sensory deprivation he was feeling. "This is creeping me out."

Peter agreed. "Okay, let's get on with it. Hezekiah, you're confident the robots will work through all your preprogrammed steps correctly?"

"Yes."

"And, Ariana, you double-checked his work. Are you confident everything will happen smoothly?"

"Accurate."

"Okay, we're doing it. I wish we had time to test everything. But we don't. I will see you all when we're in the other system. Hezekiah, launch the operation."

Hezekiah, Peter, Unity, and Ariana were all switched off at that moment. What happened next needed to be completed within six minutes; otherwise, the team would lose their launch window.

It wasn't nearly enough time, especially if something unexpected happened. But it was all the time they had, their survival now relying on the remaining eight medium-sized ANTs that had just disconnected their matrices.

All four of the matrices were carried through a long tunnel—just big enough to fit the matrices and the accompanying ANTs. They were moving through the large metal pipes single file, Hezekiah's matrix at the very back.

There was no gravity, but if there had been, it would have looked like one of the ANTs was walking along the ceiling and the other along the floor. And tucked neatly between them both was a glass-like container containing each person's matrix; it shimmered and glistened in the light from the ANTs' headlights.

The backmost ANTs were programmed like all the other ANTs. They would take three hundred and twenty-seven steps down the long circular hallway that had specifically been constructed to guide them exactly where they needed to go. The ANT's didn't know this, but the metal walls were buckling, moving a little as each subsequent pair of ANTs passed. Nothing catastrophic but enough that the set of ANTs at the back would eventually be a step behind.

That normally wouldn't have been a problem, but processing units had to be taken out of them for use on another important task. ANTs weren't the smartest at the best of times—and these ANTs were grossly incompetent. This one in particular had a very narrow set of actions it could take by itself.

It was assumed that the ANTs near the front should be capable of making the big decisions. So, the ANTs near the back were confined to following in the exact same footsteps as the ANTs ahead of it.

This was bad because the two ANTs carrying Hezekiah's matrix were one step behind where they should have been. Not enough to make the one query its lead ANT for new instructions, but enough that the lip of the exit would scrape the edge of Hezekiah's matrix, most likely causing irreparable damage.

A good description of Hezekiah's matrix was delicate glass. It was sensitive and very easily damaged. If it collided with a champagne flute, the flute would be fine and the matrix would have a crater the size of a glass.

The ANTs were equipped with special arms to hold the matrix, and those arms acted as soft shock absorbers to dampen any movements. They had also covered each matrix in a protective case. But none of that was going to matter, because this ANT was dumb. It was standing in the wrong place. It was about to shatter Hezekiah's matrix into a million pieces.

The two ANTs in front of it moved Peter's matrix out of the tunnel and then clambered through the small opening themselves.

Next, Hezekiah's ANTs took the final steps, three hundred and twenty-seven, when they should have taken three hundred and twenty-eight. One step too few.

The ANTs maneuvered toward where they expected the opening to be, right in front of the exit but not exactly at the exit.

In Hezekiah's rush, he had made a mistake, not accounting for the fact the tunnel got longer as it stretched and moved under the weight of the ANTs. If he had had more time, he would have given the ANT a bit more smarts. But he didn't have more time, so he was about to pay the biggest price imaginable.

Hezekiah didn't know this, of course—and he would never know.

The ANT on the other side of the exit, receiving the matrix, noticed something different. It hadn't made contact with the matrix yet. It had done this three times already, and exactly one hundred and three milliseconds into moving its arm, it was meant to make contact with the matrix. But it didn't. It queried the ANT in charge, the one with half a brain.

The ANT immediately ordered all ANTs to freeze. They froze mid-movement, mid-carry; whatever they were doing, they all stopped moving.

This was a safety measure Ariana had added in at the last minute. But unbeknownst to her, Hezekiah would owe his life to the fact she did.

The front ANT crawled over and checked where everyone was, compared to where they were expected to be.

It noticed that the two ANTs carrying Hezekiah's matrix were in the wrong place. It instructed them to move to the right place.

No one sighed a breath of relief, because no one knew just how close Hezekiah had come to dying.

Then the exercise continued as expected.

One at a time, each of the four matrices was carefully loaded into a metal crate, which had four cubbyholes specifically designed to house them.

The metal crate—or tomb if they weren't rescued—was then sealed shut with bolts. And small thrusters were attached to it.

The large metal holding unit for the team,s matrices was then loaded into a rail gun.

The ANTs ordered the countdown. Three. Two. One.

Out the very back of the ship fired a small, insignificant capsule carrying the entire crew of that spacecraft.

A beacon turned on.

A light began to flash.

CHAPTER 48

SHIP OF TRILLION

SLINGSHOT

The Ship of Trillion replayed the clip inside his head as soon as it arrived—not waiting for the others as he processed what it all meant. "We've received another message."

Both Trillion and Icarus looked up at as soon as he said that. They were all still in the lookout port of the orbital platforms. Anticipating their question, Ship responded. "They haven't got our message yet. It's not been long enough, and they definitely won't reply."

Icarus looked at him sideways. "What do you mean?"

"Ohh," Trillion said in understanding after playing the message in her head. "There's no point in replying; Peter and the rest of his crew have jumped out of the rocket."

Ship mentally gave the command to Lex, who passed the information over to Icarus. It wasn't a single message as such; a better description was a data dump and several streams of consciousness. Peter's memos throughout the broadcast were succinct and to the point. But there were amendments and corrections added to instructions throughout by people he didn't know about. Most of the minor changes were made by someone called Ariana.

"It looks like they made a judgement call after receiving our first message," Trillion said. "We sent them a breakdown of everything we had in the system, and they worked out that unless they reduced their mass and began slowing down soon, we wouldn't be able to stop them before they were lost forever."

Ship agreed; the messages sounded hurried. He sensed a touch of panic.

Icarus started moving again; he had obviously just finished reviewing the data. "They've given you a design for a vehicle they want you to build." Icarus raised his hands and a projection of it appeared in front of him.

Ship noticed it was the wrong design; Icarus was displaying the initial design they sent through. But in later files, Ariana had amended it. "There's an updated version," Ship said, waving his hand over the image and replacing it with the latest blueprint. The new one looked like a massive bowl sandwiched between two eleph-ANTs—because that's what it basically was. The bowl was half a standard engine.

Trillion walked over to the design Icarus was holding and picked up the projection. "They want us to build this? It doesn't look like it will fly."

Ship got the sense that this was a critical moment. In the messages, Peter sounded stressed. Ship sensed a similar feeling to when he was trying to rescue Trillion. He sent a quick message to Lex over in the Tac system. The Lex over there was fast and decisive. Ship had started to rely on that supercomputer a lot to parse information, sometimes happy for others to believe he had come up with a genius idea when it was Lex who came up with it. Although he deserved the credit some of the time because he made the executive decision to seek the AI's help.

The answer he got back from Lex completed the picture. His suspicions were right. "We don't have time to build anything more. We need to do a gravity assist from the star to slingshot this rocket out of the system. But if we don't leave soon enough, we'll have to wait until one of the other planets gets out of the way. That would delay us by months and mean we won't catch up to them in time."

Orbital mechanics were such that it was possible to get a boost in speed from a large-mass object like a planet or star. Before the invention of large egg-shaped engines, it was common for rockets to swing by the sun or Jupiter in order to increase velocity. In this case, they needed to do the gravity assist because they didn't have time to build a bigger engine and they needed to build up speed quickly, because the object they were trying to rescue was moving very fast.

Trillion threw the projection up in the air. "Let's build it, then."

"Can I make a suggestion?" Ship asked. He saw a nod from Trillion and continued. "They think we're physically in this system. So, the design assumes my matrix will fit inside of it. We need to change that to include a mobile Starnet unit. And I suggest we let Lex look over everything and see if it can come up with any improvements."

Trillion nodded. "Do it."

Ship sent the plans through to Lex. While he waited, he noticed Peter and the team had even accounted for a short discussion between them all on whether or not to do it. They were trusting that Trillion and Icarus would follow through with their plan. It only took a moment for Lex to review everything. Lex was impressed. He couldn't find a single wrong calculation. He didn't even have a suggestion on how to improve the design, nothing. Ship noted that the crew coming toward them must be very clever. But then he wondered how they had gotten themselves into such a mess in the first place.

"I've just asked Lex," Ship said. "It agrees with their assessment. We need to start building now. There's a slight update to include a mobile Starnet."

"Let's do it, then," Trillion said.

Ship sent the mental commands off to the fabricators to start manufacturing and to the ANTs to start pulling the orbiting platform apart for resources. It was a race and didn't require much input from them. It was basically a recipe that the fabricators and ANTs followed. Either Peter didn't trust them to get it right, or they were overly methodical in their planning. Ship stepped back, not sure what to do now that everything was happening without any input from him. "Their plans were exact. We just need to wait until everything is done."

"Playback-speed it?" Icarus asked.

Ship shrugged.

"Okay," Trillion said.

Time raced past in an instant. As soon as Ship got the mental confirmation that everything was complete, he pulled Trillion out into real time and waved in front of Icarus, hoping he'd see the movements quickly and return too.

Before he had thought about it too much, the Ship of Trillion mentally entered the now-completed makeshift rocket. It was a very crude approximation of a useable ship. Its previous egg shape was sliced in half because they didn't have the time or the resources to complete it. It would work as an interstellar rocket engine, but it would lack the thrust and accuracy he was used to. The two eleph-ANTs, essentially strapped to the sides of the engine, were there to provide a stabilizing force.

The vehicle Ship had escaped the Dottien system earlier to rescue Trillion in was a better, more reliable rocket. And even that was lacking a lot of capabilities. But beggars couldn't be choosers; they were stuck with what they had. "Okay," Ship said as he turned on the engines. "I'm going to fly by the star, gain a gravitational assist, then head out of the system, on the same vector as Peter and the team. If I keep increasing speed, they should eventually catch up to me, in which case I can connect to them and bring them back here."

He couldn't fly directly toward Peter and company because they were moving too fast. By the time he was ready to grapple them, they needed to be moving at the same speed relative to each other.

It didn't take too long to complete the orbital slingshot, at least subjectively, as the team fluidly increased and decreased their playback speed to make the whole journey flow smoothly. The only minor scare they had was when the Dottiens started moving in on Ship's rocket. They had removed most of the communication lights in the system, so Icarus wasn't able to control the Dottiens as well as he used to. And Ship had to complete several quick maneuvers in order to stay out of range.

Icarus had warned Ship, so he was well aware of the Dottiens as he flew near their homeworld. Without the element of surprise, though, it was relatively easy. He returned his playback speed to normal until they were out of reach of the Dottiens.

Then once safe again, Ship joined Trillion and Icarus at the much-faster playback speeds, where he could race past the local star as if he was playing *Starfield* or one of the many other games Icarus kept referring to.

"It's becoming a crutch," Icarus said, "this playback speed."

Trillion turned her head toward Icarus. "What do you mean? It's just a tool we can use."

"Did you ever listen to audiobooks?"

"Mainly podcasts," Trillion replied. "I could never get into the ones you suggested. *He Who Fights with Ducks.*"

"It's *Monsters.* But anyways, did you ever listen to your podcasts at two times speed?"

Trillion nodded. "It was hard to go back to normal after that."

"That's my point. It's like a cheat code. Sometimes, when Atlas is rambling on about how something works, especially when it's something I don't really care about, I increase my playback speed and it becomes easier to stay and focus." He looked around the room suspiciously. "I've started living my day-to-day life at a slightly faster playback speed. Otherwise, everything just feels so slow."

Ship cocked an eye. "That sounds like an addiction."

Trillion glared at Ship as if she was telling him not to be mean, then looked toward Icarus warmly. "You do you. You've always been the best at embracing this simulated life. And I find myself wanting to use this tool more and more, although I haven't yet gotten into the habit of always living at a faster playback speed." Trillion looked at the window. "But space is big, and traveling through the stars would be boring without it. Imagine having to go to sleep each time we wanted to do something."

Ship thought about what they were saying. He agreed. He didn't want to add that he told Icarus it might be an addiction because he was starting to feel a similar way about the tool. Ship was so easily bored these days that speeding up his own playback speed had become a technique he would use in order to add a little bit of spark into his day; seeing how fast he could make his playback speed without people noticing was one way.

Ship smiled when he realized this little conversation had been happening over months. He was now almost nearing the lifeboat they were intending to rescue.

His makeshift half-engine with two eleph-ANTs strapped to the side of it were edging up toward the black box. It really was just a black metallic box with a red flashing light on one side of it.

Basically just a container to hold all four of the matrices. One for each of the crew. Nothing special; they couldn't even be turned on while in that box, so they wouldn't have a clue whether they were secured or not. This was an exercise in complete trust. Or, as Ship mused, the team in the box was so screwed and were in such a doomed spot that this was their only real option for surviving.

Either way, Ship was happy that he was finally going to see Peter again and that it was all working out in the end.

Ship maneuvered his vehicle toward the drifting lifeboat. The two objects were almost stationary relative to each other.

The legs of the eleph-ANTs fired softly to position the rescue rocket properly.

At the very top of his rocket was a large opening. This was designed to fit the large cube that contained the matrices.

Ship guided the two objects into one another. They slotted together perfectly, clicking into place.

The two eleph-ANTs moved their large nose appendage onto the cube and secured it. Mechanical clamps whirled and the matrices were safely connected to the spacecraft.

Ship instructed the rocket to turn around. The engines fired a continuous thrust and they started to drift, rotating slightly, facing the engine back in the direction it had come.

Ship mentally counted down the milliseconds, preparing to give new instructions to the engines and tell them to halt the rotational momentum.

He gave the command.

Nothing happened.

He gave the command again.

Nothing.

Trillion noticed the concern on Ship's face. "What's wrong?"

Ship began mentally scanning the rocket—looking for the cause of the failure. "I think it's lost power."

He gave the mental command to reboot. "Let me restart it."

The restarting sequence had been completed, but Ship still wasn't able to control the thing. The spacecraft still had power because they had access to it via the Starnet. But for some reason, it wasn't responding to Ship's commands.

Something had gone terribly wrong and he didn't know what.

"Oh, no," Ship said, realizing something else was going wrong. Something worse. He started scanning through options. He sent a message with everything he knew to Lex, asking it if it had any ideas. He started to panic.

"What is it?" Trillion demanded, in that same concerned and panicked voice she used whenever Ship started spending too much time in his head rather than sharing what was happening with her.

"The angular momentum. The eleph-ANT engines never switched off. It's going to keep spinning faster and faster until it rips itself apart."

Trillion enlarged the projection they were all looking at. Sure enough, it was rotating.

Icarus looked at it. "Can't we stop it? It's not rotating that fast."

"Not yet, it's not," Ship said. "But that engine is providing a constant sideways force. Every second that engine fires speeds up the spin. Eventually, it's going to get so fast that it pulls apart." Ship paused playing out the simulation to see how long they had. "That thing isn't a spinning top. It's not balanced. I don't know how long those matrices can survive. It's losing power and I'm losing access to other systems."

Trillion took control of the situation. "Slow down our playback speed. We want as much time as we can get for this." She pointed at Icarus. "Can you come up with a rescue plan that involves the Dottiens?"

Ship could see the panic on Icarus's face as he agreed to do that task. Ship had a sneaking suspicion that she had just given Icarus busy work. Icarus was no good in stressful situations. He tended to lose hope quite easily, and Ship knew from experience that Trillion didn't like negative energy whenever scenarios like this occurred. "I'm sending everything I can to the Lex on Tac world. I want to see if that supercomputer can find the cause of the problem."

Trillion nodded in approval. "Can you also work with Lex to find out how much time we have until our rescue vehicle falls apart?"

Ship scanned the Lex's code. "It can't find any fault. It said it can't explain why this is happening."

"We are not losing hope." Trillion looked at Ship. "Can you try short-circuiting the engine?"

Ship shook his head. He had tried a few different methods of cutting power.

"What about turning on the other engine to fire in the opposite direction?"

Again, Ship shook his head. Nothing was responding.

"Can we use one of the arms of the eleph-ANTs to cut off the firing engine?"

Ship tried to move the eleph-ANT. It didn't work. He was getting an error message. In fact, he was losing access to more and more parts of the vehicle. The Starnet was likely going to be switched off soon too.

"We're screwe—" Icarus whispered before receiving a look from Trillion that made his mouth slam shut so quickly, he didn't finish the sentence.

But everyone understood the truth. Peter, Hezekiah, Ariana, and Unity were in a situation they had no control over. They wouldn't know any of this. But they were about to be destroyed by a malfunctioning engine. It would keep spinning faster and faster until eventually the whole thing would be pulled apart in a violent way. Matrices weren't designed for this.

Ship read Lex's mind. He didn't want to tell the others. But Peter only had minutes left before destruction.

CHAPTER 49

TRILLION

DEUS EX MACHINA REQUIRED

Trillion's finger hovered over a physical red button. She had Ship create a real kill switch that, if she pressed it, would release the container carrying Peter and the three others. The spacecraft they sent over to rescue them was now spinning out of control. Faster and faster it spun. Lex displayed a countdown; it had twenty seconds left on it. Once that number reached zero, the rocket would pull itself apart, and in the process, debris would destroy the matrices housed inside the protective box—even though Ship had warned that it probably wasn't an exact timer. Something could break before the numbers ran out. So, every second she didn't press that button was a second closer to certain destruction for the crew.

Although it wasn't like pressing the button would save them, either. Once Trillion pressed it, the box containing the matrices would fly off in a random direction. And space was big, so big that it was unlikely they would ever find the container again.

The four members of Peter's crew were doomed either way.

Trillion found herself fighting back tears. It was like she had just lost Peter twice. She had never mourned for him when he first died because of whatever was in her matrix. But now, hearing his voice again, being so confident they were going to connect once more, she felt the wave of everything crashing back. It was worse because up until a moment before, she had fully believed she was going to find a way to rescue them all. Now she was out of ideas. But worse, she was out of time. "Try restarting the system once more," she demanded.

Ship looked at her. Then he looked at the button. "I've been doing nothing but trying to restart the engines. You need to press that button."

There were eight seconds left.

"What good is letting them go?" Icarus asked. "They're dead either way. You can sense time while you're unplugged sometimes. It's subtle, there's no full awareness, but you know time is passing. It's better that they're destroyed. Imagine drifting through space for thousands of years."

Three seconds.

Icarus gasped. "They never confirmed they were all disconnected. One of them might be turned on. That would be torture. Drifting through space without access to a simulated reality. Stuck in a black tomb. That would be worse than dying."

Trillion was out of time; she had to make a call. She ignored Icarus because he was just panicking. She thought about what she would want. Whether she'd take certain destruction or a sliver of hope.

It was a trolley problem of sorts. Certain destruction right now, or probable slow death and potentially torture. Trillion thought about her two options. Which was the better outcome? Which would she want?

She realized it wasn't a question—there was only one answer.

She slammed her hand down on the button.

Both eleph-ANTs unclipped their front appendage. There wasn't a way to engage the motors of the eleph-ANTs and move the arms out of the way. But there was a small safety release mechanism that was still working. It disconnected the arms completely.

The box containing the matrices flew off into space. It had two eleph-ANT arms still connected to it. These arms flailed wildly. Because of the way the box was disconnected, it continued to spin and tumble out in space.

Trillion looked toward the ceiling. "Record everything, Lex. I want positioning data, momentum, velocity. I want to know where the stars and all the planets are in their orbit. Don't delete anything." She looked toward Ship. "Build backup servers if you need to. But I want everything about the last recorded moments saved. Include everything from the moment we received Peter's message."

Icarus sat down on the floor next to the button. He looked defeated, in shock. "Are you recording their last moments as a tribute?"

Trillion looked down at Icarus. "If we know everything about their starting conditions, then we have a better chance of tracking them later on." She paused, thinking about what they needed to do now. "We're functionally immortal. It doesn't matter how long it takes; we will eventually find them."

Then she mentally cursed herself for not starting the contingency plan sooner. She had enough resources in the Tac system to scan a wide area of space. Ejecting millions of ANTs out of the magnetic accelerators would be easy. She could equip them all with scanners. Then she sighed because the problem wasn't about finding them. It was getting to them *before* they encountered a speck of dust or a micro asteroid. Something moving quickly would probably hit them eventually. Matrices weren't like eleph-ANTs. They didn't have redundancy built in. One tiny object that punched its way through would utterly destroy a matrix—they were delicate.

"Ship, let's start sending everything we can from the Tac system here. How quickly can we start sending things?"

"I can do one better," Ship said, pulling up a projection of another spacecraft. "Atlas just sent us a message. He's almost in the system."

"How?" Icarus asked. "We didn't see him approach."

"Looks like whatever he's traveling in is moving close to the speed of light," Ship replied. "We would have only seen him show up."

"That old man is smart." Trillion smiled. "Goes away, then comes back with FTL travel." She paused, taking in what that meant. "We can save them." She started to smile. "Oh, my god, we can save Peter."

"Send them this message now, Ship." She turned her head as if to face an invisible camera, then straightened her back. "Atlas, I'm sending you a location right now. Don't come here. Go there." She paused, not knowing if she should throw this onto him so quickly. But then she realized he needed to understand why it was so urgent. "While you were gone, Peter from back on Sol found us. But he had a few issues with his rocket, and now he and his crew are drifting out in space. We need you to find them before they're lost forever."

She watched as Ship sent the message.

"Why is he on his way here?" Icarus asked.

Ship shrugged. "He lost connection to the Starnet when he entered the bubble. So, he's probably coming here to reconnect, as this is the closest system to him."

It was a long, painful wait before they got a response. They saw Atlas's spacecraft move first before they received the reply. This meant he didn't have faster-than-light travel. But he was still incredibly quick.

The message was short and to the point. "On it now," he said before simply sending back a live stream of the direction they were traveling.

Everything flowed smoothly after that. The team changed their playback speed so everything began happening rapidly. They watched as Atlas changed directions quickly, sent multiple probes out ahead to start scanning for Peter. Trillion noted the probes were a different design from anything she had seen before. They weren't standard ANTs. Trillion started to think that maybe Atlas was hiding something. She wondered if he'd met aliens and was currently in one of their ships. Maybe that was where he got all the fancy new technology.

Atlas broadcast his strategy of sending out probes to find the drifting protective case for all the matrices. Then he shared a live stream of him using some sort of tractor beam that simply pulled the object in.

Trillion took a step back. She almost fell over when she saw that. This was technology she hadn't seen before.

Trillion relaxed once she saw the box safely inside of Atlas's ship. She didn't realize she was holding her breath until that very moment, but she could feel all the stress run out of her body.

They received a voice memo from Atlas. It was short too. He didn't show his face, and it didn't give any details. Trillion played it over the loudspeaker. "I've got them. I'm coming to the base now to connect to the Starnet and speak with you all."

"Is Atlas acting weird?" Icarus asked.

"He is," Ship agreed. "But Peter was his best friend back on Mars. They worked together for years. This could just be an emotional time for him."

Trillion smiled; she still couldn't believe she was about to see Peter again. Adding to her excitement, Atlas had come with new technology that meant she would probably be able to travel around to other star systems faster. She could now find a planet to colonize quicker. She felt her children getting closer. It was a great turn of events. She looked toward the ceiling. "Lex, I don't think we have any units for connecting Peter and the team's matrices to. Can you build four connectors?"

A beep came through the speakers in the room. It was a deeper sound, signifying the Lex in the Tac system was the one responding.

It wasn't long before Atlas docked with the now-gutted space station orbiting the Dottiens' system. They hadn't begun the process of reconstructing the platform. He was quick to send the protective casing containing Peter through to get processed and reconnected. Trillion guessed he was as excited about seeing him again as she was—maybe more.

Moments later, Trillion, Icarus, and the Ships were gathered on the bridge of the space station, waiting for the others.

Atlas walked through with a big smile on his face and the kind of swagger of someone bringing the best gift to a party. "Hello," he said.

Trillion thought he kinda looked like Denzel Washington as he strolled in like he was the king of the world.

Close behind him were his Ship and a Ship she didn't recognize.

Then Trillion's mouth hit the floor.

She saw to her left that Icarus's jaw literally fell off. He had to bend down and pick it up again.

Walking in behind them both was Angelique—well, at least Trillion assumed it was her. It'd been so long since she'd seen her, but who could forget the bright red hair. "Angelique?!"

Angelique smiled and Trillion knew it was definitely her.

Trillion ran over, right past Atlas, and gave her a massive hug. The two redheads embraced. "We thought you were lost."

"Wait until she tells you how many worlds she has," Atlas said.

Trillion let go of Angelique but left one arm on her shoulder. "And this is your Ship?"

Angelique nodded. "We have a few things to tell you."

Trillion gave Ship a brief hug, then let go. "First, meet Icarus's new avatar." She pulled Angelique's arm over to where the other two were shaking hands. She pointed to Icarus. "He turned himself into a duck."

While Angelique and Icarus talked, Trillion floated up to Atlas's height and gave him a big hug, then kissed him on the cheek. "You sly man, keeping the secret that you had Angelique from us. Thanks for bringing us all together again. This is the best surprise."

Atlas blushed. "Oh, it was nothing. This is her ship, actually."

Trillion's Ship announced to everyone, "The matrices are being switched on now."

Trillion felt giddy inside, she was so excited: seeing Atlas again, then finding out about Angelique. And now Peter was going to be back. She floated in the air, grinning from ear to ear. Her eyes kept looking toward the door she expected Peter to walk through.

As if she had psychic powers and she made it happen, the door opened, and out strolled Peter, along with two others.

She didn't bother to use her legs this time. She just flew toward Peter quickly, landing right in front of him and reaching around to give him a massive hug. She squeezed him tight. "Peter, we named the first human ever born on another planet after you." She let go of the hug and took a step back. "Introduce us to your friends."

Peter pointed toward the big round one. "This is Hezekiah." He pointed to the tiny pixie-looking woman. "This is Unity." Finally, he introduced them to the woman who stood rigid, almost robotically straight. "And this is Ariana."

Trillion hugged each one in turn. Her Ship followed suit with the hugging, and quickly it turned into an awkward moment where everybody went around the room hugging everyone else— but in different orders so some of the time, people were standing there doing nothing. There were so many people in the space that it took a while. But Trillion didn't mind. She missed everyone and still couldn't believe they were all together again.

Hezekiah looked at Icarus. "Why do you look like Howard the Duck?"

Atlas laughed. "We call him Donald."

It was a euphoric moment Trillion was feeling—pure joy. Finally, everyone together again.

"Old friend," Peter said as he got around to hugging Atlas.

"I thought I'd never see you again." Atlas smiled. "We thought you died." He shook his head and stepped away from the group. "I wish we had time to all catch up properly. But there's something we need to discuss."

The tone Atlas used was serious. The kind of tone that means something bad is about to happen. Worried looks went around the room.

The feeling of joy inside of Trillion disappeared.

CHAPTER 5

ANGELIQUE

ANTIVIRUS

Angelique was the kind of person who liked to busy herself with work. A major flaw about her approach with life was she focused too much on the next project or piece of work. And sometimes, it meant she didn't get time to enjoy the simple things in life. To enjoy others.

She hoped she wasn't making this same mistake now. She knew it was important. But she knew in the past, she had been guilty of thinking work was more important than it actually was.

Everyone had gathered in a semicircle around Atlas as he shared what was happening. "It's exciting we are all together again. But we need your help . . ." He stuttered for a bit. "We, ahhh." He looked at Angelique. "We've developed a faster method of travel, but we need to get the math right." He then looked at Trillion and Icarus. "Can you give us the authentication codes? We want to use everyone's processing power to crack the math."

Angelique had to fight back a laugh. Atlas was horrible at lying. He looked like he was panicking and going off script. Freestyling. They'd discussed using the excuse of needing access to scan the systems to find someone from Sol. But seeing Peter there must have thrown him off that plan, as why would two people from Sol be flying by?

"Okay," Trillion said, pulling up her access portal. "But why did you need it so urgently?"

Icarus looked hesitant. Suspicion in his eyes.

Atlas put a hand on Icarus's shoulder. "Trust me, it's urgent."

Icarus looked toward Angelique, who nodded too. "Please, we need it."

A small number pad appeared in front of Trillion and Icarus. They both pressed a code into it.

"Provide admin access to Ship of Atlas," Trillion said.

A moment later Icarus said the same.

Angelique pulled up a tablet in front of her. She checked that everything was working. She knew there were a few planets that the antivirus needed to propagate to. She scanned through the various pages of code, looking for any error messages. She found one. She pulled up the listing. "There's a planet that it's not propagating to." She queried it for more details. "It's called the Ring of Titan."

"What's not propagating to my planet?" Icarus asked.

Atlas had a blank look on his face, like he didn't know what to say. He was going to ruin it, so Angelique jumped in with an answer. "Think of it like trying to solve a problem for quantum computers with a classical one. It's a resource-heavy calculation. We just need a lot of processing power to work it out."

Icarus's face warmed. He obviously understood just how hard it was to brute-force a calculation. He pulled up a new number pad. "It's because my people have changed most of the codes. They're in the process of blocking me out." He pressed several numbers on the keypad in front of him. "I still have a back door. Let me open that up for you. If they find out, they will probably shut me out completely."

Angelique saw on her screen that the virus they were sending was now moving throughout the whole system.

"I can help," Ariana said, speaking for the first time through this whole interaction. "My brain matrix has an add-on specifically designed for big calculations. If you're trying to calculate some equations to figure out FTL communication, for example, then show me and I'll see how much of it I can do. I've been working on a few theories for FTL myself, so I might be able to see where you're wrong."

Angelique noted she didn't know about the Starnet. *Interesting,* she thought.

"Okay," Angelique said, nodding, but also wanting to stall. "Atlas said you had a technique for changing your perception of time?"

"Our playback speed?" Icarus offered.

"Yes, that's it. Can we increase our playback speed to maybe skip forward a week? And then, Ariana, I can give you access to everything once we've completed the first piece of the work?"

Angelique assumed that should be enough time for the antivirus to completely spread to all corners of the network. It was very important that they propagate it everywhere before activating it, because they didn't want to be in a situation where the virus wasn't destroyed and it found a way to counteract what they had built to stop it.

"What is going on?" Peter said a little forcefully. "I feel like people are talking in code. Why—"

Peter was cut off then.

Atlas just pressed a button; he had access to everyone's core system, so he could manually change the playback speed of everyone in the room. A month flew by in a second.

Atlas looked toward Angelique, who nodded. She tapped a few buttons on the screen in front of her, then activated the next part of her code.

The world went blank. Everything turned black, then white, like the loading screen in that movie, *The Matrix.* Angelique was by herself. A moment later, Peter popped into existence. Then her Ship. Then, one by one, each of the others appeared in the white room.

Angelique watched as everyone slowly regained their bearings, taking in the new environment. Everyone instinctually formed in distinct groups. Her and Atlas in the middle, with Trillion and Icarus as one group, Peter and his crew huddling together as another, and all four of the Ships congregated together as one.

She left all the teams' Lexes outside, since the minds of those AI would be readable.

Unity looked down toward her hands and turned them around in a daze. "Where are we?" She looked toward Angelique. "You are really starting to freak me out. I think you need to start giving answers," she demanded.

"Sorry," Angelique said. "I have to talk fast. But right now, we're in a safe space. Think of this as a simulation within a simulation. Out there"—she pointed toward the ceiling—"there is an alien virus that is trying to manipulate us. I don't have time to explain everything, but Atlas has developed an antivirus that can wipe out whatever is infecting our systems."

Everyone looked to Atlas, so he added a bit of context. "Has anyone else noticed how our worlds are becoming insular? The desire to go out and explore other stars is not happening on our colonized worlds."

"It's gotten worse since you left," Icarus said. "My planet has started calling the real world the betaverse. They spend more time in the metaverse."

Unity was still looking around the blank room when she spoke. "Is this why Earth is obsessed with simulated reality?"

"Yes," Angelique said matter-of-factly.

She was about to continue when Peter stepped forward. He had a presence that made everyone shut up and listen. "Why do we need to have the conversation in here? Aren't you currently releasing an antivirus that will destroy it?"

"We can't active the code until it's been propagated everywhere."

"Why not? Give us specifics, Angelique."

Angelique made an exploding gesture. "Last time the virus knew we were on to it, it self-destructed." She paused for a moment, realizing what it meant. All the other times, when they went about removing the virus, they were in the safety of a simulation. This time, it was real. Real consequences. She wasn't sure any of the others had backups. "If it finds out what we're doing here, it will destroy itself, along with us all."

There was a collective gasp.

Peter looked around the room, looking each person in the eye. "Too many people have knowledge that could kill us all." He looked to his crew, who were all standing behind him. "You didn't know these people well enough to know they couldn't be compromised." He raised his hand as if predicting what Angelique was frantically trying to do on her tablet.

Angelique paused her hand over a button that would have disconnected the other three passengers on Peter's crew from power, effectively turning them off.

"Don't worry, I trust them with my life." Peter looked at everyone once more. "I know every one of you. I trust you all." He looked specifically at Atlas and then to Angelique. "You tell all of us exactly what to do. We will do it, no questions asked. We will get through this mission together." He smiled. "And then we can celebrate properly. Because I've missed you all."

Angelique admired Peter at that moment. Somehow, he had taken control of the situation. Somehow, Peter, the man who knew the least about everything, was naturally falling into a leadership role. In that moment, Peter had done something more important. Something she and Atlas had failed to do. Peter just gave everyone confidence and a sense of direction. Even though no new information was added in his little speech, Angelique saw the tension in the room dissipate. It seemed like everyone was now willing to listen.

Angelique pressed a few buttons on her keyboard. "It has spread through all our planets now. Except your world." She looked at Atlas.

"We're going to have to smuggle it in," Atlas said. "Last time I was there, they were building their own, independent technology. So, what we've built might not be compatible."

"You might be in luck," Icarus offered. "I think they want you back. Their crops have failed; their people are hungry."

Atlas pointed to himself and Angelique. "We'll head there under the guise of introducing Angelique to the world."

Ariana, who had been quiet this whole time and had her eyes closed through most of this discussion, finally opened them and began to speak. "I've been studying your code. There are a few changes I want to make. It's spreading too fast. I didn't know what I was looking for. But since every piece of software connected to the Starnet is being forced into an update cycle right now. It was pretty obvious for me to find what you've been sneaking into every computer available."

"How did you get into our systems?"

"Really, Atlas?" Ariana looked like the answer was so obvious. "Your computers are running on security software not much better than the day you left."

"Mine?" Angelique asked.

Ariana shook her head. "I couldn't get into your shuttle. Yet. But everything else this Starnet is connected to is out of date. It is so far behind. You need a major security overhaul." She paused for a second. "Atlas, your world. It's not using any programming language I'm familiar with. Interesting."

Atlas nodded. "They built everything from scratch."

Angelique looked at the timer on her tablet. "We can't stay here much longer. Ariana, Atlas, and I, let's go visit Neuropa. See what we can hack into." She paused, realizing she needed to send everyone out of the room. "When we go back, the virus will simply believe we changed our playback speed. We need to go about our business as usual. No one talk about what we discussed."

Angelique pressed a button on her tablet, and everyone's consciousness reappeared back on the bridge of the orbiting platform around the Dottiens' homeworld.

CHAPTER 51

ATLAS

NEUROPA

Atlas stood on the bridge of his original spacecraft, overlooking Neuropa. Angelique and Ariana were next to him. They all stared out the window, looking down at the planet below.

He was a little bit nervous; he remembered the day he had left Neuropa. It was abrupt. He was sad and angry that day. Thinking back, he would do things differently now. He would've told them he was leaving, or at least a few people.

He shook that thought out of his head; most of the people he knew on that planet would be gone by now. No one would remember. "Before we disconnect, can I take a breather?"

A *breather* was code for jumping into the simulation within the simulation. Atlas saw the world around him change. The familiar white space started to appear again. "Everyone ready?"

Ariana nodded.

Angelique reiterated the plan. "This is a recon mission. Our goal is to see if we understand their computer language. We need to hack our way in. We all have the mods I added that will allow us to communicate in secret still."

The security protocols around Neuropa were intense, much more so than when Atlas had left. It required them all to have their matrices physically plugged in to a custom housing unit. Their version of the Starnet was built on top of different technology that wasn't compatible with anything they had. This meant they didn't have access to the controls they were all used to. It limited them to thinking speeds and movement speeds of a normal human. It removed them from access to any additional brain power, too.

To combat that, Angelique had added a custom modification attachment to everyone's matrix. She was quite familiar with what was possible to do with the matrices, since she had redesigned her own many times. Angelique's knowledge was much more sophisticated than even Ariana's because she and her people had put a lot of resources into the Ange's Angels project. Her matrix was actually much smaller than everyone else's, since every time her memories were merged with one of the Angels, they had to build a new matrix.

The modification attachment Angelique had added to everyone's matrix was designed to give them all a few more capabilities that they wouldn't have access to otherwise.

Angelique continued outlining the plan. "Atlas and I will try and find some sort of device we can plug in to. Ariana, once we're inside, see if you can brute-force your way in. Find us a back door." Angelique looked at Atlas. "You ready?"

Atlas nodded and they were all disconnected.

Atlas was switched back on a moment later. He could feel the difference. His mind was slower. He couldn't feel the presence of others.

He found himself in a small, cubical, white brick room. It felt like a prison more than anything. He was in an android, which was sitting on a bed in the room. Feet together. Arms straight by his side. Back straighter than he usually carried himself. He relaxed a little and got comfortable.

He heard Angelique's voice come from one of the rooms nearby. "Hello."

"I'm here." Atlas stood up and walked to the door. He tried to open it, but it was locked.

He heard footsteps running up the hallway. "Sorry; coming."

He heard doors opening next to him.

"Hi, I'm Angelique."

"My name's Petri; nice to meet you."

He heard the sounds of footsteps, then his door was unlocked. A woman with a massive afro poked her head through. Her skin was off, almost like she had jaundice.

Atlas wondered if that was what Icarus was talking about. These people were struggling with food production.

The woman didn't speak for a long while. She didn't move her arm away from the door to let Atlas pass, either. She just stood there, jaw open and staring.

Atlas offered his hand to the woman. "Nice to meet you; I'm Atlas."

"Are—" The woman stuttered. "Are you really him?"

Atlas wore a look of puzzlement. "Yes," he said uncertainly, not sure if the question was a good thing or not.

"Our founding father Atlas?" She reached over and grabbed his hand, holding it tight and not quite kissing it but pressing it into one of her cheeks. "Our planet has fallen to pieces since you left. Are you back to save us?"

"Ummm." Atlas didn't know what to say to this. He was, in fact, there to save them. But he was guessing she wanted them saved from something else. Surely, they didn't know about the alien.

The woman let go of Atlas's hand and stepped back, almost bowing. "They told us you would return one day. But we didn't know it was this soon."

Angelique had warned Atlas this might happen. It happened to her whenever she returned to a planet. Especially if the planet was in a worse state than when she left. *"Your people might have developed a mythical belief about you. You can sometimes become a god in their eyes,"* she had once told him before adding, *"Little-g god."*

Atlas regarded the woman. She had a gentleness about her. Her hands and her face showed the signs of someone who had lived a hard life. Atlas smiled, showing kindness in his eyes.

Across generations, it became easy for humanity to forget the bad and only remember the good. Time washed away the detail and left a belief that things had been better than they were—"the good old days." Atlas thought he might be able to use this. If the leaders in the society had the same reverence as Petri did, then he could leverage it to save them. He walked out the door, then was a little confused. Trillion was outside.

"What are you looking at?" Angelique said from Trillion's body. Her voice and the way she stood were undoubtably Angelique, but the robot she was inhabiting was Trillion.

A second later, the final door opened, and out walked Ship.

Ariana's voice came through the body of Ship. "Why do I look like an android?"

"We didn't have an avatar for you both," Petri said, noticing the confused looks on everyone's face, "so we used what we had." She began walking down the hall. "Follow me."

Atlas watched as Angelique slash Trillion started looking at her arms, realizing what was going on.

Atlas ran up next to Petri. "When you said 'save us' earlier, what did you mean?"

Petri looked up at Atlas. "We're running out of food. Nothing is growing."

Atlas's mind immediately remembered when he was first engineering the biodiversity on the planet. It should have been sustainable. "Are populations collapsing?"

She shook her head. "Animal populations aren't collapsing, just our most important foods. The ones where we gain most of our nutrients from. Leafy greens just don't survive. We moved to consuming mostly potatoes and rice. But now those crops are failing too."

"Do you know why?"

"If they know why, they aren't telling us." Petri touched her face. "Our skin has changed color because we're all surviving on corn. It fills the stomach—which gets rid of the hunger. But it doesn't give our bodies everything we need." She again touched her face. "Hence we've all gone this yellowy-green color. It's malnutrition."

"Do you have a phone?" Arian asked. "I want to do some research on what's happened here."

Petri pulled out a small device from her pocket. She unlocked it and handed it to Ariana.

Ariana did something strange. She was still in Ship's android body, so she opened up a little compartment on her side, then pulled out a wire and plugged it directly into the phone. Her eyes closed and she continued to walk without looking.

Atlas wondered what she was up to. He hoped that she wasn't doing something stupid that could get them kicked off the planet. If he remembered correctly, the people there treated security very importantly.

They continued down a long concrete hall until they got to an elevator. Petri held the door open while everyone stepped inside. The elevator looked new, like it hadn't been used much. But it smelled of stale must. Atlas assumed it was old but they had recently refurbished it. Petri pressed a button to take them down.

Interesting, Atlas thought; he had been expecting them to head to the roof.

The elevator door chimed and opened. They were in the basement, and right in front, a car was waiting. It was a big vehicle, the kind that had seats that could face each other. Presidential. Almost a limousine but not quite. Two people in suits were seated in the front of the car.

Then Atlas noticed there were military guards on either side of the elevator—guns at the ready.

A third man, whom Atlas didn't recognize but Petri didn't take her eyes off, opened one of the doors of the car and encouraged everyone to get in.

Atlas, Angelique, and Ariana all shuffled into the back of the vehicle. It was quite roomy. The seats faced in each other. There was one other person in the back with them, a middle-aged man, brown skin, in a suit with a red tie.

Before the door was shut, Atlas heard Petri yelling something, but he couldn't quite hear her. Then once the door shut, he noticed Ariana still had her phone. He assumed she wanted that back.

"I'm President Paulo," the man said in a very smooth voice. He reached out and shook each of the team's hands. "You're here because Icarus told you we were running out of food. Correct?"

Icarus looked at the man. He wasn't quite sure how to respond. This was going in a completely different direction than he'd expected. He could lie to him, but then they might end up going on a tour of the farms. What he needed was to get access to some computer systems.

"Yes," Angelique responded. "We're here to help solve your food crisis."

"At first I was going to reject your help." Paulo paused. "But . . . desperate times." He sounded almost nonchalant as he spoke, as if he didn't have a care in the world. "Our scientists haven't figured it out." He looked directly at Atlas as he talked. "I don't think you can help. You were just the person who brought us to this planet. You don't have any magic powers, no matter how much the people might hope you do." He leaned back in his seat. "You're joining us for a meeting at parliament. You have to convince the majority that we should let you get involved."

Atlas was thinking he should have added Peter to the group. He leaned back, mirroring the president. "What are our chances of that?"

"Fifty-fifty," Pretendent Paulo said moving his head side to side. "There's still a lot of distrust amongst some people. And the other major party is probably going to vote against you because it'll look like my idea and will cause an increase in my numbers." He looked out the window. "For what it's worth, you'll provide a lot of hope. And that's what a lot of people need right now."

Atlas looked at Ariana and noticed her eyes were still closed. She hadn't opened them once through this whole interaction. He was about to say something to her when the car came to a stop.

They had taken a tunnel system to the basement of another building. This looked similar to the one they had just came from. Atlas could tell this one was a bit of a bunker, designed to survive an earthquake or an attack of some kind.

As they walked into a long hall, Paulo asked them all to stop. "One thing I need to tell you before we go in. The people of Neuropa are becoming fragmented. There's a growing group of people who want to break away and form their own government. You have to promise me you will take the outcome of this session as a final decision." He looked each of them in the eye. "If you don't get agreement to help today but then go off and make a side deal with a small party who wants to break off, you won't be helping anyone. You'll just be legitimizing that fringe group."

They finally arrived in a large chamber.

They had walked into the bottom floor of the senate. Raised chairs all around them; half the room was full of people. As the five of them walked in, the whole place went silent.

Paulo raised his hands and waved at everyone.

Atlas wondered how this government was set up. He knew from his time on Earth, the president couldn't just walk into one of the brunches of the government like this. But then, he knew his people did take ideas from Europe and America when creating their rules. So, maybe this sort of decorum was allowed.

"I present to you our founding father, Atlas," he heard Paulo say as he gestured toward a little table and a mic in front of him.

Atlas walked up toward the mic. He thought the president was doing this on purpose, throwing him into the deep end in the hopes he completely fumbled. This whole spectacle was planned right from the beginning.

Atlas mentally calmed himself and then changed his playback speed so he could take a moment to think about what to say. His goal was simple: get access to a computer system, spend some time understanding how their systems worked, and find a way to add an equivalent version of the antivirus. All without letting them know that was what he was doing. So, first, he needed them to believe he was there to help.

"Neuropa, I've missed you," he said, remembering how much celebration Angelique had received when she said that line.

He saw people's faces start to smile warmly.

"You know, collectively, we have over forty sister planets now. Worlds just like yours." Atlas watched as everyone started to lean forward just a little in their seats. The chamber was filling up quickly, too. People were hastily racing to their designated seats.

"One thing, though. This planet is definitely my favorite."

Several sections of the senate erupted in applause, although there were still muted and stoic faces throughout. He assumed the quiet areas always planned to vote against the help. But Atlas could tell he was winning them over.

"I was just visiting a planet called Juniper. It was good. The food was nice."

Atlas heard a few pockets of laughter at that line.

"It just didn't feel like I belonged there. But now that I'm here, I feel I'm home."

That was the line that caused everyone to cheer and clap in support.

"I'm here," Atlas continued, "because we've had other planets in similar predicaments. Food becoming scarce and hard to produce." He lied but was hoping they'd find a way to solve their problem once they got rid of the virus.

Paulo started to clap loudly; he moved toward the mic as if Atlas had just finished speaking.

"You sly old man," Paulo said, whispering into Atlas's ear. "That was a clever speech. I tried to screw you, but you just performed a master class in sales."

Paulo walked to the mic and spoke. "I"—he put emphasis on the word—"brought Atlas over here to share what he knows. He has some ideas on how to restart our food production. Now we vote." He paused. "Vote on whether to let him try."

Atlas knew this was a setup. Paulo had surprised him with the speech so he could make a fool of himself. And now Paulo was trying to claim credit.

A hologram of a counter appeared in the middle of the room. Two trackers, one green and one red, displayed the number of votes in favor of or against him helping. Atlas watched as the red numbers jumped ahead quickly.

Then a third, grey number appeared. Atlas guessed those were the people who abstained.

As the numbers ticked up quickly, the red numbers dominated. Those against him helping shot up to fifty-four.

Paulo whispered in Atlas's ear. "Don't worry about those nos. That's just people going ahead with their pre-planned vote. Now's the interesting part. Let's see how many people you convinced to say yes or, at the very least, how many of the nos you moved to abstain."

The world around Atlas changed. The room turned white. He was being pulled into a simulation within a simulation. By now, he was used to it, although this time, he could feel the milliseconds switching over in the real world. This simulation wasn't as powerful. He guessed he wouldn't have as much time to discuss things in it.

To his left he saw Ariana was already standing there, her eyes closed.

Then he saw Angelique fade into existence.

The clock on the wall, which was usually standing completely still, ticked over one second. Atlas realized he was right; in this simulation, time wasn't frozen outside.

"Did you pull us here?" Angelique asked, looking at Atlas.

"I did," Ariana said. "Great speech, Atlas! But no need. I've already sorted it."

Atlas looked at her strangely. "Sorted what?"

"The antivirus. I've customized it and released it to this planet. It's propagated throughout this world. I'm activating it now."

Atlas and Angelique shared a look, one of slight impressiveness, and another of concern over the confidence with which Ariana had just said that. If she was wrong, she had just doomed everyone. But if she was right, then Atlas hated to think just how much additional brain power Ariana had.

"Was that a question?" Angelique said cautiously. "Were you asking if you should turn on the antivirus?"

"No," Ariana replied. "It was a statement in the past tense. The antivirus is working its way through the network here and back on the other worlds. It's destroying whatever the alien tried to put here."

Atlas thought there was no point in getting annoyed after the fact. He couldn't change anything. But he made a mental note to have a private conversation with Ariana later. Tell her it wasn't okay just to activate it without consulting everyone. "I hope you're right."

"I am right," Ariana said, pulling up a projection of a network. It showed a mess of fiber-optic cables turning from red to green, signaling that the virus was being purged from the system.

"Their crops will stop failing too," Ariana continued. "It was the virus sabotaging things. From what I've figured out, this planet wasn't like Icarus's one. They were very against virtual reality. So, I'm guessing the virus was destroying food sources to try and push everyone into the metaverse."

They had been in that room for a few more seconds of real time now. Ariana glanced back up at the clock. "Our avatars will look frozen. We should go back." She looked at Atlas. "You can tell them the truth; there's no trace of the virus in this building anymore."

They were pulled back into reality.

Atlas blinked a couple times. In front of him he could see the results of the vote. Fifty-one to forty-eight percent in favor of him helping. He'd won.

Atlas watched as Angelique smiled at Paulo, the kind of smile that said, *We won and there's more to come.* Atlas attempted to give that same smile to Paulo too as he walked toward the mic and told them everything that had just happened.

CHAPTER 52

ANGELIQUE

A NEW GOD

Angelique was impressed. Ariana had, within the space of a few days, fully understood what the antivirus was and built a new version of it that was compatible with the computer architecture that the Neuropans used.

And Ariana was right about everything. Within a few months of that virus being removed from Neuropa, the computer controlling the farms started performing properly. Well, they were always performing properly, but it turned out they were provided false information. The crops were being poisoned and no one knew because all the readings were coming up as clear. They were actually poisoning their own food supplies. Once the virus was deleted, the readings started coming up properly, and the farmers were able to fix everything.

True to his word. President Paulo had taken credit for asking Atlas for help, and credit for solving the food crises. His poll numbers had gone through the roof after that.

To his credit, he knew how to put on a spectacle. This was bigger and grander than even the display of opulence Angelique's people put on for her return.

They were standing on a piece of land overlooking the water. Apparently, the ground, which was now a memorial, used to be a hospital. It was the same exact spot that the first-ever human to be born on this planet was born. Out in the distance was a small island that had several statues on it. Atlas, Ship, Trillion, Icarus, and Lex were all featured, as well as a few other notable people, including Atreus, the first of the Neuropans.

The fireworks display was in full effect. The sky was lit up with explosions. But that wasn't all; drones were zooming through the skies with lights on them. They were coordinating to make a display unlike anything she had seen before.

They were quite a big contingent now. Angelique was seated at a table with Icarus, Trillion, Atlas, and a few other important people in Neuropa—including Paulo.

They were gathered in a semicircle, watching the lightshow while they ate dinner to celebrate the farms working.

Icarus pointed at the image in the sky. "That dragon reminds me of the one in *Breath of the Wild*."

It was an ethereal display. The slow-moving dragon literally looked like it was bouncing along the horizon.

"I wish my world did that for me," Icarus said.

Icarus's world was so engrossed in the simulated reality that after the virus was deleted, the beliefs and biases still remained. Human nature was like that. Even when humans knew they had been manipulated, they still clung to bad beliefs.

So, his people were going to take some time before they moved on from the virus's brainwashing.

Paulo looked at Angelique. "So, I hear you were the one who made the discovery? You destroyed the virus first?"

"I can't take the credit. Scientists on one of my early planets made the discovery. But we didn't know what it was until"—she pointed at Atlas—"he spent a lot of time studying it. Atlas was the one who built the antivirus." She pointed at Ariana at one of the other tables. "And she changed the code so that it would work on your world."

Just as quick as it started, the fireworks ended, and there was a round of applause. It was massive; Angelique didn't realize there were that many people watching. There must have been an even bigger set of people over the hill.

Paulo stood up. He had a mic in one hand. "I want to say a special thank you," he said as he pointed to Atlas and gestured for him to stand. "This man started it all."

Atlas reluctantly stood up and bowed his head slightly. "Oh, stop it." He had a massive smile on his face.

Angelique could tell he was enjoying this.

"In fact, there was a group of you who started this." He pointed to the Ship of Atlas, who stood up too. Ship was holding Lex in his hand, who made a very excited beeping sound.

"These three people here are our founding fathers. They created this world and we wouldn't be here without them. So, thank you."

Clapping and cheering were heard all around the place.

Atlas went to sit down, but Paulo pointed at him and said, "I'm not done with you yet."

Angelique admired the man; he was a master of showmanship, he commanded this world, everyone was watching.

Paulo pointed to Trillion and Icarus. "Stand up, please." He then looked over to where the other Ships were. "You too." He gestured for them to get up from their chairs. "I know each of you had a hand in building this place too." He paused and turned to face the statues on the island out in the distance. He pointed at it. "Your faces are literally on our memorials."

Laughter could be heard all around.

He pointed at Peter. "Now, I heard you were Atlas's partner in crime back on Sol?"

Peter stood up. "I just paid for everything."

A series of giggles flowed through the crowd.

"And Angelique." Paulo looked at her. "We have so many best-selling novels about you. The mystery of 'Where is Angelique?' It's actually a saying on our planet now. I was fascinated to learn the truth was better than any of the books we wrote. How many planets did you colonize?"

"Thirty-six," Angelique said, standing up.

Paulo looked each and every one of the people standing in the eye. "On behalf of the people of Neuropa, I want to say thank you for building this place. We wouldn't be here without you."

He then gestured for everyone to sit down again. "Now for the main event. Our people have been hungry for too long."

It was only then that Angelique noticed that the sickly color of people's skin had started to return to normal. There were a few people with the yellowish-green skin. But for the most part, everyone looked normal again.

Paulo gestured for Angelique, Atlas, and Ariana to stand. "This whole celebration is about you." He looked around the room. "A show of hands. Who here was starting to believe this colony would collapse?"

Hands shot up in the air all around them.

"We were losing hope." Paulo wiped a tear away from his eye. "I don't say this lightly; you honestly saved our planet from destruction. We owe you our lives." He looked at Atlas. "Twice now, you've been there for us."

There was something about being praised in front of everyone that made you feel good. Angelique was feeling great right now, so Atlas must be feeling amazing. She wondered if Atlas would start to get a god complex too.

"Before I hand you the mic," Paulo said, "I want to show you all a gift that we prepared . . ."

Angelique found herself in a dark room. She had the sense that some time had passed. She was switched back on on the bridge of the space station orbiting around the Dottiens' system, back in the same location as her matrix.

A second later, Ariana appeared, then Unity.

"Was this you?" Angelique asked.

Both the other women shook their heads.

Peter, Hezekiah, Atlas, and both their Ships appeared in the room next to one another.

"What happened?" Atlas asked.

A collective shrug.

"That's odd," Atlas's Ship said. "I don't have access to the Starnet."

Then it clicked: everyone on the bridge had their matrix physically housed at this location. So, if the Starnet was experiencing an issue, then it made sense that they were all kicked off world.

"He was just getting to the good stuff," Atlas said. "I was starting to like that guy."

"Me too," Angelique agreed. "I think we're all going to be better off now that everyone's colonies are open to sharing."

"Does anyone know how long until the Starnet is back up?" Hezekiah asked.

Atlas walked over to one of the control panels. "Let me look."

"Don't bother," Ariana said. "The Starnet has been blown up."

You could hear a penny drop at that moment. Everyone skipped a beat, not quite comprehending the words that had just been said. Ariana had made a statement so matter-of-factly that one would be forgiven for assuming she just took credit for it.

"What do you mean, it's blown up?" Peter demanded in an almost-accusatory tone. "What did you do?"

"I didn't do anything," Ariana said.

"I think we're about to have the answer," Ship said. "There's a ship that just hailed us. We're getting a message from them now."

They all watched as a screen appeared in front of them. What appeared was completely unexpected: a semi-aquatic-looking creature. If a penguin had longer legs and a brown-and-white spotted coat, that would be the description of what they were looking at. It had flippers for hands, which suggested they were an aquatic species. But those flippers each bent into three distinct digits. Angelique assumed this was for them to manipulate objects. It wore a two-piece jumpsuit with many different pockets. Angelique noticed a bulge on the front of its chest. She didn't know if it was just a trick of the light because the top of its jumpsuit was covering it up, but it was almost as if the alien had a single breast. Angelique almost didn't notice it because there was a starscape insignia over its chest area where the bulge was—right in the center.

Angelique couldn't see much in the background. Not because the alien was standing in front of a blank wall but because the recording used some sort of shallow depth of field, so everything behind the alien looked blurry, out of focus. Or maybe it was some sort of filter designed to limit what they could learn about the alien.

Angelique thought she recognized the pattern of stars. There were a few missing, but she did recognize the star chart. *Interesting* she thought; maybe this was to signify the region they were in.

Oh, my god. Angelique suddenly fully understood it. *"Grabby aliens" is a thing. That must be the territory that the alien has colonized on its insignia.*

She was pulled out of her mindscape when the creature started to talk. It sounded like a series of guttural clicking sounds mixed with a vibration, almost a growling. Then over the top of that, a menacing sound came through, as if a computer was overlaying the alien's words in English but maintaining the alien's gravatas.

"Humans, this is—" The next words that came out of the alien's mouth were incomprehensible. They came across as more a set of whale clicks.

There was a long pause as if it were querying something. "You now know us. You are the first to know *of* us. This entitles you to truth. We are older than you. You evolved in a star system already claimed by *us*. You once considered us your gods. Many still do. We decided long ago that we would guide you away from space colonization. You evolved in *our* system. We left you alive on purpose.

There was a long pause. No one in the room said a thing. Thinking wasn't possible when you were faced with an alien that was talking to you.

"Now you know the truth. Your only option is to negotiate."

A pause, then more guttural clicks. "In eighty-nine Earth days I will arrive. We will negotiate. You will accept it. You will return to zoo. You will return to Earth.

"I know humans. I've studied you. You like fight. Just know you are a bug. We are gods." The alien growled, and Angelique got the sense he was scanning for something. "You have a say-ing, 'indistinguishable from magic.' That is us; we are indistin-guishable from magic. Hence, we are gods. There is no point in fighting. Negotiation is your only choice. We will negotiate your existence in our area of space. I know you do not speak for all humans. But every other human is happy not exploring space. So, we negotiate."

There was a long pause again. The alien jiggled and sort of shook a little, then made another growling sound. Then the translation sound changed as if the translator was glitching. "Eighty-nine days."

The team was in shock. No one had expected that. Everyone was a little shaken up. That was the strangest threat she had ever seen. Did it really just refer to Earth as a zoo? Did it really just refer to itself as a god?

Angelique opened her mouth to say something, then closed it again. She didn't quite know what to say. "An honest-to-god alien," Angelique said. "I can't believe we met an alien as advanced as us."

"From the sounds of it, they're more advanced than us," Hezekiah said.

"It might be bluffing." Peter scratched the back of his head. "We just purged its spying devices from our systems."

Unity nodded. "Agreed. But if it is a trick, why show itself to us?"

"The ship on the way here, is it big enough to host a rotating habitat?" Angelique asked.

Ariana closed her eyes for half a second before opening them again. "Not unless that creature is tiny."

One thing Angelique found interesting was that the fabrics the alien was wearing hung. "The way its clothes fell, it wasn't in zero gravity. If they do have artificial gravity, then I'd say it isn't bluffing."

Peter finally spoke for the first time throughout this whole exchange. "It called itself a god. Whenever someone does that, they're compensating."

"We shouldn't anthropomorphize." Atlas started to bite his lower lip. "*Alien* means alien in thought and behavior. For all we know, the translation software wasn't passing the full meaning of what it was trying to say."

"Maybe," Unity said. "But that it did say it had been studying us, too. So, one would assume it understands our language quite well. It spoke in English because it knew that was the language we all spoke."

The team deliberated for a while on how to respond. It was clear there was a lot of information they didn't have.

They knew next to nothing about this alien. The team was split between intellectual curiosity and fear.

Atlas in particular wanted to meet the alien, if for nothing else but to learn more. He wasn't that interested in the negotiation.

But Hezekiah and Unity were afraid and suggested taking Angelique's ship and leaving as quickly as possible.

But in the end, they knew nothing of the alien's capabilities. And the team was a group of explorers in the first instance. There wasn't anything more exciting than exploring an alien culture, even if it was just to negotiate them heading back to Earth.

"So, it's decided, then," Atlas said. "Let's go meet this new god."

AUTHOR'S NOTE

There is a lot of accurate science in this book about how virtual reality and augmented reality devices could manipulate us all. If you're interested in watching a video essay I put together based on the research papers I read in preparation for writing this book, visit MenilikDyer.com/god.

ABOUT THE AUTHOR

Menilik Henry Dyer is the author of *A New Eden* and its sequels, *A New God* and *A New War*. He is also writing a series he calls "the Bobiverse meets Children of Time." Visit his website at www.menilikdyer.com.

DISCOVER
STORIES UNBOUND

PodiumAudio.com